Stacey, my dear friend

SECURE
THE
RANCH

JOYCE OROZ

Outskirts Press, Inc.
Denver, Colorado

Secure the Ranch
All Rights Reserved.
Copyright © 2010 Joyce Oroz
v2.0

Outskirts Press, Inc.
http://www.outskirtspress.com

ISBN: 978-1-4327-5892-9

Outskirts Press and the "OP" logo are trademarks belonging to Outskirts Press, Inc.

PRINTED IN THE UNITED STATES OF AMERICA

Secure the Ranch is dedicated to Lorraine,
my dear deceased friend

I would like to thank my friends and family for their help in producing this book. They each played a part. Carolyn was my honest and wise mentor, Wendy was my logic police, Marlene was my editor, Avery was my photographer, Dorothy and Joyce were my cheerleaders and Art was my lovable and knowledgeable final authority on most things. And special thanks to Tomi for the tile, etc. and Michael for his much appreciated 24/7 tech support.

Chapter One

A fortuitous phone call instantly recharged my sluggish brain cells. I gleefully envisioned gobs of money filling my checking account, settling overdue mortgage payments, way overdue taxes and a couple credit card bills.

As the owner of Wildbrush Mural Company, I constantly searched for good clients and job security for myself, my two employees and my four-legged dependant, Solow. Unfortunately, the last six months had been pretty lean, work-wise. Mural prospects were intermittent to say the least, thanks to a recession. But when Mrs. Munger phoned, it was a sign that better times were coming.

My basset hound stood by the front door, his head turned in my direction.

"Want to go out, big guy? OK, Solow, secure the ranch." I called it a ranch, but really it was my little century-old adobe home perched on a hill, surrounded by a sprinkling of oaks and cooled by ocean breezes. It was real country living, from the dusty gravel driveway, to the retro wood burning stove and the rickety wooden stairs leading to the loft. Only one mile from the wee town of Aromas, it was a California paradise.

I followed Solow out the door. His long thick body circled twice and finally settled into his favorite doggie bed. I sat on the porch beside him, bare legs in the sun, estimating in my head the distance between Aromas and the new jobsite. I figured it would be a one-hour drive for me and forty-five minutes for Alicia, my number one friend and employee. Kyle would take a half hour from Santa Cruz.

I thought about my new client, Theda Munger, and the 9,000 square foot mansion she and her husband were building near the little mountain town of Boulder Creek.

My mind wandered back to three weeks earlier when the Wildbrush Mural team traveled ninety miles north to San Francisco. We painted faux marble finishes on eight sets of elevator doors. The four-story office building presented several hurdles, such as scarce parking and overactive elevator doors. The Munger job sounded like a sweet cupcake by comparison. What could possibly go wrong in Boulder Creek?

I spent the rest of Monday afternoon rounding up paint supplies from my rusty shed behind the house. I reviewed my inventory and ordered several quarts of paint from Nova Paint Company. Trigger, Alicia's ten year old son, had turned me on to the very durable paint. At ten-years old he already used his computer to find all sorts of things while mine collected dust.

A familiar voice assured me the quarts of cadmium yellow, raw umber, cobalt blue, and chromium oxide green would arrive by UPS in three days or less. She took my credit car number. I held my breath. Seconds after I hung up, Kyle called.

"Hey Jo, got your message. Like, what's this about a big job, man?"

"Hi, Kyle, ready to go back to work?"

"Like, no, but I gotta' make some dough. Actually, my rent is overdue."

"I think we can lock-in this job, Kyle. The Mungers are building a mansion near Boulder Creek. We all need some work right now, so cross your fingers. The woman sounded a bit weird, sad actually, like she just lost her best friend. I hope she's not going to flake on us."

"So, ah, library, nine-thirty, like you said?"

"Yep, see you there." I hung up feeling like my biggest loose end, the talented Kyle Larsen, was ready to paint for money again. I curled up on the sofa and lost myself in the world of "Mr. Monk" TV reruns. Mysteries were my passion. Painting had been a passion until seventeen years ago when my husband was run over by an 18-wheeler. At that point I had to get serious about painting or work in a stuffy office somewhere. I chose to support myself by becoming a professional muralist.

As a fifty-year-old widow, I had managed fairly well, but my recent gall bladder operation, puny insurance and truck repairs had put me in the seriously red category. At times I felt I would never get out from under my bills, but that Monday night I had hope.

Tuesday, seven in the morning, I sprung out of bed and bebopped down the hall to 'La Bamba' blasting from the radio. I swayed to the rhythm of one tune after another as I showered, dried my unruly auburn hair and pulled on a clean blouse and shorts. After a light breakfast, I powered my mature reubenesque body into the driver's seat of my red Mazda pickup and left Solow snoring in his front porch doggie bed, securing the ranch.

After the usual slow and go through Aptos and Soquel, the freeway cleared and my ten-year-old truck crept up to sixty-five. I left the freeway at Scotts Valley and drove eighteen slow, curvy miles through the redwood forested valley, past Felton, Ben Lomond and finally into Boulder Creek. I made a left on West Park Avenue and a right into the library parking lot, pulling into a space next to Kyle's yellow Honda motorcycle. He sauntered up to my truck, leaned down and put his face in the open window.

"Like, this place is 90 degrees and it's only nine-thirty."

"Yeah, it's hot. I'm glad you made it, Kyle. Have you seen Allie and Trigger?"

Kyle swiveled his scrawny neck to the left, revealing a new red and black tattoo. It was a hand holding a pineapple with wings? The intrinsic meaning escaped me.

"Ah ... like, I haven't seen ... oh, there they are." The

Quintana's late model Volvo station wagon pulled to a stop on the opposite side of Kyle's motorcycle. Trigger, never known to be slow, slammed his door and sprinted to my truck.

"Hi, Auntie Jo," he grinned, his dark eyes anticipating adventure as usual.

"Hi, Trigger. I've missed you, buddy."

Alicia joined us in all her natural 'south of the border' prettiness. Five-foot-nine, slim, with shiny black hair in a stylish cut. She stood out in any crowd. She had been my closest friend ever since we met at Jasmine's Yoga Class four years earlier. We were both painters so we teamed up on a mural in downtown Los Gatos and had worked together ever since. I hired Kyle two years later when he was a freshman at UC Santa Cruz, painting sets for the drama class.

We turned our heads when a silver Lexus SUV rolled to a stop next to my truck. The driver was pretty silver looking herself. The shoulder length hair was a silver-gray pageboy, the tank top a silky gray, and the white shorts were short, for a middle-aged woman. She climbed down from her seat, leaving the door ajar. With right hand extended, and a forced smile on her lips, she joined our circle.

"Hi, I'm Theda Munger," she said. We took turns shaking hands as I introduced the team members and Trigger. Theda glanced back at her sport utility vehicle.

"I think we'll all fit in my car," she said with a barely

detectable slur. Maybe the gin breath had something to do with it. But it was too late to protest as everyone was already seated when I reluctantly climbed into the front passenger seat and buckled my seatbelt extra tight.

"How many miles to your house?" I asked, hoping it wouldn't be far.

"Just a couple miles," Theda cooed, as we gained speed. The winding mountain road caused us to jerk left, then right, then left, or maybe it was Theda's driving. Without warning, my right shoulder hit the door as Theda cranked the Lexus into a hard left turn up a steep, unpaved, terrible excuse for a driveway. I looked back at Bear Creek Road, wishing we were still on it. Theda glanced at me as if reading my mind.

"Our driveway is scheduled to be paved in a few weeks," she smiled.

"Whoopee, lotta' good that will do us," I thought.

"Cool. This is fun," Trigger and Kyle said in unison.

So who was the ten year old and who was almost double that? No time to ponder that question when the minutes of my life seemed to be numbered. On our right, a cliff dropped hundreds of feet into a river canyon. Perspiration trickled down the back of my neck as I held the door handle with a death-grip.

"Oh, what a cute little cabin, and look, a barn," Alicia said, pointing to the left.

"That's where we're living while the new house is being built," Theda said, as she took her left hand off the wheel to point. "You can see why I'm anxious for the new house to be finished. My husband, Warren, wants the new construction to be one hundred percent complete before we move in. That's why it's wonderful that you nice people are free to start work right away."

"Do you, like, have any neighbors?" Kyle asked.

"Not really. The whole hundred acres is ours." Theda waved her left hand as if pointing to property lines far away. Loud scraping noises made my heart skip a beat as we side-swiped blackberry bushes on the left side of the driveway. Mrs. Munger over- correct to the right, the cliff side. I prayed hard and it must have worked because she miraculously kept three tires on the road.

The glorified deer path finally funneled into a three-acre flat clearing on top of the mountain, crowned with one of the largest Italian villa-style mansions I had ever seen, and I had painted in some big ones. The building featured several second story balconies with ornate balustrades and a tower of windows at the west end, capped with a dome.

A dozen or so pickups were parked randomly around an unpaved circular driveway. It looked like bees on caffeine with workmen everywhere, digging up the front yard, painting the house and installing heavy terra cotta tiles on the roof. We gladly climbed out of the "vehicle from Hades" the second it stopped.

"Theda, it's lovely," Alicia said, as she steadied herself against the SUV.

Color was returning to Kyle's face. "Like, it's awesome, you know." Who would believe the college kid, with spiked red hair and a nose ring, painted like a master?

Theda led us past the six-car garage to the sunroom on the east side of the house. The solarium alone was as big as my whole house plus my neighbor's carport. A dozen wicker chairs and three small tables had been placed against the north windows. Hammering, sawing, scraping and drilling noises echoed wall to wall.

We followed Theda's silver flip-flops through the kitchen into the dining room, oohing and aahing all the way. She stopped in front of a gianormous north-facing window, rested her silver braceleted hands on her skinny hips and pointed at the opposite wall. She raised her voice over the construction noise.

"This dining room wall is twelve feet high by twenty-four feet long, and here is where you will paint a Tuscan pastoral scene. I have samples of the seat cover and drapery fabrics to help you with colors. The walls are smooth and ready to be painted.

Whoa, she sounded smarter than the average mural customer, I thought to myself. I pulled a pen and note pad out of my purse and jotted down the measurements.

"Mrs. Munger, do you have scaffolding we can use?"

"Chester will take care of that." The image of an old man with a limp, dragging in the heavy metal setup, popped into my head.

Theda stepped back into the kitchen and the gang

turned to face the humongous window. We silently stared at the tops of ancient towering redwood trees poking their pointy heads up from the mountainside. As I marveled at the dense forest stretching to the north, range after range, a hawk carved circles into the bluest sky I had ever seen.

A minute later our guide was back with fresh gin on her breath. I wondered how long it would take to walk back to Boulder Creek. Theda relaxed her shoulders, took a couple deep breaths and resumed the tour. She led us down a wide hallway, turned right and stopped inside a manly, mahogany everywhere den. My crew was not as quick to stop and piled into each other's heels, looking like "The Three Stooges". Theda didn't notice the pile-up behind her as she pointed to the coffered ceiling.

"The inner ceiling area measures ten by twelve feet and will be decorated with blue sky, clouds …."

"Puffy clouds and maybe a couple cherubs in the renaissance style?" Alicia suggested.

"Yes, I see we're on the same page." Theda gave Alicia a weak smile, turned and walked out of the room. We followed her to the music room located at the southwest corner of the first floor. All the rooms had high ceilings, but that one was two stories high with a dome at the top. Sunlight filtered through a round stained glass window ensconced in the top of the cupola. The intricate design involved a spray of yellow and purple wild flowers. We stood with our necks crooked, admiring the sunlit display of color.

Two tall windows facing south and two more facing west provided most of the illumination for the music room. Through the southern windows we watched a tall and tanned young man, his blond hair pulled back in a ponytail, carefully inspect the outer stucco wall. Theda opened a window and introduced Chester as her contractor and the person we should go to if we needed anything. Chester gave Theda a quick glance, smiled and saluted us with two fingers.

"At your service, folks."

Theda turned away from the window and walked to the middle of the room.

"The north wall will be painted as a meadow full of wild flowers, redwoods in the distance and ...."

Suddenly the glass ceiling exploded and a renegade roof tile plummeted through the wildflower picture, smashing onto the tile floor. Everyone jumped, ducked and covered their heads. We screamed like banshees as shards of glass rained from above.

The tile had barely missed Theda's silver-polished toenails. Her tan immediately turned milky and her body seemed to list to one side. Alicia quickly stepped forward and caught the woman's elbow.

"Yeow!" Trigger and Kyle yelled out in unison.

"Oh my God!" I said, heart pounding like a jack-hammer. Chester yelled outside.

"Who's up there? What do you think you're doing? Get your butt down here NOW!" his face turned red, but still no answer from the roof. We watched with shock frozen on our faces as Chester made two fists and kicked the wall with his work boot. When he realized we were all watching him, he shrugged his broad shoulders.

"Accidents happen on any project like this," Theda said, shaking from head to toe. She turned her back to us, wrapped her arms around herself mummy style and stretched her chin upward, gazing at the hole in the ceiling. Finally, she took a deep breath and turned around.

"Josephine," she cleared her throat, "would you please work up an estimate on the three rooms we've discussed today and call me? I have a few more places for your work, but we can discuss those later. I'll have Chester drive you back to the library." Suddenly my blood pressure dropped like a rock, all the way back to normal.

We followed Mrs. Munger down the hall, made a right into the massive two-story front room, passed the elegant staircase and walked through the foyer to the front yard. We watched Theda tramp unsteadily over to Chester at the western corner of the house. She said something, he nodded and approached us wearing an artificial smile which didn't fool anyone. He pointed a thumb at the SUV and we quickly piled in.

As we motored down the rutty driveway, our bodies swayed and bounced to the same beat. I was first to break the silent tension.

"How about that mansion, you guys?"

"Like, awesome, you know?" Kyle yelled from the

backseat. The drive up had seemed long and exhausting, but the drive back was a snap. I sat back and enjoyed the views from the front passenger seat. Chester sat quiet as a stone until he parked the car in the library lot. The motor idled as he spoke.

"Don't worry folks, this tile thing was just an accident and I intend to get to the bottom of it. See you guys later." I held my door open.

"Just a minute, can I have your phone number in case I need to arrange for some scaffolding before we paint?"

"Good idea, Josephine," he said as he dug through his wallet and handed me his business card. I thanked him, slammed the door and he was gone. The sun was straight up and the Library parking lot offered zero shade.

"Thanks you guys for coming," I said. "Call ya later if we get the job."

Chapter Two

I fired up my truck, pulled into Highway 9 traffic and left Boulder Creek and the Munger mansion behind. Driving home, I decided to stop off in Santa Cruz to see if Mom and Dad were around. Chances were good they were out rollerblading, biking, hiking or swing dancing. They always said they wanted to stay active before they turned eighty and knowing them, it would take more than being eighty to put on the brakes.

Mom and Dad had lived on Walnut Avenue in Santa Cruz since I was born. When I left the nest they found plenty of things to do and have been rocking ever since. I wanted them to continue their busy lifestyle on a fixed income, which was why I down-played my financial troubles.

I turned onto Walnut Avenue and parked at the curb in front of a modest, cream with brown trim, restored bungalow. Sitting on the roof was a woman who looked a lot like me, but older. She wore a green t-shirt with a yellow slug printed on the front, khaki shorts and high-top tennies. Dad stood on a ladder handing her fake-wood shingles. Leola sat like a lady as she swiveled her derriere to the left, took a shingle from Dad, pivoted back to her right and tapped the thing in place with a hammer. The activity was repeated again and again. Finally, they saw me walking up the sidewalk and stopped their work.

"Hi, honey," Dad yelled, a big smile spreading across his leathery face. Mom made a beeline for the ladder and followed Bob down the aluminum rungs.

"Hi, Mom, Dad. I didn't mean to interrupt your project. I just happened to be out this way."

"Honey," Dad cleared his throat, "we're replacing the shingles that blew off last winter and we have all summer to finish. Besides, your mother baked banana bread this morning. I think she knew you would show up in a day or two." As a creature of habit, Dad tried to put his hands in his pockets, but his Spandex biking shorts had no pockets. His tank top had a wet patch down the back and he was still sucking in lots of air.

Mom was breathing hard too, but managed to give me a Sumo hug and a peck on the cheek. "Good ... to ... see you ... Josephine."

I did most of the talking and much of the eating once we were inside. By the time I left, they were as excited about Theda's murals as I was, maybe because I left out the part about the falling tile.

On my way home I stopped at my favorite market in Watsonville to stock up on Solow's kibble and a few goodies for myself. My short and chubby grocer friend,

Robert, had just finished bagging an order when I rolled my cart up to the register.

"Hey, Jo, how's it goin'?" his young freckled face broke into a full smile.

"Well, next time I see you I'll be paying with green backs, not a plastic card. Got a big job in Boulder Creek working for the Mungers. I ran my card through the machine, held my breath and signed the ticket.

"Not the Mungers from San Francisco, I hope." He squinted one eye as the smile vanished.

"Well, they are from the City, but so what. I'm sure there are tons of people with that name. What's the big deal, Robert?"

"Don't you remember? Last year on the news the Munger's daughter was missing and she still hasn't been found." Robert robotically bagged my groceries as he talked. "They suspected foul play by the uncle, but there's no body and no evidence so far. There's no proof of murder, but I'd be careful if I were you."

"Thanks for the heads up," I said, as Robert stowed my groceries in the bed of my truck. I drove home with the windows down and the music up. My little pickup sped south along the mostly straight, two-lane road, past hundreds of acres of strawberries, raspberries, lettuce and cabbage, and then up into the Aromas hills.

Solow welcomed me home with a low-pitched howl and a tail that wouldn't be still. I usually called him 'big guy', hoping to help his self-image. The poor basset only stood fourteen inches tall on a good day and spent much of his time asleep in his bed on the front porch recovering from cat chases with Fluffy.

After putting the groceries away, I decided to spend some quality time walking the neighborhood with Solow. He lived for short walks and long naps.

"Solow, let's walk down to David's house and see Fluffy." His ears perked up when he heard the 'Fluffy' word, even though she was his nemesis and always made him look ridiculous. After our walk and a good cat chase, Solow was ready for a nap. The phone was ringing when I entered the house. I made a dash for it, "hello."

"Hi, Josephine, it's Alicia. Just wondered what you thought about that terrible accident today."

"Theda was a basket case, but she seemed distraught even before the accident," I said, remembering her demeanor and trips to the bottle.

"I feel sorry for Mrs. Munger," Alicia said, in her typically soft voice.

"Allie, do you remember a news story about a year ago involving the Munger family from San Francisco … something about a missing daughter?"

"Yes … so that's where I heard the name before. Was their daughter ever found?"

"I don't think so, but what if our Mungers are those Mungers?"

"That's so sad," Alicia whispered. My friend had told me how sad life could be. Before she was adopted by a loving family, she was a six-year-old orphan living in the streets of Tijuana, Mexico, selling chewing gum to tourists.

"Allie, I'm going to call Theda tonight with prices. Is your schedule clear?"

"Yes, of course. What a magical place to work with redwoods all around. Let me know what Mrs. Munger says."

I put the phone down and rummaged through the fridge. I heaped liverwurst and tuna on a hot dog bun slathered in sweet mustard, trimmed with lettuce and thin slices of red onion. I settled into a chair at the kitchen table, my left hand manipulating the sandwich while the right hand scribbled a few figures on a scratch pad. I estimated as close as possible the number of days my friends and I would need to complete the three large murals Theda wanted. The walls were already nicely prepared, but I added an extra couple days in case the unexpected came up. I had a gut feeling something would.

After multiplying the number of days required by our daily rate, I called Theda. The phone rang at least ten times and I was about to hang up when a soft, slow voice said, "hello."

"It's Josephine. How are you this evening?" I heard her mumble something and then a sigh. "Here are the figures you asked for." I gave her the estimate for each mural and told her we could start in the morning. After a long pause, Theda sighed again.

"See you ... in the morn ... ing." I took that as a yes and proceeded to call my cohorts. They promised to be on time, lucky people--they only had to show up. As the originator and owner of Wildbrush Murals, it was my responsibility to bring all the paint supplies including things we might need under strange and unpredictable circumstances.

With a fading sun at my back, I made three trips to the shed, lugging heavy tackle boxes full of paint, one at a time, dropping them into the truck bed beside two of my ladders. The six-footer lay kitty-corner on the bottom with the eight-footer on top, hanging over the tailgate. Then came a cardboard box full of quarts of paint and three canvas bags full of painting supplies including brushes, palettes and dozens of recycled plastic tubs, newspapers and plastic bags. Finally, I pulled down the spring-loaded metal truck bed cover and took a deep breath.

The sky turned from red to purple to black, bringing on a splash of twinkly stars. Suddenly I remembered the blond hunk. I should have called Chester sooner.

He picked up on the first ring.

"Mathus Construction."

"Hello, Chester, this is Josephine Stuart ... we met to-day. Sorry to call so late."

"Yeah, what's up?" he asked, sounding not as per-turbed as I had expected.

"We start work tomorrow and need scaffolding in the dining room, about six feet high and the length of the room. I'm hoping to start painting about 9:30."

"No problem. I'll have my guys set it up before you get there. So, you're OK working for the Mungers? You looked a little shaky after the incident."

"Incident?"

"I meant, accident."

"Whatever," I said, "I'll see you tomorrow and thanks for the help on such short notice. Oh, by the way, how's Theda?"

"She's managing."

We hung up and I turned my attention to gathering photos of the Tuscany countryside from my over-flowing files. I drew a few pencil sketches to get us started. The rest of the ideas lived in my fertile little brain, along with a nagging desire for ice cream. I satisfied my 'new job jitters' with rocky road extra creamy, put out fresh water for Solow, set my alarm for seven-thirty and hit the sack.

I hated it when my body collapsed, but my brain kept running in every direction on overdrive. I thought about poor Mrs. Munger hitting the bottle like there was no tomorrow. Theda's pale, frightened face haunted me for what seemed like hours. I wondered what my friend and neighbor, David Galaz, would think about the accident that didn't seem very accidental. I wondered who was on the roof when it happened.

Finally, I fell asleep listening to Solow's rhythmic snoring across the room. I dreamt about a mansion in the clouds and a very long, steep slide at the back of the building. Someone pushed me down the slide. I hit the bottom hard and rolled under a thorny bush. I was lying on the ground in the dark, not able to find my way back to the mansion, when Solow found me and licked my cheek.

Chapter Three

It was seven o'clock Wednesday morning. Disco music blasted from my clock radio as dark dreams slowly evaporated. I think Chester starred in the one after the slide nightmare. I couldn't remember much, just a bad feeling that lingered. Solow followed me into the bathroom licking my heels.

"I love you too, big guy." I dragged myself into a steamy shower and a few minutes later my body started to come alive - even my brain showed signs of life. I toweled off, dried my hair with the hair dryer, flossed, brushed, creamed, plucked, and powdered until I looked my natural best.

I searched through my closet for a hot-weather paint outfit. Should I wear the yellow t-shirt with blue and green paint smears to match my green eyes or the white t-shirt speckled with red, yellow and brown? I yanked the yellow one off its hanger, pulled it over my head and jumped into a pair of Levi cut-offs with holy pockets and smears of white paint. I smiled at myself in the mirror. I would be easy to spot in a crowd.

I buzzed milk, protein powder and a cup of frozen blueberries in the blender and downed the frothy shake. With my other hand, I scooped kibble into Solow's bowl, then made my favorite sandwich, peanut butter on each slice of bread with slices of Fuji apple in the middle. I packed the sandwich and a few other food groups into my little cooler, grabbed my camera, purse and folder and headed out the front door.

My cell phone rang. I set everything down on the gravel driveway and answered the call.

"Hi, Jo, it's Alicia. Kyle called a minute ago to say he has a doctor appointment this morning. He said he was lucky to get in so fast."

"So what you're saying is he didn't want to tell me himself because I might give him a bad time. I told him he'd get an infection from that raunchy ring in his nose."

"No, Jo, the one on his nipple is infected."

"Oh, well, that makes all the difference. Can he make it to work at all?" I tried not to visualize the problem area on Kyle's skinny white body.

"He wanted me to tell you to pick him up at the library at ten."

"OK, thanks, Allie."

I made sure Solow was safely securing the ranch from his porch lookout, threw my purse in the front seat and took off in a cloud of gravel dust. The air inside the truck was already hot from the morning sun. I opened my sliding back window, cranked up the volume and shared my Susan Boyle tunes with the world. It felt good to be employed again.

One hour later, I turned off Bear Creek Road and headed up the Munger's driveway. Theda's SUV was parked at the cabin so I decided to pull in for a chat. She answered the door in her silk robe, looking pale and frazzled.

"Hi, Josephine, anything wrong?"

"No, just wanted to pick up those sample fabrics you talked about yesterday. I'd like to mix several paint colors today."

"Just a minute," Theda turned, walked across the living room and disappeared down the hall. I wasn't invited in, but from the open door my eyes made a quick tour of the front room. Open beamed ceiling, river rock fireplace, oak flooring and lot's of small paned windows. The cabin had obviously been restored, using the best and most expensive materials. The little house probably looked a thousand times nicer than the original cabin of well over a hundred years ago. Theda returned to the front door and handed me a plastic bag with the fabrics neatly folded inside.

"Thank you. This will be a big help," I turned when I heard the roar of an engine coming up the driveway and caught a glimpse of the back end of Alicia's dark green Volvo through the dust. Trigger waved madly.

"So far, so good," I thought to myself as I aimed my truck up the mountain. I approached the rough-cut circle drive just as Alicia parked her station wagon. Quick as lightening, Trigger leaped out of the car and ran toward a short haired, brown dog lying in the shade at the edge of the clearing. I had always been a dog lover, but even my first glance at the over-sized dog made my hair stand on end. Trigger was crazy about Solow, but this dog wasn't a sweet old basset.

Alicia ran after her son shouting, "Trigger, stop, come back here right now. We don't know this dog!"

Too late. The dog stood up and snarled with all her teeth exposed. She started after Trigger, who spun around and ran toward his mother. The dog was fast and able to reach the boy in a split second. Its drooling jowls tore a hole in the back of Trigger's baggy soccer shorts, just missing his little bum. I watched in horror as Trigger tripped and fell on the uneven ground, doing a perfect face plant in the dirt. Alicia screamed.

I watched the whole drama, which seemed to be in slow motion, through my windshield. My mind raced. I took my foot off the brake and drove ahead a few yards into the scuffle with the horn blowing. The dog paid no attention, and by that time its jaws were around Trigger's arm. My heart was pounding and Alicia was hysterical.

One of the workers, a short stocky man with broad shoulders and a mustache, picked up his shovel and ran to Trigger's side. Without hesitation, he raised the shovel over his head with both hands and let the dog have it. Even from inside my truck I heard the cracking of the dog's skull. Then the animal went limp.

The man bent down to see if the dog was breathing, pulled the jaws apart and freed Trigger's arm. Two little streams of blood dripped from under his torn t-shirt sleeve. Trigger sobbed as Alicia crouched and held him. Normally I couldn't stand to see an animal hurt, but all my tears were for Trigger, the one boy in the entire world I loved most. The son I never had.

"Allie, is he OK?" I shouted, as I leaped out of the truck. My legs wobbled and nearly folded. The slow motion was gone. Instead, things seemed a little fuzzy. The brave man with the shovel backed away as if wanting to disappear. With tears streaming down my cheeks, I caught up to him.

"My name's Josephine. I want to thank you Mr. ...?"

"My name ees Manuel. I did not do so much," he said, his eyes trained on my sandaled feet. I felt so emotional, I hugged the man with all my wobbly strength.

"Thank you, Manuel."

He smiled for a second, but was obviously embarrassed. He turned and drove his shovel into the ground where he had been working. Two laborers watched from the other end of the ditch. At first, Chester was nowhere in sight, but he must have heard the ruckus and came running from behind the garage.

"Where did this dog come from?" he shouted, as if we knew where all dogs came from. He circled around Alicia and Trigger. "Anyone hurt?"

Alicia gulped in some air, her eyes blinking rapidly as she looked up. "Trigger needs to see a doctor right away."

"I'll take you," Chester said, in a husky voice. "Wait here and I'll get my truck."

I walked closer to Trigger, bent down and kissed his dirty little forehead.

"Allie, don't worry about anything here, take your time." She nodded, but could not muster a smile. Chester's truck pulled up next to me. I helped Trigger into the back seat and Alicia crawled in beside him. Chester grabbed the carcass of a female mastiff and tossed it into the bed of the truck.

"I'm going to hand the dog over to Animal Control. Maybe they can tell us if it was sick," Chester said, as he swung himself into the seat of his 150 Ford pickup and slammed the door. I hadn't thought about rabies.

I watched the top of Trigger's head, studded with dusty black hair, through the little backseat window. My shoulders finally began to relax as the truck made a half circle and disappeared down the mountain in a cloud of dust. I checked my watch and remembered I was supposed to pick Kyle up at the library. It was already 10:30.

"Well, Kyle, I'm coming. Next time leave your stupid nipple alone," I said to the windshield as I followed Chester's truck down Mungers' Mountain.

The small town of Boulder Creek probably hadn't changed much in the last hundred years. Same western style storefronts, same firehouse and park, but the people were different. Many walked from place to place with a cell phone held to one ear. If they weren't talking or listening, they were texting.

I pulled into the library's lot, my truck idling behind Kyle's motorcycle. He sat on a bench with a phone at his ear. My eight fingers thumped the steering wheel while Kyle slowly ended his conversation, dropped the phone into his pocket and meandered over to my window with his yellow-flamed helmet under one arm.

"Like, you're late, Jo."

"We had an unfortunate incident at Theda's this morning. I'll tell you about it on the way up there. Get in." It didn't take a genius to know I was in a bad mood. He quickly ducked into the passenger seat, buckled up and piled a canvas bag, folder and helmet on his skinny lap. I talked and drove while Kyle listened attentively. He finally spoke.

"So where did the dog come from? Like, who owned it?"

"I haven't a clue, but you and I need to get busy painting. Alicia has enough on her mind right now. They won't be back for awhile, if at all." Poor Trigger. Replays of his frightened little face as he started to run from the dog ran through my mind, non-stop.

As we approached the mansion, I noticed Theda's Lexus parked near the sunroom. It looked like she had just arrived. She smiled when she saw us and seemed unaware of anything unusual happening. I parked beside the SUV.

"Kyle, everything in the truck goes to the dining room. I'll be there in a sec."

"Like, even my helmet?" he snorted.

I rolled my eyes, "get real, Kyle." With that, he carried an armload of supplies into the house while I talked to the boss.

"Theda, do you happen to know who owns the brown mastiff that was here this morning?"

"What mastiff? Aren't they awfully big? I've never seen one around here. A few of the workers bring their dogs, but no mastiffs, just labs and I saw a cocker the other day. They usually sleep in their owner's truck all day. Why do you ask, Josephine?"

I told Theda everything that happened as gently as I could. In a matter of seconds she unraveled right in front of me. Fear flashed in her gray eyes and her hands trembled as she leaned against the stucco wall for support. I reassured her everything was under control, but it seemed she was looking at the larger picture, like, why were so many ghastly things happening?

I took Theda's arm and led her, as if she were a five-year-old, into the sunroom where she melted into a wicker chair. She said nothing, just stared straight ahead. I decided to help Kyle unload the truck and planned to check on Theda later.

We managed to unload everything and set up shop in record time. The dining room hosted some sturdy scaffolding six feet high and twenty feet long. Chester really aimed to please. Another plus to the new job was the fact that the carpet had not been installed, so we didn't have to be concerned about paint messing up the floor.

Kyle walked into the dining room carrying a box crammed full of paint cans. I spread the tarps and pointed to a corner of the room where I wanted the supplies to go. Like a happy puppy, Kyle followed directions and had already forgotten my grumpiness.

"Hey man, this room is radically rigged, you know."

"Is that the last of the stuff?"

"Like, yeah."

"OK, you can tape off the wall, top, sides and bottom, and then open the gallon of white and the different quarts of blue. Fill a container with water for our brushes ...."

I found a piece of green chalk and a level, climbed six feet up and crouched on the platform. I drew a rough horizon line at the same height as my knees, the length of the wall. Next, I drew an outline for the hills at roughly the height of my chin, which left approximately four feet by twenty-four feet for the sky.

"Kyle, it's just you and me, old buddy. Let's see if we can get the sky painted before the Quintanas' return."

I mixed four batches of blue for the sky in four different shades. Kyle knew the routine, first person paints the darkest blue across the top of the wall, end to end. Number two person works his second darkest shade into the bottom of the still wet darker paint. First person doubles back and follows the second person, blending in a lighter shade and then the second person comes along with the last and lightest blue. We needed a one foot by twenty-four foot splotch of each shade. The idea was to work fast, blending the layers before the acrylic paint dried.

Kyle applied the darker blue and I followed with the second darkest color, working it in with a three inch brush and a lot of wrist action. My adrenalin was pumping as I thought about the mastiff. Kyle had just started the last color when his cell phone made an obnoxious buzzing noise. He slipped his paintbrush in a plastic bag and pulled the tiny metal irritation out of his back pocket.

"Ah, hello. Kellie, I can't talk now, ya know?"

"So why did you answer the phone? We're at a critical point here. The paint's drying fast," I pleaded with Kyle.

"Like, I have to go now ... sorry." He was still listening to her, blushing like crazy and my blood pressure was going through the roof. Kyle whispered into the phone as if I wouldn't hear him, "OK, sweetie, ah ... bye."

Even though Kyle's mind was far away, he managed to finish his portion of the sky. At least three hours had passed and we were both exhausted and hungry. On our way to my truck, we passed through the solarium. I noticed Theda was gone, but of course she would be. Rats! I had promised myself I would look in on her, but I had forgotten to do it.

"Hey, Kyle, where's your lunch?"

"Like, I didn't bring one."

We sat in the truck sharing the food I had packed in my cooler. I looked into my friend's lovesick eyes and asked about Kellie. Kyle had never been a man of many words, but on that subject, he was a boy with no words, just a quirky smile. I guessed it was personal and I should butt out. I put the key in the ignition and asked what station he liked. As soon as Kyle was happy with the noise he called music, I announced I was going to take a walk.

"Like, don't go near any dogs, Jo."

"OK, I'll be careful." I laughed to myself at the spiky haired worrywart, put all negative thoughts behind me and took off down the driveway. The air was warm and flush with woodsy smells. Small specks of incredibly blue sky peeked through the trees. I guessed it would take about ten minutes of fast walking to reach Theda's cabin. It turned out to be a pretty close guess. I tapped on the cabin door. It opened a crack.

"Theda … hi." The door opened a bit more.

"Come in Josephine," she said. I entered and was directed to a soft suede sofa. It felt great to take a load off my feet. Theda sat down in a matching chair and took a sip from the glass she held tight. She didn't look like she was fully recovered yet, but she was feeling no pain. Her eyes were red and puffy and the room was less than tidy.

A framed photograph on the mantle caught my eye. A young woman and an older man posed, arm in arm, in front of a baby blue Mustang. Why did they look familiar?

"Theda, is there anything I can do for you while I'm here?" Well, that did it. The tears poured.

"I hardly know you ... Josephine, and yet I feel like ... like you care, really care what happens to me," sniffling, she continued. "I called Warren at his office in San Francisco. Sniff. He doesn't think things are so bad ... says we should expect a few problems on a project the size of this one. His work is all he cares about, his stupid tanning salons ... stupid ... stupid salons." She took another sip from her glass.

I felt sorry for Theda and wondered what kind of miserable man her husband was, leaving her alone to deal with all the problems of construction.

"Does your husband come to Boulder Creek very often?"

"Oh, sure, he's here almost every weekend, but nothing bad happens on the weekends. He doesn't understand what it's like to handle ... things, you know," (another sip) "Josephine, I'm sorry to worry you ... I just ...."

"That's OK, Theda. Sometimes it helps to talk it out."

"Last month," Theda continued, "one of the workers was injured when his truck caught fire and he tried to save his dog trapped inside." Tears were streaming down her cheeks. She set her drink on the coffee table and wiped her eyes. "Would ... you like something to drink, Josephine?"

"No, thank you, I just finished lunch. How did the fire start?"

"No one seems to know." She stared out the window as if looking for answers. "The man's dog was always wandering off so he put it in the cab of his truck. It was awful. Juan never came back to work ... and I don't blame him."

"Theda, do you stay here alone when your husband's in the city?"

"I have been living here for the last six months," she said, slowly. "My housekeeper stayed with me on the weekdays, but poor Juan is her brother and she was too upset to come back, you know, after the fire and all. We do have a night watchman every night from seven at night to seven in the morning. He drives by the cabin now and then, but most of his time is spent at the new house."

It seemed like the longer I stayed, the more emotional Theda became and I needed to get back to the job so, I said, "I should go now, but when you're feeling better, I'd like to go over some sketches with you. Make sure we have the same vision."

"Yes, of course, I want to see them, and Josephine ... thank you for coming down here to see me." We both stood up and intuitively hugged.

The front door closed behind me, and then the snap of the lock. I began my trek to the top of the mountain, knowing it would take at least twice the time it took coming down. I had been walking only a few minutes when I heard a truck grinding its way up the mountain. Chester stopped his dusty pickup and I hopped in before he could officially invite me. Three smiling faces looked at me from the back seat.

"Wait a minute, I said, who's the fluffy one?"

Trigger laughed as if I had reached back and tickled him. "She's mine, really! We saw her in the window of Donna's Pet Shop in Scotts Valley next to the clinic. Do you like her, Jo?" He held a tiny bundle of white and gold fur with brown eyes peeking out from under his good arm. A sling held the bandaged arm.

"Let me see, prominent nose, honest eyes and fur everywhere. She's adorable."

"It's a Sheltie," Alicia said. "Isn't she the cutest thing you ever saw? It's kind of like getting back on the bike when you take a tumble. You know what I mean?"

"Good thinking, Allie." I looked over at Chester, but couldn't read his face. The truck stopped in front of the sunroom and we disembarked.

"Kyle and I finished the sky, Allie, and if you feel up to it, I'd like you to paint in the clouds. Not too many, kinda' wispy, like you painted at the Hannon's, remember?"

"I'm ready to paint. Don't worry about me, Jo. Trigger is going to take it easy in the sunroom, aren't you, Trigger, honey?"

"Sure, Mom, I can play with Tansey."

"Tansey?" I laughed. "Where did that name come from?"

"My doctor's name is Doctor Tansey." Trigger said. "Do you like her name?

"A perfect name for a perfect little dog. Oops, almost perfect." A little river of puppy pee ran down Trigger's leg, but he didn't seem to care. He was in love and the injured arm was almost forgotten. Alicia, Trigger and Tansey went inside, but I decided to round-up Kyle, who was still sitting in my truck with a phone to his ear. I walked up to the open window and faked a little cough. Kyle jumped in his seat, hitting his head on the roof of the cab.

"Sorry, Kyle, are you busy?" He shook his head and put the phone to his ear.

"Ah ... like, I gotta' go ... cause my boss wants me to." He listened to the other party with ears as red as his hair, and finally said, "I know, like, I'll call you later."

"OK, college boy, time to wash brushes, open the greens, yellows and browns and locate the sponges. Allie's putting in the clouds right now. I'll be there in a few minutes." I headed across the front yard, dodging holes and equipment as I watched Chester off-load planks from a lumber truck to be used as forms for cement walkways. He looked up.

"What's up, Josephine? The scaffolding OK?"

"It's perfect, but we'll want it lowered to three feet for tomorrow. Now, what about that horrible dog? Is it being tested for rabies? Do you know anything yet?"

"Take it easy, they're running the tests and they'll call the mother as soon as they know anything. I figure a couple more hours. Doctor Tansey said the boy would need further treatment if they find the dog had rabies.

She's already started him off with one shot, just in case. The labs testing flesh from the bite and the dog. Can't be too careful." He put a hand on my shoulder and told me to relax.

"Thanks, Trigger is very important to me. You really took care of things today. By the way, I talked to Theda. Somebody had to tell her what happened with the dog and all." A scowl washed over Chester's ruggedly handsome face. "Do you think she should be staying in that cabin all by herself? Poor lady looks like she's being trampled by a never-ending stampede of accidents."

"You're probably right, but who wants to stay with her in these mountains. Her maid took off weeks ago. Besides, the new house will be finished in a month." He grabbed a plank from the back of the truck, letting me know our conversation had ended.

I took the long way back to the sunroom, around the west and north sides of the building where giant redwood trees rimmed the mansion and its immediate grounds. On the north side, enough trees had been taken out to allow for a view of mountain after tree-covered mountain stretching up the coast toward San Francisco. Eventually I arrived at the solarium where Trigger and Tansey were chasing a tennis ball. I laughed.

I made my way to the dining room where Alicia was busy painting while Kyle studied my sketches. There were no more distractions to keep me from getting serious about the mural and Alicia's clouds were an inspiration.

Kyle and I went over the sketches and then we mixed up three shades of green paint, each one going lighter and bluer than the last.

Kyle and I set up shop at the opposite end of the scaffold from Alicia. I sat with my legs dangling over the side, leaning low, painting the far away mountains. Kyle sat Indian fashion with his long body folded in half, applying a lighter green in places to give dimension and establish the light source. When my mountains finally stretched end to end, I started all over again applying the lightest green, highlighting here and there. Kyle finished up with his green while Alicia finished the clouds. We climbed down to the floor for a better look.

"Mommy, I think Tansey's getting hungry." Tigger said, in a strained voice. I had forgotten he was with us and I had forgotten the time.

"Mommy finished her clouds and she can take you home now," I said.

"Are you sure, Jo?"

"No problem. Kyle and I are going to clean up and leave pretty soon. You guys get out of here. It's been a long day." Trigger hugged me before they left.

"Kyle, did you know it's already four-thirty?" No answer. I felt sure the big puppy was thinking about his girlfriend.

By five we were pulling into the library parking lot. Kyle hopped aboard his motorcycle, pulled on his flaming helmet and roared onto the road in front of me. I followed him through the valley wondering what kind of girl had stolen his heart. Kyle was a bit odd, kinda' shy and I didn't care for his taste in tattoos, but I did care that nothing bad happened to him, including a broken heart.

Rush hour traffic on Highway One was constipated as usual so I concentrated on oldies music from the radio. I was swinging to the beat as I changed lanes, when some guy in a dump truck waved to me with his middle finger, but I didn't let it upset me.

I left the highway, wound my way through Watsonville to my favorite pet shop and purchased a small doggie bed lined with fluffy white wool. I paid the cashier with plastic and held my breath until the credit card was approved. Solow would have loved the bed. After all, he was an expert on relaxation and sleep.

I climbed back into the truck and headed for Alicia's place on the east side of Watsonville. The Quintanas owned a modest two-story house with a million dollar view of Drew Lake. The giant back lawn extended all the way to the water and they had a dock for Trigger's peddle boat. Alicia answered the door and led me to the backyard where her husband, Ernie, sat watching Trigger and Tansey run in circles on the grass. Ernie stood.

"Have a seat, Josephine. Would you like a cold beer or iced tea?"

"Iced tea, please." Alicia headed for the kitchen. Trigger ran to me and we hugged as if we hadn't seen each other in weeks. He scooped up Tansey with his good arm and handed her over to me. Never had I held anything so soft. She settled into my arms and I was her slave.

"What's in the bag, Auntie Jo?"

"Something for a certain new puppy. Go ahead, you can take it out of the bag." I pulled on the bag as he grabbed the bed with his good arm. Alicia arrived with my drink and smiled when she saw Trigger showing the bed to Tansey.

"In my experience with dogs, one can never own too many doggie beds," I said. The Quintanna family knew Solow personally and they laughed at the thought of him securing the ranch from his cushy bed.

"Josephine, can you stay for chili rellenos? And, by the way, we got the call. The dog was not sick." Alicia's eyes were wet and mine were getting wetter. "Can you celebrate with us?"

"Well, if you put it that way, how can I say no? However, I have to eat and run because my hound needs his dinner." I helped Alicia carry the food out to the patio table. The chili rellenos with rice and beans were better than any fine restaurant could have produced. I forced myself to leave right after the strawberry shortcake. There were hugs all around and then I was on my way home.

Fifteen minutes later I arrived at my house with its red brick walkways and two front windows sandwiched between teal green shutters. Each window had its own flower box full of parched marigolds. No lawn. Lawns were unadvisable in Aromas as water was very expensive and my budget didn't allow for such extravagances.

Solow heard my truck, lifted his head and thumped his tail. A package from Nova Paints sat by the front door. I opened the box, checked to see if the colors were right, dragged the whole thing over to the truck and hefted it into the bed with a grunt.

"Solow, come and get it," I said as I entered the house and filled his bowl. I noticed the blinking light on my answering machine and pressed the button, fearing another call from a bill collector, but it was Theda asking me to please call her back. She answered on the first ring and didn't sound the least bit intoxicated.

"Hi, Theda, what can I do for you?"

"Josephine, I'm going to set aside my pride and ask you for help. If you say no, I'll understand. It's just that ... I'm alone up here and ... nervous. What would you think about living here at the cabin, just the weekdays, until the house is finished? We would pay you extra and you would have the guest bedroom. What do you think?"

"Actually, that's something I would be very happy to do. I've been worried about you, Theda, and I know if I were in your place I wouldn't want to be alone in the mountains. I hope you don't mind if I bring along an old hound dog?"

"Josephine, I wouldn't mind if you brought the dog and all his relatives. I'm just so happy you didn't turn me down."

My chili rellenos did a little flip-flop as I imagined

what it would be like at night in the forest. But what the hay, I had been living alone in the country for seventeen years. "This won't be bad," I thought to myself, "just a lot more trees."

"I'll pack my things tonight and see you tomorrow morning."

"Thank you, Josephine. You're a dear." We hung up.

"I'm getting extra money for something I want to do. Yippee!" I shouted, dancing around the room. Solow stopped eating, his eyes following me as I leaped over my ottoman for the fun of it. "Pack your bed, big guy, we're going to blow this joint." He ignored me and went back to his kibble.

I made a mental list of things I should pack, filled two small suitcases with my clothes, toiletries and a can of pepper spray Dad had given me and stuffed Solow's belongings into a big cardboard box. He would need his two beds, leash, water bowls and a bag of kibble. I wondered what I would do if I didn't have Solow in my life, and then I remembered to call David. I threw a couple chew toys in the box and dialed my neighbor. He picked up on the first ring.

"David, it's Josephine. I'm going to be away on a job for a few weeks, but I'll be home on the weekends. I was just wondering if you could keep an eye on my property."

"Be glad to. Don't worry about a thing. Hope I see you on the weekend."

"I hope so too," I said and hung up as a flash of warmth

moved up to my face. After all, the man was single, very attractive with thick graying hair and dreamy brown eyes and I was pretty sure he liked me. I was still smiling as I made one last phone call, explaining to Alicia why my truck would be too full for another passenger the next morning. She said she would be happy to pick up Kyle at the library.

When everything was packed, I crashed on the sofa, fell asleep and dreamt foresty dreams of rabbits, squirrels and bears wading in quicksand that looked and smelled like chili rellenos. It all seemed wonderful until I got stuck in the stuff and couldn't move.

Chapter Four

It was another sunny California morning. My spirits were up as I motored down San Juan Road, hoping I didn't forget to pack anything important. I went through my 'things to pack' mental list as I headed into Watsonville. I was on my way to Boulder Creek with my faithful navigator in the passenger seat, head out and ears flying like two floppy kites.

A few blocks before the freeway entrance, I remembered not packing my toothbrush. We made a quick right turn and cruised over to my favorite Watsonville grocery store. Good time to pick up some fresh fruit, yogurt and a packet of salad greens.

Robert had just arrived for work, saw me and began walking beside my cart.

"How come you're shopping so early in the morning, Jo?"

"I'm on my way to work and I'm moving into Mrs. Munger's cabin until her house is finished. I'll be home on the weekends though." Robert scrunched his eyebrows.

"Sounds creepy to me. What if the uncle shows up, the one they suspect of murder? You better be careful, Jo."

"Thanks, Robert, I'll be alert." I threw a toothbrush on top of a bag of sliced almonds and rolled the cart up to the checkout stand. I held my breath as I ran my credit card through the machine. Luck held and five minutes later Solow and I were on the freeway sailing north again. It's funny how short a trip seems when you have someone to talk to. Solow was always a good listener. We even liked the same music.

After a jarring ride halfway up the Mungers' driveway, I parked my truck beside Theda's Lexus in front of the cabin. She opened the door wearing pink shorts and matching top, four-inch purple sling-back pumps and multiple silver bracelets, dangly earrings and a choker. More bling than a Christmas tree.

"Hello, Josephine. Who's your partner? He's adorable."

"This is my best buddy, Solow." I helped Mr. Tubby out of the truck. My back felt like it was at the breaking point. I promised Solow I would put him on a diet as he hit the ground running with his nose sniffing everything in sight.

"Will he run away?" Theda asked.

"In the first place, he's a slow runner. Second place, why run away from food and a soft bed?"

"I see your point," she laughed. Theda helped unload the suitcases while I set out Solow's water and two beds, one in the extra bedroom and the other on the front porch. As soon as the second bed was in place, Solow just had to try it out. I knew he wouldn't move again for several hours.

I heard a familiar noise and turned just in time to see Alicia's Volvo bouncing up the mountain road. She waved and kept on going. Kyle and Trigger were in the back seat holding on for dear life and laughing like two ten year olds.

I stocked Theda's nearly empty fridge with my groceries and then took off for work. In no way was I prepared for what had happened to the mansion over night. I parked my truck and watched two workmen roll white paint over large black letters spray-painted on the southern wall outside the music room. The first coat of paint didn't cover the, "LEAVE OR DIE" graffiti very well.

I shivered and then my blood began to boil as I marched over to the massacred music room wall where Alicia and Chester stood in serious discussion. I heard him explaining that the mural was damaged, but he was sure that the Mungers would pay for the extra time it would take to repaint it.

"Did you say, mural?" I sputtered.

"'Fraid so," Chester said.

"Where are the boys?" I asked, trying not to imagine the mural in a state of ruin.

"The boys are taking Tansey for a walk," Alicia said. "She's almost trained, but the poor little thing wet on Kyle when we hit a pothole driving up here."

The three of us marched into the house, straight to the dining room wall. Our mouths dropped open, then my jaw clenched. An unexpected groan escaped from my dry throat. At the same moment, Alicia gave out a sad sounding sigh.

"Jo, don't worry, Chester said he'll have two coats of paint on it by tomorrow."

"Oh ... my ... God!" were my first words. The mural had big, black, spray painted letters across the sky, "LEAVE OR DIE".

"Don't worry, Jo. Remember, it's only paint," Alicia said.

"The painters will have the wall repainted and ready for you by tomorrow morning," Chester said.

"Hey guys, it's not the paint I'm worried about. What about the freaking painter, the creep who did this? I thought this place had security."

"Take it easy Josephine," Chester said, as he wiped beads of sweat off his upper lip. "I got here at seven-thirty this morning, a half hour after Ace Security left, so it must have happened between seven and seven-thirty. I called the Ace people and told them to have the guard stay until I, or one of the workers arrives in the morning, from now on. The security guard will arrive at five in the afternoon instead of seven. Locks will be installed today along with the alarm system. A little ahead of schedule, but that's OK."

"I'm still wondering who would do this and why,"

I said. "Should we be afraid, or is it just a prank? Does Theda know what happened?" My mind jumped back to the falling tile incident. I remembered Chester shouting at whoever was on the roof in English? Maybe he forgot that most of his workmen speak very little English.

Chester seemed unable to answer my questions. He just shrugged his shoulders and walked off. I looked around the room. Fortunately, our paints and supplies were untouched. From the large dining room window, I watched Kyle and Trigger running in circles outside, chased by a little ball of fluff with four tiny feet. Trigger's bandaged arm didn't slow him down. My shoulders relaxed a tad, but the pinch was still in my neck.

"Allie, there's nothing we can do today so you might as well take off and we'll try again tomorrow. OK?"

"Sure, we'll be back tomorrow. You look awful, Jo. Get some rest and don't worry," Allie said, giving me a much needed hug.

I went to a window and watched my friends leave, wondering if I should tell Theda about the graffiti or not worry her and just let it go. I was still undecided as I walked into the music room to see if there was any damage in that room. Looking out the window, I saw that Alicia's Volvo was gone, but in its place was the silver SUV. Theda just sat in her Lexus with her mouth open. After a couple minutes, she threw it in reverse, whipped it around and drove away at the speed of light.

I ran to my truck, sped down the mountain and parked

in front of the cabin before the SUV's dust had time to settle. I helped Theda as she stumbled to the door. We sat quietly in the beautifully appointed living room. Finally, Theda spoke.

"Josephine, I'm so sorry I brought you into this mess. I'm at a loss. I don't know why all these things are happening and I don't know what to do about it. Someone must hate us, but why?" She was eyeing the liquor cabinet across the room.

"I talked to Chester and he said he has taken care of everything, more security, locks on the doors and the alarm system will be installed immediately. Try not to worry," I said as I wiped my forehead with the back of my hand. I needed to get Theda out of the house and away from the liquor cabinet, pronto.

I went to the kitchen, found two glasses and filled them with water. Theda thanked me for the water as if it was a wonderful new tonic. I clinked my glass to hers and said, "it's time we had some fun. Monterey or Carmel for lunch?"

"Are you serious, Josephine?"

"Absolutely. Where would you like to go?"

"Monterey!" her eyes sparkled, "what do you think?"

"Monterey is fine with me. I'll leave Solow in the house while we're gone."

I pulled some clean clothes from my suitcase and exchanged them for the paint-smeared ensemble I had been wearing. A little costume jewelry, and I looked fairly decent for a small-town, middle-aged artist.

Since the outing was my idea, I figured I would be the driver. And for that small mercy I was grateful. I fired up the truck and we bucked our way down the hill. After the driveway, the rest of the trip was easy. Ninety minutes later, I angled my Mazda into an empty space at the municipal parking lot near Fisherman's Wharf.

Most of the coastal morning fog had dissipated and the ocean air was warming up nicely. Seals barked, gulls screeched, waves pounded and people seemed happier in Monterey. We sauntered down to the end of the wharf and halfway back before we decided on a place to eat. There were a dozen or more restaurants, all very tempting. The one we chose was dark inside except for a bank of sunlit windows facing the water.

A young woman wearing a white peasant blouse and short black skirt led us to a table with an outstanding view of the ocean. She handed each of us a menu.

"Would you ladies like something to drink?"

"Iced tea, please," I said.

"That sounds good. I'll have the same." No mention of booze from Theda so far. "It's like a different world here," she cooed, "the waves crashing over the rocks, the fishing boats, and tourists everywhere. This was a good idea, Josephine, but don't think I don't know that you plotted it all to get me away from my worries." We laughed and enjoyed our afternoon at the shore. The food was good and Theda never indulged in anything stronger than iced tea.

It was late afternoon when we arrived back in Boulder Creek. Instead of turning right onto Bear Creek Road, I turned left and parked the truck at the public library.

"Theda, do you mind if I pick up a book at the library? I forgot to pack one."

"I'll go with you. I've never been inside this library." Her voice was clear and strong and there was a bounce in her step. We entered the library and proceeded down a wide entry hall. The walls where decorated with framed newspaper articles and old photographs. One of the sepia colored pictures caught my eye. I stopped and stared while Theda looked over my shoulder.

"Do you see what I see?" I asked.

"I do. That's our cabin with a horse and buggy in the front yard. What year was it, Josephine? Look at the newspaper clipping under the picture."

"I'll read it to you. May 10, 1923, Amos McFee and his wife Sarah, holding their son, Herman, pose in front of their home in the Boulder Creek Mountains. The McFee land was cleared in 1893 by Amos's father, Daniel McFee and deeded to his son in 1918. Amos manages the farm and the mine and belongs to the Boulder Creek Volunteer Fire Department. Recently, Amos helped create the Valley Water District. He and his family will be honored at the annual Western Days festivities in July."

Theda's usually restrained voice doubled in volume. "The baby in that picture was the previous owner of our property, Herman McFee. Herman was almost ninety when he died and left everything to his son, Kenneth, who sold it to us."

"Why did Kenneth sell the place?"

"I don't know why Kenneth sold it, but his three sons had been living in the cabin with their grandfather and were not happy about having to leave. We bought the property five years ago and let it sit for three years. When we finally decided it was time to remodel the cabin and build the new house, we found three young men still living there. The sheriff had to be summoned to remove them."

"Where did they go? Have you seen the boys since?"

"We don't know what became of them. They were certainly a rough lot."

I stared at the picture, focusing on every detail. The faded black and white picture showed Amos McFee wearing overalls and a plaid shirt. He was ruggedly handsome with a bushy head of dark hair and beard, broad shoulders and long legs. Sarah was a small woman with dark hair pulled into a bun. She held baby Herman in her arms. A shock of straight dark hair stood up on his tiny head.

"Theda, let me get this straight, each generation inherits the property until it gets to the three boys and they get zilch?"

"I guess so, but I'm sure we don't know the whole story."

"Where's the mine? What is it, a gold mine?"

"I have no idea. I didn't know the mine existed until

a moment ago. We have never seen the whole hundred acres, only what can be seen from the top of the mountain, tree tops, that's all." Theda looked up at the ceiling for a moment. "I remember the plat map showing a road winding around the base of the mountain. Warren asked about it and our realtor, Mrs. Bates, said it disappeared years ago. Overgrown, I guess."

"Do you think anyone knows where the mine is? What about Kenneth?" I was becoming more curious by the minute.

"According to Nora Bates, Kenneth moved to the bay area right after high school. Years later, when Kenneth's wife died, his three boys moved in with their grandfather, Herman. They didn't leave until three years after he died. Not until we forced them out."

I wondered if Nora Bates had any more stories about the place. The Munger history and land fascinated me. I lost interest in finding a book and Theda hadn't found anything either, so we left the library empty handed. I dropped Theda at the cabin and continued up the mountain. It was almost five o'clock. Only one of the workers remained at the mansion and he was literally up to his neck, shoveling a ditch.

"Hello, Manuel, how's it going?" He paused, looked up into the sun for an instant and then turned back to his 'pipes-in-the-ditch' project.

"Nice day, don't you think?" I said, trying to pry him from his work.

"Si, ees nice day." Another shovelful of dirt flew out of the trench.

"Have you worked for Chester very long?"

"Si, very long."

Just then an Ace Security truck rolled into view. An oversized senior citizen decked out in a sky blue uniform with badge, gun, club and the works, slammed his door and strolled over to see what Manuel was working on. Maybe he just wanted to meet me. His large body, encased in a too small uniform, practically bounced over the uneven terrain. Something about him reminded me of a retired cop. But why would a retired cop work a low paying job like Ace Security at the Mungers' estate?

"Hi, folks. I'm security round here." A little tobacco juice escaped from the corner of his mouth. "Just call me Stan." He touched the brim of his blue cap in a show of chivalry, as he smiled and gave me a wink.

"Hello, I'm Josephine and this is Manuel." Manuel dutifully looked up for a moment.

"You must be one ah them mural painters they brought in," Stan said. "Nice tah meet ya. Guess you folks can go home now. I'll be here until tomorrow mornin', keepin' watch." I couldn't resist asking a couple questions.

"Have you seen the perpetrator ... I mean, do you know who wrote on the walls?"

"Oh yeah, Chester called in about some mischief up here. Too bad." Stan lowered his thick eyebrows and shook his head slowly. "Kids!"

"It's a little nerve wracking if you know what I mean. Have you seen any strangers up here, or a Mastiff? What do you think is going on?"

"Ma'am, I don't know what's goin' on, as you say, but I did see a truck come up here in the middle of the night last week. Them boys saw me and took off in a hurry. Didn't see no dog."

"Do you happen to know the former owners of this property?"

"I never met old man Herman, but I did have a few run-ins with those crazy grandsons of his. Years back, I was a deputy sheriff and them boys was always in trouble. Not big trouble, they was just light fingered, pot smokin' troublemakers. Think I saw Damon's truck parked in front of Mac's Bar the other day. Hard to miss a pickup with that much rust." My blood moved a little faster as my heart pounded and my brain strained to connect the dots.

"What color is the truck? Could it be the same one you saw here, in the middle of the night?"

"Damon's truck is mostly spots of gray primer, except for all that rust." Stan scratched his bristly chins. "It's a big ol' Dodge. By the sound of the engine, might be the same truck. Maybe, maybe not. Couldn't say, bein' it was dark and all."

"Do you know where the McFees live?"

"No, ma'am, don't know. Excuse me, gotta' check the grounds. I do that everyday. Nice meetin' ya, ma'am." Stan turned and shuffled off to the back of the mansion. I noticed Manuel had been following our conversation. It occurred to me that he might understand more English than I thought.

"Manuel, have you ever seen the truck Stan was talking about?"

"Si, I see it on Bear Creek Road near dee bridge. Two brown dogs in dee back."

"Did you see the driver?"

Manuel lowered his eyes, "no, I no see anyone." I decided to give up for the time being. He climbed out of the ditch and brushed himself off.

"See you later," I said as I climbed into my truck.

Back at the cabin, Theda sat on the floor in the living room with the front half of Solow stretched over her lap. They looked content to stay there so I offered to make dinner. A light supper would do. I scrounged through the fridge and the cupboards only to come up with lettuce, cucumbers, yogurt, peaches and a package of sliced almonds.

I whipped up a yogurt dressing, a green salad with slivered almonds on top and peaches and cream for dessert. I filled Solow's bowl with kibble and called Theda to the kitchen for dinner. She pulled out a pricey Chardonnay from the fridge and did the pouring.

The kitchen had been a real surprise to me. It had new granite countertops, stainless steel appliances and all the bells and whistles of a great kitchen. We settled into our chairs and clinked our glasses to a new friendship.

The evening slipped away without our noticing the time. We discovered that our birthdays were only three months apart, same year, and we agreed that turning fifty was not a big deal. Theda grew up in Los Gatos and as a teen, visited the Santa Cruz Boardwalk frequently; I grew up in Santa Cruz, and spent a lot of time at the boardwalk and the plunge. We both loved children, animals, music and chocolate.

Finally, after an evening of conversation with Theda, I felt comfortable enough to ask the question that had been burning in my brain all day.

"Theda, where have I seen that picture before? It looks so familiar," I pointed to the silver-framed 8x10 photo on the fireplace mantle. A couple minutes passed. I was beginning to think she hadn't heard me, when she finally spoke.

"That's my husband and next to him is our daughter. You probably saw the picture on the news programs last year. She has been missing …" Theda stared at the floor, took a deep breath and continued with great effort, "since one year ago last Tuesday. I had a hard time getting through that terrible anniversary, the anniversary of the worst loss in my life. Dear Emily disappeared without a trace, our only daughter … our only child." Theda's eyes were about to overflow.

"I don't know what to say, Theda. Are you OK talking about it?"

"I suppose I am. I never get used to it and I never stop hoping. Emily was a junior at San Francisco State, a good student, even took summer classes. She had lots of friends, never a problem. She drove her car to school one day to find that her nine o'clock chemistry class had been canceled. Her friend, Kate, said she saw Emily drive away in her Mustang a little after nine, and she has not been seen since."

"Warren and I had tried to get her to apply to UC Santa Cruz because we planned to retire here in Santa Cruz County, but she was having a hard time with that. Her friends were very important to her."

"What about her car?"

"It hasn't been found." Theda wrapped her hands around her shoulders as if it were a cold day. "Warren gave Emily a restored baby blue Mustang Convertible for her birthday. Probably the car he wished he had for himself, instead of the big pretentious cars he thinks he needs to boost his image."

I don't know a lot about marriage, having been married only three years before Marty was run down by the eighteen-wheeler, but this marriage sounded very unhappy. I hadn't heard one kind word about Warren. Somewhere I heard that losing a child often breaks up the marriage. I wondered if there was something I could do to help the dismal couple. I tried to take Theda's mind off Emily, at least for a moment.

"Say, how about a card game?"

"I'm sorry Josephine, I wouldn't be able to keep my mind on the game, and besides, I'm feeling sleepy. You might want to open your window tonight. The crickets make lovely music." She stretched, I yawned.

"I'm going to bed right after I take Solow for his constitutional." After much coaxing, my reluctant pal trundled outside with me. The night was warm and moonlit, crickets chirped and the forest smelled of rotting leaves and fragrant laurel.

I almost lost track of Solow as he sniffed his way to the back of the cabin and then another sixty feet to the barn. He sniffed at the side door and howled, nagging me about how slow I was. I followed the best I could, given there was no official path across the uneven ground.

I finally caught up to Solow, opened the side door to the barn and ran my hand up the wall in search of a light switch. The switch was exactly where I guessed it should be. Two long rows of florescent lights blinked on, revealing a shop with workbench and all sorts of woodworking tools. In one corner a rickety old high-back wooden chair was pushed up to an equally old wooden desk, probably from the twenties.

I noticed a door on the other side of the room, so for the sake of Solow's curiosity, I opened it. At least a minute went by before my eyes adjusted to the darkness and even then, I could barely see the straw scattered across the earthen floor of the large interior. I didn't find a light switch, so I called Solow back into the workshop and we snooped around a bit more. Many of the tools looked like antiques, but others were newer plug-in types. The workbench had acquired its character from paint spatters and pounded hammer and chisel indentions.

"Time for bed old buddy. Come on, follow me." He followed without ever lifting his nose off the ground. The house was quiet as Solow padded straight to his bed. I locked the doors, front and back, and turned off the lights, except for the antique lamp in my bedroom.

I guess you could call me snoopy, but I couldn't help myself. As I hung a few shirts in the small walk-in closet, I noticed half a dozen outfits pushed to the far end. Two pairs of shoes sat on the floor under the clothes, a pair of white leather sandals and a pair of navy tennis shoes. No bling on the shoes, so I concluded they belonged to the daughter, which meant I would be sleeping in Emily's room.

I decided to empty the contents of my suitcases into dresser drawers. Pepper spray went in the empty nightstand drawer. What was I thinking, packing that stuff? I thought Dad was crazy when he gave it to me for protection. My protection was peacefully snoring in his bed, securing the cabin. Soon we were snoring in concert, as I dreamt about an owl that kept watch over the barn. The bird caught fire and its ashes fell on my feet.

Chapter Five

Wafting through the cabin was the most heavenly, freshly brewed coffee aroma. It took a minute for me to shake the dust bunnies from my brain and remember where I was. I raised my head to look at the clock on the nightstand. It was almost eight. I finally realized it was Friday morning, I was in Emily's bed and I should get ready for work.

Across the room Solow opened one bloodshot eye, groaned and went back to sleep. "That's OK, old boy. You don't have a worry in the world." I left Solow with his dreams of Fluffy and followed the coffee aroma to the kitchen.

"Good morning, Josephine. Did you sleep well?"

"Yeah, like Solow after a good Fluffy chase. And you?"

"It's been a long time since I slept so sound." Theda pointed to the coffee maker. "Coffee?" I nodded. She poured a mug for me and refilled hers.

I sipped coffee strong enough to straighten my hair, and

washed down two pieces of blackened toast. Obviously Theda was not the most talented cook on the block, but her attitude was chipper. We discussed front-page stories from the Sentinel, I in my faded cotton nightshirt, Theda in her designer silk robe, like two old school chums.

"By the way, Josephine, the shower is yours. I'm finished in the bathroom." That's what bothered me about little old houses. They usually had only one bathroom. At my house I hated sharing my bathroom with guests. Inevitably, just when I needed to use the powder room, my guest would be taking an extended shower on my water bill!

"I'll get in the shower now," I said. "Don't let my dog get excited and fall out of bed while I'm gone." It was nice to hear Theda laugh.

Twenty minutes later, I was clean and dressed for work. On my way out, I gave Solow a quick ear-rub. My truck didn't even have time to warm up before I parked it in front of the mansion. Alicia pulled in beside me. The boys were laughing as usual and Tansey yipped and twirled as we all walked toward the house.

"So, what was it like to spend the night in a cabin in the forest?" Alicia asked.

"Not bad. Theda is a very nice person and the house is comfortable. Solow and I explored the barn last night in the dark. No problem. I really like it here. How's Trigger doing with the injured arm?"

"Oh, you know him, a little too stoic for his own good, like his father. He woke me up last night with one of his nightmares, second night in a row."

"Does the nightmare have anything to do with a dog attack?"

"I don't know, Jo. He went back to sleep as soon as I tucked him in."

Trigger and Tansey played in the sunroom while Kyle, Alicia and I examined the dining room wall where our mural had been. Alicia sighed.

"We had a good start, didn't we? I guess it was just practice. What do you want me to do, Jo?"

"Kyle and I will paint in the sky. I loved your clouds, Allie, so you get to create them all over again. In the meantime, mix up three colors for the mountains, going from an earthy green to a faded bluer-green. Kyle, I need you to bring in the box of paint from the back of my truck." He came back carrying the box and set it down.

"Like, Chester says your truck's in the way." He watched me roll my eyes. "Ah, like, I'll move it for you, Jo." I smiled, handed him the keys and he ducked out.

I mixed four shades of blue paint while Alicia worked on the greens. When I finally looked around and realized Kyle could have moved my truck to Nova Scotia in less time, I went looking for him. I spotted my pickup at the far side of the circle drive with a certain goofy looking college student sitting in the driver's seat, talking on the phone. He saw me coming and jumped out of the truck, the phone still held to his ear. I didn't say a word, just turned and walked back inside.

Kyle was a model worker the rest of the day. No more phone calls to anyone. We sped through the sky painting process, Alicia did her magic with the clouds and by the end of the day we even had mountains.

I said my good-byes, hugged Trigger and watched the Volvo disappear down the mountain. Since I didn't have a long commute home, I decided to walk to the front yard trench project and see what Manuel was up to.

"How's it going today? I see all your help went home." Manuel leaned against his shovel.

"Si, they all go. I wait for Stan." There were only two vehicles parked at the villa, mine and Manuel's older blue and white Chevy pickup. His truck was parked under an oak tree just a few yards away, dusty, but well maintained. I noticed a black lab mix lying in the back, eyes closed, paws twitching.

"OK, Manuel, gotta' go. Have a good weekend." He almost smiled. I climbed into my truck and took off. Halfway to the cabin I rounded a turn, frantically slammed on the brakes and wrenched my pickup up a leafy bank as the Ace Security truck roared up the narrow driveway. Stan smiled and waved as he whizzed by.

When I arrived at the cabin, Theda greeted me at the door. Solow dragged himself up from the floor and beat his tail against my legs.

"I hope you don't mind, Josephine, we have a little change of plans. Warren just called and said he's running late, but he will be here at eight or nine. What do you say to dining in Boulder Creek?"

"Works for me, just give me a minute to shed this paint outfit. I'll wear my 'Monterey luncheon' ensemble again since it's all I brought with me." I went to my bedroom and discovered Theda had tidied things up. When I returned to the living room Theda stood ready, her purse on her shoulder and keys in her hand. It was a warm evening, but a shiver ran up my spine when I remembered the last time I rode with her. I told myself to forget that terrible Tuesday, the one-year-anniversary of Emily's disappearance, and concentrate on the new Theda who was all smiles and no gin breath.

Theda's driving had greatly improved, but the driveway hadn't. Eventually we turned right onto Bear Creek Road. As we passed over the Bear Creek Bridge, I noticed a green forestry truck parked at the side of the road, just like the one I had seen the day before.

"Must be looking for steelhead poachers," I said. Theda nodded. Boulder Creek was humming with cars and people. Johnnie's parking lot was packed and cars lined Central Avenue in both directions. Luckily, Theda found a parking space at the curb just two doors from The Brewery.

"Is The Brewery OK with you, Josephine?"

"I've never eaten there. Looks fine." We entered and found a table by one of the front windows. The place was old, full of dark wood, brass and glass, and beautifully restored. I admired the plank floor, paneled walls, giant hand-hewed beams across the ceiling and the long carved walnut bar.

Two young women worked behind the popular counter where a dozen men drank beer while sitting on high stools that swiveled. The men swiveled a look when we walked in, then swiveled back to the young women. Seems we were on the wrong side of thirty.

The music was western, but the menu could have easily come from the Fairmont Hotel in San Francisco. It was long and pricey with truffles, calamari, ahi pole, pesto chicken penne, tiramisu and on and on. We decided there must be a real chef in the kitchen because the food was very good.

After dinner we sipped decaf and watched the sun disappear behind the mountains. It was all very pleasant except for an annoying muffler noise outside. Looking through the front window, I saw an old rusty Dodge pickup roll by making a guttural racket and belching black smoke from its rear.

"Theda, look, did you see that truck?" Theda looked confused and shook her head. "I think I just saw Damon McFee's rusty old truck. You know, the McFee family that lived in your cabin about three years too long."

"Sorry, I try not to think about those days. Are you ready to go? Warren will be arriving soon." Theda paid the bill and tipped Annie, our perky and thoughtful waitress. We drank in the fresh evening air, walked a short distance to the SUV and climbed in.

Back on Bear Creek Road, near the bridge, we passed the forestry truck. "Working late," I thought to myself. Immediately after the bridge, we passed another turnout space and then the Munger's driveway began. Theda hung a left and we bumped and wound our way through the forest to the cabin. The headlights beamed onto another vehicle, long and dark, turning into the cabin's parking area. Something else caught my eye, a faint light from the barn, and then it was gone.

A man I recognized from his picture stepped out of the long black Lincoln. As soon as my feet touched the ground, Warren reached out for a handshake.

"Hello, I'm Warren. You must be Josephine," he said, pumping my hand. "Theda has told me all about you and I want you to know we appreciate your staying here. Theda never did like being alone."

"Yeah and she's had to be alone a lot, thanks to you." I thought to myself. To Warren I said, "Hello, Warren," and I did not roll my eyes even though I wanted to, really, really bad, as I watched him give Theda a practiced hug.

"I hope you two will excuse me, I need to take Solow for a walk," a perfect excuse to get away from the happy reunion. I dragged Solow out of his bed. Once he was outside, the smorgasbord of smells tempted him like catnip to a cat. Nose to the ground, ears dragging, he headed for the barn.

The darkening sky still had tinges of red and purple, but only specks of light pierced through the canopy of trees. I strained to see my way to the barn, opened the side door to the workshop and immediately noticed the smell of cigarette smoke.

I flipped the light switch. Everything looked the same as before, so I peeked through the second door into the main part of the barn. Nothing there. I was just about to turn off the shop lights when I noticed something I was sure I had not seen the night before. On the work bench, plugged into an outlet, sat a cell phone charger. No phone in sight. I switched off the lights and let Solow lead me back to the cabin. Quickly, I loaded one suitcase and one doggie bed into the truck. It was time for us to go home.

By ten-thirty I had gathered my mail from the mailbox at the end of my driveway and parked the truck in front of the house. Solow followed me inside. I flipped on a light, dropped my purse, mail and suitcase just inside the front door and fell into my favorite chair. The answering machine blinked. I pushed the PLAY button.

"Hello, dear, it's your mother. Hope your new mural project is going well. We're having ribs Saturday afternoon. Hope to see you then." Mom and Dad still didn't know about my financial difficulties, and I hoped I wouldn't have to tell them. They had so much living to do and not a lot of money to support all the fun they planned to have.

The next two calls were from bill collectors doing their miserable jobs. I punched the ERASE button with more force than necessary, turned on another light and sorted through my mail. Since I didn't win any sweepstakes and there were no hand written letters, the stack of mail could wait.

I turned on the TV just in time for a rerun of Monk, but my mind was elsewhere. Even my financial worries had taken a backseat to Theda's problems. I wondered if Emily was still alive, since no one had found her body or her car. Was Stan telling me everything he knew about the McFee boys? Who wanted the Mungers to leave their beautiful villa? Who was in the barn and why? Finally my thoughts shifted to things I was thankful for, like being home.

I don't know who fell asleep first, probably me because I don't remember hearing Solow snore. Maybe he heard me for a change. I dreamt about Theda's barn and a bearded gentleman who sat on Theda's porch, quietly carving furniture out of tree limbs. Suddenly the man's long fluffy beard slipped off, revealing his handsome face. He sounded like David when he spoke to me and Solow seemed to know him.

Chapter Six

Saturday morning began early with a cold, wet nose on my cheek. I opened one eye at a time. Staring back at me were my favorite bloodshot eyeballs. Out of patience, Solow finally let out a mournful howl, letting me know that he meant business.

"Need to go to the john so early?" I stumbled down the hall, opened the back door and watched Solow run through the weeds chasing Fluffy. David's big white cat circled Solow several times. I drank my morning coffee and counted eight buzzard hawks circling above the patio, probably in hysterics. I felt my energy rising as I laughed out loud and let Solow back in the house, panting and exhausted.

After breakfast I cleaned the kitchen and then hauled my laundry outside to the washer and dryer. The machines sat on a cement slab my deceased husband, Marty, had created many years ago. It was all very convenient. Winter wash was a little dicey, but summer laundry was a breeze. I stuffed a weeks worth of laundry into the washer, added soap and water and by noon everything was clean and dry. I mopped the kitchen floor, watered the marigolds and read the mail.

It was time to go to town. I left the house wearing white shorts and a red, short-sleeved knit top, the best I could do for my favorite summer holiday, the Fourth of July. Solow rested in his bed on the front porch, securing the ranch.

My truck found the Watsonville Market out of habit. I planned to dash in for flowers and a bottle of wine for the folks. Good old Robert was putting his weight into pushing a long row of carts toward the store entrance. He saw me walking across the parking lot and let the carts come to a stop.

"Hi, Jo, heard about the murder in Boulder Creek?"

"What are you talking about? I was just there yesterday."

"I heard it on the radio this morning. KPIG said a forest ranger was missing for a couple days. They found him in the creek, dead." Robert loved to be the first with the news, good or bad. "What do you think about that, Jo?"

"What makes you think he was murdered?" I asked, as an image of the green forestry truck parked near the Bear Creek Bridge flashed before my eyes.

"A grown man wouldn't drown in a little river, and besides, KPIG said he was murdered." He looked at me to see if I looked creped-out, or at least worried.

"I hate bad news like that. Excuse me, Robert, I need

to buy a couple things and drive to Santa Cruz," I said, entering the store. I left Robert wrestling carts into their holding pen, and quickly took care of my grocery needs. All the way to Santa Cruz, I pondered the fate of the forest ranger. I had no conscious memory of driving to Santa Cruz, but somehow I ended up in front of my parent's house on Walnut Avenue.

From my truck, I watched Mom and Dad on the roof, patching the brick chimney with grout. After a couple minutes the job was finished and they skittered down the aluminum ladder. We hugged and eventually congregated in the backyard. I was startled by a loud bang, a firecracker going off somewhere down the street. Feeling a bit jittery, I handed the wine and roses to Mom before another firecracker went off.

"Honey, thank you, the roses are beautiful and we'll enjoy the wine. We're so glad to see you're alright, you know, with that murder and all." Mom gave me the 'eye'.

"Hey, you two, I'm fine and what does the murder have to do with me, other than it happened near my work?"

"We're just glad you have Alicia and Pyle up there with you," Dad said.

"Dad, his name is Kyle."

"Yeah, and those little towns up in the mountains are full of weirdos."

"Did I tell you that my boss, Theda Munger, hired me to live in her cabin until their mansion is finished? It's beautiful up there, quiet and woodsy, and no hectic commutes." Dad turned his back and walked across the lawn as Mom forced a smile. "She pays me a hundred dollars a day to live there and then buys me fancy meals."

Another bang, very loud. I jumped and whipped my head around, following the bang and sulfur smell. I watched Dad crouch down near the back door and light another cherry bomb. He jumped up and stepped back, howling with laughter when it went off. Actually, I couldn't imagine my parents ever growing up and becoming dull.

Promptly at four o'clock, Myrtle joined Dad and me at the picnic table. Myrtle lived next door and my parents invited her to every holiday celebration because she was a widow and her selfish kids and grandkids never included her in their plans. Her plump little body was stuffed into a black polyester pantsuit like a sausage in its casing. Her double chin peeked out from the red, white and blue patterned scarf tied at the neck. Fuzzy white hair sparsely covered her head and she spoke in a husky, ex-smoker voice.

"Hello, Jo, it's good to see you, dear. Everything going well at work these days?" I nodded and smiled "I hear you're working in Boulder Creek, of all places. How do you like those mountain men?" she winked a saggy eye.

Translation, "Isn't it dangerous working way out in the boonies. Meet anyone you want to marry, yet?" I could read her ancient little mind like a book. After all, we had known each other since before Marty and I were married. I always knew Myrtle's heart was in the right place, I just didn't know about her mouth. She was the one we trusted to pass on gossip, inaccurately.

Mom changed her clothes and joined us in the backyard. She wore a red sari and gold sandals. Not bad for a woman nearing eighty.

"Myrtle dear, don't you look nice, and how are you feeling, you know, the rash and all?" Mom asked with concern in her voice. Myrtle automatically scratched a spot behind her ear.

"Oh, Leola, it's nothing to worry about. Doctor Cowden thinks I'm allergic to Toppsy. If he thinks I'm getting rid of my cat, he has another think coming. By the way, did you hear about Fred Pasco, the forestry officer? They say he was shot, died instantly. You just can't trust those mountain people up there in Boulder Creek," she crabbed, looking at me to see if she had made an impression.

"Yes, Myrtle, we read about it," Dad said. "Crime is everywhere these days, but not in my neighborhood." He knocked his fist three times on the wooden bench he was sitting on, stood up and walked quickly to the flames leaping from the BBQ. He calmly put the top on the old Webber and announced the ribs would be ready in five minutes.

Mom and I brought out side dishes, drinks, plastic ware. We feasted while the rockets flared up and down the street. I washed down the last bite of charred meat with a good dose of Mom's slippery potato salad.

"The corn was fabulous, Mom. Where did you buy it?"

"Shopper's Corner - is there any other place to shop?" That's a Santa Cruzan for you, loyal to the oldest store in town, to the end. "Honey, I wish you would call us more often. You're working in a safe neighborhood, I trust?" I hated being scrutinized by my parents as if I were a ditsy teenager.

"Don't worry, Mom. I'm working with dozens of people, like, roofers, landscapers, wood finishers, painters, electricians, you name it. It's a good group and the place is drop-dead gorgeous. Theda and Warren hope to move into the house in a few weeks. Maybe you can drive up and see the villa when it's finished."

"So why are you staying at the owner's cabin?" Dad asked.

"Theda's lonely, way up there in the mountains. Her husband works in San Francisco on the weekdays. Warren is pleasant enough, but he's gone so much of the time. Sometimes I wonder if their marriage has lost its magic." I looked at Dad with his hand resting on Mom's. "Not everyone knows how to keep it together like you two." Myrtle smiled and nodded.

Fourth of July in Santa Cruz had always been a foggy affair and that year was no exception. We were just lucky the fog held off until after dinner. Wet, chilly air finally forced us inside where we indulged in banana cream pie and decaf while Myrtle filled us in on the murder details.

I silently wondered if she was related to Robert, maybe in another life.

"I read in the Sentinel that Mr. Pasco had been testing the water in the creek where he died. Poor man couldn't even do his job without lunatics interfering. They said he was shot in the back from a long distance."

I kept a poker face as everyone watched me, looking for signs of fear. Apparently I passed the test and they finally moved on to other subjects. It was getting dark outside when I finally stood up to go.

"Think I'll run along now. Thanks for the great meal. I'll call you." I had the front door open before Mom and Dad could object. Dad met me at the door and shoved a handful of firecrackers into my purse. Poor Dad, he should have had a son.

"What do I want with these?" I asked.

"I don't need them, you have fun with them," he smiled at me as if I was ten years old and he was giving me something I had always wanted. In truth, I never got a charge out of setting off fireworks.

"Thanks, Dad." We hugged, and then Mom and Myrtle stepped up for their hugs. I stepped outside under street-lights that made the fog look like yellow cotton candy. The muffled sounds of fireworks boomed through the drizzly air as I shivered my way into the driver's seat. I would have stopped for gas at the cheapest gas station in Santa Cruz, but I was freezing in my shorts so I drove all the way to Watsonville on fumes. Finally out of the fog, I pulled into a gas station, ran my card through the slot and began filling the tank.

"Nice night for pumping gas," a familiar voice said, startling me out of my day dreaming. I turned. Ernie Quintana smiled as he filled the Volvo's gas tank. I should have recognized the family station wagon the minute I pulled in.

"Ernie, what are you doing out here on the Fourth of July?"

"We watched the fireworks display at the fairgrounds and Trigger fell asleep on the way home. Alicia and my mom decided it would be fun to make s'mores tonight in the backyard. They're home building the fire while I shop for the ingredients. Thought I would gas up while I'm in the neighborhood. Why don't you join us? Mom hasn't seen you since the hospital, when Trigger fell out of the tree. She always asks about you."

"I'd love to, Ernie. I'll follow you over there." Mrs. Quintana was a very nice lady with a cute Spanish accent. No wonder Ernie was a real gentleman, like my neighbor, David. I wondered if David was celebrating the fourth.

Alicia greeted me at the gate to the backyard, and Tansey was all over me as if we hadn't seen each other in a month. I picked up the little fur ball and we snuggled. I never could get enough puppy smell. We strolled over to the patio.

"How are you, Maria?" Maria sat, smiling with her whole round face.

"Josephine, I am very fine, gracias. Come sit over here. It is good to see you."

Ernie sat in a lawn chair on the other side of Maria. Alicia began toasting marshmallows on a stick over the BBQ. She sandwiched the browned marshmallows and chocolate squares between graham crackers, creating s'mores. The sky was clear and inky-black, the perfect background for fireworks on the other side of the lake.

"So, Ernie, did you hear about the murder in Boulder Creek?" He nodded, and I continued. "You're the biologist, why do you think the ranger was testing the water?"

"I'm not sure, but usually they test for pollutants such as lead, arsenic, nitrates and anything else that endangers fish, animals and especially people. Sometimes people up-stream poison the water with sewage, garbage, pesticides, you name it," he frowned.

"If the murder took place where I think it did, there are no houses around. It happens to be the Mungers' property, just forest everywhere." I waved my arms.

"Might be some farming going on, if you know what I mean." Our heads went up, eyes following the fireworks as he spoke. "I hope nothing illegal is going on."

"Murder's illegal," Alicia quipped, passing around a plate of s'mores. I figured it wouldn't be polite to refuse such a delicacy, even though I was already full to my chin with banana cream pie.

"Just one, thank you. Gotta' watch my girlish figure," I laughed. "Too bad Trigger is missing one of the best food groups, the indulgence group."

For the second time that night I encountered billows of chilly fog blowing in from the west, blocking out the fireworks. Everyone decided to go inside except me. It was time to call it a night and I had already popped the top button on my shorts. Besides, I needed to go home and feed my dog.

Driving in fog is always eerie, but that night was beyond eerie for me. A man had been shot in the back while doing his job. Why? As I parked in my driveway, the headlights caught Solow running toward the truck. I bent down and ruffled his ears. He walked me to the front door and I flipped a light switch. He made deep basset sounds as I poured kibble into his bowl. I left Solow and checked the answering machine.

"Howdy, neighbor. Fluffy and I miss you. How about breakfast at the Grange tomorrow?" It was hard for me to even think about breakfast with my belly stuffed full of desserts, but I did want to see David so I called and left a message.

"David, thanks for the invite. Meet you there at nine." The pancake breakfast was a once a month event at the Aromas Grange with the profits subsidizing the library's budget. It was a lovely way to do our civic duty and I was looking forward to good pancakes, omelets and extra good company.

I slept in Sunday morning until eight. By nine I was showered and dressed in a lavender summer dress and white sandals. Lavender always brought out the red highlights in my wavy hair, not that I really cared.

The grange was jammed, but I quickly spotted David saving a chair for me. He stood as I sat. His Levis were a titch too short for his long legs and his hair was overdue for a haircut, but his smile was warm and welcoming. He had retired two years earlier when he turned fifty. Too bad David's ex-wife took off with the preacher ten years ago and missed his retirement, but not too bad for me.

"Hi, beautiful," David said, just before he gave me a quick kiss on my cheek. People around us had knowing smiles, probably thinking we made a nice couple, when actually, we were just good friends.

"Hi, yourself, good lookin'." I loved to lead these people on. "How's the coffee?"

David didn't wait for a junior volunteer server to come around; instead, he found a coffee pot on his own and poured a cup for me. Maybe he knew me well enough to know I'm a nicer person after I get my morning caffeine.

Between the two of us, David and I knew quite a few people in Aromas, especially ones who had lived in the area for ten years or more. It was a place where families settled and usually never moved again. We talked with the people sitting near us, ate our omelets and pancakes, and enjoyed the warm summer morning.

"Ready to go?" David asked. I looked around and

noticed many of the pancake connoisseurs had already left.

"Ready," I said. "Want to come out to my house and watch the weeds grow?"

"I have a better idea. I'll cut your weeds for you."

"Well, a girl doesn't get an offer like that everyday. Sure, if you really want to."

David had a tractor-mower that was way too much fun. He rode it every chance he got. I couldn't have stopped him from mowing my five acres if I tried. My whole property was covered with tall green grass going brown. The neighbors always cut their grass as a fire prevention measure and this wasn't the first time David had rescued me from my weeds.

I drove home and a short time later heard David's noisy mower coming up the gravel driveway. Solow raised his head and thumped his tail twice, the equivalent of a big smile. Looking like a real farmer, David had changed into overalls, an old straw hat and a bandana around his neck. At first glance, who would guess he was well educated and had retired at an early age with a nice pension from IBM. His apricot orchard was just a hobby.

"Close your windows," David shouted. "I'm gonna' stir up some dust." He bumped over the uneven, hilly terrain to the closest oak tree and circled it, looking like a rodeo contestant making a tight turn on a bucking bronco.

Not wanting to suffer the dust, I went inside and closed the windows and doors. I decided to catch up on my chores. I dialed Chester's number, expecting him not to be home. He surprised me and answered on the second ring.

"Mathus Construction."

"Hi, Chester, it's Josephine. I just wanted to remind you to take away the scaffolding. Actually, you could set it up in the den, six feet high and ten feet long." There was no sound on the other end so I did a little nervous chit chat. "We won't start work till nine or so, plenty of time to get your guys to break it down."

"No problem, Josephine."

"Oh, by the way, anything going on up at the mansion, you know, with the murder and all?"

"DEA and sheriffs all over the place asking questions. I tried to catch up on work Saturday. Didn't get much done." I tried to imagine what Theda was going through.

"How is Theda holding up?"

"How do you think? She's a wreck. Warren took her to Los Gatos today to see her parents." He cleared his throat, "so, how much do you know about this Fish and Game thing?"

"I haven't even read a paper or seen a newscast. I just hear what people are saying. I saw a forestry truck parked near the Bear Creek Bridge a couple days in a row. I guess that's where it happened. Am I right?"

"Yeah, that's where it happened, only up the creek a few hundred yards."

"Did it happen on the Mungers' property?"

"Sure did, that's why the Feds and the deputies are asking questions at the mansion. Don't worry about the scaffolding. We'll handle it for you."

"Thanks. See you tomorrow." I put the phone down and peeked out the window. David was making progress. I could tell because the air was thick with dust and bits of grass. I could barely see poor David with his safety glasses clouded and the bandana up over his mouth.

I decided to check for email. Yikes! Over four hundred messages. An hour later I was still sorting and trashing spam. Suddenly I realized the mower was quiet, and then I heard a knock on the back door.

"David, what happened to you?" I suddenly felt queasy. David stood at the door, hat in hand, his hair matted with blood.

"I was cutting under one of the oak trees when a sneaky little branch hung down and got me. Probably looks worse than it is. My hat got the worst of it." He wore a foolish little grin as he entered the kitchen, his filleted hat dropped to the floor.

"Sit here, Indiana Jones," I chuckled. "I'll clean you up a bit and we'll see how much damage you did to your noggin." I pulled a clean hand towel from a drawer and soaked it with warm water. After a little swabbing, I realized the scratch wasn't very deep. Heads always bled a lot. I washed his forehead, noticing how smooth his skin looked, but the dark chocolate eyes were his best feature.

"You sure know how to show a guy a good time," he said.

"Anytime, sailor. You're clean and medicated, but I hope you don't plan to go back out there and finish."

"Nope, I'll work on it tomorrow. Mind if I leave the machine here overnight?"

"Of course not. It's already three, how about a bite to eat?" He nodded and I began foraging for food. I ended up slicing potatoes and sausages into a baking pan, added sauerkraut on top and baked up a "bratwurst surprise" in the oven while I made a green salad. After our late lunch - early dinner, David and I caught up on stuff. He asked how the new painting job was going.

"You won't believe what's going on up at the Munger's. First day we're up there, a roof tile falls through the glass ceiling and almost sends Theda to the big mansion in the sky. Next day Trigger's attacked by a Mastiff and a workman kills the dog with his shovel. Next day we see that someone has written, LEAVE OR DIE, on the walls, including our mural! As if that wasn't bad enough, Saturday morning, a forest ranger was found shot to death on the Mungers' property."

"Jo, I'm worried about you working up there. Can't you find a job somewhere less dangerous?" he asked, eyes intense, jaw pulled tight.

"Never mind all that. It's really a great job. They even pay me to live in the cabin on the weekdays. I'm a little curious about a light I saw in the barn and the shop smelled of cigarette smoke. Maybe one of the workmen wandered down there."

"Where in Boulder Creek did you say this place is located?" David didn't take his eyes off me for a second. I wished I could have retracted a few details.

"The Munger's driveway begins about a mile from town, just past the Bear Creek Bridge. Doesn't your friend, what's his name, live out there somewhere?"

"Yeah, Jake Dynes, you met him a couple years ago. He worked with me at IBM. He and Lois rattle around in their big house on West Park Avenue. They love it up there in the redwoods." He talked on and on about Jake and the years they worked together at IBM, never mentioning Susan and her friend the preacher. My hair stands on end when I think about that woman leaving David after almost twenty years of marriage for an unsaintly man like the preacher. David looked tired.

"Shall I make some coffee?"

"Oh, no, gotta' go home and feed Fluffy." He stood up. "Thanks for the chow."

It's funny how we both used our pets as an excuse to go home when we were tired.

"I'm the one who should be saying thank you, after you sliced your head open trying to cut my grass." He bent down, kissed my forehead and was out the door. I watched him until the wild lilacs blocked my view.

Chapter Seven

Monday, eight-thirty in the morning, I parked my Mazda next to the silver Lexus in front of the Mungers' cabin. Theda must have heard me drive up. She opened the front door wearing her silver robe and a weak smile. I handed her two bags of groceries and went back to the truck for two more. I was not about to live in a house with no food, and I didn't trust her to buy any.

"Where's Warren? I didn't see his car," I said, as I carried in the last two bags.

"He left for the city an hour ago. Has a meeting or something."

I tried not to think bad thoughts about Warren, but it was impossible not to. After all that had happened, couldn't he stay with his wife a little longer? Not my business, I told myself, as I loaded the fridge with fresh fruit and veggies.

"I had way too much good food this fourth of July. How about you?" I asked.

"Warren and I spent a lovely Sunday afternoon with

my parents in Los Gatos." After a long pause she sighed, "I'm afraid I was a bit of a basket case Saturday when the detectives questioned us. Warren was about to lose his temper and I about to lose my mind. What a pair." She slumped into a chair in the kitchen. Minutes later Solow was asleep, his chin resting on her feet. "Sunday was a nice little respite," she smiled, watching Solow at rest.

"I'm glad you were able to get away for awhile." I thought Warren should take her on a cruise to the Bahamas. "I see my dog isn't shy around here."

"I don't think you need to worry about him. If only I could fall asleep that easily." She reached down and patted Solow's head. I finished putting groceries away and decided to unpack my suitcase later, after work. I grabbed my little cooler full of lunch and walked to the front door.

"See you later, Theda."

"Josephine, I almost forgot, I have a hair appointment today, but I'll be home by four," she smiled and waved from her seat in the kitchen.

I backed my truck onto the rutty road and headed toward the top of the mountain. Alicia was right behind me. Looking at my rearview mirror, I saw the boys bobbing up and down in the back of the station wagon. We parked a couple hundred feet from the house in a field of dry grass, keeping our distance from a cement truck pouring concrete into the sidewalk forms. Another truck idled, waiting its turn.

Several workmen were bent over, smoothing wet

concrete as fast as they could before it dried. One man's job was to spray the cement with water from a garden hose so it wouldn't dry too fast. I couldn't imagine how the cement trucks made it to that altitude in the first place, using the same skinny, rutty road I had just driven.

Trigger ran to my open window before I could climb out of the truck, and held up Tansey for my inspection.

"Do you think she's bigger? Grandma says she's growing."

"Sure looks like it to me. What are you feeding her to make her so pretty?"

"Oh, just kibble and leftovers, but she always looked pretty."

I pocketed the truck keys and followed my crew around the cement chaos to the unfinished mural. The room looked bigger without scaffolding.

The next step was to paint the lower half of the wall with earth and grass, adding trees, vineyards and farmhouses later. The worst was always last, the foreground, which would be the bottom two feet of the mural. We would have to do all kinds of contortions to paint that close to the floor.

While Kyle mixed up some gold and a couple greens that matched Theda's fabric samples, Alicia and I walked across the hall to the manly den. Scaffolding was in place, just as I had requested.

"Would you like to paint clouds today?" Alicia shrugged her shoulders.

"Sure, I'd love to." Which could mean anything since she never complained about the neck-wrenching ceiling work.

On our way back to the dining room, we doubled back to the music room to see if it had a new glass ceiling yet. It didn't. I looked out one of the southern windows just in time to see a silver SUV skid to a halt behind my truck. Theda stumbled out of her vehicle, wiped her eyes and looked around as if she had accidentally landed on the moon.

"Allie, I gotta' run. You can start the clouds anytime now." I tore through the house and around the concrete-pouring obstacles to Theda's side. As soon as she saw me she burst into tears, rivers of tears.

"Hey there, what's the matter?" I put my arm around her shoulder. That caused more rivers. Finally she was able to control everything except a couple hiccups. Theda coughed out a few words.

"Josephine, I'm so sorry ... so sorry ...."

"What's wrong, Theda? It can't be that bad, can it?"

"I'm so sorry ... Solow ran away." She put a hand to her chest, "I didn't know what to do so I came here ... to tell you."

"We'll find him, don't worry," I said, feeling more desperate than confident.

"Can you drive?" She nodded. "I'll take the truck and meet you at the cabin."

I don't remember driving down the mountain. All I

thought about was my sweet hound dog who had never runaway from home before. I remembered feeling a tinge of jealousy earlier that morning when he had looked so happy to be with Theda. What would I do without Solow? I couldn't bare the thought.

I helped Theda out of her Lexus. Her body shook with each little sob. I asked her to tell me everything.

"I took a shower," she began, "and when I came back to the kitchen, Solow ... was gone. I think he pushed the screen door open. I ... walked around the cabin and over to the barn, calling his name ... nothing. (Sob)" I walked my friend into the house and watched her collapse on the sofa.

"Stay here and relax. I'm going to look around." I darted out the door, quickly circled the house and headed for the barn. A powerful odor attacked my nostrils. It was so strong it made me gag and I wanted to barf. The pungent odor of skunk was getting to me so I held a hand over my nose and mouth while I looked under logs and into gullies.

I opened the shop door. The air was half decent inside so I gulped some air and took a quick look around. The cell phone charger was gone and Solow was nowhere in sight. I quickly opened the second door and checked the main area of the barn. Nothing there but straw.

"So ... low, So... low, come here baby." I started putting one and one together and realized he had probably chased a skunk thinking it looked rather like a cat. I decided to follow the smell, no matter how far it took me. My eyes stung as I scanned the open area around the house and barn. Nothing bigger than a grasshopper was moving.

"So ... low," I repeatedly called. I spotted a cigarette butt on the ground behind the barn and kicked it with my foot. Heading away from the barn in a westerly direction, I entered the forest. The foul smell was fairly strong. I followed a narrow deer trail, sandwiched between wild lilac and blackberry bushes, pushing back branches and climbing over vines as I made my way down a gentle slope. I finally decided blackberry thorns were more than Solow would have endured, turned and started back up the trail.

Suddenly rocks rolled under my feet, my butt went down and my feet flailed in the air. Helplessly, I rolled over and over, down the steep cliff, feeling every rock until a redwood tree stopped my descent. The tree was unscathed. I was wobbly to say the least and there was still no sign of Solow. Even if he could have made it that far, he wouldn't.

I hiked around on spongy soil under a canopy of green, searching for a way to climb back up the cliff. After a hurried search, I discovered a path with steps cut into the hard clay hillside. I quickly climbed to the top, following the trail all the way to the open area behind the barn. I pushed through bushes and branches at the end of the path. Camouflage? No wonder I hadn't seen the trail before.

I thought I heard a whimper, rounded the barn and

headed for the cabin. The closer I came to the house, the louder the whimpering and the stronger the smell. My hopes were rising, my heart was pounding and my throat was gagging.

"So ... low, come here boy."

Suddenly the whimper became an all out howl. My eyes stung as I peeked into a crawl space under the back of the cabin. Two pitifully bloodshot eyes blinked back at me, then came another mournful howl. Theda did a fast walk to the backyard when she heard Solow. We laughed and the tears flowed, but my buddy didn't budge.

We called and coaxed Solow, promised him a juicy bone, but nothing worked. Another howl. I got down on my hands and knees and crawled into the space with him. I had a strong urge to throw up or at least turn and run. Instead, I crawled closer. Solow moaned, eyes blinking fast. I grabbed his collar and tugged while talking to him in my most persuasive voice. I kept pulling. Inch by inch we crawled through the dirt until finally we were out from under the house and I was able to stand up.

"Oh, Josephine, I've been so worried," Theda cried as she helped me to my feet. "Poor Solow is shaking worse than we are." I stumbled to the porch and collapsed.

"Bring his leash. It's hanging on my bedpost." Theda ran inside and a minute later I fastened the leash to Solow's collar and walked him to the corner of the house where I tied the other end of the leash to an outdoor faucet.

"Now I need to buy a big can of tomato juice. I've

never had to do this before," I said, "but David told me the juice helps to neutralize the smell."

"Josephine, I hate to tell you this, but you're in no condition to go to the store. You're filthy and there's blood on your knee and some on that elbow, not to mention the scratches and dirt on your face. I'll buy some juice at Johnnies. Don't worry about a thing." Before I could say a word she was in the house collecting her keys and purse. A minute later she backed her SUV onto the infamous Munger driveway.

I decided to use soap and water on Solow while I waited for the tomato juice. Solow was sullen. He tucked his tail tightly under his bum while I soaped him up and rinsed him off with cold water. Only his eyes moved, still blinking and burning. Mine were on fire too.

Theda came back with a half-gallon can of tomato juice. I slowly poured it over Solow's squat backside, rubbing it into his coat as I went. He didn't budge except for a shiver now and then. When the juice was gone, we left him tied to the faucet to dry in the sun. Solow stretched out on the front porch and hung his head over the side.

Theda ran a nice bubble bath for me. Normally I would have considered it a luxury, but that particular bath was a necessity. A little later, I reloaded the tub and had a second bath followed by a short shower. The warm water made every ding sting and the soap kept them stinging. My body was scratched and bruised, but Solow was back. I pulled on a clean outfit, found my cell phone and called Alicia.

"Hi, Jo, where are you?" she asked.

"I'm at the cabin. You won't believe what happened. Solow was skunked!"

"Is he OK?"

"Don't worry Allie, he'll live. I'll see you after lunch." I ended the call and slipped on my sandals. I would let the summer sun dry and fumigate my hair. Theda appeared at my bedroom door.

"How about a little squirt of Chanel No. 5?"

"Thanks, but I have some Scent of Vanilla with me if I can find it in this messy purse. Oh, here it is." I gave my bare arms and legs a few big squirts of the stuff. "Yikes!" My scratched limbs stung all over again.

"Now, don't I smell like bakery goods?"

"I wouldn't go that far, but you do smell better than Solow." Theda slowly shook her head from side to side, and then turned on a big smile. "I made peanut butter sandwiches for lunch." I checked my watch.

"Thanks, Theda. It's already one o'clock. I'll eat my sandwich while I drive. You can leave Solow where he is. See you around five." I wrapped my sandwich in a napkin and ran out the door. Solow was asleep on the porch, still tied to the water pipe, looking like a botched hybrid tomato experiment.

My little truck roared up the mountain until it came upon a cement truck on its way down. I stopped, shoved my Mazda into reverse and prayed for a wide spot to pull into. There were no wide areas, but I saw a low bank behind me, off to my left. I swung the truck over the bank, and down the other side, landing against a toppled tree in the late stages of decay. A soft landing, really, compared to hitting a live redwood.

The driver of the cement truck didn't bother to see where I had gone. He had enough to do, maneuvering Big Bertha between the edge of the cliff on one side and a bank on the other. I watched as the giant churning truck disappeared around the bend.

My truck stalled. I turned the key and we were in business again, stirring up loose mulch and scraping the underbelly on dead branches. My peanut butter sandwich was nowhere in sight. I figured I would find it someday if I decided to clean the interior.

I parked as close to the villa as I could, turned the ignition off and just sat staring at all the activity. The roofers were roofing, the cementers were cementing and I hoped the muralists were muraling. To know for sure, I had to be there. I took a deep breath and made my way around the chaotic construction activity, all the way to the dining room.

"Jo, I've been worried about you," Alicia said, looking me up and down and squeezing her lips together. "Why are you all scratched up?"

"Yeah, like what happened, Jo?" Kyle asked. "And what's that smell?"

Trigger looked up from his dinosaur book and said, "wow, Auntie Jo, you look like you met up with a stinky Tyrannosaurus."

"It was something like that only smaller. You wouldn't think one pesky skunk could do all this, would you?" I winked and he laughed.

"A little skunk did all that?" Alicia snickered.

"After Solow was skunked, I went looking for him in all the wrong places. Finally, Theda and I found him under the house smelling worse than a bucket of chicken manure on a hot day. How's the painting going?"

"The clouds are finished, that is, if you think they're finished." We walked to the den. I agreed the clouds were finished, and fabulous.

"Allie, I know you can handle painting the cherubs, but that's a lot of ceiling work for one day. Would you like to start them tomorrow?" Alicia wrapped one hand around the back of her neck.

"Yes, tomorrow would be better. Thank you, Jo." We returned to the dining room where the boys were engrossed in dinosaur facts from Trigger's book while little Tansey napped on a tarp.

"Why don't you two take some time off and explore the area, get some sun and exercise?" I said. Kyle and Trigger immediately dropped the book and fled the room.

Alicia and I worked toward each other from opposite ends of the dining room. We created the basic terrain; hills, fields and a stream. Our styles of painting were quite similar, always trying for realism. Time passed without our noticing.

Rumpled, dirty and out of breath, Trigger and Kyle

burst into the room. Tansey woke up and raced to her master. Trigger scooped her up.

"Auntie Jo, we had a great time, didn't we, Kyle?"

"Like, it was crazy, man. We almost got lost, but Trigger climbed a tree and remembered the way back."

"Mom, you should see the waterfall we saw. We hiked down this trail into a dark place where you can't see the sun because of all the trees. I picked up a slug. It was cool."

"Yeah, like, way cool. Trigger's not afraid of anything."

"Trigger, when you reached the end of the trail, were you able to hear the workmen and the noise they make hammering and sawing here at the house?" Alicia asked. Trigger looked at the ceiling for a moment.

"No, I don't think we heard anything except the water in the stream."

"Honey, that means you went too far. Next time not so far."

"OK, Mom," Trigger said as he sat down on the floor and opened his book.

"Kyle, you can take over Allie's spot. I think she needs a break. And speaking of breaks, Chester told me the downstairs powder room in the main hall is up and running. No more blue plastic outhouse for us." We all did high-fives.

At four o'clock, Kyle and I took a break and joined the Quintanas in the solarium. I was starving. I opened my little cooler and indulged in a late lunch. Trigger and Kyle ate all the cookies I had packed. Watching the cookie monsters made me smile, and despite the interruptions, I felt we had made good progress on the murals. I sent everyone home a little early.

I sat on the wide front steps breathing in fresh air and enjoying the splendid forest around me. The mansion was quiet, for a change, since all the workers except Manuel had gone home. He shoveled in his usual trench, waiting for Stan to show up. I waited because I had a couple more questions for Stan regarding security. At five-thirty Stan still had not arrived. I walked over to Manuel's project.

"What do you think happened to Stan?"

"He ees late."

"I see your dog is awake today. Does he like to run?"

"Si, he runs very much."

"I see a rope in your truck. Would he run with me?"

Manuel nodded. "Sueno want to run very much." He unbuckled the dog's leash from the metal tie-down near the back of the cab and handed it to me.

As soon as I took the leash, Sueno yanked me across the driveway like a wild bull pulling a butterfly. We crossed a freshly poured sidewalk, leaving paw and foot prints in the soft cement. As I struggled to stay upright, Sueno circled and pulled me across the walk again in the opposite direction. I held onto the leash with all my strength as he led me in a wide oval back to Manuel's truck. He grabbed Sueno, heaved him into the truck bed and lectured the dog in Spanish. We ran to the sidewalk to assess the damage.

"Muy malo!" Manuel said, stamping his foot and shaking his head. He turned, charged over to his truck, grabbed a trowel from his toolbox and hurried back to the sidewalk. He bent down on one knee and carefully, but with some effort, smoothed the wet cement until the prints disappeared.

I thought to myself, how nice it would be to have a sidewalk at home with Solow's paw prints forever embedded in it. I was smiling at the thought and washing my sandals with water from a hose, when an Ace Security truck pulled up next to my Mazda.

The man inside was definitely not Stan. The new Ace man climbed down from his truck and marched toward us. He was about my height, five-six, but very thin with thick curly brown hair under his blue cap. His uniform was baggy at best and his belt full of hardware hung low.

"OK, people, you can go now," he said, as if to an unruly crowd.

"What happened to Stan?" I asked.

"Didn't show up for work," he said, looking around, twitching his nose. He was probably trying to figure out where the bakery-skunk smell was coming from.

"And you are?" I said, wondering about the young man with the puffed out chest.

"Name's Russell Vandiveer. I'm taking over for Stan." He turned his back to us and walked toward the house. I looked at Manuel and he looked at me as if to say, "Who made him King?" Like good little subjects, we left for our separate residences.

I parked my truck beside the SUV, just a few feet from where Solow was tied to the faucet. He opened his eyes, raised his head and gave a mournful groan. His head sunk down again to rest on his paws, but his eyes never left mine. I reached down to pet him and that's when the smell hit me.

"Hi, little buddy. Guess you're gonna' be an outdoor dog tonight." I probably didn't smell much better than Solow. Theda greeted me at the door, her hair looking freshly styled.

"You smell a little better Josephine, but I don't think you're ready for eating out. I'm making dinner myself, if you don't mind."

"Mind? I think that's wonderful. What are you making?" And then the reality of Theda's cooking hit me. Oh well, she looked happy and that was the important thing.

"I'm making spaghetti the way my mother-in-law makes it, with Italian sausage. The marinara sauce comes from a jar, but I spice it up a bit."

"Your spaghetti sounds good. That reminds me, I need to give Solow another rinse. I'll just be a minute." I pulled on Solow's collar until he stood directly under the water faucet. He looked miserable when I turned the cold water on and began rubbing tomato juice residue off his body. Gradually he relaxed and seemed to enjoy the massage. His fur gradually changed from pinkish-orange to a pale peach and, of course, he had to shake before I had time to step back.

I scrounged up a ten-foot piece of rope from my truck and tied one end to the faucet, the other end to Solow's leash, giving him access to the porch and a few square feet of front yard dirt. After a good rubdown with a towel, he was ready for a siesta.

The spaghetti was fantastic. Too bad the garlic bread was burnt and the salad was bitter. Can't win 'em all. We cleaned the kitchen and then we each hauled a wooden chair to Solow's front porch. The sun was down behind the mountains and the crickets and frogs had begun their nightly concert. Even as a child, I loved that magical time of night when light fades into a restful twilight. I relaxed and let my thoughts drift off to David and his bucking mowing machine. I smiled in the dark.

Chapter Eight

Very early Tuesday morning I awoke with a start, tangled in the sheets and sweating from head to toe. My dream had turned into a nightmare when I realized someone in a truck was trying to run over my dog. I couldn't see who was doing the driving and I couldn't get to Solow because my ankles were tied to a giant faucet.

The bedside clock flashed the time, two-twenty am. It was dark; even the crickets were asleep. After a long tossing and turning session, I pulled on my robe and slipped into my sandals. Ouch! Pain shouted from every muscle and nerve. I decided to try a little ice cream to help me sleep. I loaded a bowl and carried it outside so I could give Solow a bit of company. When I sat down, my bum hurt.

"You have no idea how sore I am after falling down a cliff looking for you," I said as Solow rested his head on my knee, just inches from the bowl. "Next time you run away you're on your own. How about a little ice cream, old buddy? It's strawberry."

Solow moaned, sat up and licked his privates; His way

of saying yes. I plopped a spoonful into his empty dinner bowl. Before I had time to blink, the scoop was gone. Then came the sad eyes looking for more.

"Ok, you win, here's two more spoonfuls, but the rest is mine." When all the ice cream was gone, I decided to take Solow for a little walk in the moonlight. He pulled on his leash, following his nose, as usual, straight to the barn. This time the side door was locked. I scratched my head and wondered if Theda had locked it for some reason.

We walked back around the barn to the big double doors at the front. Hinges squeaked as I pulled one giant door open. I paused, listened and then stepped inside. The darkness was complete except for a reflection of moonlight on the shop doorknob. Solow pulled on the leash, yanking me across the straw toward the shop. The door was open, but as I went over the threshold, I tripped and landed on my shins.

Feeling like a fool, I slowly gathered up my aching body and turned on the florescent lights. At first the light was blinding, but after a few seconds my eyes adjusted. I looked around and discovered the cell phone charger back in its original place. I unplugged the gadget and dropped it into my robe pocket, planning to show it to Theda. There were plenty of outlets in the cabin, so why would she use the barn?

I closed the barn door and we trundled back to the house. I tied Solow's leash to the rope outside and went back to bed.

Five hours passed. As light streamed through my window, I thought I had dreamt about a trip to the barn until I saw the battery charger on the bed stand next to the clock. When I felt my sore shins I knew for sure it was not a dream. It was after eight o'clock and time to get up, but my body hurt all over.

Solow wandered into my bedroom and gave me a big puppy lick on my cheek. Theda was right behind him.

"I think Solow smells good enough to pal around with us again, don't you?"

"If he's good enough for you, it's OK with me," I said. The skunk odor was present but bearable. "I'll share my shower with him just to make sure. He'll like that."

Solow and I came to breakfast smelling like lavender soap and vanilla. We smelled much better than breakfast, which consisted of oatmeal paste and burned toast, to be washed down with coffee sludge.

"Theda, I couldn't sleep last night so Solow and I took a walk to the barn. Do you use the barn or the shop for anything?"

"No, and I don't think Warren does either. What would we use it for?"

"Twice now I noticed a cell phone charger on the work bench, plugged in. Last night I brought it back with me to show you." Theda looked puzzled,

"Couldn't it have been left here by the McFees?" she asked.

"One problem with that. I've been to the barn twice

when the charger wasn't there. Someone is using it. Any idea who?"

"Josephine, that's a scary idea that someone has been in our barn."

"Did you lock the side door to the shop?" I was even more curious now, not to mention freakedout.

"We don't pay any attention to it one way or another. We never thought anyone would trespass so close to the house. No one lives around here."

"To tell you the truth, Theda, I saw a light in the shop window once and I smelled smoke from a cigarette. I found a cigarette butt on the ground behind the barn, and now the charger. I don't know what to think." I felt the hairs on the back of my neck stand at attention.

"Should I call the sheriff?" Theda asked in a voice thin as thread.

"I wouldn't unless something is stolen or wrecked." We finished our breakfast in thoughtful silence. I threw a few edibles into my cooler and took off up the hill. The mural gang sat in the solarium, relaxing.

"Hi, guys. Ready to rock?" We walked to the dining room and began the mural work. After the morning break, Alicia began painting cherubs on the ceiling of the den. By lunch time, I figured her neck and my whole body were ready for a break. The solarium was jammed, but we managed to find an empty table with chairs. The smell of Mexican cuisine permeated the room and had my stomach begging for food. The workers around us had it made when it came to lunches from home.

"Allie, how's your neck?"

"Its fine, Jo, don't worry."

"You can work on cherubs tomorrow. I want you to work with Kyle and me this afternoon." I swallowed another bite of my egg and tuna sandwich, stood up and excused myself. The sun was straight up, its rays cooking the driveway and my little truck. I touched the door handle and winced. My fingers felt like they would blister. I opened the door to the cab with my shirt tail and climbed in. At least the fried fingers helped me to forget my sore bones for a minute as I called Theda on my cell phone.

"Hello, Josephine?"

"Yes, it's me, just wanted to see if you're alright."

"I'm fine," Theda said. "I was just thinking I would like to drive up to the house and take a look at the mural."

"While you're up here, maybe you should have Chester arrange a change of locks on the barn doors and the cabin too. What do you think?"

"I think I'm a smart woman to have a friend like you. See you in half an hour."

I walked on the new concrete sidewalk, checking for traces of footprints. The walk looked fine, thanks to Manuel's quick repairs. As I entered the sunroom, my band of painters stood up and we all marched to the dining room. Trigger and Tansey fell asleep on a folded tarp in the corner of the room.

"Is Trigger having any more nightmares?" I asked Alicia.

"Last night as a matter of fact. Ernie's mother wants him to stay with her for a couple days. I think he would like that."

I heard a female voice outside the room and expected to see Theda walk in. Instead, a young woman with hair dyed even redder than Kyle's entered and looked around. Her heavily mascaraed eyes found their man.

"Kyle, we need to talk."

"Hang a minute, Kellie." He looked at me. "Josephine, like, I need to go outside for a minute, you know?" He and Kellie disappeared into the kitchen. Their voices were muffled. I couldn't make out the words, hard as I tried, but they came back holding hands. I hoped that didn't mean interruptions and phone calls when Kyle should be working. He finally remembered his manners and introduced Kellie. She flashed us a pearly white smile followed by a little theatrical curtsy.

"Like, Kellie plays Queen Gertrude in Hamlet, you know, at UCSC. She's really cool," his eyes were glued to her smooth skin and dark eyes.

"Kellie, it's nice to meet you. I'm afraid Kyle will be busy here for a couple hours, and then we set him free."

"That's OK. I thought I'd look around Boulder Creek and see how these people get their kicks." Kellie cocked her head and rolled her eyes as if to say mountain people were a strange life form she knew nothing about. Kyle finally let go of her hand.

"Like, later, Kellie." She exited the room with a 'princess wave' to Kyle.

Alicia painted trees, Kyle worked on a farmhouse and I painted a vineyard. We periodically reviewed the sketches and photos spread across the floor. Trigger woke up and took Tansey outside. When he returned sometime later, Kellie was with him, holding the little Sheltie. I checked my watch. It was almost five.

"Hey guys, let's clean up and go home." I watched Kellie and Kyle making eyes at each other. When all the brushes were clean and the paint was stowed in the corner, we left as a group. The two redheads climbed into Kellie's green Miata, top down, of course. I waved good-bye to Alicia and Trigger and hoofed it about twenty yards to where Chester was climbing aboard his pickup.

"Chester, did you talk to Theda today?"

"No, didn't see her." He slammed his door, but the window was open.

"She wants you to have new locks installed at the cabin and the barn, ASAP. She said she was going to talk to you about it today. I wonder what happened." Chester stuck his head out the window.

"Well, it's a little late now, but we'll get to it tomorrow. Why does she think she needs new locks?"

"Just can't be too careful, you know?" I wondered how Theda would have answered that question, and by the way, where was she? Just then Russell appeared, riding his bucking blue Ace Security truck. Chester climbed out of his truck, tramped over to Russell, bent down to the driver's side window and said something to the cocky little security guard. I wasn't close enough to hear and resisted the urge to join them, uninvited. I didn't want to seem overly inquisitive so I left.

The SUV was gone and Solow was alone in the cabin. I put some kibble down for Mr. Loveable and changed my clothes. Chester's Ford roared down the hill just as I fired up my Mazda. I waited for the dust to settle before backing out.

Tuesday evenings were fairly quiet in Boulder Creek. I checked out the cars up and down Central Avenue and spotted a silver Lexus parked in front of The Brewery. I parked behind Theda's car and entered the restaurant. A couple chairs swiveled my way and back again. Theda sat at a little table in the far corner, slouched over a drink. She was talking to Annie, who sat at the same table, patiently listening to her customer. She stood up as I sat down.

"May I join you?" I said, pulling a chair out from the table.

"Oh, Josephine, do you know Annie?" She waved her hand at the fourth chair. "Sit down. Oh dear, you are sitting. Would you like ... something to ... drink?"

"Yes, thank you," I looked up at Annie, "I'll have an iced tea, please." I didn't see any food on the table and asked Annie to bring a plate of buffalo wings. She nodded and headed for the kitchen.

"What time is it Josephine? I think ... I didn't feed Solow," Theda babbled.

"He's been fed, don't worry. How long have you been here? Have you eaten anything?" She stared into her glass and sighed.

"I planned to come up to see the mural today ... but the time just went ... and I don't know how I got here, but ... here I am. Warren called and I told him about the charger thingy ... he sounded angry. He thinks we made ... it up."

"Don't worry, Theda, I told Chester what you want and he said he would have the new locks installed tomorrow."

"What would I do ... without you ... Josephine?" Annie came back with iced tea, a plate of spicy wings and two menus tucked under one arm. She whispered in my ear.

"I made a very weak drink for your friend. I'm afraid she was already snockered when she got here." I thanked Annie and ordered dinner for both of us, including coffee for Theda. We ate slowly, talked and sipped another round of coffee with dessert. As the sun dropped behind the mountains and many of the customers left, Theda became herself again.

"How about a walk down the street?" I asked. Theda nodded, paid the bill and gave Annie a hefty tip.

Outside, the air was still warm, but refreshing. We walked toward Johnnie's Grocery store, looking into shop windows as we went. The front door to Mac's bar flapped open and several old buzzards leered at us from their barstools. We laughed and kept on walking, talking and enjoying the rustic ambiance. We jay-walked across the street and stepped into Johnnie's, intending to buy coffee, eggs and ice cream, but left the store with two big bags of food we didn't know we needed.

One block later, we crossed the street again and passed by Mac's just as two shaggy young men were leaving the bar. The tallest one had long straggly black hair in a pony-tail. The other man was a bit shorter, stockier and sported a full black beard and mustache. Their filthy clothes, greasy hair and body odor made an ugly statement.

I told Theda I would rather smell a skunk than those guys. They walked in front of us, then turned left down a side street and hopped into a very rusty old Dodge pickup.

I leaned in toward Theda and whispered, "did you see that? Those must be the McFee boys, men, actually. And that's the truck I told you about."

"Really?" Theda said, as she stared into the window of a dress shop. The truck fired up, followed by a lot of muffler noise and black smoke.

We walked up the street another block to our separate vehicles and headed home. I drove with my windows open, enjoying the night air. As I crossed the Bear Creek Bridge, I noticed the McFee's rusty old Dodge idling in the open area just before the entrance to the Munger driveway. I pretended not to look, made my turn, bumped up the drive and parked in front of the cabin. I stepped inside the cabin, right behind Theda. Solow greeted us with the usual howl, tail wagging and happy vibes.

"Did you see the McFee's truck down by the bridge?" I asked Theda, as I put groceries away.

"No, I'm sorry, I didn't." It seemed like the more curious I became about the McFees, the less Theda cared. Maybe she had learned not to care about much of anything, just to keep herself from hurting. I knew what it was like to lose someone. I remembered when Marty died. You never get over it completely.

I gave Solow a good ear-rub, clipped the leash to his collar, picked up a flashlight and we took a walk in the forest. We tramped through areas we hadn't covered before, but eventually I followed Solow's lead, straight to the barn.

The side door was locked so we skirted around to the big front doors and entered. I thought about oiling the squeaky hinges, not that squeaks were a big deal. My flashlight made it easy to find the shops inner doorknob. I opened it and flipped the light switch. I grabbed a small oilcan from the bottom shelf and turned to open the door. I couldn't believe my eyes.

"Oh, my God, look at the hole in this door," I said to Solow. "Looks like someone was really angry and punched a fist clear through the door. Wonder if somebody wants their charger thingy? What do you think, Solow?" I decided not to bother with the door hinges and set the oilcan on the workbench for later. I wanted out of that creepy barn before the big-fisted Neanderthal came back.

Solow strained at his leash, making it a very fast trip back to the house. Had he run across the scent of another skunk, or was he spooked like me? Solow sat in front of the TV, panting. A minute later, he was stretched out on the floor snoring, his feet still chasing a skunk or a smelly trespasser. I decided to call David while Theda watched her favorite quiz show. I dialed.

"Hello." David sounded like I woke him from a snooze in the recliner.

"Hi, David, it's Jo. How's it going?"

"I'm glad you called, Josephine. I finished mowing your yard yesterday without suffering any serious wounds. Guess we won't see you until Saturday, unless you invite me up to see the big mansion."

"Gee, David, that's a great idea." I gave him directions, even though he was familiar with Boulder Creek's one main street and one signal light. "Don't forget, just after the bridge you'll see a turnout. At the end of the turnout is Mungers' driveway. Your Jeep would be a good choice, better than the Miata."

"Can't wait to see the place. Think I'll look in on old Jake while I'm in the area."

"So what time do you think you'll be here tomorrow?"

"Lunchtime, if you can get away."

"I'm the boss. Lunch sounds good. See you tomorrow." I was smiling at the thought of David driving all the way to Boulder Creek just to see my murals. I hung up the phone and turned to Theda.

"My friend David is coming here tomorrow. I hope you don't mind. I had told him all about your beautiful villa and now he wants to see it … and the murals, of course."

"That's lovely Josephine. I can't wait to meet him."

I had Theda's attention and could have told her about the hole someone punched in the shop door, but why ruin her good mood.

"Josephine, you told me you lost your husband many years ago. Why haven't you remarried?" I usually ducked such questions, but decided to answer, for a change.

"At first I was devastated and thought no one else could take Marty's place. A few years later I began looking around and discovered I was right. After a few more years and a couple failed relationships, I gave up. My life is good now and I intend to keep it that way."

"Did you ever want to have children?"

"Of course. I used to volunteer at the library, reading stories to preschoolers. That helped to fill the emptiness." I smiled when I thought about Trigger. "Being close to Trigger helps a lot and David has a darling little four-year-old granddaughter. I see Monica once in a while when David's son is in town." Theda gave me a soul-searching stare. I shrugged and said, "Life is good."

"I think life is what you make it," Theda said, "and I'm trying to make mine better, but it's not easy." She looked down at her perfectly manicured toenails.

"You've had a lot more to deal with than the average woman," I said, "Hang in there. I think you and Warren will be OK once the house is finished and you move in together. It will be a new beginning."

After the Ten O'clock News and some microwave popcorn, we retired for the night. I kept my bedroom window open, hoping the crickets and frogs would sing me to sleep. Solow, on the other hand, fell asleep instantly.

It seemed like I had just fallen asleep when I suddenly woke up to screeching tires, loud laughter, smashing of glass and the roar of a truck racing up the mountain. I instantly had visions of the "falling tile" incident and shuddered. Solow was up and barking.

Theda and I bumped into each other in the dark hall as we groped our way to the living room. I opened the front door and poked my head outside. Solow whined and growled behind me, while Theda turned on the porch light. Whoever the creeps were, they were gone. I looked down at the cement porch just in time to avoid stepping on the remains of a smashed Jack Daniels bottle with my bare feet.

Solow pushed past my legs and galloped to the middle of the driveway. I called him back to the porch and listened for the nasty truck's return. After all, what went up the mountain had to come down. My heart raced as I grabbed Solow's collar, yanked him into the house and threw the latch. His ears perked up as we all heard distant noises, like skidding tires, rough engine and screaming boys getting louder by the second. I turned off the porch light and peered out the front window. Solow howled.

Suddenly there was a crash, metal on metal, scraping and the sound of glass breaking followed by loud yelling and laughing. I saw sparks and headlights swerving away from the cabin. A little Ace Security truck, identified by the ferocious twirling yellow light on the roof, escorted the first pickup down the mountain.

"Theda, call 911! I'll see what they did."

"Be careful, they might come back," Theda whispered. I heard her teeth chattering as my own heartbeat pounded in my ears.

I stepped into a pair of flip-flops, put the porch light on for the second time and gingerly stepped outside. I walked slowly around the back of the SUV. Nothing wrong there, I told myself. Then I saw it. My dear little truck had a smashed rear end. The tailgate was folded in on the right side where the tail light used to be.

Hot anger rose up to my throat until I could barely speak. Call me crazy, but I've always had feelings for my truck, as if it could feel pain. Theda walked up to me in her robe and slippers, holding my cell phone to her ear.

"Josephine, what do I say?" Theda handed me the phone. Her mouth dropped open as she gazed at my truck. I cleared the bile from my throat.

"I want to report a hit and run. It happened less than five minutes ago." I explained that we needed an officer pronto because the yahoos might come back and harm us.

The minute I got off the phone, a blue Ace Security truck chugged up the driveway and turned into the space next to my mutilated truck. Russell stomped around my vehicle, looking like a little blue rooster with his feathers in a twist.

"Did they do this?" He pointed at my truck.

"They sure did. Do you know who they are?"

"The truck got away." Russell checked his notebook. "The license plate was bent, impossible to read, besides, it was dark."

"Was it a Dodge?" I asked, standing in my flip-flops and knee-length nightshirt.

"Like I said ma'am, it was dark." I clenched my teeth together and silently dared him to call me ma'am one more time.

"Personally, I think you should stay here all night in your truck and protect your employer." I pointed to Theda, trembling in the doorway under the porch light.

"First I need to fill out a report." Clueless began inspecting my Mazda with all the panache of a "Barney Fife".

I walked Theda into the house. She slumped onto the couch, with an eye on the liquor cabinet. I hurried to the kitchen and made a pot of chamomile tea, poured two cups and we sipped the brew as we tried to gather our wits.

Half an hour later, an official sheriff's car quietly pulled in next to the Ace pickup. I watched from the front window as the sheriff talked to "Inspector Clouseau" for a couple minutes before he knocked on the front door. When I opened the door the sheriff stood for a moment, badge in hand, quietly studying my rumpled appearance and agitated demeanor.

"I'm Sergeant Machuca. Looks like you ladies had some trouble up here. Did you see anyone?"

"No, we didn't. We heard an old truck with a bad muffler, but it was too dark to see very much." I sized up the deputy sheriff as I ran nervous fingers through my hair.

Machuca was a big man with dark eyes, curly black hair and a king-size hook nose, probably fortyish.

"I don't think there's much I can do for you folks right now, but I'll be back here first thing in the morning when it's light and take a closer look at the damage. In the meantime, Rusty will stay close and radio if anyone comes back."

"His name is Russell. I guess we'll be OK with him around," I said. The sergeant must have sensed my lack of confidence.

"Don't worry, ma'am, I'll be cruising Bear Creek Road hourly, unless I get called away on an emergency. I'm covering the whole valley tonight." He turned to leave.

"Thank you, Sergeant," Theda said as he disappeared out the door.

"It's almost three in the morning. Think I'll try getting

some sleep," I yawned.

"Wait a minute Josephine. I want to know if you really think the McFee's are involved in this malicious behavior?"

"Sure do." Apparently Theda had been paying closer attention to the whole situation than I thought, and maybe she couldn't ignore the facts any longer.

"When Sergeant Machuca returns tomorrow, I think we should tell him everything we know," Theda said, caving into a soft chair. I agreed.

"I think he's the one to talk to about the cell phone charger, the hole in the door and tonight's incident."

Theda tilted her head, "Hole in the door?"

"I didn't want to worry you, but yes, there's a hole in the shop door. I think someone saw that the charger was missing, and punched the door." Theda's eyes widened.

"So you really think someone is coming and going on this property? You think it's the McFees, don't you."

"Unequivocally, yes," I said as I stood and walked to my room. "Goodnight." At that point I felt like a stressed out, beat up, old basket case in need of sleep. Solow had already passed out in his bed, his paws twitching as if he were tracking down those evil boys who hurt my truck. I wished him luck.

My dreams took me to a dimly-lit arena where a gladiator type of competition was being held. The crowd roared as giant cement trucks with whiskers and ugly warts chased little crippled trucks and beat the snot out of them.

Chapter Nine

My clock flashed seven. The house was quiet except for doggy snores. I saw my chance to have a decent breakfast for a change and tip-toed to the kitchen. I filled Mr. Coffee with water and the correct amount of coffee grounds. Next, I washed a juicy ripe peach, several large strawberries and peeled one banana. I sliced the fruits and scooped them into two cereal bowls with a dollop of vanilla yogurt on top.

Coffee aroma filled the kitchen and floated down the hall to Theda's room. She shuffled into the kitchen with a smile on her sleepy face.

"Good morning. It smells good in here."

"I'm preparing an egg scramble for breakfast," I said. "Do you like onions?"

"A small amount would be lovely," she said.

I whipped the eggs with a fork, added chopped green onion and red bell pepper, a dash of oregano and black pepper. I fried the scramble and sprinkled some shredded Monterey Jack on top. We loaded our plates, but before we had time to sit there was a knock at the front door. Solow howled and charged through the house to the door. Suddenly I was reminded of the terrible, middle-of-the-night events. Still wearing my nightshirt, I let Theda answer the door. At least she had her robe on. I listened to Sergeant Machuca talking to Theda.

"I'm going to see if I can get some tire prints," he said, starting to turn away.

"Won't you come in?" Theda asked. "I think we have something to tell you." She led the officer to the kitchen where I offered him a chair and a cup of coffee. Finally my chance had come. Justice would be done.

"Sergeant, you're probably aware of the vandalism up at the mansion," I said. He nodded. "We've noticed some odd things happening here at the cabin." Machuca took out his pad and pencil and I continued.

"Last Friday night I noticed a light coming from the direction of the barn. It only lasted a second. I decided to go there and look around and discovered a cell phone charger on the workbench, plugged into the wall. A few days later it was gone, but I found a cigarette butt on the ground and the air smelled like smoke.

Machuca's large body squirmed in the small pine chair, as he scribbled his notes.

"One night the shop door was locked. Theda says she and Warren never go to the barn for any reason. I found the charger plugged in again Tuesday evening. I unplugged it and brought it to the house to see if it belonged to the

Mungers. It didn't. Anyway, the next time I went to the barn, there was a hole the size of a fist punched in the door."

"My advice," the sergeant said, "is to install an alarm system in the house and in the barn."

"So you think someone is trespassing?" Theda's eyes were like saucers.

"That's what it sounds like, ma'am. I'll search the area after I finish the hit and run report. And I'll need to see the charger for fingerprints." He took two more gulps of coffee and lumbered out the door.

"I think the alarm system is a good idea," Theda said.

"That reminds me, Chester will be down here pretty soon to talk about new locks. Wait till he hears we need alarms too." I finished my breakfast and took a quick shower. When I came back to the kitchen, Theda was reading the paper out loud to Solow.

"Josephine, I'll clean the kitchen and thank you for breakfast. It was lovely."

I thought about packing my cooler, and then remembered David was coming for lunch. I smiled at Solow, already working on his first nap of the day.

"I'll see you later," I said to Theda as I walked out the door. The sheriff leaned against his car, looking up from his notebook with cryptic eyes.

"I'm finished with the truck. I'll take a look around the property now."

"Thank you officer," I said as I climbed into my

bashed-in, but still functional pickup. When I arrived at the mansion, Kyle was already painting on the landscape and Alicia was down the hall creating cherubs on the ceiling of the den. Alicia looked down from her perch when she heard me walk in.

"Jo, I saw your truck on the way up here this morning … and a sheriff's car. What happened? Are you alright?"

"We had a rough night. Some drunken yahoos clipped my truck and kept on going. It's never dull around here."

"Does the sheriff know who did it?"

"No, but I can guess who has the best motive. I'm thinking the McFee's are familiar with this place and were kicked off the property once already. Sounds like a motive to me. Trouble is, it was dark and no one got a license plate number, or even a good look at the truck."

"How do you like my first cherub, Jo?"

"Allie, you're the best. Michelangelo would be proud. I'll be working with Kyle until noon."

I passed by the music room, looked up and felt sad about the hole in the ceiling, the hole in my truck and the hole in Theda's heart. I stared out the southern window, watching Manuel hacking away on the trench with a pickax as four other men unrolled long strips of grass that would become lawn. Finally I pulled my thoughts back to the production of murals and joined Kyle in the dining room. He sat on the floor painting a second farm house.

"Kellie seems like a nice girl," I said, gathering brushes, palette and paint. "Did you two meet at your drama class?"

"Actually, like, we met at Score More Tattoos when I had my, ah, never mind. She was having, like, a really bad butterfly tattooed on her …."

"How sweet." I painted grass and trees while trying not to think about tattoos, wherever they might be. I made a mental note to order more chromium oxide green and raw sienna and call my insurance agent as soon as possible. I decided there was no time like the present and rummaged through my purse for the illusive cell phone and a card Barry had given me two years ago in case some idiot ran into my truck. I dialed.

"Hi, Barry?"

"Barry Lowe speaking." Barry's name was deceiving. He had a high-pitched voice like a girl, but if you saw him, he was a real stud muffin.

"This is Josephine Stuart, and I want to report a hit and run on my truck."

"Do you have a police report? Was anyone hurt?"

"No one hurt, just my truck with a mashed rear end, and yes, I have a police report. Do you need anything else?" I juggled the phone as I painted in a cypress tree.

"Josephine, I'm going to call you back. Is that OK?"

"Sure," I said, and gave him my cell number. Kyle was looking at me with curiosity. I told him what had happen and watched his jaw drop. Alicia walked into the room rubbing the back of her neck.

"I'm going to give my neck a little rest. What would you like me to paint in here?"

— 123 —

"Remember the cart and the old man in one of those pictures over there?" I pointed to the folder by the window. "Paint him in front of the house Kyle painted yesterday. Allie, I miss Trigger. Is he with your mother-in-law today?"

"Yes he is. I miss him too."

I looked up. A tall, good-looking friend of mine appeared in the doorway.

"David!" Is it noon already?" Before he could answer, I said, "Kyle, this is my neighbor, David. David, you remember Alicia?"

I immediately dropped my brush in water and took David for a tour through all the rooms in the house, upstairs, downstairs, even the wine cellar. After the tour we made our way outside, skirting around the landscaping projects, to the parking area. David's green Jeep sat next to my truck.

"I don't remember your truck looking like that," David said as he ran his hand across the broken tail light and crumpled tailgate.

"That happened at two o'clock this morning, right in front of the cabin. Some drunks hit my pickup and kept on going. Can you believe it?"

"Must be a form of entertainment up here in the mountains, right?" David grimaced.

"Right, a very expensive form of entertainment when you consider the Mungers have to install another alarm system, plus the money it'll cost the insurance company to fix my truck, not to mention the deductible I have to pay." David nodded and I changed the subject. "So what did you have in mind for lunch?"

"Thought you might be able to recommend a place," David said.

"I've only been to one restaurant in Boulder Creek, but it's good. It's called The Brewery, and it's a place where I won't feel too weird in my paint clothes. Will it bother you, my looking like this?"

David squinted his eyes and pretended to look me over. "You'll pass."

"We should stop at Theda's on the way down the mountain. Maybe she would like to join us for lunch." David didn't say much until Theda opened the cabin door and gave him a warm smile.

"Hello, Mrs. Munger. It's a pleasure to meet you," he said as they shook hands. Solow howled and wagged his tail as he galloped over to his favorite neighbor-friend. He thoroughly sniffed David's pant legs, probably wondering if Fluffy had come along for the visit.

"Please call me Theda. Won't you come in, David?"

"Just for a minute Theda, we're on our way to lunch at The Brewery," I said. "Would you like to join us?"

"I'd love to, but I told Chester I would be up at the house right away to make some appliance decisions."

"When will the alarms be installed?" I asked.

"Chester said Ace will put them in later this afternoon." She looked up at David. "We just couldn't go through another night like last night. You two have fun now." She shooed us out the door with a wave of her hand.

The Jeep bumped down the mountain on its tight springs, entertaining us like a carnival ride. We were still laughing as we cruised through town and parked near the Brewery. The place was packed with people, except for one empty table by the windows.

"Must be ours," I said. Annie appeared and waved her hand toward the table.

"It's yours if you want it," she smiled.

David was impressed with the menu and even more impressed with the actual food. The day was hot, the beer was cold and the lunch hour was over way too fast. David paid the bill, thanked Annie and we stood up to leave. As we walked toward the door, I thought I recognized a customer, but couldn't place him right away.

The man was big with bushy eyebrows and very little hair on top. He sat at a table near the door, giving all his attention to a long rack of ribs. Sauce ran down his chin onto a napkin stuffed into the neck of his tee shirt. When he looked up I noticed he had fresh black stitches above his left eye. I imagined the man wearing a blue cap on his head.

"Stan. Hi. Haven't seen you at the mansion for awhile," I said. "This is my friend David."

"Well, if it isn't the mural lady." He wiped his hands on his greasy napkin and licked his lips. "I'm takin' a little time off. Ol' Russell will do a good job. He's new, but he catches on pretty fast." Yeah, like there's so much to catch on to. How to eat donuts sums it up pretty good, I thought to myself.

"Door hit you in the head?" David asked, smiling.

Stan looked down at his pork ribs and mumbled, "yeah."

"Take care, Stan," I said, but he was already working on the ribs and didn't look up. David held the door for me. We looked at each other, I rolled my eyes and we walked out into the sunlight, each of us blinking and fumbling for our shades.

"Well, that went well," David said.

"Don't worry David. It's his problem. You were just trying to be friendly."

David pushed a clump of salt and pepper hair back from his forehead. "I feel right at home in this town, stitches and all."

"Oh no, you had to have stitches? Guess I'm not cut out to be a nurse."

"Monday my little injury was red and puffy. I went to the Doc and he cleaned and stitched it. I take a pill twice a day."

"You're on antibiotics? I can't believe it. Now I feel guilty for letting you cut the grass."

"It was my idea and besides, now you can feel sorry for me." He crinkled his eyes and gave me a devilish smile. What kind of friend was I? I hadn't even noticed his stitches until he pointed them out to me.

As we motored through town, my head automatically swiveled a look down the side street near Mac's Bar. Sure enough, the rust bucket was parked at the curb.

"David, turn right, I see the McFee truck." He turned and curbed the Jeep. I jumped out and trotted up to the pickup's dirty headlights. Nothing new. No red paint on the bumper. No new dents or scrapes that I could see, but of course, the truck was already garbage so it was hard to tell for sure.

David gave me a questioning look as if to say, "Don't you ever mind your own business?" but didn't say it out loud. On the way back to the villa I explained my theory concerning the McFees. David frowned.

"Now that you've inspected the truck, has your theory changed?"

"No." Call me stubborn.

We motored up the mountain, past the Ace Security truck parked in front of the cabin, and didn't stop till we reached the mansion's parking area. I turned to look at David who had been unusually quiet.

"Thanks for lunch, David. Are you going to see your friends, Jake and Lois this afternoon?"

"I'll see Jake. Lois is visiting her sister in Canada."

"Tell Jake hi from me." I gave David a little wave, turned and walked to the house. I felt his eyes watching me, then the Jeep fired up and he was gone.

Kyle was already back to work in the dining room and Alicia was gracing the ceiling in the den with another cherub. I wondered what Warren would do in his oversized playroom. Set up a tanning booth?

"It's really coming along Allie. I'll be in the dining room if you need me." Kyle was in his own world and didn't know I was around till I started painting beside him.

"So is David like, serious?" Kyle asked with a silly grin on his face.

"We are seriously good friends. That's it," I laughed. Was that a hot flash I felt?

"So, how do you like my cows, man?" Kyle pointed at his latest creation.

"Man, they're bad, radical even. Actually, they look like happy California cows." I heard myself sounding as goofy as Kyle, just before we both cranked our heads toward excited voices in the kitchen. I didn't know what they were saying because I know very little Spanish, but it sounded serious. I decided to snoop.

Manuel stood at the kitchen sink, his forearm wrapped in a bloody shirt. The shirtless young man standing next to him grimaced as he pushed the lever on the water faucet up and down, but nothing came out.

"The water isn't connected yet, but the powder room is working." I pointed to the other end of the house where we muralists were allowed to use the restroom. The rest of the workers were still using blue plastic outhouses.

The two men followed me down the hall to the bathroom. Manuel unwrapped the shirt, exposing a three-inch gash on his arm. The younger man worked the faucet as Manuel rinsed his injury. Feeling queasy, I stood behind him, looking at the floor, but ready to steady him if his knees should buckle.

"Manuel, how did this happen to you?" I asked. The younger man answered in perfect English.

"Sueno saw a rabbit and chased it down the hill. Manuel cut his arm on a broken bottle when he rolled down the cliff looking for his dog." He wrapped Manuel's arm with paper towels. "We need to find a doctor. Do you know one in this area, ma'am?"

"The only place I know is, 'Doctors On Duty' on Scotts Valley Drive. You don't need an appointment there." The men left, but I couldn't put the whole thing out of my mind. I followed the drops of blood through the house and outside to Manuel's truck. No black Lab in the front or back.

"Sueno, here stupid dog," I called as I headed west about fifty feet from Manuel's truck, where the flat land ended. I looked over the side at a series of steep sandy cliffs, ending far down the mountain under a canopy of redwoods. I climbed down one little bank, then slipped and slid several feet down another bank. One sandal came to rest on a broken bottle with its golden label glistening in the sun. A Jack Daniel's bottle smeared with Manuel's blood.

"Here Sueno. Come here you stupid dog," I wailed, gripping a greasewood root.

It broke just as I grabbed another root with my other

hand. Manuel must have held onto the same bloody root. I decided to work my way to the left instead of trying to climb straight up the bank. I clung to roots and branches, stepped over rocks and climbed over boulders until I found a narrow path. The path was steep with little to hold onto.

I heard rustling noises off to my right, then panting and a sharp bark. Sueno caught up to me, dragging his leash, and affectionately jumped up to lick my face, sending me backwards down the hill about ten feet. As I tried to stand up, he loped over to me, aiming his front paws at my shoulders.

"No Sueno. Down boy," I screamed as the dangerously frisky dog raced past me and effortlessly scampered to the top of the mountain. When I finally arrived at the top, Sueno was standing in the back of Manuel's truck panting and wagging his tail as if nothing had happened. I was scratched, scraped and bruised, not to mention angry. I tied the end of Sueno's leash to the handle of Manuel's toolbox.

It was my turn to go to the powder room and clean up. The cold water felt good on my hot, dusty skin. Manuel's blood ran off my hand and swirled down the drain. I thought about the broken bottle and wondered who threw it over the cliff. When I was clean and dry, I trundled down the hall and stepped into the den.

"Allie, let's rest that neck of yours."

"I need a rest? Have you looked in the mirror lately?"

"Actually, no. A mirror hasn't been installed in the powder room yet."

"Just one more minute and I'll have this foot finished," Alicia said. I watched her paint on the fifth toe and then climb down six feet of scaffolding to the floor. "What was all the fuss awhile ago?"

"Manuel cut his arm looking for his dog. Sueno's back now and Manuel went to the doctor for stitches. A doctor could make a lot of money in this town on stitches alone."

Alicia and I walked down the hall to the music room and out of habit, gazed at the same old broken glass ceiling. I described how I thought the field-of-flowers mural should be painted and where the forest would start. She suggested a couple of deer at the edge of the meadow. I agreed and planned to have the pale blue sky color blend into the light blue wall color at about ten feet. Wispy clouds would float around the room all the way up to the dome. I figured two people and five days should get the job done.

"Allie, I'm going to look for Chester. We'll need help with scaffolding tomorrow, so why don't you and Kyle clean brushes and call it a day?"

"Jo, are those new scratches on your arms? And look at your knee."

I looked down at my knee. The skunk wound was open again and leaking a little blood. The old bruises had faded a bit, making way for the fresh ones. My cut-offs were dirty and the sole of my left sandal gaped in the front. Not a pretty sight.

"Allie, I'll tell you all about it after I find Chester." We parted, she to the dining room, I to the front yard. Chester's truck was parked near the garage, so he had to be around somewhere. I asked one of the painters where I might find Chester, as he repositioned his ladder outside the music room. The painter grunted, making it clear he did not speak English.

"You lookin' for me?" Chester asked, as he walked toward me from the back of the mansion. "I heard from Ace that all locks and alarms are in. You'll have to learn the codes."

"That's great," I said, "maybe I can get some sleep tonight. What I wanted to tell you is that we would like to have scaffolding in the music room tomorrow, four feet high on the two walls opposite the windows. The den will stay as is until Alicia finishes her angels."

"No problem," he said over his shoulder as he walked to his truck. Several trucks followed him around the loop and down the mountain. Alicia and Kyle stirred up more dust as they headed home. The place was suddenly quiet. No hammering or sawing noise, just the sound of wind in the trees and two blue jays squawking cantankerously.

An older model Nissan pickup with paint splashes on the tailgate and a metal frame above the bed for ladders was the only vehicle, besides mine, still in the parking area. Obviously, a painter was the designated person to wait for

Russell. The sound of an engine straining to conquer the mountain told me his wait was over. The minute the Ace truck came into view, the painter fired up his truck and drove away. I walked up to Russell's truck.

"Hello, Russell. How's the investigation going? You know, who smashed into my truck?"

"What are you doing here?"

"I live here, remember?" I smiled sweetly. "Find any clues at the cabin?"

"I turned my report in to the sheriff, confidential, you know."

"Right," I said, "That means you didn't find a thing."

"I wouldn't say that."

"Then what did you find?"

"We found traces of white paint on the Mazda's tailgate."

"That's it?" I frowned in disgust.

"It's not like they hurt anyone."

"When my truck gets smashed, I'm hurtin'," I said.

"I'm sorry about your truck, but that's all I can tell you."

"Thanks, Russell." I left him standing in my dust. I loved the no-commute lifestyle. Fire up my truck and I'm halfway home. Theda's SUV was not at the cabin. I tried the door. Locked. I pulled out my key and opened the door. The house was quiet except for a soft humming sound coming from the wall beside the front door. Finally, I realized it was coming from a newly installed panel of numbered buttons with a flashing red light. My cheeks flashed red. "Oh my God, what do I do now?"

My cell phone rang. "Ah, hello."

"Josephine, this is Barry, your insurance agent. Is something wrong?"

"Dang, I mean, Barry, you caught me at a bad time. We have a new alarm system in the cabin where I'm staying and I think I triggered the alarm. How do I turn it off? I don't know the code." Solow must have sensed my panic and belted out a series of howls, making it difficult to hear Barry's response.

"Better hope it's not one of those systems that goes straight to the sheriff's office."

"Did you call the company that installed it?"

"I just got home." I shouted, over the howling. "Hang on a minute." I began pressing buttons, combinations of numbers, but with no good result. "Barry, what should I do? I'm pushing buttons, but the red light is still on and so is the humming noise."

Solow howled urgently. "Quiet!" I shouted. My poor puppy dropped his head down and tucked his tail between his legs, making me feel even worse.

"Barry, are you still there?" Suddenly tires squealed outside, Solow wailed and my heart pounded double-time.

"Call ya later." I dropped the phone and peeked out the front window just in time to see two deputy sheriffs, guns drawn, crouched behind their white sheriff's car. A rack of red lights revolved in circles, silently, from the roof of the official vehicle.

"Come out with your hands up!" shouted one officer. They had my attention. With legs like Jello, I walked to the door and slowly opened it. Both hands reached for the sky, just like in the movies. Things weren't supposed to happen like this in real life. Sergeant Machuca stepped forward as he holstered his gun, but the other sheriff kept his gun trained on me. Machuca rolled his eyes.

"I see you took my advice and had an alarm put in."

"I'm sorry to get you up here like this," I said, "but the door was locked and I don't have the code numbers yet."

"Just happens we were in the area, no harm done." Machuca waved at his partner to holster his gun. "You'll have to pay a fine if it happens again."

"By the way, I heard there were white paint fragments found on my truck," I said, hoping to lead the sheriff into a disclosure of evidence.

"Who told you that? Must have been Rusty."

"Russell," I said. "Is that all you found?"

"As a matter of fact, an older white Dodge pickup was stolen and taken for a joy ride that same night. We hope to match the tire tracks. That's all I can tell you."

"Are you sure it was a white truck?" I said, in disbelief.

"You got it straight from Rusty, didn't you?" Machuca and I were discussing the new alarm system when Theda drove up. She leaped out of the SUV.

"What happened now?" She looked at the open front door, and then put a hand across her mouth. She stared at me for a moment and then her mouth dropped open.

"I was shopping … you didn't know the code." She took a couple deep breaths. "I'm so sorry, Josephine."

"These gentlemen said they'll let this one slide," I said. "Guess I better learn the code."

"If you ladies need us, call 911." Sergeant Machuca said, as he touched his cap and drove away.

I helped Theda bring in a couple bags of groceries, including one bag that felt warm and smelled like roasted chicken. We set the bags down and she showed me how to deactivate the alarm. Four little numbers was all I needed to know.

"Emily's numbers," Theda said. "She was born on the twelfth of December. The code is 1212." Her lips made a sad smile.

"Do I smell dinner in that bag?"

"Yes, I thought deli roasted chicken might be nice and I bought a pasta salad." Theda set two places at the table while I put the groceries away. By the end of the meal, we were relaxed and laughing about the deputies and their weapons. Probably the most fun they had had in a long time.

The phone rang and Theda became involved in a conversation with Warren. It was time for Solow's evening walk. He reluctantly agreed to go when I bribed him with a piece of chicken skin. He stood up and devoured the tasty morsel while I attached the leash to his collar.

For the first time since he arrived at the cabin, Solow wanted to explore the driveway. He pulled me down the hill about 300 yards to where a giant redwood had fallen against the bank and would forever lean across the road at an angle. A squirrel scampered the length of the tree above us, daring Solow to chase him.

We had started out with Solow pulling me down hill, but I knew that going home would be grueling. I tugged, pleaded and finally managed to turn him around and point him up hill. Solow's stubby legs moved slower and slower. His ears dragged on the ground like a lop-eared rabbit. It was almost dark when we finally reached the cabin.

That particular evening we did not go snooping, didn't even consider it. Neither of us had enough strength left to walk to the barn. Actually, I looked forward to a quiet evening, lacking excitement of any kind.

Chapter Ten

Thursday morning I drove the short distance to work, parked and found Alicia and Kyle setting out paint and brushes for another day of mural painting. My poor old carcass ached from the Sueno escapade the day before. Bountiful bruises had bloomed into yellow and violet splendor.

The minute I arrived I knew something was different at the mansion. Carpenter noises were minimal, the men worked slower than usual and some just stood around as if they had nothing to do. But the solarium had plenty of business.

"Hi, Allie, Kyle. Is it just me or is something different around here?"

"Ah, like, Chester isn't here today. Is that what you mean?" Kyle said.

"Jo, I wonder if the scaffolding is up in the music room," Alicia said. I had the same thought at the same moment.

"Good question. Let's go see," I led the way. The three

of us marched through the house only to find the music room empty. Not a stitch of scaffolding in sight.

"Anyone know if Manuel came to work today?"

"Is he the number two boss?" Alicia asked.

"Yes, and I sure hope he's here today."

"Like, he looked pretty bad yesterday," Kyle said, grimacing.

"I'll look for Manuel. Kyle, you can finish painting in the dining room and Allie, you can work in the den. If I don't find someone to help us, we'll just have to take apart the scaffolding ourselves and reassemble it in the music room. I trudged through the house, looking into each room I passed. Several workmen had gathered in the solarium for a cigarette break. Theda wouldn't like that. I walked up to the group of men.

"Hi, anyone here speak English?"

"I speak English. Name's Jose. What do you need?"

"Must be nice to be bilingual," I said, admiring his helpful demeanor and broad shoulders. Jose smiled ear to ear. He was tall and wide with brown skin and a crew cut. Probably the last person I would have picked for a conversation in English.

"I'm working my way through college. I need both languages to get by," he said, with no hint of an accent.

"Since Chester isn't here today, I was hoping to find Manuel."

"Afraid you're out of luck. Maybe I can do something for you?"

"Actually, maybe you can. Do you know how to put up scaffolding?"

"Who do you think does that for you?" He pointed a thick thumb at his massive chest and widened his smile.

"How about putting some scaffolding up in the music room?"

"No problem."

"Meet me in the music room at ten, OK?"

"OK." He turned and walked out to the unfinished garage where paint supplies were stored along with wheelbarrows, saws and pieces of scaffolding. Twenty minutes later, precisely at ten, Jose stood ready in the music room, his coworker beside him. I recognized his partner as the painter who had waited for Ace Security to arrive, before going home.

"This is Norman," Jose said, smiling and shrugging his shoulders. "I know what you're thinking. His full name is Norman Castro Garcia. His parents wanted to give him a head start at being American." I put my hand in front of my mouth and faked a cough, keeping my reactive smile to myself. The young and very handsome Norman stared out the window as I pointed to the two windowless walls in the room.

"Jose, we need scaffolding the length of each wall and four feet high. Is that doable?"

"No problem," Jose said. No sign of comprehension from Norman.

"Thanks, guys." I walked down the hall to the den.

Alicia looked down from the cherub she was painting.

"Jo, did you find Manuel?"

"No, but I found Jose and Norman. They're putting up the scaffolding as we speak. Looks like this room might be finished today. What do you think?"

"I think you're right, but before you go, tell me if this cherub needs more hair?"

"Not really. It's adorable. I wouldn't change a thing." The cherub had wisps of short, curly blond hair, pink cheeks and a chubby body straight from the Sistine Chapel. Alicia was certainly talented and I was lucky to have her working with me. "Think I'll go see how Kyle's doing." I walked to the dining room and discovered Kyle sitting on the floor, a phone at his ear. He looked up and a flood of red washed over him.

"Kellie, like, I gotta' go." He hung up immediately, making me feel like an old meany boss.

"We can finish off this room in a couple days, don't you think?" I said in my kindest voice. The truth was, Kyle had done a beautiful job so far and I didn't want to come down on him for one little phone call.

"Yeah, sure, a couple days. Do you, like, want another barn over here?" Kyle pointed to land near a painted farmhouse.

"I'm picturing a small barn and a vineyard over here. We'll put in a row of cypress trees leading up to the villa on the hill and we need some of your contented cows over here. I'll paint the vineyard and cypress trees and the rest is yours."

We painted for a couple hours to the lively beat of Mexican music coming from a boombox in the sunroom. It's amazing how much can be accomplished when the music is fast. The hard part was keeping my body still and the brush steady. Around lunchtime the music suddenly stopped along with the hum of the worker's conversations. I heard Theda ask where Chester might be. Then silence. I put my brush in the water can and walked through the kitchen to the solarium.

"Hi, Theda. What's up?"

"Josephine, I'm looking for Chester. We have an appointment to talk about light fixtures." I noticed a thick manila folder tucked under her arm.

"All I know is, he's not here, but I wanted to ask you about the faux finish project when you have some time."

"It looks like right now would be a good time to look at the columns."

Theda walked ahead of me, her bracelets clinking all the way to the foyer where four giant pillars, sporting Corinthian capitals, looked as if they were holding up the high ceiling. Their smooth plaster surfaces had been sanded by hand, under Chester's direction. White primer had been applied to the columns and sanded again. When we were finished with them, they would look like travertine marble.

Theda opened the over-sized front door and looked outside for Chester's truck. It was nowhere in sight and all the workers were in the sunroom eating their lunches.

"He didn't call to cancel our meeting. I wonder if he forgot. Anyway, getting back to the columns, I think you have the sample of real travertine, don't you?"

"I have it, no problem. I was wondering about the capitals. We could make them gold or whatever you want them to be. I have pictures of gold ones if you'd like to see. Theda stood back from the door and stared at the ceiling.

"I'm picturing gold capitals on the columns and cherubs on the ceiling, just two of them and wispy clouds. Did I tell you I want a patina on the stair rail?" She thumbed through her folder and pulled out a magazine advertisement showing a magnificent staircase, almost as wonderful as her own. In the picture, the ornate bronze railing had a slight greenish cast which made it look rich and old. I could easily imagine the same thing for the Munger's elegant staircase. The teal patina on bronze would make a nice contrast with the reddish mahogany steps.

Through the open front door I saw a familiar looking old blue and white pickup pull up and park next to Alicia's Volvo. A pretty olive-skinned woman in her forties jumped down from the driver's seat and walked up to the front door. Long black hair covered the back of her tank top, all the way to her blue jeans.

"Hello," she said as she peered in the open door. "Mrs. Munger?"

"Yes, I'm Theda Munger."

"I'm sorry to bother you. My name is Juanita Cortez

and my husband, Manuel, wanted me to tell you that his doctor said he won't be able to work for two weeks, hard labor, that is."

"I'm sorry he was injured yesterday. Of course he needs time to heal," Theda said, with concern in her voice. "Don't worry about anything, Juanita."

"How is he doing?" I asked, remembering his bloody arm.

"Fourteen stitches in his right arm. He's driving me crazy. Wants help with everything. He can't even brush his teeth left-handed." Juanita rolled her eyes.

"My name is Josephine. Please tell Manuel that we miss him and to hurry up and get well. I'll always be grateful to him for saving my little friend's life when he killed that evil dog with his shovel." Juanita's eyes were as big as poker chips.

"What dog?" she stammered.

"I guess brave men don't brag about their deeds," I said. "Ask Manuel about the Mastiff sometime."

"I'll be sure to ask him," she said. "Good-bye." She turned, still shaking her head and walked to Manuel's truck. Sueno sat in the passenger seat, his head hanging out the window and drool running down the door.

Theda and I finished our discussion, she left the house to go home and I walked back to the dining room where Kyle painted happy cows. I wondered what it was like to be a Kyle, and then shook the thought from my head. I wondered if Theda liked the mural so far. I wasn't getting any feedback from her, but sometimes that's a good thing.

"Hey, Kyle, it's lunch time." Even as I said the words, I heard the noon siren go off a mile away at the firehouse. Kyle dropped his brush into the water can. Alicia joined us and we walked to the solarium. All the whicker chairs were taken so we sat on the kitchen steps and ate from our coolers, only Kyle didn't have a cooler so he shared mine. Alicia gave him a can of root beer and an apple. Just like an old hound dog, all he had to do was look at us with sad eyes until we gave in and threw him a scrap of food.

Jose and a few of his friends finally got up and went back to work, so we made good use of their chairs. Four beer-drinking roofers had an intense card game going at their table. In the far corner of the room a workman slept in his chair until someone turned on the boombox full blast. The music sounded happy like a merry-go-round, but we couldn't hear each other talk over the racket so we went back to work as soon as all the food was gone.

I walked down to the music room to inspect the scaffolding. It was perfect. Just what I had ordered. I glanced out the front window just as Norman, riding a very tall extension ladder, toppled slowly to the ground. Unfortunately, his bucket of peach colored paint got away from him and splattered my view.

A workman raced to the scene with a water hose, squirting the windows and wall. I was looking through a blurred mixture of water and paint as Norman stood up, staggered a couple yards to a light post and wrapped his arms around it.

The window finally looked pretty clean. I walked up to it for a better look. Oops. It looked like the sidewalk had taken most of the paint. The man with the hose looked angry as he sprayed the sidewalk long and hard. Norman ambled off to the garage.

I went back to painting cypress trees with Kyle.

"You won't believe what I just saw. Norman rode his ladder all the way to the ground and didn't even get hurt."

"That's bad, man." A few minutes later, Jose burst into the room asking for paper towels. I handed over the whole roll and followed him outside.

"What's going on?" I asked as if it were my business.

"Norman got a punch in the nose from one of those belligerent roofers and he bled all over the unfinished doors in the garage. The blood soaked into the wood. Now we have to sand the dang things all over again," Jose growled.

"Why are you upset with Norman?" I asked. Jose looked around.

"The idiot was drunk and fell."

"I saw that part. He rode the ladder like a trapeze artist. So why did the roofer punch him?"

"It was the roofer's ladder and now its all bent out of shape."

"I know for a fact that the roofers were drinking, too,"

I said as we stepped into the shady interior of the garage.

"Norman, aqui!" Jose tore off a length of paper towel and handed it to Norman who sat on a sawhorse with his face tilted up, pinching his nose.

"Gracias." Norman said.

I saw the victims of Norman's blood, the two doors resting on sawhorses. They would need extra man-hours for sure. Returning to the house, I noticed three of the card players were still playing poker and the boombox still boomed. I joined Kyle in the dining room as he slipped his phone back into his t-shirt pocket. Even if I hadn't seen the phone, his red ears would have given him away.

At four-thirty we cleaned our brushes and called it a day. Alicia and Kyle left in the Volvo, followed by mushrooming clouds of dust. I looked around and discovered I was the only person left on the grounds. I decided to stay and wait for the Ace man. Trying to escape the midsummer heat, I walked to the back of the mansion and took in the view. Beer cans and cigarette butts were strewn across the bank. I had the feeling Chester's tight ship was taking on water.

I pulled up an empty five gallon paint bucket and sat with my back leaning against the back of the house. A hawk circled, and the soft drone from a small airplane drifted down to earth. My eyes felt heavy.

I awoke to the sound of footsteps and clinking noises from Russell's overloaded belt.

"I thought that was your truck I saw," Russell said.

"It's the only one around with a smashed rear end," I reminded him.

"I hear they found the three guys that did it. Seems they took a stolen truck for a joy ride. Kids!" Russell rolled his eyes. "Only one was old enough to drive, let alone drink." I wasn't sure I had heard Russell correctly.

"They were young kids? Are you sure?"

"Actually I read it in the Sentinel this morning."

"I didn't read the paper this morning," I mumbled, still feeling sure the McFees were to blame. It seemed all the clues I had gathered were summarily dismissed by the authorities. "Pull up a paint bucket and have a seat."

"Maybe later. Gotta' check the grounds, you know." He marched his straight little body toward the back entrance to the solarium and disappeared inside. I strolled over to my truck, fired it up and left the mansion with a bad taste in my mouth. I opened the front door at the cabin and Solow greeted me with a passionate howl, but didn't leave Theda's side.

"I thought we might eat out tonight," Theda said. "What do you think?"

"Wonderful. I'll clean up for dinner." I noticed Solow's food and water bowls were full. I gave my face a splash of cold water and applied moisturizer, mascara and lip-gloss. I looked in the mirror. Not bad for a half century of wear. Next, I went to my room and dialed Barry on my cell phone.

"Barry, it's Josephine. I need to know where I should

take my truck to have it fixed." I slipped into clean clothes as we talked.

"I compiled some information for you, including a list of body shops, and I mailed it today," he said in his soprano voice. "You should get it tomorrow or Saturday." He sounded like he was in a hurry so I let him go and dropped my phone on the bed.

Sporting knee length pants with matching yellow shirt and gold loop earrings, I was ready to go to town.

"Don't you look smart?" Theda smiled as she hooked her alligator bag over a bony shoulder, causing her dangly silver earrings to dance.

"Theda, have you lost some weight?"

"I don't think so," she said, looking down at Solow. "He's such good company for me. I took him for a walk down the driveway today. You're so lucky to have him."

"He's all I have," I said. I could almost read Theda's thoughts. I'm sure she was thinking about Emily and wishing she had the comfort of a daughter. All she had was Warren and sometimes I wondered if she even had him. Personally, I would rather have Solow any day.

We took off in the SUV, bouncing our way to Boulder Creek and our favorite food hangout, The Brewery. It was only six, but the place was hoppin'. Even the bar was full. We stood just inside the door, waiting for a table. A burly patron opened the door, squeezed past us and sat down with an older woman at a table in the far corner. I did a double-take and realized it was good old Stan. Was he not feeling friendly or did he just not see us standing in his way at the front door?

Finally, a young couple paid their bill and left the restaurant. Annie waited for the busboy to take away the dishes and then seated us.

"So how's it goin', ladies?" she said, in her usual sunny voice.

"Just hungry," I said. "Looks like you're really busy tonight."

"It's only gonna' get worse. Tomorrow is the beginning of Western Days. Things will get pretty wild around here." Annie ran the back of her hand over her forehead and took a deep breath.

"That sounds like fun," Theda said. "Will there be a parade?"

"Sure, starts at noon Saturday." She handed us each a menu and disappeared into the backroom. Three other waitresses rushed food to their customers as country music competed with the noisy clientele. A warm, friendly atmosphere prevailed, except for Stan and his woman in the corner who ignored us completely.

We sipped iced tea, waiting for our dinners to be served. I couldn't help overhearing four noisy lumbermen sitting at a table close to ours. They drank beer, ate buffalo wings from a huge platter and took turns telling inflated stories, everything from dating the fattest woman to catching the biggest fish. I figured most of it was pure fiction and I paid little attention until one man spoke.

"Hear what happened to Mathus?" The other two men shook their heads. Somebody rear-ended him. Sent him over the cliff and sixty feet down to the river. Lucky to be alive," the man said. I looked at Theda, twirling her straw in the tea.

"Isn't Chester's last name Mathus?"

"Yes, that's his name, why?"

I leaned closer to her, "the man behind me said someone named Mathus had a bad accident and he's lucky to be alive."

"Do you think it might be Chester?" she dropped the straw as her eyes widened.

"I sure hope not. From the sound of it, it was bad." I made a mental note to check the newspaper and wondered if people in the mountains ever lived long enough to die of natural causes. I nibbled at my dinner. It was good, I think, but my mind was elsewhere.

"Everything OK?" Annie asked as she passed by us carrying a tray full of entrees at shoulder height. We both nodded with our mouths full. A little later I was feeling the pinch of my waistband.

"How about a walk to Johnnie's before we go home?" I asked Theda.

"Yes, a walk would be lovely." She paid the bill.

At seven-thirty the sun was riding the top of the western mountain range, ready to slip down the other side. We crossed to the other side of Central Avenue and wandered through an antique shop and then a candle boutique. I bought a Sentinel from the news rack outside Johnnie's Market. We decided not to go inside the store because the fridge was still bulging from the last shopping trip.

The sun disappeared and a balmy evening began. We crossed the street and passed by Mac's open door. Rowdy men stood three deep around the bar. I didn't see the McFees or their rust bucket of a pickup truck anywhere. Maybe they liked the bar when it wasn't crowded.

It was dark when Theda made the left turn onto her dreaded driveway. Halfway to the cabin she suddenly slammed on the brakes as the headlights glommed onto a huge redwood tree lying across the narrow roadway. It was the same tree that used to slant up over the road and worked as an overpass for squirrels.

"What the ...!" I was incredulous.

Theda turned off the engine, sat back in her seat and stared straight ahead. I climbed out of the Lexus for a better look. I figured a carpenter could build several houses out of the monster tree and have wood left over. But I didn't trust my eyes, as all we had were headlights. I walked closer, felt the end of the log with my hand and climbed back into the SUV.

"Someone cut down the tree with a chainsaw while we were away."

Theda just stared through the windshield. It occurred to me we would have to walk all the way up to the cabin in the dark, but that was as far as my plan went. I opened the glove box and fished around for a flashlight.

"Theda, I think we have to leave the SUV here and hike up to the cabin. What do you think?" Theda was definitely on overload. She turned her head at the sound of my voice, but I don't think she heard the words. I repeated the plan and she obediently climbed down from her vehicle and slammed the door.

"Do you have your cell phone with you? I left mine at the cabin."

She shook her head, "No."

I grabbed my purse and Theda's, along with the flashlight and newspaper. We walked to the end of the tree where it rested against the bank, about three feet off the ground. There was just enough room for us to squeeze under with maximum stains to our pretty summer outfits. My hair caught on a small branch on the underside of the tree. I dropped the purses, paper and flashlight. After a struggle I was finally able to untangle my hair and stand up on the other side. Theda followed, managing the feat in a more coordinated fashion.

"I guess Russell must be securing the mansion right now."

Theda finally came to life. "Do you think he heard the chain saw?"

"Probably not, we're almost a mile away." I wondered how much the Mungers had to pay Ace Security for all the useless protection. By the time we reached the cabin we were way out of breath and too tired to talk. Theda unlocked the door and neutralized the alarm. Solow yawned and pounded his tail a few times.

"Theda, how about a cup of green tea?"

"That sounds lovely, Josephine." She fell back into the sofa with a sigh. I went to the kitchen to make tea and to read the paper. I heated the water on low heat, giving me more time to read. I didn't find anything about Chester, but I did find an interesting article about my truck getting smacked in the rear end. It seems three high school students with no past record of misdeeds met an unnamed man at the Boulder Creek Park. He gave them each a bottle of whiskey. They drank until they were drunk at which time the man gave them the keys to a stolen truck and made a bet they couldn't drive to the top of a certain mountain. The boys drove up the road they were shown and did damage to a vehicle on the way back. The man has not been identified or located and the boys are in Juvenile Hall.

I carried the tea to Theda, not saying a word about what I had just read. If she read the paper the next day, fine. I was not about to add to her misery.

"You look tired, Theda. That was some hike we had. Do you take sugar?"

"No, thank you. These ginger snaps will go nicely with the tea. You think of everything." I wished I could think of everything.

"I did think of one thing. How are the workers going to get to the villa tomorrow morning? Maybe we should make a few calls before it gets any later." I saw the worry and stress pulling Theda's shoulders down. "I'd be happy to do the calling if you can give me the numbers."

She pointed to the fat manila folder full of mansion ideas and a list of trades people. I decided to call Chester first. The phone rang four times, then Chester's voice answered, "Mathus Construction, leave a message after the beep." Just as I expected. I looked at the list again, but didn't see Jose's name. I dialed Manuel's number and his wife picked up. "Juanita?"

"Yes, who is this?"

"My name is Josephine. We met this afternoon at the Mungers. I was wondering if you have Jose's phone number. It's very important."

"I will ask Manuel." After a couple minutes she was back. "My husband gave me a list of names and numbers."

"Jose's number is all I need."

I jotted it down and dialed. Jose sounded shocked to hear about the tree and suggested calling a tree service. He volunteered to call Gunther's Tree Service right away. I crossed my fingers and hoped Gunther would show up early in the morning. I asked Jose to take care of Theda's SUV. I told him it was unlocked, keys under the mat.

Theda drank tea and watched the news, better known as the great escape. I took Solow for a short walk under the stars, but didn't let him go near the barn. I was in no mood for more trouble and my legs ached. We walked back to the cabin. I set the security alarm and noticed Theda had already retired to her room.

"It's dreamland for us, big guy." Solow happily followed me into the bedroom. We curled up in our beds and dreamed the night away. I dreamt a giant albino squirrel was bouncing on a fallen redwood tree. Unfortunately my leg was caught under the trunk. Solow ran for help and came back with Fluffy because David was busy.

Chapter Eleven

I awoke Friday morning to the buzzing roar of distant chainsaws and someone knocking on the front door. Solow raised a brow, opened his eyes and began to howl. He jumped out of his bed, nose to the floor and headed for the living room with me just a step behind. Dressed only in a ratty old night shirt, I opened the front door a crack.

"Sorry to bother you. I think someone's cutting trees on the property," Russell, our friendly security specialist, said.

"Why don't you drive down the mountain and see who it is? Isn't that your job?" I asked, after being rudely awakened.

Russell fired up his little blue truck and headed down the mountain. I went back to bed for a couple more hours of much needed sleep. The second time I awoke it was to the smell of coffee brewing. I laughed to myself when I remembered telling Russell to drive down the mountain and see for himself.

Theda wore a sleeveless pink shift, matching pink pumps and a serious expression. She looked up from the newspaper when I walked through the doorway.

"Did you sleep well, Josephine?"

"Mostly. How about you?"

"Fine. I was just reading a story in the paper about the boys who ran into your truck. It seems a man gave them alcohol. Can you believe that? What kind of man would give alcohol to children?" I had a hunch what kind of man would do that, but decided to keep it to myself. Theda was in a fairly good mood, so why spoil it. As we ate breakfast, Theda announced she was going to drive to Santa Cruz and shop for light fixtures and bathroom accessories and would not be home until dinner time.

"Josephine, would you consider having dinner with Warren and me tonight?"

"I should go ...."

"Oh, please. I want you and Warren to become friends ... like we are. She gave me a pleading look. I couldn't say no.

"Sure, I'd love to go with you and Warren," my last words as I left the cabin.

I counted six pickups plus Alicia's green Volvo already parked at the villa. The fallen tree must have been cleared away nice and early, thanks to Jose. Obviously a very capable young man, I thought to myself.

I walked around a pile of sand and jumped over an open ditch. The obstacles were everywhere, but I finally reached the house, and then the dining room. Kyle sat on his heels painting a rock wall bordering a pasture full of happy cows. I squeezed several colors of paint onto my palette and began painting rocks along a stream meandering through the Tuscany countryside.

"Jo, like, what happened with the tree we passed? Did it fall last night?"

"Yes it did, but with help. Someone cut it down while Theda and I were in town. By the way, did you see her car down there?"

"Ah ... like, was I supposed to?" Kyle cocked his head. I hoped Theda's car had been taken care of. After an hour of painting, I put my brushes in water and packed up most of the supplies I needed to start the mural in the music room. On the way there, I looked into the den.

"Allie, the cherubs look great."

"I just finished. I was looking at the ceiling to see if anything is missing. What do you think?"

"You know I love it. Grab the gallon of white paint from the dining room and meet me in the music room." She nodded and took off down the hall. I entered the sunny, high-ceilinged music room and set my paint box and canvas bag down on the floor under a window. Already heat poured into the room from the southern exposure. Working on that side of the house would be a challenge as the AC was not up and running yet and there were no blinds to close.

Glancing out the window at the work projects, I caught

sight of Theda walking the gauntlet of a pre-landscaped front yard. Her pink pumps wobbled side to side, but she made it to the front door without a mishap. I went to see if she needed anything.

"Josephine, Jose delivered my Lexus washed and gassed up. That boy is a hard worker. I asked him to take charge of construction here at the house until Chester or Manuel come back to work. Do you think I did the right thing?"

"I think Jose is young, but very good at all sorts of things," I smiled.

"I couldn't wait to tell you about Jose. Now I'm going shopping. See you around six," Theda smiled and gave me a little girly wave as she left the house. It felt good to see her happy.

Alicia and I blended light blue paint onto the blue wall color, ten feet above the tile floor. Jose raised the scaffold again and we painted clouds all the way up to the domed ceiling. Perspiration ran freely and I was desperate for water. Alicia wiped her brow periodically and the back of her t-shirt was soaked like mine.

By noon, the clouds were finished and we were exhausted. Alicia and I headed down to the sunroom and picked up Kyle along the way. We sat on the kitchen steps as all the chairs were taken. The card players had a game going at a table across the room from us near the boombox.

I looked around and was surprised to see Trigger

walking toward me holding Tansey in his arms. He dropped the ball of fluff into Alicia's lap and wrapped his arms around my waist.

"Hi, Auntie Jo, look what I found today," he said, pulling some little rocks from his pocket.

"Nice rocks," I said.

"Not those ... this." He pulled a baby lizard out of his pocket by its tail. We had one quick look before the lizard dropped to the floor and ran for cover behind a table. Trigger stood holding the lizard's tail, wondering what had happened. It felt good to have him back on the job with us again.

"Cool, Dude. Like how'd ya do that?" Kyle's eyes were big and staring at Trigger with admiration.

"I didn't do it, the lizard did it. Mom, how did he do that?"

"Honey, the lizard is made that way in case he's captured by a curious boy." Alicia and I had a good laugh. Even the boys were laughing. Kyle finished the other half of my peanut butter and pear sandwich, stood up and walked outside, probably to make a phone call to a certain girlfriend. I wondered if Kellie was as lovesick as Kyle.

"Allie, I'll be right back. I need to go to my truck and use the cell phone." I usually kept my phone plugged into the dash as a convenient way to keep it charged. It also kept me from being bothered by calls when I was busy painting. I wasn't one of those people who walk through the stores chitchatting about their personal experiences for everyone to hear. As I approached my truck, I saw Kyle's red hair in the side mirror.

"What's this, the local phone booth?" I teased, trying to sound gruff.

"Like, I just wanted some privacy, ya know?"

"I know. Just hand me the phone. Over there, to your left." Kyle handed the phone out the window.

"Thanks Kyle, and hi to Kellie." I found a bit of shade under a bay tree and dialed David's number. No answer. Just a message to leave a message, so I did.

"Hi, David. I'll be coming home late tonight. I'm having dinner with the Mungers." He seemed to keep track of my coming and going and I didn't want him to worry. All my neighbors looked after each other's properties.

Kyle and I finished our calls and walked back to the house together, he with long strides and me with shorter ones. He went back to the Tuscany mural and Alicia and I to the music room. Trigger and Tansey followed us and fell asleep on the floor in the shadows created by scaffolding.

I drew horizon lines with chalk and we began painting the distant forest. A couple hours later I decided to go to the cabin to give Solow a walk since Theda was going to be gone all day. I parked in front of the cabin next to a big black Lincoln. Warren stood near his car looking lost. I leaned my head out the window.

"What's the matter, Warren?"

"I don't know the code. I was just about to go looking for you."

"The numbers will be easy for you, Warren. They're Emily's birthday numbers, twelve and twelve." I watched his face to see if he wore the same pain as his wife. I didn't see any revealing changes.

"Thank you, Josephine. You saved me a lot of trouble getting into the cabin. I wanted to surprise Theda and arrive early."

"She's shopping in Santa Cruz today and won't be home for several hours," I said, climbing out of the truck. "I came down here to take my dog for a walk. Theda usually takes care of him while I work." Warren opened the front door. Solow met us at the door and did a little "woof woof "as if he wasn't sure if Warren was a stranger or not. I clicked the leash to his collar and we turned to go.

"Mind if I walk with you? I've been sitting in the car for the last two hours."

"We don't mind, do we Solow?" Solow led the way as usual, snout to the ground, velvety ears dragging. He headed for the barn, pulling on the leash with all his might.

"I see who's boss in your family," Warren laughed. "Do you have a big family, Josephine?"

"No, just Mom and Dad and a few stray cousins I almost never see … and my Aunt Clara. Actually, my parents are great. They're all I need and, of course, Solow." We walked to the shop door. I tried the knob. Locked. "So, where are you from, Warren?"

"You probably think I'm a city guy, but my grandparents lived in Boulder Creek most of their lives. They had a house half a mile out Two Bar Road on eighty acres. I remember going there when I was a kid. After they died, my dad sold everything." The story sounded familiar.

"Did the Mungers and the McFee's know each other?" I asked as Solow sniffed wild mushrooms and then jogged toward the double doors at the front of the barn.

"Oh, yes, they knew each other, but not as friends. They shared a property line and I guess it was in dispute for many years. It seems the river changed its course over time and the river had been the boundary line, so of course somebody was shortchanged. I never understood why the McFees cared so much since each family had a lot of land and not much of it was being used."

"This property used to belong to the McFees, right?" I asked. He nodded. "You mean this property wasn't being used?" I said as Solow energetically sniffed the crack under the barn doors. "It was just a house and barn, no little farm or mine?"

"I have never seen anything but the house and barn. Do you know something about it?" Warren cocked his head to one side.

"Theda and I read a newspaper article from 1923 about the McFee's property and it mentioned a farm and a mine. It didn't say what type of mine." I tried one of the old barn doors. It swung open on noisy hinges.

"If there really was a mine involved in the dispute,"

Warren said thoughtfully, "that might explain the hard feelings between the two families." I could tell he was chewing on the idea. He finally noticed I had opened the door.

"Isn't this barn supposed to be locked?" Warren asked.

"I thought so," I said. "Let's try the inside shop door." He walked into the dim light ahead of me. Solow strained at his leash to be first.

"It's locked," he said, jiggling the knob. "I guess the shop is all that matters anyway. The rest of the barn is basically empty." We walked back to the cabin satisfied that the shop was locked.

"Is there any way to go from one property to the other, like a road?" I stepped into some shade beside the cabin. Warren paused.

"In the old days they always had a road to the river, but those old roads become overgrown when people stop using them. When I was a kid, there was a path down to the river. I think my grandpa built his house around 1925, close to the time of the article you read. I'll ask my dad if he remembers anything about a mine next time I call him."

We entered the cabin. I unleashed Solow and in a nanosecond he flopped down on the cool wood floor in the hall. I think he was asleep before he landed. Warren went to the kitchen for a glass of water. I followed him.

"Isn't it hard for you and Theda to be apart so much?"

I asked and then bit my lip, thinking I probably shouldn't pry. "I'm sorry, it's not my business." I turned to go.

"Well, Josephine, our lives were so disrupted a year ago with Emmy missing and all, we just haven't been as close as before." Warren's dark eyes made me feel sad. This man was truly hurting just as Theda was hurting.

"Warren, I hope you two can get it together before there's too much water under the bridge. Try flowers once in awhile. Maybe if you make the first move ...." He didn't answer and I left the cabin feeling like an intruder spouting hackneyed clichés.

Back at the villa, the murals were happening according to schedule. So far the Mungers had shown little excitement over the paintings, just steadfast approval, smiles and nods. Clients were hard to figure. Some were overjoyed from the start and others waited to see the finished product before they made comments of any kind. Some had to wait for a spouse or friend to comment before they knew how they felt about the artwork. If my brain ever slows to the point that I need someone else to tell me what I like, just take me to the pound and put me to sleep.

Actually, the villa project had become very personal for me. Most of my energy went into trying to keep Theda out of total melancholy. I painted out of habit, exerting very little conscious energy on the murals. Thank goodness for Alicia and Kyle and their extraordinary work. I walked fast, dodging construction at every turn, vowing to focus on the murals instead of the Mungers for a change.

The dining room was empty so I took off for the music room. Trigger ran by me, chasing Tansey toward the kitchen.

"Hi, Auntie Jo," he yelled and kept running. I entered the music room. Alicia and Kyle were chatting with each other as they painted the distant forest which would eventually border the yet-to-be-painted meadow flush with wildflowers. They didn't hear me coming over the noisy fan in the far corner which basically made noise and pushed hot air around. Kyle finally looked up.

"Jo, like, I couldn't make the cows look happy anymore so I'm helping Alicia." He was sweating to the extreme with rivulets running down his forehead and dripping off the end of his nose. The end of his nose caught my attention.

"Kyle, no ring on your nose?"

"Like, Kellie doesn't want me to wear it." He turned back to the trees he had just created with practiced strokes before his face inevitably turned red.

"Have you seen Trigger?" Alicia asked.

"Ran past me a minute ago headed for the solarium, I think."

"I'll check on him in a few minutes," she said.

"We can all take turns," I suggested. "Why don't you spend some time with him, Kyle?"

"OK," he said, dropping his brush in water and leaving the room with a smile on his sweaty face.

"Thanks Jo. I guess I felt Trigger was safe when Chester

was around. Things just aren't the same without him."

After many breaks for liquid refreshment, four-thirty arrived and we gratefully cleaned our brushes and prepared to go home. Home, however, would not happen for me right away. I had promised Theda I would go out to dinner first. All I really wanted to do was enjoy my favorite chair in my favorite house on five acres of freshly mowed weeds. Poor David. I hoped his head was healing. Obviously nursing was not my thing.

When Alicia and I finally exited the mansion, Trigger ran up to his mother, pulled a handful of rocks out of his pocket and held up an arrowhead made of flint for us to examine. Alicia took a careful look at the Native American artifact.

"Honey, that's a wonderful find. Indians must have made it long ago. Ohlones maybe." Alicia beamed as if she were looking at the crown jewels. "What's that in your other hand?" Kyle stepped closer, adjusting Tansey who was asleep in his arms.

"Like, he found a gold nugget in the water. Almost as big as a raisin."

"We searched the whole beach and the shallow water, but this was the only piece of gold. It is gold, isn't it, Mom?"

"It certainly looks like gold and it will be a valuable addition to your rock collection. Now, let's get in the car and go home." Alicia was the last to buckle up and off they sped. I stepped back, coughing, and waving at the dust.

Across the empty parking area I noticed Jose loading a toolbox into the back of his little yellow pickup. I strolled over to his truck.

"Jose, haven't seen you all day. Your new position keeping you busy?"

"Oh, hi, Josephine." He leaned his large frame against the cab, allowing himself a moments rest from a long day. "I had business in town. Is the scaffolding in the music room satisfactory?"

"I hate to bother you, but we're already finished with the scaffolding," I said, trying to be pleasant, despite a flock of pesky gnats in my eyes and dust in my throat. Jose blinked a cloud of gnats away from his eyes.

"Don't worry. The scaffolding will be gone when you're ready to work Monday."

"Thanks a lot, Jose. See you Monday." I waved good-bye and fired up my dinged-up truck. Jose seemed like an exceptional young man compared to all the other work-men who had evacuated the villa by two o'clock because Chester wasn't around.

I found the cabin empty except for a sleepy old dog, who showed his love for me by lifting his head and pounding his tail. I showered and made a special effort to style my wayward hair. I jumped into the one clean outfit left in the closet. It wasn't dressy, but it looked better after I put on my practically genuine gold earrings and necklace. I could never keep up with Theda's glitter and style, but I didn't look like a dud either.

I clipped Solow's leash to his collar and we strolled out the door, right into the fresh dust from Theda's Lexus. She hopped down from the driver's seat wearing a whole-face smile, obviously successful in her hunt for treasures. The back of the SUV was jam-packed with lamps, area rugs and bags of household accessories.

"Josephine, guess what I bought?"

"Haven't a clue. What did you buy?" Solow strained at the leash. She reached over to the passenger seat, pulled out a large plastic bag and handed it to me. I handed the leash to Theda and pulled out a genuine alligator purse, probably worth more than the resale value of my whole truck. I gulped air and managed to say, "gee ... thanks!"

I had never owned an alligator anything because I didn't believe in killing an animal just for its skin. Besides, I could never afford such an extravagance. We hugged. Theda began unloading her vehicle and I took Solow for a short walk. He pulled me forward, sniffing like crazy, straight to the back of the barn where he stopped in his tracks and sniffed at something on the ground. Another cigarette butt. Whoever was leaving butts was still leaving butts.

Silently I scolded myself for being way too curious and headed back to the cabin. I tied Solow to the outdoor water faucet and helped Theda unload the last of the loot. We stashed most of it in Warren's almost empty walk-in closet.

"By the way," I said, "Warren was here this afternoon.

Wanted to surprise you."

"That's nice." A tiny smile stole across her brilliantly pink lipstick. "I wonder where he went. He doesn't know anyone around here." We both automatically glanced at our watches and came up with six o'clock. As if on cue, Warren's Lincoln could be heard powering up the rough grade.

Theda excused herself to go do a little primping before dinner. I heard her close the bathroom door just as Warren stepped into the house carrying a bouquet of long stemmed yellow roses and baby's breath, displayed in an exquisite crystal vase.

"Hi, Josephine," Warren said, cheerfully, "I explored Boulder Creek today."

"Theda's dressing. She'll love the roses. So what's new in town?"

"You piqued my curiosity earlier today." In an animated voice, Warren told me about his afternoon. "I was about to pay for the roses when I suddenly remembered that Nora Bates, our realtor, has lived in this town her whole life. Probably forty or so years, and knows lots of people and gossip. When she sold this property to us, she yammered on about the town and how it was going to the dogs. Then, she'd catch herself and say that Boulder Creek was a great place to retire," he chuckled.

"Well, I told the florist to keep the flowers refrigerated while I paid a visit to Nora, and I would be back around five to pick them up. The woman eyed my wedding ring and gave me a sly smile." Warren popped open a can of cold soda and offered me one. "Makes me wonder what kind of woman Nora is."

"No, thanks on the soda." I poured myself a glass of water. "So, what do you know about Nora Bates?"

"To put it bluntly, I'd never trust anything she says. She was pressuring us to buy this property, but we wanted it on our own. It was our second choice after we tried to buy my grandparent's property on Two Bar Road. They've been gone for many years, but I have good memories of the place."

"So, your grandparent's home was for sale at the time?"

"No, but I thought the owner might sell if the price was right. We had Nora make offer after offer, but the answer was always no." He emptied the soda can and threw it in the recycle bin under the sink. My impression of Warren was on an upswing. He continued. "Anyway, today I asked Nora if she knew anything about the Two Bar property. She avoided my question and said something like, 'how's your new home coming along? Must be almost finished by now.'"

"She sounds a little wacky," I said, rolling my eyes to the ceiling.

"Listen to this ... I asked her again, straight out, and she admitted she owned the property herself. You could have knocked me over with a potato chip." He shook his head and balled his lips together. "You know what that means? If she owned the property five years ago, she was rejecting our offers herself. I don't know if she has a ton of money or she's screwy. Maybe she's both, but I wonder why she tried to hide the fact that the property was hers."

"Did you ask her about the mine?" I was forgetting to breathe at that point.

"Nora said she never heard of a mine in the area. She said in the old days most of the valley residents had jobs to go to, plus vegetable gardens and orchards at home to help with living expenses." Warren fiddled with the flower arrangement as his mind wandered from the subject of discussion.

"I noticed your truck really got clobbered. Even dented that custom bed top. Too bad. You know we will make up any losses you suffer."

"Theda has been quite generous." I didn't feel like small talk at that point. "About Nora, did you ask her if the Mungers and the McFees hated each other?"

"Yes, I did. She told me she had never heard of any problems, but said she didn't know much of the history." He cocked his head to one side. "Seemed like Nora knew a lot of history and gossip five years ago when I talked to her."

"Anyway, she looked like she was sitting on a hot poker, nervous, distracted, that sort of thing. She said she had an appointment to see a client, so I left. After I picked up the roses I passed by her shop window. She was on the phone."

"Not a person you can trust," I said. "This conversation only adds fuel to my speculations." Before Warren could ask about my thoughts, Theda made her entrance in a baby blue silk pantsuit. They hugged a modest hug and Warren complimented her on how she looked. She saw the roses and walked across the room to smell them.

"Thank you, Warren. What's the occasion?" she asked, batting her eyes.

Warren smiled, "I hired a manager to run the office beginning two weeks from now. At that time, I'll be able to focus on the move to Boulder Creek and work on finding a caretaker for our house in the city. Actually, I already put a 'help wanted ad' in the Chronicle this morning to sort of test the waters."

Theda and Warren were opening up to each other and sharing their week in an amicable way with me hanging around like the third party in a duet. I excused myself and walked to my room carrying the phone book in one hand and my new alligator purse in the other.

I had a naggy bad feeling about Chester's accident and thought I might find him at the Dominican Hospital in Santa Cruz. I found the number and called. Sure enough, he was in room 243 in the west wing. I jotted down the room number on my scratch pad and dumped the contents of my old purse into the new one. I checked my hair in the mirror and walked to the front room where the Mungers stood, ready to depart.

"I made reservations for seven," Theda said. "If we

leave now we'll just make it."

"That's for Scapazzi's, I take it," Warren said. She nodded. I quickly dumped some kibble into Solow's bowl, locked the door and joined the Mungers in the Lincoln.

Scapozzi's was packed, but we had a reservation and were assigned a table on the front deck in less than ten minutes. The hot day had turned into another balmy evening, which was just peachy, except that I felt like the chaperone for a couple of goo-goo eyed teenagers.

Warren was warm and affable toward his wife and she looked more relaxed and radiant than I had ever seen her. Theda sat opposite her husband with me at the side. She glanced at her menu and looked up at Warren.

"Glorious night isn't it, dear? I'm so glad you and Josephine are getting to know each other," she smiled. Warren gave me a wink.

I was very happy with the Mungers' new togetherness, but it was hard for me to stay focused on the conversation. My mind kept drifting away, trying to analyze the information Warren had gleaned from his earlier trip into town.

Two hours later, after coffee and Brandy, the three of us settled our well nourished bodies into the Lincoln's cushy leather seats. Riding in the Lincoln was like riding on air until we turned onto the notorious driveway.

Back at the cabin, I took Solow for his constitutional, thanked the Mungers for dinner and headed home. However, going straight home would have been too easy.

Chapter Twelve

As I drove through Boulder Creek, Solow at my side, I spotted a real estate office just two doors down from the florist shop. The small wooden storefront was white with green trim and featured a black Dutch door. The blinds were down on the two front windows. Affixed above the door was an unlit neon sign which read, BATES REALTY. A small CLOSED sign hung in the window-half of the door, blocking much of the dim light from inside.

The old town was alive with pedestrians, young couples mostly, enjoying the starry night. All the bars and restaurants were still open, making it difficult to find parking. After two passes through town, I remembered seeing a PARKING IN THE REAR sign at the entrance to a narrow alley between the Candle Boutique and Bates Realty. I motored down the alley and parked in the only spot left, beside an old rusty Dodge pickup. My ticker did a back-flip.

"Stay, Solow." His head hung out the passenger window,

tongue flapping. "Secure the truck until I return."

I told myself I was just going for a little walk, maybe to Johnnie's to buy ice cream. The alley was darker than Theda's coffee until I rounded the corner of the building where street lights illuminated the Central Avenue sidewalk. I turned left and casually walked the couple yards to Bates Realty. I put my hands to the front door window and leaned forward to see who might be inside.

I looked past the dark front room into a connecting, well-lit, backroom and counted three people. As they talked and moved about, I caught glimpses of a heavyset woman with Dolly Parton hair and a tall, dark-haired man swigging a can of beer. I recognized the third person as the McFee brother with the bushy beard. So why were these men here with a woman who looked twenty years their senior?

The tallest man, the one with his hair in a pony tail, glanced at the front door for just a second. I couldn't tell if he saw me, but my guess was that he did. I sidled away from the door, turned and marched up the sidewalk to Johnnie's. I experienced a sense of safety as I entered the well-lit store full of evening shoppers. My shoulders re-laxed a bit as I strolled down the aisles dropping eggs, ice cream, a pound of ground beef and two boxes of Watsonville-grown strawberries into the cart.

With the new gator purse over my shoulder and two bags of groceries in my arms, I walked back to the truck. It was a lovely evening until I entered the dark alley. Goose bumps popped up all over my body as I imagined McFees hiding in every shadow. I finally reached my Mazda, opened Solow's door, shoved the groceries under the dash and hurried to the driver's seat. Breathlessly, I whipped my truck around and sped down the alley. Solow broke into a long serious howl.

"What's with you big guy?"

Then I heard it, coming up fast from behind, the roar of an engine propelling a truck with major muffler problems. It backfired. I jumped a couple inches in my seat and my heart skipped several beats. Headlights flashed in my rearview mirror. Solow howled again, his head stretched out the window as far as it could go. I made a right turn onto Central Avenue, stifling the urge to stomp on the gas pedal. The truck behind us followed at the same speed until we left the streetlights behind.

Highway nine was a windy two-lane road that followed the San Lorenzo River through the redwood forest from Boulder Creek, all the way south to Felton. There were no street lights, just sharp turns, narrow bridges and steep drops down to the river.

"Brace yourself, big guy." I put my foot down hard, the engine coughed, and we sped up only to slow down for a sharp turn. And so it went, turn after turn with the Dodge bearing down on our tailgate like an eight-cylinder cat playing with a four-cylinder mouse. I had a white-knuckle grip on the steering wheel, sweat running down my back and my jaw was tighter than a double-knotted shoelace.

I had driven through the valley many times and knew my way around, but the McFee's had the "home advantage". I felt a hard jolt from the right rear of my truck. Solow yipped. In slow motion, we spun to the left on two wheels, across the other lane and instantly turned someone's closed garage door into a million toothpicks. The one-car garage, perched high above the river beside a rustic cabin, stood about five yards from the highway. The little house was typical of many in the area, probably built in the thirties or forties when building codes were lenient or nonexistent.

Thankfully, we stopped before my pickup could break through the back wall of the garage and drop eighty feet down to the river. I heard Solow whine and didn't blame him. I felt like a good cry myself. Shaking like crazy, I cautiously opened the door and climbed out. Once I had my balance, I stumbled down a dark path to the cabin. The porch light blinked on and the front door opened. A very distraught elderly couple dressed in pajamas looked at me as if the Martians had landed.

I stepped into the light and apologized profusely. Feeling wobbly, I wrapped my arm around a porch pillar. I always hated it when females fainted in the old movies, and I never wanted to be a fainter. But there I was, feeling numb and shaking like a maple leaf. Next thing I knew, I was laying on a couch too short for my body. My feet were up on the armrest with pieces of peanut butter sandwich clinging to the toe of my right sandal.

"So that's where Theda's sandwich went," I mumbled. The plump little old lady patted the goose egg on my forehead with a wet cloth. "I'm so sorry I ruined your garage door. I'm sure my insurance will pay for a new one." I looked up and thought I was hallucinating. A huge caribou head hung on the wall behind the couch. Its yellow marble eyes glared down at me accusingly.

"Relax, dear," the frizzy-haired woman said. "You've had a terrible shock." The elderly man stomped into the house with his pajamas in a twist and announced that his collection of stuffed animals was a complete loss. It seemed odd to me that he wasn't nearly as concerned about his garage door as he was about some silly stuffed animals.

"I'd be happy to buy you some new ones," I said, feeling horribly guilty. The little lady looked like she was ready to split a gut.

"Honey, you can't buy them. You have to kill the mangy animals and then they're stuffed and ready to spend thirty years in the garage, or until a nice accident takes them out." She couldn't hold back any longer and let loose with uncontrollable laughter, slapping her knees and wiping her eyes. Her husband stomped out of the house. Finally she calmed down, but her smile never went away.

"I'm Mrs. Vandiveer, but call me Mary. The geezer is Herbert, my husband of fifty-seven years." The name sounded familiar, and then I remembered.

"Nice to meet you Mary, my name is Josephine. Any

one named Russell in your family? Maybe a security guard." Mary crossed her hands over her heart.

"Glory be, Josephine, you must be the famous artist Russell has been telling us about. He's our grandson, you know." I wondered what Russell had said about me. If he could lie about the famous part, what other distortions might he tell his grandparents?

"I'm not really famous, although I have painted for a few famous people."

"Well, Russell just thinks you're the 'cat's meow.' Now, lie back and let me take care of that bump on your head." She giggled her way into the kitchen. I watched her wrap a sack of frozen peas in a dishtowel, giggle her way back to me and place the peas on my forehead. I rested quietly with frozen vegetables on my head for several minutes, until I remembered Solow.

"Oh, my God, Solow," I gasped. I hadn't a clue how he took the crash. I jumped up and raced out the front door. Herbert had the light on in the garage that looked like Hurricane Josephine had hit it. I rounded the truck and opened the passenger door. Solow practically fell out. I helped him to the ground, noticing his whole backside was crimson. I stifled a cry with my hand. Tears welled up as I embraced the best dog-friend a person could have. Down close, hugging him, he smelled like strawberries.

Once I realized Solow was wearing strawberries and a few other food groups, I relaxed considerably. He had polished off a pound of ground round, a pint of 'cookies and cream' ice cream and a dozen raw eggs. He had been literally rolling in groceries under the dash. Every dog's dream!

I walked Solow to the house and introduced him to Mary, then tied his leash to a porch pillar. He looked like he'd been in a food fight and lost, but he and Mary took to each other like hot fudge to ice cream.

"Mary, may I use your phone? I need to call the sheriff."

"Help yourself my dear." She walked me over to a green rotary phone, probably the last one in California. I called 911 and reported the accident. The dispatcher said a sheriff's deputy would be right out. Over the phone I had called it an accident, but I knew better. Mary sat beside me on the couch and began to knit.

"Now, tell me what happened, Josephine, you'll feel better." Her needles clicked into high gear.

"Has Russell told you about the trouble we've been having at the Munger's mansion?" Mary slowed the needles.

"Russell has been a little worried, but he said he's about to break the case wide open." Her wrinkled lips smiled with pride as she bumped the needles up to top speed.

"Well, the bad guys are still out there, but I'm sure your grandson is on the job even as we speak." So much for explaining what happened. I rested my head on the back of the couch and positioned the sack of peas squarely on my forehead. The accident wasn't bad enough to set off the air bags, so I figured my dog and I would be fine just as soon as all the bruises went away in a month or so. I felt like inflicting a few bruises myself. After all, the McFees could have killed us. Perhaps that was their intention. I shivered all the way down to my peanut-buttered sandal.

"My dear, would you care for a cup of tea?" Mary was already halfway to the kitchen before I could say a word.

"Yes, Mary, that would really hit the spot," I said as Herbert finally returned from his sulking place somewhere outside.

"Fine dog you have out there, once you clean him up."

"He's a good dog. Mr. Vandiveer, I'm truly sorry about your collection."

"Don't give it another thought, my dear," Herbert whispered. "It's time I let it go. Don't tell Mary I said so."

Mary must have known Herbert was back in the house because she balanced a tray with three teacups and a bowl of sugar, setting it down on the coffee table.

"Sugar?"

"No, thank you." I tried to smile, but my face hurt. A car door slammed outside. In unison, the three of us turned our heads toward the open front door and Solow gave one of his happier howls. Sergeant Machuca filled the doorway with his bulk.

"Evening folks. What's going on?" He looked at me. "Ms. Stuart, we meet again."

"Sergeant Machuca, this is Mary and Herbert Vandiveer.

They were kind enough to help me out after I destroyed their garage." I stood up and began explaining what happened and why, according to my theories. Machuca was not an instant believer, but the old folks were taking it all in, their eyes wide and mouths gaping.

"Have anything to drink tonight?" Machuca looked at the ceiling. "I have to ask."

"Just tea." I raised my cup.

"Do you have any injuries?"

"No, not much."

"What about that goose egg on your forehead?"

"It's feeling better already, but I'm not sure about my truck."

"Let's go take a look," the sergeant said, as he followed me out the door. I fired up the truck and backed it up a few feet. The right rear was so dented from the first hit-and-run it was hard to say if there were any new dents. Other than a face full of feathers and fur, my pickup seemed to be OK. A bear's claw dangled from the grill, a small piece of what had cushioned our crash so nicely. A pile of heads, horns, legs and wings told a tale of animals being collectively murdered for the second time.

The sergeant seemed satisfied that my vehicle was drivable; however, he gave me some advice.

"I want you to go straight home tonight and don't be surprised if you get stopped for a fix-it-ticket. You'll be getting the tail light fixed soon?"

"Right away." I brushed feathers off the side

mirror. "Guess you'll be looking for the McFees?" I said as I searched his inscrutable eyes for a glimmer of cooperation.

"I'll make out a report and get back to you," he said.

"Monday, I'll be working at the Mungers if you need me." I hoped something would be done about those moth-eaten, beastly brothers and I would certainly make myself available to help.

"You realize they tried to kill me?" I said. Machuca pushed his lips together and rolled his eyes upward.

"I have a few questions for the folks, but you can go now," he said, turning toward the cabin. I didn't need to be told twice. I grabbed Solow's leash, we jumped into the little Mazda garbage truck and headed home. How I wanted to be home. It was already well past midnight, the adrenaline was gone and I was exhausted.

David would never believe this one. I wondered if I should tell him and then I thought of Mom and Dad. If I told them, they would want me to quit the job and I was not about to do that. In my head, I played out all the pros and cons of telling friends and family and concluded I should keep my trap shut. Solow snored as I drove, his paws twitching now and then.

"Go get 'em boy, get those dirty McFees!" I parked close to the front door of my darling little house. It looked so welcoming with the porch light on and the perky marigolds looking watered and cared for. I walked inside, turned on a light and noticed a neat stack of mail on the coffee table. David always did the nicest things.

Solow dragged his fat belly to bed, expelling air from both ends of his ballooned body. I would deal with the filthy truck and my food-crazed dog in the morning. I fell into bed and slept like the dead. My dreams that night included a food fight with the McFees and a tea party with three Vandiveers in tall black felt hats. I was wrestling a caribou while trying not to spill my tea, when Solow burped, looking like a balloon when it loses all it's air.

Chapter Thirteen

A wet lick on my cheek and the smell of raw foods brought me to wakefulness. The sun was up and the clock said, "can't be," but it was, noon. I had slept through several phone calls as indicated by my trusty message machine. Mom, David, Mary and Barry had all called me. I zoomed through all the messages. Barry's was last. He told me he had arranged for my truck to be worked on right away. All I had to do was drop it off at The Body Shop in Watsonville, Saturday between eight and two, and pick up a rental car there. I began to perspire when I realized it was already twelve-thirty and I still needed to clean the truck.

In an attempt to save time, I pulled a reluctant, but reeking Solow into the shower with me and closed the glass door. In no time we were both lathered and rinsed. I left Solow in the shower stall where he could shake himself dry. Twenty minutes later, I was dressed in shorts and a t-shirt, hosing down the pickup. I let Solow out of the shower and returned to the truck to scrape out the interior. I washed my hands, threw on some jewelry and lipstick, and cruised into a parking space at The Body Shop with four minutes to spare. The girl at the desk looked ill when she saw me. She had probably anticipated Saturday afternoon off instead of taking care of me.

"Can I help you?" she whined, with one fake eyelash askew and a hickey on her neck.

"I'm Josephine Stuart. I'm dropping off my truck and picking up a rental." She shoved a clipboard at me with two forms to fill out. I sat down in a cheap plastic chair and began to fill in the blanks. I only mentioned one hit and run accident. No one would believe I had two in the same week. Besides, all the damage was in the same place.

The shop seemed to be vacant except for me, the girl at the desk and a mechanic who had just walked in with keys in his hand. I gave the completed forms to the girl and the young mechanic gave me keys to a rental car.

"Your Ford is right over there." He pointed out the window to a maroon compact car all shiny and clean in the summer sun. He eyed the girl behind the desk and she smiled coyly. They were happy to see me go.

I jumped into my Ford rental, took a few minutes to check out all the gadgets, lights, wipers, etc. and then headed for a fast food restaurant and an Asian chicken salad, my first meal of the day. I tried to be careful, but a few crispy noodles got away from me. The car had been broken in with noodles on the floor and anointed with a smudge of salad dressing on the door. Solow would clean the car in a jiffy.

After lunch, I turned onto Highway One heading north to Dominican Hospital in Santa Cruz. The little Ford zipped along side-by-side with huge trucks and cars, making me feel small and vulnerable. I turned into the hospital parking area, found an empty parking space and slid in with gobs of room to spare.

Once inside the hospital, I asked a nun where room 243 was. She very kindly pointed to a staircase and explained some right and left turns on the second floor. The door to room 243 was open so I walked in. I was shocked to see Chester lying on his back, one leg suspended from a contraption, head bandaged, neck collared and one arm in a major cast from shoulder to wrist. He opened his swollen eyes when I spoke to him.

"Hey, Chester, how are you feeling?" I bit my lip. He blinked and stared, trying to remember me. Guess I wasn't as unforgettable as I thought. An old starchy nurse walked in, took Chester's blood pressure and flashed me a stern look.

"You can visit ten minutes." She bustled out of the room.

"So, I heard you had an accident," I said.

"Yeah, they got me pretty good."

"Who got you? I heard you fought with someone before the accident." Chester sipped water through a straw.

"McFees, know 'em?"

"Do I know them? If I knew them any better I'd be dead or at least in the hospital like you." I felt my forehead to see if my goose egg was still there. It was, but after seeing Chester, I knew I had gotten off easy.

"Do you know which McFee did this, or was it all three?"

"Damon and George." Chester croaked, taking another sip of water.

"Is it true you fought with them and then they ran you off the road?"

"Yeah," he tugged at one of his pillows. I reached over to help and unfortunately tipped over the pole-hanger holding the IV bag of medicine being piped into his arm. He opened his mouth, but didn't make a sound. A real gentleman.

"Is there anything I can do for you?" I asked as I repositioned the hanger.

"No."

"How do you happen to know Damon and George?"

"We went to the same high school for a couple years." He closed his eyes as if to recharge his batteries.

I figured my ten minutes was up so I said, "Bye," and left the hospital to the sick and the injured. Since I was already in Santa Cruz, I thought I might as well drop by and see if Mom and Dad were home.

Walnut Avenue looked like a quiet neighborhood from the forties, or even the thirties, except for all the yuppie cars parked against the tree shaded sidewalks. Mowers were mowing and children were skating, along with my parents. Mom and Dad wore matching tank tops, shorts and roller blades. As soon as they realized it was their daughter getting out of the little maroon car, they rolled up to me and stopped.

"What's that bump on your forehead, dear?" Mom shaded her eyes with one hand as she leaned forward and squinted for a better look.

"You know how it is in the painting business with ladders and all. We're always getting dinged up." I wiped the sweat from my lumpy forehead. I should have invented a hairstyle that would hide my bump, but it was too late. The inquisition was on.

"Honey, did you sell your truck?" Dad asked.

"Oh, no, this is a rental. My truck needed a little work."

"Well, what do you think about our vacation plans?" Dad asked me. I walked and they skated to the front door.

"What plans?"

"Didn't you get my message?" Mom pulled off one skate and then the other. When all their skates were parked by the front door, we went in and made ourselves comfortable at the bar in the kitchen. I admitted I had not listened to my messages, except the one from Barry.

"Honey, your father and I have rented a cabin in Boulder Creek for ten days beginning tomorrow. Are you surprised?

"Nothing you do surprises me, but why Boulder Creek?"

"Because Myrtle's son is going to Atlanta on business and he rented it to us cheap." Dad explained. "Tom lives there year-round, you know. Now your Mom and I can see you more often and get in a little fishing." He was beaming. I smiled back.

"That will be wonderful," I said. "We can get together after work. I know a couple good dinner places in town." I squirmed on my barstool.

"Are you hungry, dear?" Mom asked. "We were planning to have an early dinner at Stagnaros on the wharf. You know how your father loves clam chowder with sourdough bread. Of course, I'm no slacker when it comes to seafood either. Want to go with us?"

"Sure." I'd be the last person to turn down dinner on the wharf. We rode away in Mom's Subaru. Stagnaros was located near the end of the mile-long wharf in Santa Cruz and hadn't changed much in the last fifty years. It was only five o'clock so we were not surprised to see a few empty tables. The sun shone through over-sized picture windows, casting a glow behind one familiar looking couple as they ate shrimp cocktails and watched sailboats skim across the water. As we walked by their table, earrings and bracelets clinked. Theda turned her head and smiled.

"Josephine, imagine meeting you here." Her smile was ear-to-ear. Warren stood and gave me a hug.

"Hi. I'd like you to meet my Mom and Dad. Theda,

Warren, meet Leola and Bob Carl." My Dad was immediately shaking Warren's hand with vigor. Mom bent down and put an arm around Theda who was still sitting, mainly because there was no room in the aisle for standing. The girl holding our menus asked if we would all like to sit together.

Warren and Dad both nodded they would. The ladies were too busy talking to hear the question. I spoke for everyone.

"That's a great idea. Thank you."

Theda and Warren followed us to a larger table with the same incredible view. A waitress retrieved their shrimp cocktails. I settled onto a comfortable bench seat and checked out the menu while the Mungers and Carls got to know each other. I was starting to feel like a piece of furniture until a certain subject came up, and then I wished I was a piece of furniture. Mom started it.

"Theda, dear, have you had any more trouble with your building project?"

"Just the hit and run Wednesday morning," Theda looked at me. "Josephine, are you having your truck repaired?"

"I dropped it off today." Thanks a lot. My cheeks felt hot.

"Honey, what happened? You didn't tell us someone hit you." Only a Mom could coax a confession out of her fifty-year-old daughter.

"They didn't hit me. They hit my truck while I was in

the house. The boys were caught and my insurance will take care of everything. No big deal."

"You're sure everything's OK up there? What do you think, Warren?" Dad said.

"Actually, Bob, we have the latest in security systems already up and running. We also have Ace Security on the property whenever the workmen are gone. The estate is really quite safe." Warren smiled and popped a shimp in his mouth. Theda and I exchanged glances as if to say, "You don't know the half of it." Warren continued his boast.

"We had our house designed after a villa we visited in Tuscany a few years ago. You should come by sometime."

"Well, it just happens we'll be in your neighborhood all next week," Dad said.

"Love to have you come up and see the place," Warren said, between shrimps. "I'm afraid I won't be there Monday through Friday, but Theda can show you around."

Apparently, the Mungers had not heard about my accident Friday night, as it was never brought up in the subsequent conversation. The five of us ate, sipped wine and discussed everything from building codes to terrorists to how to grow violets.

Outside our window gulls swooped, pelicans dove and surfers surfed the famous, steamer lane. By seven, the familiar summer fog bank had moved in, giving the world a softer, wetter appearance. We walked outside into the gloom and said our good-byes to the Mungers.

"Thanks for dinner," I said, as we cruised down Walnut Avenue and parked at the Carl abode. "'Fraid I gotta' run home now and feed Solow." Actually, I figured he wouldn't be ready to eat again for a long time, not until his belly shrank, but I was tired and ready for some downtime at home.

We exited the Subaru, Dad hugged me and Mom said, "We'll see you next week, honey. You still have your cell phone with you?"

"Sure do. See ya soon. Love you, bye." I automatically looked around for my truck. The little maroon Ford caught my eye and I remembered what I would be driving home. By the time I reached Watsonville, the fog was miles behind me and the sun still shone on my favorite grocery store. I hoped Robert was on duty and ready to reveal all kinds of facts and rumors. I found him on the canned food aisle.

"Hey, Robert, got any new stories for me?"

"Hi, Jo. It's been pretty quiet around here, but not for you, right?" I studied his freckled face for a clue.

"What do you mean by that?"

"You know, Mr. Mathus, the contractor … works for the Mungers. I read it on page three in the Sentinel. He got in a fight and then the guys chased him halfway through the valley and ran him off the road. He's in stable condition and lucky to be alive according to the paper." Robert straightened a stack of canned tuna. "You probably know more about it than I do."

"Not really, but I did hear that he knew the guys who did it," I said. No response from Robert. "Any fresh salmon in the meat department?"

"The salmon is probably gone by now. People buy it up early in the day." He stopped his canned food straightening. "So, who were the guys, Jo?" I shrugged. "I heard that the DEA might get involved in the Mathus case," he said. "Must be drugs."

"No, I hadn't heard about that. What else do you know?"

"The A's beat the Giants."

"Thanks, Robert. Now I know everything." I gave him a wink and continued my shopping. The groceries I bought at Johnnie's were a total loss, so there I was again, cruising the aisles. At least I had money to buy a whole new batch of stuff. No more paying with plastic for me, not since Theda paid me for five days of living in her house.

When I finally reached home it was dark. Not even a porch light to greet me. Solow stood at the front door barking his head off until he realized who it was in the little maroon car. He hurried to my side, leaned against my leg and whined. He was not usually a whiner, but he was whining and crying. I wondered if his tummy hurt. It should. I also wondered if he was mentally traumatized from the night before.

Once the groceries were put away, I concentrated on comforting my short legged friend. I sat on the floor, yoga style, with most of Solow's body crushing my legs. I stroked his ears and said sweet things in a soft voice. A few minutes later he was snoring peacefully while his stomach made gurgling noises. Galloping garbage was my diagnosis.

Chapter Fourteen

Sunday morning I remembered I hadn't called Mary or David. Why did I always put David last? I played Mary's message again and wrote down her number. Solow seemed to be feeling better. He crunched some kibble while I dialed.

"Hello, Mary? This is ...."

"Josephine. I'd know your voice anywhere. How are you, dear?"

"I'm fine. The bump on my head is almost gone and Solow is doing better too. I'm sorry I didn't get back to you yesterday."

"I didn't get a chance to say good-bye when you left our house," Mary said. Herbert and I enjoyed having tea with you."

I was dumbfounded. I ruined their garage, destroyed the dead animal collection, and all they could say was they had enjoyed having tea with me? Their social life must have been pretty limited.

"I enjoyed the tea and I hope I'll see you again

sometime." I found myself talking to her as if we had just met at a garden party. Must have been Alice's tea party.

"You take care of yourself now and don't stay out so late at night. Good-bye, dear."

"Bye, Mary." One more call to make. Why do I not know what to say to David? Tell the truth or beat around the bush? Lord, help me to say the right thing, whatever that might be. David picked up the phone on the second ring.

"Josie, how are you?"

"Oh, just fine. I'm doing chores around the house." I'd been at it since dawn, but I didn't want to bore him with house-cleaning details. The real reason for my early start was Solow wanting to terrorize Fluffy at the crack of dawn. I was foolish enough to let him out, thus ending my attempts at sleep.

"How are you, David? I wanted to thank you for turning on the porch light the other night and for keeping my marigolds alive and mowing my grass and bringing in the mail." I wished I could be half the good neighbor David was.

"You're welcome. I was wondering if you had a little time today to help me with a paint project. I'm planning to paint faux bricks on a cement wall in the backyard."

"That's a great idea. I'll bring lunch. Bye." Good, a project to talk about and keep us busy instead of questions about the dangers on Mungers' Mountain. I put together a cardboard box full of odds and ends, like giant sponges, masking tape and special formula paints for concrete. I added a couple throw-away plastic trays and a stir stick, and put the box in the back seat of the car.

David usually liked my cooking, or else he was a saint and ate it anyway. I decided to make my tri-dip special. First dip: three hardboiled eggs smashed up with mayonnaise, salt and pepper. Second dip: two avocados mashed up with lemon juice and salsa. Third dip: hummus with chopped onion and red bell pepper. Everything was designed to be eaten on a corn chip. I filled a picnic basket with prepared food and stowed it in the back seat of the Ford. I added a watermelon in case David was still hungry, and boosted Solow into the passenger seat.

The trip to David's included a drive down my driveway and then up his, the equivalent of less than two blocks. David greeted us at the door wearing a ratty t-shirt, an old pair of cutoff Levis and sandals that had seen better days. Regardless of the clothes, he looked tan and fit.

"Come in. I'll take that." David took the watermelon at the front door and set it down on his black granite counter top in his recently renovated kitchen. We walked back to my rental car and gathered up the basket of food and the box of paint supplies.

"Having your truck repaired?"

"Yes, I dropped it off yesterday. It was such a busy day, visiting the folks and all. By the way, they're spending ten days in Boulder Creek. A little vacation, you know. So, what have you been up to, David?"

"I'll show you." He walked me to the backyard. Solow tagged along, alert and scanning the yard for Fluffy.

"Oh, David, it's marvelous!" I was blown away with the work he had done. "The pond is lovely and the brick paths, and the ferns over there ... oh, the gazebo is wonderful too. How long did it take to do all this?"

"Remember the last time you were here, on my birthday in April? That's when I decided to build a pond. One thing led to another and this is how it ended up." We sat down on cast iron chairs near a matching little table where I had set the tri-dip platter.

We ate lunch and sipped iced tea sitting in the gazebo, listening to the sound of water trickling into the pond from a little waterfall. I felt like I was in a delicious trance and the world was beautiful, kind and full of goodness. The villains had taken a hike from my consciousness. Solow snored while he chased Fluffy in his dreams, and Fluffy watched him from the kitchen window.

"This dip idea was a good one," David said, "almost as good as a dip in the pond." He grabbed my hand, pulled me over to the shady pool and kicked off his sandals. David stepped into the shallow water and I followed. We sat on large, flat rocks with our feet dangling in the cool green liquid. Tame stuff compared to my parent's kayaking, but fun all the same. He pointed to a two-foot-high cement wall. It extended about twenty feet and held back a bank of lush green ivy.

"That's the wall we're painting," he said, pointing to it.

"I think I can match up the faux bricks with the real ones. I brought a few things to help us." I turned my head to see David's face. A smile crossed his lips.

"I figured you'd take control, this being a paint job," he gave me a wink.

"I just want to help, after all, you help me all the time."

"Guess that's settled." He splashed some water over his legs. I splashed some more water on him and he returned the gesture. Pretty soon we were soaked, sputtering and laughing like teenagers.

"Now you know why there aren't any fish in the pond. The filter system keeps the water clean so I can cool off whenever I want too. You're welcome to join me anytime."

"Too bad you can't heat it up in the winter," I said, between giggles.

"Oh, but I can. It doubles as a hot tub. The other side is deeper you know."

"David, that's incredible!" I was truly impressed with his ingenuity, and knowing him, he probably did all the work himself. We started painting midafternoon. The relentless sun beat down on our backs, but whenever the heat was too much, we just took a splash in the pond. I wished all my painting jobs could have been that much fun. Three hours later, our fake brick wall was finished.

"How are things going at the mansion?" David asked as we walked into the house for a cold drink of water.

"Oh, about the same," I felt there was a lot of truth in that statement.

"I was kind of wondering about that lump on your forehead and the bruises on your arms. And I noticed a bit of a limp when you walk. The painting business must be pretty rough."

"I guess I can't fool you, David. There was another incident." Once I got started on the truth, I couldn't stop. I told him all about Friday night, including Solow eating the groceries and rolling in the leftovers. David's expression bounced from disbelief to worry to hysterics over Solow's food binge, and then he was quiet for a moment.

"Do you think there's a chance you'll outgrow that curiosity of yours?" He gave me a concerned look with lowered brows.

"It's just a habit. I'll work on it." I turned away from his stare, wishing I hadn't gone into so much detail.

"The faux bricks look great, Josie. How about we clean up and go to the barbecue at the Grange?"

"What about the bump on my head and all the bruises?"

"No one else will look at you as closely as I do," he said. Suddenly my cheeks felt hot. "Go clean up and we'll have a great time." His pleading smile and positive energy sold me. I drove Solow home before he had time for an encounter with Fluffy, which must have been quite a letdown for him.

"Sorry, old boy, you had all afternoon to find that silly

cat. Too late now." I showered and worked my hair into a casual style that hid the lump and looked OK. I slipped into a yellow shift with a loose-knit white bolero, which covered my bruised upper arms. White sandals and an alligator purse completed the ensemble.

I had just finished applying lipstick when the doorbell rang. I opened the door. David's brown eyes looked great against his light blue button-down shirt, tucked into Levis.

"You look great Josephine, you even hid the bump. Don't you want people to know how dangerous your life is, how you rid the world of bad guys?"

"Very funny. But seriously, David, I just thought of something. I don't think Chester told the police who ran him off the road, otherwise they would have an APB out for the McFees, and those creeps wouldn't be hard to find either. I wonder why he didn't tell them. Just a minute, I have to give Solow his kibble and then we can go."

We left Solow in his bed on the front porch, his dinner bowl close by as he secured the ranch. Ocean breezes had cooled the air considerably and the Grange Hall party was in full swing when we arrived. The extra large, crowd-pleaser barbecue was positioned on the east side of the building where the breeze carried the scent of roasted ribs and chicken two blocks down-wind into town. I couldn't decide whether to have ribs or chicken, so, of course, I took some of each with all the fixin's. David wasn't shy about helping himself either.

When we were quite stuffed, we sat back on foldable wooden chairs and watched a trio, three brothers, playing Mexican music. The youngest looked ten or twelve. He wore a smaller version of the same decorative costume his big brothers wore, from the sombrero down to the fancy vest and boots. When the sky darkened, the musicians and their followers carried their chairs into the Grange and the dance began.

A perky polka lured us onto the dance floor along with twenty or so other couples. The nine-to-thirteen crowd danced on the outer fringes of the dance floor. The noisy youth were constantly bumping into us. After three polkas, I was ready to collapse on my couch for a week or two. David took my arm and walked me off the dance floor.

"We worked pretty hard today," he said. "Let's take a rest. How about ice cream and decaf at the Ducky Deli?"

"Sounds ... wonderful," I gasped. And it was wonderful. The short walk to town, the coolness of the Deli with its ceiling fan on high speed and, of course, nothing beats ice cream when your body temperature reaches triple digits.

"David, it's been a wonderful day," I said on the way home.

"I'm glad," he said, smiling that inscrutable smile of his. And like a gentleman, he walked me to my front door and kissed the lump on my forehead. I almost let myself hope there would be more, but I was way too tired to act on my wishes. If there was to be more, it would have to be in my dreams.

Chapter Fifteen

Monday's commute from Watsonville to Santa Cruz turned out to be a real bummer. In the wee hours of the morning, an eighteen-wheeler carrying fresh lettuce from Watsonville, missed a turn and flipped over into the ice plant. The semi slid down the slippery ice plant embankment and back onto the highway, resting on its side.

Solow and I watched as a gigantic crane righted the rig and an impressive tow truck hauled it away. Caltrans workers began scraping, shoveling and sweeping broken crates of mangled lettuce off the road. Two tanker trucks arrived and workers washed down the asphalt. The freeway was backed up for miles, making me late along with a thousand other unlucky commuters. I reminded myself that I was actually pretty lucky. My boss would not fire me, she loved Solow too much. I smiled at my pal sleeping in the seat next to me.

Looking four car lengths ahead, I recognized a green Volvo station wagon. The top of Trigger's head was barely visible in the back seat. I wouldn't be the only one late to work on Mungers' Mountain. I tried to think about my mural responsibilities, like plotting out who would paint what. That only lasted a minute before my mind wandered to other things, like why didn't Chester tell the police who tried to kill him and did Warren understand the danger we were in?

Finally, the cars ahead started moving, but it was slow going as three lanes of traffic funneled into one. I watched Alicia take the off-ramp to Highway 17. As I followed her to Boulder Creek, I remembered my last trip through the redwoods. Daylight was comforting.

Alicia pulled into the library parking lot to pick up Kyle. I made a right on Bear Creek Road and dropped off Solow, a suitcase of clean clothes and a few groceries at the cabin. Theda met me at the door and helped put things away. She filled Solow's water bowl and massaged his droopy ears with her perfectly manicured nails.

"Did you miss Auntie Theda?" she purred. I knew my dog was in good hands. I felt like I was leaving my only child at Grandma's house.

I headed up to the mansion feeling anxious to get the mural painting finished. To my surprise, Manuel was standing in the parking area wearing a sling on his bum arm and directing three new workers pushing wheelbarrows full of bricks. I hardly recognized him without a shovel in his hand, but decided to talk to him later when he wasn't so busy. I parked and made my way toward the house.

One of the three bricklayers stared at me in a strange way that made me very uncomfortable. He was medium height with greasy blond hair and had a bloody knife tattoo on one bony shoulder. I didn't stick around to see more.

Alicia's Volvo ground to a stop near the almost finished garage. She, Kyle, Trigger and Tansey joined me at the solarium. Trigger chased his puppy into the dining room and we all followed.

"Auntie Jo, guess what Tansey can do?"

"I give up, what can she do?"

"Watch this. Sit," and Tansey sat. "Speak," and Tansey barked. "Lie down," and Tansey wagged her tail. "I'm working on that one," he said, with hands on hips.

"Nice work, Trigger," I said, "she knows a lot for a little puppy. OK, painters, it's already ten-thirty. Let's get busy." We girls shuffled off to the music room, leaving Kyle to add more happy cows and cypress trees to the Tuscany landscape.

Alicia and I set up shop, ready to paint fields of wild flowers. Out of habit, I looked up to see if the stained glass had been replaced.

"Allie, look up there. Isn't it beautiful?" I pointed to the newly installed stained glass window at the top of the domed ceiling. It took my breath away.

"Heavenly," she said. "Don't look now, Jo, but the scaffolding is still up." We gazed at it for a minute.

"What the ...? I told Jose I wanted it down." I rubbed

the back of my neck. "I'll be back in a few minutes. Why don't you help Kyle in the meantime?"

"OK, Jo. I'd love to."

I took off down the hall, practically stumbling over Trigger and Tansey as they chased a tennis ball across my path.

"Sorry, Trigger. Have you seen Jose today?"

"No," he said. I looked everywhere until I finally found Manuel.

"Have you seen Jose?"

"No," Manuel said and continued measuring for the ornamental brick wall which had a good ten feet finished and was looking beautiful. With one arm bandaged and in a sling, Manuel seemed determined to keep working.

"Jose, call me last night. He say he eese muy sick."

"Oh, that explains it. I had asked him to take down the scaffolding. Now what do we do?" I scratched my head, further dramatizing my predicament.

Manuel walked over to the bricklayers and told them I needed help and to follow me. The men dropped their trowels in a bucket of water and walked with me to the music room. The oldest of the three wore a belt full of tools around his waist, everything they needed for just about any job. The greasy guy with the tattoo stood in the doorway and watched the other two men break down the scaffolding and haul it away.

Once the men were gone, Alicia and I settled down to our work. The sun was already heating up the room and the fan wasn't much help. I carried a clean bucket down the hall to the powder room and filled it with cold water.

"Look, Allie, we can use these rags to cool ourselves." I dipped a piece of cotton cloth in the water, rang it out and ran it over my neck, arms and legs. Alicia grabbed a rag and did the same. Not a whole lot of work was accomplished before the noon siren blasted. The old Boulder Creek fire siren could be heard for miles in every direction, a throwback from the volunteer fire department days.

Apparently Manuel had a better handle on things than Jose. We ate our lunch in the solarium where the boombox music was not too loud and the card players were gone. I noticed two of the new workers sitting in the far corner eating burritos. The scrawny one was missing. Just then, the fire siren from town went off again. We were used to hearing it, so naturally no one paid any attention until Alicia mentioned the fact. Kyle cocked his head to one side and I became alert as the siren droned on.

"Ah, maybe it's, like, a fire?" Kyle suggested.

Trigger grabbed Tansey and ran outside. As soon as the door opened we smelled wood smoke. I walked outside and stood with Trigger, listening to fire sirens getting louder and louder, closer and closer, and then one by one they went silent. The hair on the back of my neck stood up as I felt a weakness in my knees. Alicia and Kyle stood frozen, eyes glued to the driveway. I thought about the worst thing that can happen in a forest, a forest fire with only one road out.

Suddenly Tansey freaked, leaped out of Trigger's arms and streaked across the parking area, disappearing down the driveway. Trigger darted after her, but could not catch up. It looked like fear had taken hold of the little Sheltie and given her super speed.

Alicia and I charged after Trigger. She repeatedly ordered him to come back, but Trigger only knew he had to catch his beloved puppy before she got into trouble. The driveway sloped gradually at first, but eventually became steep and difficult to navigate. We rounded the first turn with Trigger many yards ahead and Kyle loping along behind us. Alicia shouted again. Trigger kept running with only one purpose propelling him forward.

Two more turns completed and we three artists had our tongues hanging out, sucking in smoky air. We heard crackling sounds getting louder. As I ran, it occurred to me that Theda and Solow might be in danger. Extra strength came to me at that moment and I was able to catch up to Alicia. Kyle had slowed to a walk and was somewhere behind us, out of sight. After two more turns we saw red flames through the trees, shooting forty feet straight up into the air.

Finally, the cabin, surrounded by fire trucks, came into view. One fireman shot water at the cabin's already drenched roof. The barn was consumed in flames and the flaming ash caught a couple surrounding trees on fire as we watched. Two hoses were aimed at the trees and two at the barn which, anyone could see, was a total loss. I frantically looked around for Theda and Solow, but they found me first.

"Isn't it awful, Josephine?" Theda coughed. She put a hand on my arm and held Solow's leash with the other. He circled behind Theda and nuzzled my leg, whimpering.

"Thank God, you're OK," I said, as I hugged Theda and then my pooch.

A second tanker truck arrived along with the Chief in his red SUV. The two tanker trucks were necessary because there were no water hydrants that far from the main road. The Chief waved us back up the driveway where we were out of the way and the smoke wasn't as bad, but we still had a perfect view of the barn.

"Jo, look, Trigger found her," Alicia said, her arm around Trigger who held Tansey tightly to his chest. Kyle came strolling down the mountain and joined us as we watched the fierce battle only fifty yards away. One of the burning trees was doused only to have another catch fire next to it. The battle raged and we were mesmerized.

At least ten helmeted men carrying shovels leaped out of a forestry truck before it came to a complete stop. They spread out around the barn and used their shovels to put out small fires in the dry grass before flames could grow into big fires and threaten the whole mountain, maybe the valley.

My knees felt weak again so I moved to the side of the road and sat down beside Trigger on a moss-covered log.

From a safe distance, we watched the completely surreal scene play out before our eyes.

"Are you alright, sweetie?" I put my arm around Trigger.

"Sure, I guess so." Tansey was asleep in his arms after her Olympic run down the mountain. "Do you think Mrs. Munger is sad?"

"Honey, I think she's probably very happy that the cabin didn't burn. Everything is going to be alright," I said, sounding more positive than I felt. Alicia sat down on the other side of Trigger, not letting him out of her sight. Half an hour later, the main fire was out, but the mop-up continued. One truck and three firemen stayed to make sure every ember was dead.

Theda drove her weary muralists up to the villa, Solow in the front seat, painters in the back seats. She stayed with us for almost two hours, seeming to need the comfort of our company. We were all pretty shook up except for the sooty smelling canines that rested peacefully. Just before she left the music room, Theda looked up at the ceiling.

"Isn't it lovely? Flowers from heaven." We all agreed.

After work, I drove down to the cabin with Solow at my right. I thought about the fire and all the other things that had happened since the mural job began. It had become one big roller coaster ride and I thought I was ready to get off, but when I walked into the cabin and saw Theda on the phone talking to Warren, I knew I couldn't quit. I couldn't let her down.

Theda saw me and wiped the tears from her cheeks. I acted like I didn't see them and walked to my room where I stared out the window at the ghostly remnants of a barn. Solow and I had had many curious moments in that barn, like the time we discovered a fist-size hole in the shop door and all those times we smelled cigarettes and found a few of them on the ground. I would not miss the barn's entertainment value, but wished I could have found answers to my questions. Theda entered my room.

"You probably surmised I was talking to Warren." I nodded. "He said he'll drop everything and be here in a couple hours. I think he finally understands some of what you and I have been going through. He actually sounded angry." She turned and shuffled down the hall. I followed.

"Hey, Theda, we have a couple hours. Let's go to town and check out that new dress shop next to the barber shop."

"What if we have an iced tea at the Brewery and then try on dresses?"

"Good idea. I think we both could benefit from a cold one. I'll drive. Just give me a minute to change into something presentable."

I hurried back to my closet and began the transformation. Trouble was, I had gray ash everywhere. After a very short shower, I slipped on a skirt, peasant blouse and all the trimmings. I was looking forward to getting away from the smell of wet ashes as we walked to the Ford. Three firefighters looked up from their work. Wear a skirt and they always look.

My ash-covered car was humble transportation, but there were no complaints. We decided to leave our worries at home and have a good time. It was after six and the Brewery was practically empty. I figured the town was resting after a weekend of Western Days excitement. Two barstools swiveled as we walked in.

"Want to sit at the bar?" Theda asked.

"Sure, why not." We climbed onto stools at the opposite end of the bar from two young men bent over their beers. Annie delivered two iced teas.

"Did you hear about the fire?" she asked. "I heard it totaled a barn."

"Oh, it was totaled alright," Theda said. "I know because it was my barn." Annie's eyes grew bigger and her mouth opened, but no sound came out. Finally she was able to speak.

"Oh dear, I'm so sorry." Annie put a hand over her mouth for a moment. "I thought I smelled smoke when you walked in. It must have been just awful."

"We're here to drown our sorrow in iced tea," I said. The three of us laughed, dispelling the seriously sober mood. Annie darted into the back room and minutes later came back with a plate of buffalo wings.

"On the house. Enjoy, ladies," she turned and walked away. I wasn't sure who had been more upset about the fire, Theda or Annie.

"So, Theda, how are you doing? Is Warren being supportive? Forget that, of course he is. What am I talking about?"

"Things have improved, but I don't know if I'll ever feel really close to him again. There's such a big hole in my heart." The tears came just in time for Annie to see them. Annie's eyes were instantly wet as she turned away, looking embarrassed.

"It's going to take time for you and Warren to get over Emily. After Marty died, I suffered for over a year until I finally realized that happiness is a choice. Not an easy choice, but a good choice." She nodded her head and smiled.

Just then, a young man in worn Levis, black tee shirt and cowboy boots entered the restaurant and sashayed across the floor. He smiled at Annie and threw her a kiss.

"Howdy, Miss Bates. You're the prettiest thing I've seen all day." Annie giggled as the young man climbed onto a bar stool next the other two men. All three were in their twenties and seemed to know each other.

"Here's your beer and try to behave," she laughed.

I jabbed Theda in her side and whispered, "Did you hear that?"

"Hear what?" she looked puzzled.

"Annie's last name is Bates, same as your realtor's name."

"Josephine, what are you talking about?"

"Never mind. I'll tell you later." Annie passed by us on

her way to the kitchen.

"Annie, is your name really Bates?" I asked.

"Sure, why?" She gave the counter a nervous wipe with her towel.

"Just wondered if you're related to the real estate lady here in town."

"She's my mother. Why?" More counter wiping. My cheeks were hot.

"I'm always curious about people," I said, "just my nature." I pretended to lose interest in the conversation and stared at a couple coming in the door. Annie hurried away to greet the new customers. I wondered how a nice person like Annie could be the daughter of the lying Nora woman with Dolly Parton hair. Theda and I made short work of the tea and wings.

"Ready to look through Deena's Dress Boutique?" I asked.

"Oh, sure." She slung her purse strap over a shoulder and slid down from her bar stool. I did the same. Deena's was directly across the street from The Brewery. A GRAND OPENING sign stretched over one window, the other window displayed summer outfits for the thirty and older crowd. Theda tried on a light-blue cotton knit shorts and top outfit which made her look way too thin. I shook my head. We tried on hats and checked out the costume jewelry. Shopping was a release from the stress we had been under and a fun pastime, but we didn't actually buy anything.

Next, we walked past Bates Realty, which was closed

on Mondays, to the ice cream shop where we treated ourselves to double scoops. We sat on a bench in the shade of an oak tree near the post office.

"Theda, I was interested in Annie's last name because it seems she's the daughter of Nora Bates, your realtor. Warren told me how you two had tried to buy his grandfather's old place on Two Bar Road. Now we know that Nora owned the place all along and was lying about it. Why would she do that? On top of that, Nora is quite friendly with the McFee boys. Did you see how upset Annie was about the barn burning down?"

"I appreciate your concern, Josephine, but really, what does it all mean?" Theda went back to licking the top scoop of mint chip.

"I don't know what it means exactly, but there was another incident I haven't told you about. Last Friday night, after I left the cabin, I peeked through a window at Nora's real estate office. I was surprised to see her with two McFee brothers. They saw me, chased me down Highway 9 and ran me off the road, just like they ran Chester off the road. Theda gasped and I continued. "Luckily Solow and I weren't hurt, but Chester's in bad shape. Something's going on around here and we need to get to the bottom of it."

Ice cream dripped down Theda's wrist as she stared straight ahead.

"I never meant to put you in danger, Josephine. I just wanted company. You're right, things have gone too far.

But what can we do?"

"Sergeant Machuca knows all about my crash, but for some reason Chester didn't tell the authorities who ran him off the road. He told me it was the McFees, but I'm not telling the police. I don't want those maggot-infested brothers going after Chester again."

"Will Chester be all right?" Theda's eyes stared into mine as if she were trying to read my brain.

"Eventually, I think." I held my ice cream cone away from my skirt and let it drip. We had the same idea at the same moment. We dropped our remaining ice cream into a garbage can and walked to Johnnie's Market to use the restroom. When our hands were clean, I suggested we take a little ride out Two Bar Road.

"Sure, sounds like fun," Theda said as she scrunched down into the car.

"I want to see the house that Warren's grandparents owned."

"It's a lovely old place." Theda went on to describe the swing in the backyard and the huge weeping willow in the front. Sure enough, the willow took up a good portion of the front yard. The old, two-story Victorian sat about a hundred feet from the road with the ubiquitous gravel driveway circling to the back. The place looked straight out of the 1920's, except for a big black Hummer parked near the front porch.

I pulled off the road and stopped the car in a grassy wide spot directly in front of the house, and thought I saw a window curtain part for just a second.

"Someone knows we're here," I said, looking south, past the house, to the forest. "Does that forest go with the house?" Theda nodded.

"Eighty acres." She heard a car approaching and craned her neck to see who had parked behind us. "Oh my, it's Warren. Can you believe it?" Warren walked to Theda's window and bent down to look in.

"Imagine meeting you two here," he chuckled. "I was driving along when I saw two pretty ladies in a maroon car turn onto Two Bar Road. What do you think of the place, Josephine?"

"Very beautiful and quaint, except for the Hummer." Warren turned to look for himself.

"Must be Nora's. And I thought I cornered the market on big black vehicles."

"We were just out for a drive," I said, "to settle our nerves, you know?"

Warren touched Theda's shoulder, "how are the nerves? Are you two OK?"

"I feel fine as long as Josephine entertains me," Theda smiled.

"Theda, why don't you go home with Warren? I have a few errands in town." She obediently opened her door.

"Thank you, Josephine, for everything. We'll see you later," she said before they drove off and I was left behind to do a little research. I headed straight back to The Brewery. Good old Stan sat at a table in the far corner hunched over his beer. I sat down in the chair across the table and leaned forward.

"Hi, Stan, remember me?"

"Course I remember you. You're always gettin' in my way."

"I missed you too. Anyway, I have some serious questions to ask you."

"I'm not in the mood." Stan's eyes glazed over and his head hung low like an old hound dog.

"My dog and I were almost killed Friday night. Know anything about that?"

"I mighta' read somethin' in the paper." He squirmed in his chair. I hadn't thought to look in the newspaper. Good grief, maybe Myrtle read about it and told everyone, and Robert would read the story for sure. I tried to focus on Stan without upsetting him as I leaned forward again.

"I need to know why you have those stitches in your forehead, and do the stitches have something to do with you not coming back to work?" Annie watched us from behind the bar. Stan gulped some beer.

"I told you how I got them stitches."

"I don't happen to believe you." My jaw was tight and my patience was short. Stan looked around the room, but said nothing. "I'll tell you what happened and if I'm right, you just give a little nod?" He stared deeply into his half-empty mug as I continued.

"I think someone wanted you off the Munger property.

True?"

He didn't look up, but I detected the tiniest nod.

"Was it the McFees?" Just then the door slammed and a woman marched straight to Stan's table. She pushed some unruly red hair with gray roots out of her eyes and sat down beside him. She looked at me with poison darts in her dark eyes.

"Stanley, who's your friend?" she asked, and smiled too sweetly. Stan sat up straight.

"Flo, meet Josephine. She works for the Mungers."

"Is that so?" Flo laid her hand over Stan's arm and held the phony smile in place. Just when I was finally getting the scoop from Stan, the perfumed hussy had to wreck everything.

"Excuse me, gotta' put my order in." I walked over to the quiet end of the bar and climbed onto a stool. Annie asked me what I wanted.

"I'll have a glass of water, please." She walked away and came back with a tall glass of water, lemon and a straw.

"You know Stan?" she asked.

"Sure. He used to work for Ace Security up at the Mungers' house."

"You know him?" I asked.

"I should, he's my dad. Mom and Dad were divorced when I was ten. My father and I live in Felton, but he comes here a lot to see me."

"So, do you know how he got those stitches?"

"He told you he ran into a door, didn't he?" Annie wiped the already clean counter with a wet towel.

"That's what he said the first time, but now I know the truth." The country music stopped. Annie stepped into the backroom and the music started up again. When she came back, she began scrubbing the counter all over again.

"Annie, can I ask you something?"

"I guess so." She looked at Stan who was listening to Flo yammer on about her friends. "What do you want to know?"

"Do you know the McFee brothers?" Stan turned his head our way and Flo was quiet. Annie answered in a low voice.

"I know who they are. So what?" She turned, walked over to the three guys at the other end of the bar and re-filled their pitcher of beer from the tap. I sipped my water slowly and hoped for another opportunity to talk to her.

Flo was ruffling the few hairs still growing on Stan's head as I tried to suppress my gag reflex. I tried to imag-ine Stan as Annie's father, but he looked more like her grandfather. Annie was blessed with large blue eyes, thick brown hair and clear creamy skin. I decided her I.Q., speech, manners, good looks and sensitive nature must have come from someone other than her parents. Flo got my attention when she pulled Stan out of his chair - no small feat.

"Stanley, honey, you know where I wanna' go. You take

me to Mac's or I'll find someone who will." Stan threw money on the table, walked to the front door and glanced back at Annie as he held the door for his lady friend. Flo was a titch taller than Stan with narrow shoulders and wide hips that barely missed the doorjamb. Annie gave her dad an inconspicuous little wave.

The sun went down and the restaurant cleared out. I thought about going back to the cabin, but I wanted to talk to Annie again. She walked behind my stool. I swiveled around and asked her how long she had worked at the Brewery.

Caught by surprise, she said, "Little over a year. I went to UCSC until my father got sick. He's better now ... at least he was."

"I'm sorry. Sounds like you've had a rough time. Does Nora help out?" I watched Annie's face for any clues to their relationship. She looked at the floor.

"We work in the same town, but that's it. My dad could have died from his heart attack ... she didn't care." Her eyes were about to overflow as she darted into the kitchen. I decided to give Annie a break and leave. I left a nice tip and walked out into the night.   My Ford was parked close by and soon I was cruising through town past Joe's and Mac's bars in full swing. I guessed Western Days hadn't lasted long enough for some people.

The Ford tackled Mungers' Mountain admirably. I pulled in next to a white sheriff's car cooling its wheels in front of the cabin. I opened the front door and walked into a three-way conversation. Something about cigarettes. Warren stood when he saw me. Sergeant Machuca looked up from his notetaking.

"Hello, Ms. Stuart. We'd like to hear your opinion on the fire. Won't you join us?"

"Sure. What do you want to know?" I sat on the sofa next to Theda who was staring out the window, holding a mixed drink.

"Apparently, the fire was started by a cigarette," Warren said, "but we don't know if it was an accident or deliberately set. The Sergeant says you knew about the cigarettes."

"I found them on the ground near the barn several times and I told everyone who would listen." Warren looked a little taken-aback. "How will we know if the fire was intentional?" I asked, looking at Sergeant Machuca for an answer. Solow walked over to me, lowered his body to the floor and laid his head on my feet.

"The Fire Inspector will be here sometime in the next couple days. Maybe we'll get an answer then." Machuca fiddled with his cap as he spoke. "Personally, I think it was probably an accident. After all, it was the middle of the day with the homeowner and a dog in the house."

"Josephine has a theory and I tend to think she could be right," Warren said. "But as far as motive goes, seems kinda' silly for the McFee's to do this sort of thing a couple years after we had them kicked off the property."

"What I don't understand," Theda said, "is how

someone entered our barn, but we never saw their car. It's a very difficult hike from the main road, so why would anyone put themselves through all that?" I made a mental note to see if there might be a place somewhere along the driveway where a person could park and not be seen.

It was almost ten when Sergeant Machuca said he needed to get going on his rounds. We followed Machuca to the front door, hoping to hear about another clue or last-minute idea from law enforcement, but the man was quiet. Warren quickly closed the door behind the sergeant, trying to keep the acrid smell of wet ash from polluting the inside air. Everyone sat down again.

"Josephine, you've been through a lot," Warren said. "Theda brought up the fact that you had been in an accident and Sergeant Machuca told us the details of your crash Friday night. He said you thought it might have been an intentional hit-and-run."

"Intentional, yes. The McFees, absolutely. I'm exhausted, see you in the morning." I walked to the bedroom shaking my head like a teen arguing with parents suffering from dementia. What kind of proof do people need? I fell asleep pondering that question. Solow didn't ponder, he snored.

Chapter Sixteen

A long night had finally passed. I decided fitful sleep was worse than no sleep at all. It was five-thirty in the morning when I climbed out of bed, putting an end to ugly nightmares featuring bearded pyromaniacs prowling the grounds. I pulled on a pair of cutoff jeans, a t-shirt and my sturdy sandals.

Solow was reluctant to leave his bed, but a tug on the leash convinced him he could have fun going for a walk with me. We stole out of the cabin and headed down the driveway. Down hill was easy and the crisp morning air invigorated us.

"Now, big guy, let's march right along, head up, shoulders back and no sniffing." Solow ignored every word and sniffed under every bush. We had just passed the mysteriously fallen redwood tree of last week, when I decided to explore a flat open area beside the driveway. It was a six-foot wide strip of terrain heading west, ending in a downhill drop. The strip of land lacked serious vegetation, just some low-growing blackberry bushes, poison oak and stinging nettle. It could have been a wider-than-normal deer trail or maybe an overgrown dirt road from the past. Trees surrounded the area on both sides, making it barely visible from the Mungers' driveway.

"OK, Solow, I've seen enough. It's time to go back to the cabin." Solow chose that moment to lie down in a grassy spot and search his body for fleas. I sat on a rock, still breathing hard from the walk. Suddenly, Solow stopped scratching and pointed his nose down the driveway. A second later I heard the roar of a truck engine tackling the mountain. Around the bend came an old blue and white pickup with the top half of Sueno hanging out the passenger window. I stood up and waved.

"Yippee, our rescuers have arrived," I told Solow.

Manuel saw us and pulled to a stop. My hound and I crowded into the cab with Sueno who sniffed Solow as much as was possible in tight quarters.

"You're a lifesaver, Manuel. You can let us out at the cabin." The cabin was quiet, but someone had made coffee. The aroma greeted me as I walked into the house, tired and hungry. I ignored the urge to eat, took my shower and prepared for a day of painting. When I finally entered the kitchen, breakfast was in full swing with Warren behind the spatula. The pancakes and sausages smelled divine.

"Good morning, Josephine."

"Good morning. Solow and I took a walk down the mountain earlier and found a secluded parking place. Someone could park a vehicle there, but why would they go to all that trouble?"

"You must have been up early." Warren flipped a pancake. "Please don't put yourself in danger, Josephine, that's Sergeant Machuca's job. Promise?"

"Sure. How do you make perfect pancakes like that?"

"A splash of cream. It's my mother's recipe and I've made them a million times." He flipped another pancake. Theda sashayed into the kitchen dressed for "tea with the Queen", wearing a peach-colored suit, long dangly crystal earrings, matching necklace and bracelets. Her sling-back pumps were loaded with bling, her lips were shiny peach and her eyes were bright.

"Good morning. What a lovely day," Theda said. "Did Warren tell you he's taking me to Carmel today?"

"That's wonderful. Have a great time." I licked my lips after my sixth pancake and figured I better quit while I could still walk. "I'll see you two tonight?"

"Warren has to go to work tomorrow, but yes, you'll see us later tonight." She gave her husband a very private look that made me think of second honeymoons.

At the Villa it was all work and no play, unless you count Trigger and Tansey running up and down the new sidewalks. The decorative brick wall was taking shape and the new lawn was bordered by hydrangeas, peonies, and hibiscus. I walked all the way to the front door without any obstructions and almost ran over Kyle, squatting on the entry floor, mixing paint for the columns.

"Morning, Kyle. How's it going?"

"Like, I'm trying to match this cream color on the sample." A ten-by-ten inch, real marble sample lay on the floor in front of him.

"If anyone can do it, you can." I had total confidence in his abilities.

I found Alicia in the music room with the fan on the highest speed, but already she was perspiring.

"I'm here. Don't despair," I said rummaging around for a palette and paint.

"Very funny, Jo. Do fires always affect you that way?" she laughed.

"Actually, I think I'm a bit rummy from getting very little sleep. You know me. I always need a good eight hours. How did the fire affect you ... and Trigger?" I suddenly realized I hadn't even talked to Alicia about the effects on Trigger.

"We almost didn't come to work today. Ernie tried his best to talk me out of it. He made me promise to call him at lunch time and again after work. He's very upset."

"Allie, I don't blame him. I'm starting to rethink this whole job, like, is it really worth it?" Alicia was quiet for a moment as she wiped her brow with the back of her hand. She looked at me with a brave smile.

"I think Kyle, Trigger and I will be fine up here where there are plenty of other people. You're the one I'm worried about. You need to be more careful, Jo. I mean it. We care about you."

"Thank you, Allie. I'll try to be careful." It was my

second warning and only nine-thirty in the morning. I began painting and sweating, fearing it would be a long hot day. But a half hour later I realized the sunny music room was actually getting cooler, way cooler. The two air vents in the room were spewing cold air, enough to make us feel like popsicles.

"Feels like the air conditioner is running," Alicia said, cheerfully. "I think this house is close to being finished."

"Sure is, if we get our part done." I checked on Kyle to see if he was able to come up with the correct color. He already had three other shades mixed and was busy blending two of them with a rag on the first column.

"Call me, Kyle, if you need anything."

"Yeah, OK, Jo," he kept his eyes focused on the column as he deftly worked the rag, blending shades of color into faux marble.

Back in the music room, Alicia had opened a window to let in some warm air. The cooling system obviously needed an adjustment. I found Jose down the hall doing his best to work the kinks out of the thermostat.

"Jose, how's it going?" I started to walk away when he didn't answer.

"Sorry, Josephine, just trying to figure this thing out." He looked whipped.

"Don't give up, you'll get it," I said. "By the way, have you heard from Chester?"

"No, but I read about your careless driving in the Sentinel." He smiled like a Cheshire cat.

"Is that what they called it, careless driving?"

"Yes, but they're investigating to see if there's more to it."

"You can bet your toolbox there's more to it." I turned and marched back to the music room.

"Everything OK, Jo?" Alicia asked.

"Oh, sure. What could be wrong?" I picked up a brush. "Sorry, Allie, guess I'm a little on edge today." Jose eventually corrected whatever was wrong with the AC, just before it was time for us to go home. I told Alicia and Kyle to leave at four and I would do the cleanup. I washed the last batch of brushes, stacked the plastic bottles of paint away from the windows and covered them with a tarp just in case the AC conked out. It's never good to let paint boil, or so I had been told. I heard footsteps in the hall, turned and saw my own likeness, but older, followed by my Dad.

"What a surprise," I said as I hugged Mom, then Dad.

"Seems everyone in Boulder Creek knows where the Munger mansion is," Dad said. He put his head back and stared at the stained glass ceiling. "Isn't that something?" Leola agreed that it was really something.

"Honey, your mural is beautiful," she stared at the walls for several minutes. "The clouds are whimsical, charming really. Are there anymore murals like this?"

"This is the music room. I'll take you on a tour and you can see for yourself?"

"It's a deal," Dad said. Half an hour later the folks had seen everything upstairs and downstairs.

"I need to go down to the cabin and clean up. Want to meet me there?"

"We'll follow you dear," Mom said.

We motored down to the cabin. The Lincoln was gone, hopefully to Carmel where the Mungers might create some special memories. I remembered how they were at breakfast, like teens on a first date, and how they were learning to pull together after their barn disaster.

I poured iced tea for the folks, excused myself and exchanged paint clothes for street clothes. I wandered through the house looking for Mom and Dad and finally found them outside, standing near the barbecued barn. Solow leaned against Dad's leg.

"Smells like a recent event." Dad watched me squirm.

"Yep. Happened yesterday. Ready to go?" I turned and started walking back to the cabin.

"Honey, was it one of those controlled burns?" Mom looked a little pale in her raspberry sheath.

"No, not controlled. Just an accident from a careless cigarette." We entered the cabin. "The Mungers never used the barn anyway."

"Get your purses, ladies, and let's go to town." Solow looked up from his nap as if to say, "What about me?" Mom and I did as we were told. I thanked God we were off the fire subject as we cruised into town hungrier than the average family of three.

"We can have Mexican food, deli, California cuisine or retro-elegant on the deck." I repeated the choices while the folks thought about it. I knew their food preferences pretty well and I was betting on California cuisine. My parents had very little retro in them, except maybe their ages.

"What do you like, dear?" Mom asked, looking at me for help.

"The Brewery."

"Is that the California Cuisine?" Dad asked. I nodded. They smiled at each other and I knew it was the obvious choice for all of us. Dad parked the Subaru and we walked one block to the restaurant.

A young blond waitress I had seen once before greeted us and showed us to a table away from the swiveling bar stools. She gave us menus and ice water.

"Is Annie here tonight?" I asked the waitress.

"No."

"Too bad. I wanted my Mom and Dad to meet her."

"Sorry, I didn't realize you were a friend of Annie's," she said. "I'm afraid I was a little short with you. See, Annie's having trouble with her Dad again, you know, trying to keep him sober and all. Seems he mixed it up pretty good with those McFees brothers again and landed in the hospital. Well, you know Annie, always taking care of him and such." She took a quick look around the room to see if she was needed anywhere.

"My name's, Josephine, and this is Leola and Bob."

"My name's, Summer, and I'm so happy to meet you all. Too bad Annie isn't here. She works six and sometimes seven days a week. What a terrible way to get a day off, her Daddy hurt and all. He's a good man, just too honest."

"What do you mean by too honest?" I couldn't help asking.

"When Stan was a sheriff, he didn't like stuff that was goin' on in the department, so he quit. You know, took the high road. Well, he's done it again on that Munger job. I'm sure Annie already told you what happened. He's an honest man, alright." She looked around again in time to see an African-American family of five walking in the door. She hurried away to greet them with menus in hand.

"You didn't tell us about anyone named Annie," Dad said.

"Actually, I barely know her, but Miss Summer thinks Annie and I are blood sisters to hear her talk." I laughed.

"Summer's a sweet girl," Mom said.

After dinner we decided to walk off a few calories and see the town first hand. The sun was down, but the night was warm and people swarmed the quaint historical town settled by pioneers in the gold rush days. But people didn't come to town because of history, they came for the restaurants, bars and shops.

We meandered through several little shops. Mom bought an interesting wind chime made from redwood and copper. Dad was pretty bored and didn't hide the fact, so we eventually took pity on him and headed back to the car. The truth was, we had seen just about everything in town.

As we passed Mac's Bar on the way back to the Subaru, shouted profanities accosted our ears. A grungy, unshaven old coot practically flew out the door, knocking Mom into Dad who caught himself by grabbing onto a light pole. Mom screamed and the man apologized. He wobbled precariously, turned around and stumbled back inside. He was quickly thrown out again on his skinny butt.

"I think it's time to get off the sidewalk," Dad said, ushering us into the street. We walked single file between the parked cars and the Central Avenue traffic, past Joe's bar and all the way to the Subaru without further incident.

"This place reminds me of a few western movies I've seen, only rougher," Mom said with a laugh. "Guess I'm a city girl." If Mom thought that was rough, I wondered what she would think of the really dangerous stuff happening at the Mungers. Dad drove us back to the cabin and dropped me off.

No one was home except Solow, so I decided to take my hound dog for a little ride in the Ford. We parked next to Russell's security truck a few yards from the mansion and found the Ace-man nearby. He sat on the newly constructed brick wall near the wide well-lit flagstone path leading to the front door. Flowering shrubs bordered the walk and a lush green lawn spread out across the grounds.

Russell looked surprised to see us.

"Oh ... hi, Josephine. What are you doing up here so late?" I checked my watch.

"It's only ten and Solow doesn't have school tomorrow.

"Right, that's a good one," he chuckled, as if he were comfortable with me and my dog invading his privacy in the middle of the night.

"Did you hear about my accident Friday night?"

"Just what it said in the paper, and a first hand account from my grandparents."

"Did you talk to Sergeant Machuca? I'm wondering how the investigation is going."

"Investigation of what?" Russell's eyes were trained on mine.

"The attempt to murder me, of course." His eyes were blank. "You did hear that it was the McFees who ran me off the road ... right?"

"No, not exactly."

"You, too?" I kicked the brick wall. "Ouch. Nobody believes my story, but the truth is that the McFees followed me from Bates Realty all the way to your grandparent's house. That was where they ran into the back of my pick-up, sending Solow and me across the road and almost over the bank into the river. The only thing that saved us was the garage and Herbert's stuffed animal collection."

"Did you tell the sheriff all this?" he asked, eyes round.

"Yes, I did. I'm just not sure he believed me. We seem to have a communication problem." I hung my head, adding a little drama to make my point.

"I'll see what I can find out," Russell said. "I have contacts, you know." I turned my head away and rolled my eyes. Right, "Mr. Fife", or is it "Dudley"?

"So, do you know why Stan quit working here as a security guard?" I asked.

"Yeah, most of it. I went to school with his daughter, Annie. Last time I saw her at the Brewery, she told me someone wanted her dad to stay away from this property and he refused. The guy hit Stan in the head with a two-by-four. That's all I know."

"That sounds awful. Why would someone do that?" I said. "Poor Stan. No wonder he didn't want to talk about it."

"Your dog just peed on my shoe." Russell stood up and shook his foot.

"Sorry, Russell. Bad dog, Solow. Well, we gotta go. Bye." Solow ran toward the Ford, jerking the leash and practically dragging me forward. Russell followed us to the parking area, pointing his over-sized flashlight at the ground ahead of us. Solow whined.

"What's the matter with you, big guy?" Got a foxtail somewhere?" I loaded him into the front seat, thanked the Ace-man and cranked up the music. I parked next to the Lincoln a couple minutes later. I felt silly knocking on the front door, but I didn't want to walk in on anything I wasn't supposed to. Warren answered the door with shiny peach lipstick on his chin.

"Hi, Warren. How was your day?" Seconds later I was the recipient of a big hug from Theda.

"We had the best time in Carmel, and we bought this for the new master bedroom," she pointed to a large oval mirror in a very ornate antique gold frame, leaning against the wall.

"It's beautiful! Must have been fun getting it into the car."

"Josephine, you don't know the half of it," Warren said, laughing and Theda joined in.

"I'm afraid I was rather insistent that we take the mirror home with us today instead of waiting for it to be delivered." Theda laughed at her own stubbornness. Whatever the story was, it was theirs and I needed to go to bed.

Chapter Seventeen

Wednesday morning I awoke to the sound of knocking on the front door. I blinked several times, trying to focus my eyes enough to see the bedside clock. It read eight-twenty. I rolled out of bed, noticing that Solow was not in the room. I heard Theda talking to someone in the front room. The door slammed and a minute later I heard the same voices outside my bedroom window. I pulled the curtain to one side.

Theda and a uniformed Fire Inspector stood with their backs to my window discussing the sad remains of the barn. Conveniently, my window was halfway open. Theda had Solow on leash beside her as the tall, trim gent told her that traces of sodium nitrate had been found in a hole six feet under the former barn structure.

"What is sodium nitrate used for?" she asked the inspector.

"It's used as a fertilizer, but could be used as an explosive."

"And you say there's a large hole under the barn and

that's where you found evidence of this chemical?" He nodded. "Was there a trap door or some other way to get to this hole in the ground?"

"Not enough of the structure survived to know for sure. You said you heard an explosion before you saw the fire. A small amount of chemicals could have been the cause. A larger amount would have taken out more than just the barn." Theda shivered.

"What do you think caused the sodium nitrate to explode?" she asked.

"That's where the cigarette comes in. It looks like a burning cigarette was left on the boards above the hole. Straw covering the earthen floor provided more fuel for the fire as it burned through the wood, dropping ash on the chemicals below and the rest is history."

"Someone had to be in the barn before the explosion," Theda said, her voice barely audible.

"That's right." The inspector wrote something in his notebook. "Any idea who?" Theda stared at the cremated barn, just fifty feet from where they stood. I had heard enough bad news, and it was time to get ready for work.

I arrived at the mansion minutes before Alicia and Trigger. Trigger ran up the sidewalk and gave me a hug, probably not having a clue how bad I needed one. My dark disposition instantly brightened.

"Hey, Trigger, where's your little pup?" He turned his back to me so I could see Tansey's head and front paws peeking out the top of his backpack.

"Hi, Allie, ready to paint millions of flowers today? Where's Kyle?"

Racing ahead of a plume of dust, a familiar looking Miata convertible made a quick stop just feet from where we stood. Kellie waved hello, but Kyle looked too pale and windblown to speak.

"Does that answer your question?" Alicia said, as she coughed the dust out of her lungs. "Good morning Kellie and Kyle."

"Hi, you guys. Sorry I can't stay," Kellie purred. Kyle swung one long leg at a time over the closed door, making it look like the easy way out of a convertible. Kellie clapped her hands in admiration, then stirred up more dust with a hard left turn and disappeared from view. I imagined little forest critters running for their lives as she thundered down the mountain. Kyle paid no attention, just headed for the front door. Alicia and I made our way to the music room.

"Allie, about how long will it take to finish this room and the cherubs in the foyer?"

"I'm thinking Friday, or maybe Monday." Kyle stood in the doorway.

"Kyle, how much time do you need to finish the columns?" Kyle concentrated very hard, at least the serious expression on his face made it look that way.

"Like, I should be able to finish by, like, the end of the day on Monday."

"Thanks, you guys. I'm not trying to pressure you, I

just need to know. If I start on the stair rail today, I think the patina will be finished Monday. Unless the Mungers come up with more work, Monday might be our last day here." I had mixed feelings about that. I loved the 'no commute' thing, the town, the people, but the downside was very real. I'd had it up to my eyeballs with worry over all the scary things that had happened.

"I'll miss this beautiful forest," Alicia said.

"Like, even Kellie likes it here."

The mansion's AC worked perfectly all day, keeping the temperature at a pleasant seventy-five degrees which, for me, was very conducive to creativity. Each of us worked at our separate projects until noon. Upon hearing the noontime fire siren, my friends and I gathered in the sunroom for lunch. Unfortunately the siren also served to remind me of the toasted barn. Trigger handed Kyle a sandwich.

"I made a peanut butter and jelly sandwich for you, Kyle." Trigger dug down into his backpack and brought up a second sandwich. "And I made this one for me."

Just then Mom and Dad walked into the sunny lunch room. Dad carried a very large pizza box. Mom carried a one gallon thermos of homemade lemonade and a sack of paper cups and napkins. Trigger put down his sandwich and joined in the pizza feeding frenzy. Kyle ate his sandwich first, and then joined us for pizza.

Mom poured lemonade for everyone, including the other workmen. They smiled and thanked her, some in

English and some in Spanish. She and Dad spoke fluent Spanish after taking night classes. Mom easily picked up French and Italian after that. Mom never met a person, subject or language she didn't like.

"Come on, Kyle, have another piece," Dad said. Kyle looked ready to burst.

"That's OK, Mr. Carl, like, thank you, sir."

When the box was empty, the smell of pesto and roasted chicken remained. Not exactly traditional pizza unless you lived in Santa Cruz.

"Alicia, would you mind if Leola and I took Trigger for a swim at The Junction?" Dad asked. "It's only a mile from here, and we'll be in the water with him." Trigger was jumping up and down, silently mouthing the word, 'please'.

"That would be lovely. He deserves a break, and it's very sweet of you to take him." Alicia looked at Tansey who was focused on eating crumbs under the table. "Tansey will stay with me."

"OK, Mom, see ya later." Trigger ran to the Subaru and opened the door for Mom. She bent down and kissed his forehead. I knew they would have a great time at the river and wished I could be there too. I was curious to know if Mom was still into bikinis or had she moved on to one-piece, old-lady swim suits.

Three hours later the sunburned and water-logged trio arrived back at the mansion. Trigger curled up with Tansey on a tarp and fell asleep in a nanosecond. Mom and Dad said they were going fishing.

"See you tomorrow?" I asked.

"If we finish our hike to Castle Rock in time," Mom said. Everyone hugged everyone and the old folks left. Our work continued another hour, and then we called it quits. I hung around in the shade by the front door until Russell showed up driving his official Ace Security pick-up. He looked way over-heated as he walked toward me wearing all his important security equipment hooked to his belt. I almost felt sorry for him, always acting big, but having no actual power.

"My air conditioner quit on me," Russell complained, as he wiped his forehead.

"Sorry to hear that, it being summer and all. Don't you guys have uniforms with short pants and sandals for the hot weather?"

"That wouldn't be regulation gear. You're probably thinking of UPS drivers." Russell took off his cap and fanned his red face.

"By the way, do you know anything about sodium nitrate?" I asked. "Apparently there were traces of it found under the barn. The inspector thinks a small amount exploded after a cigarette started the floor on fire." Russell's tight-lipped facial expression was beyond serious.

"That stuff is used as fertilizer, usually, until some sick-o terrorist gets hold of it. Who was smoking the cigarette?"

"That's the problem. None of us at the cabin smoke. Someone's been leaving cigarettes on the property for weeks. Now it's not just a trespasser -- it's a pyromaniac on the loose," I said. Russell scratched his head full of wet ringlets.

"It was a barn, right? Maybe fertilizer was accidentally triggered by the cigarette. Has there been any farming going on?"

"My guess would be, no." I said, "I'll try to find out. There are a few old apple trees in the area around the barn, that's all. There's a steep cliff and then endless forest as far as I can tell. Actually, I had a personal encounter with the cliff." Russell cocked his head to one side.

"My dog ran off and I was trying to find him. Turned out he was under the cabin the whole time." I scratched my ankle, remembering how panicked I was for Solow, and all the dings I sustained looking for him.

"So, Russell, do you have any friends in the Forestry Service?"

"Actually, my sister is married to one. He works in Yosemite and they live in Oakhurst. Why?"

"I was just wondering if there's any more information on the forest ranger who was shot on the Munger's property. Seems like I saw something in the Sentinel about sodium nitrate in the creek water?" I leaned over and scratched my ankle again.

"Probably conjecture. The DEA keeps things pretty much to themselves until investigations are over. Guess it's not over yet, but I'll ask around," he said.

"Last question … do you know how long Nora Bates has owned the property on Two Bar Road?" Russell grimaced.

"Yeah, since right after she took Stan for everything he had. She got a divorce and all the money Stan inherited from his mother. She even got custody of Annie, but Annie went to live with her dad as soon as she turned sixteen. I'd say Nora's had the property about ten years. Stan should have put up a fight, but I think she had something on him. Something he didn't want Annie to know."

"Well, Russell, I gotta' go now, but thanks for brainstorming with me."

"No problem," he said as his chest swelled.

I ducked into the Ford, put the key in the ignition and glanced down at my right ankle. No wonder I'd been scratching it. I discovered patches of itchy, lumpy red skin on my ankles and wrist. Good grief, I had poison oak. I thought back to the exploring Solow and I had done the day before. The area had an abundance of blackberry bushes, stinging nettle and poison oak. I thought I was being careful at the time. Apparently I wasn't careful enough. I scratched with one hand and drove with the other.

Theda and Solow had taken a little walk and were returning to the cabin just as I arrived. Solow wagged his tail and howled. Theda laughed at him and greeted me with a hug.

"Are you hungry, Josephine?"

"Starving." I imaged something like grilled mahi-mahi or Chicago baby back ribs with a Caesar salad. Actually, a good old pork chop would do. My stomach couldn't even remember the pizza I ate for lunch.

"Jose told me about this little Mexican restaurant right here in Boulder Creek," Theda said. "Does that sound good to you?"

"It sounds great. Give me five minutes to change. Oh, do you have anything for poison oak?"

"Not really."

I gave Solow a couple quick pats on the head, dashed into the house and changed into my brown slacks and yellow knit top. Lipstick, a quick brushing of hair and a pair of gold-loop earrings completed "the look". My poison oak would have to wait. I grabbed the gator and was out the door. Theda looked shocked to see me back outside so soon.

"Josephine, I need to do a few things before we leave. You might want to check the answering machine." She handed the leash to me with a sly smile on her lips, and disappeared into the house.

"Hey, big guy, miss me? No, I guess not. Not with Theda to take care of you."

Once we were inside the house, Solow flopped down on the cool floor. I pressed the play button on the answering machine. David's voice made me smile.

"What are you up to Josie? Hope you're staying out

of trouble. See you soon." It was short, but I could tell he was concerned for my safety.

The cabin was stuffy and hot so I stepped outside where the mosquitoes could feast on my bare arms. Hopefully, they would catch poison oak in the process. A familiar little blue pickup skidded to a stop in front of the cabin. Russell leaned out the window.

"Everything OK here?"

"Sure, why?"

"I was thinking, from now on I'm going to check the cabin every half hour. The company's going to wonder why I'm using so much gas, but that's the price of protection." He turned the truck around and headed back up the mountain. I had to give him points for good intentions. Theda stepped outside, ready to go.

"Who was that?" she asked as she watched a cloud of dust float up the driveway and around the bend.

"It was Russell to the rescue, if we needed to be rescued." We laughed as we climbed into Theda's SUV. Theda was in a spunky mood, as demonstrated by her driving. I barely had time to buckle up before we parked at Hoffman's Tacos.

"Hoffman's Tacos? What kind of name is that?"

"The restaurant belongs to the Garcias, parents of Norman Garcia," Theda said. "When they bought the restaurant it was called Hoffman's Hofbrau."

"Now I understand, I think." We walked into the colorfully decorated 1950's Tijuana style dining room. A plump woman about my age, her dark hair pulled back in a bun, asked if we wanted to sit outside. We looked past the crowded dining room, through the open French doors, to the patio. Theda looked at me and I nodded.

"The patio would be lovely." The woman led us to the one and only empty table and gave us our menus.

"How about that Mexican music?" I said, looking around at a dozen or more tables where people laughed, talked and ate to the lively beat blasting from speakers. I expected to see a crowd of people break into a fast polka at any moment.

"Isn't this a happy place?" Theda tapped her foot to the music.

"I notice you've been in a happy mood the last couple days."

"Josephine, do you realize it's only ten more days until Warren and I move into our new house together?" She ordered an appetizer and a couple iced teas. "Things are much better, and Warren is much more understanding these days." Her cheeks flushed.

"Good. I'm glad things are better." I felt like my job was coming to an end. Theda wouldn't need my help much longer as Warren was already taking over. We ordered margaritas and combo plates. My ankles itched, but I hardly noticed. Instead, I concentrated on the music, food and good company. The plump little woman I assumed was Norman's mother served our drinks.

"Everything is lovely, thank you," Theda said. I

nodded my agreement. My strawberry margarita was not only tasty, it made my shoulders relax for the first time in three weeks. I scanned the patio, enjoying the happy crowd, until I noticed a familiar- looking woman eating dinner with one of the workmen from the mansion. She had Dolly Parton hair and he had a tattoo on his scrawny white shoulder.

All of a sudden it was as if I had never had a margarita. The tension in my neck and shoulders returned. Theda looked at me.

"Josephine, you look like you just saw a ghost."

"No such luck. Just a couple of shady characters." I tipped my head in the direction of the odd couple. "The heavyset woman in the see-through white blouse, sitting with the young guy in black leather pants and vest."

"Interesting," was her comment. "The woman looks familiar."

"She should. She's your realtor."

"I only met Mrs. Bates once, you know. Warren conducted all the business with the lady."

If ever there was a misnomer, "lady" was it. I sneaked another peek at the pair just as Nora laid a one-hundred-dollar bill on the check plate. The smiley woman with her hair in a bun picked up the plate and thanked Nora. I watched her slip the bill into a pocket on her way to the indoor dining room.

"Theda, excuse me a minute. I need to go to the ladies room." I followed the bun lady inside and caught up to her when she stopped to pick up some menus.

"Mrs. Garcia?"

"Si?" she smiled warmly.

"My name is Josephine. I work with your son, Norman."

"You know my Norman? That ees nice. He ees a good boy."

"Yes, too bad he doesn't speak English."

"Oh, but he speak good English, mucho bedder dan me"

"Maybe he's just the quiet type." I changed the subject. "I was wondering about the young man sitting with Mrs. Bates."

"Oh, dat ees her son, Woody. He stay out of trouble deese days."

"Woody works for the Mungers," I said.

"Si, my Norman help him to be hired."

"Did Mrs. Bates pay for the help?" Mrs. Garcia looked over her shoulder and back to the menus.

"Si, she pay." With that, she turned, walked to the kitchen and I headed back to the patio. As I walked through the French doors, Nora bumped into me coming from the other direction. Her perfume was one of those earthy scents, "mildew on road kill", that hung in the air like a flock of gnats.

"Pardon me," she said, as she elbowed her way through the crowd and kept on walking. Her greasy-haired son, smelling of beer, followed. I finally made it to our table where Theda was still tapping her foot to the music as she sipped her margarita.

"Theda, who's in charge of hiring the laborers at the new house?"

"It used to be Chester, then it was Manuel, then Jose and now it's Manuel again." I figured Jose probably hired Woody last Friday, unless Manuel did it Monday. I decided to put the problem out of my mind so that I could enjoy the rest of the evening.

The stars came out, many people left, but Theda and I sat and talked for another hour. She told me what a beautiful child Emily had been, bright and full of dreams but, as usual, the topic brought tears to her eyes and ended in a long silence.

"Theda, do you think Johnnie's is still open?" I checked my watch, nine forty-five.

"I think it stays open until ten. Why?"

"I want to see if they sell anything for poison oak."

"Oh, dear, Josephine, I forgot all about your rash."

"I have a rash? I thought it was just a few bumps."

"Maybe it started out that way, but it's going up the back of your leg."

"Let's go before it covers my whole body." We chuckled, she paid the bill and we said good night to Mrs. Garcia. It was a short two blocks to Johnnie's so we walked. I found a bottle of calamine lotion on the shelf in the drug section and decided it was worth a try. I paid for the chalky-pink medicine and we headed down the sidewalk toward the

SUV. Even from a block away and under dim street lights, I thought the vehicle looked different somehow. Shorter. A closer look made my skin crawl.

Theda put her hands to her mouth as a tortured cry escaped from her mouth and cut through the quiet night. She stood like a plaster statue while I sputtered.

"I can't believe ... who in the ... what kind of people do this?" I kicked one of the four flat tires. Each tire had been slashed. I looked up and down Central Avenue, but saw nothing out of the ordinary, just a few pickup trucks parked in front of Mac's and Joe's. Except for the bars, the town had closed up for the night. I rested my hand on Theda's shoulder as she sat on the curb with her head in her hands, her body rocking back and forth.

"Theda, do you have your phone?" She robotically handed me her purse. I found the phone, called 911 and they put me on hold. I was really steamed. My poor friend was beaten down again and I wasn't feeling so good myself. My face felt hot as I slammed the phone shut, opened it and tried the number again.

"Nine, one, one, please state your emergency," a female said. I was practically tongue tied with rage, but managed to spit out a few words.

"I want to report four slashed tires on my friend's vehicle. We're stranded in Boulder Creek and need help."

"Ma'am, have you called your insurance or towing service?" For a second I thought, yeah, I should do that, and then I thought better of it.

"Ok, Miss," I said, "a crime has been committed here and for all we know the criminals are still in the area, possibly ready to harm us. We need you to send a deputy immediately."

"Ma'am, stay on the line ... the sheriff is on his way." Theda looked up at me.

"It's going to be OK. Sheriff's on his way," I said. Her head dropped again.

I was in no mood to be 'ma'med' by a 911 robot, but I decided to concentrate on first things first. I dropped the phone into Theda's purse and helped her into the passenger seat. I grabbed our purses and my calamine lotion off the sidewalk, hopped into the driver's seat and locked the doors. We sat in silence for over an hour until a sheriff's car finally pulled in behind the Lexus. The officer cut the engine and strolled up to my open window.

"Evening, ladies." Sergeant Machuca circled the SUV, wrote on his notepad and returned to my window. "Have any idea what happened here?" Theda just stared at him.

"No," I said. "This is how we found it and no one in sight." I stepped out of the SUV and walked to the sidewalk where the sergeant stood, taking notes. A streetlight illuminated a little something near the right rear tire. I pointed to it.

"Sergeant, that cigarette butt looks like the ones I found at the barn." He kicked it.

"Lotta' people smoke that brand."

"Do a lotta' people get their tires slashed?"

"No, not really." Machuca rubbed his chin. "Aren't you two out kinda' late?" I tried not to sound as indignant as I felt.

"Is there a curfew here?"

"Well, no."

"We've been ready to go home for a long time now. Can you give us a lift?"

"Sure, hop in." He held the door open while I guided Theda into the back seat of the cruiser. As we rolled through town, a call came in. The dispatcher informed Machuca of an accident on Two Bar Road. Instantly we were jerked back against our seats as the car leaped forward, siren blaring.

"Hang on, ladies," he said, after our necks were already wrenched. Two minutes later we were looking at a black Hummer wrapped around a giant redwood tree just a few yards from the Bates' front yard. The Hummer must have been going fast, missed the turn, rode the bank and skidded on its side until all four tires hugged the tree trunk.

Seconds later we heard a far away siren getting closer. A fire engine parked along side Machuca's car. A young, lanky fireman ran to the Hummer carrying a fire extinguisher and promptly sprayed a smoky area at the rear of the vehicle. A second fireman-paramedic ran to the mangled vehicle carrying his medical case.

Theda and I watched from the back seat of the car. We heard a female voice emitting hysterical cries for help. Before I could count to one, Machuca and the paramedic were standing on the Hummer pulling Nora, feet first, up and out the passenger window. Her bulk barely squeezed through the space and her Dolly hair had unraveled into a rat's nest. The whimpering woman was lowered down to the fireman on the ground, fitted with a neck brace and inspected briefly by a paramedic.

In the meantime, the other fireman pointed his flashlight through the Hummer windshield at the driver. He yelled to the paramedic.

"He looks like he's passed out. Get the jaws." I got out of the car for a better look as the windshield was forced open. Three firemen pulled Woody out and lowered him to the ground. His body was splayed in the moonlight with fresh blood covering half his face. He didn't move. The paramedic checked Woody's pulse and let his mother know that he still had one.

Nora half walked, half crawled to her son's side, looking panicked and disoriented. I climbed out of the cruiser and stood in the shadows about ten feet from the victims. Moonlight reflected off something metallic attached to Woody's belt. Machuca stepped back to let the paramedic have more room. I stood a couple feet behind the sheriff.

"Isn't this just awful?" I said. "What's that shiny thing in Woody's belt?"

"I'll take a look," Machuca said. He walked a half-circle to the other side of Woody and leaned down for a closer look. From there I watched him walk to his car, check on

Theda and call in a report to headquarters. Another siren fell silent.

An ambulance pulled into the Bates driveway. Machuca directed two guys with a stretcher to the patient. Eventually he returned to my side.

"What was it?" I asked. The sergeant answered without taking his eyes off the drama in front of us.

"A switch-blade."

I decided to check on Theda myself. I walked off with good intentions, but was distracted by a familiar defective muffler noise coming from behind the Bates's house. Even though it was pitch-pot dark, I circled around the west side of the old Victorian and ended up on the back deck beside a gravel driveway which headed south toward the mountains. I stared into the darkness seeing very little until brake lights flashed just before the old Dodge disappeared around a turn.

A tap on my shoulder sent me into a fast pirouette with arms raised to protect my head from ... I didn't know what.

"Sorry, I didn't mean to scare you," Machuca said, his hands up in a defensive posture. "What are you doing back here?" I lowered my arms, breathed deeply and thought about my answer for a second.

"I just had to get away from that awful accident. I hate gory things, don't you?"

"Oh, sure. Doesn't everyone?" He smirked, turned and walked back around the house. I followed and found

Theda standing near the sheriff's car talking into her cell phone. An improvement from her earlier catatonic state. She was obviously talking to Warren.

"I'll call the insurance company first thing in the morning. Yes, dear, I'm alright, really I am. Yes, dear, I'll call you tomorrow." She dropped the phone into her purse.

"Everything OK?"

"Warren's so angry he's threatening to sell our property and leave his Boulder Creek dream behind. I don't think he really would sell, but he's sure having a hard time with all of this."

"Yeah, I feel like having a hissy myself," I said and clenched my teeth together. We watched Woody being loaded into the ambulance. His mother and the EMT climbed in, someone shut the doors and they took off. A tow truck arrived and Machuca talked to the driver for a minute as he wrote in his notebook. Finally, he drove us home.

The little cabin looked so inviting, especially my sweet old dog who greeted us as if we had been away since the civil war. He needed a walk real bad so I took him for a short one, making sure not to go where there might be poison oak. The stuff was driving me crazy.

The first thing I did when we got back to the cabin was smear calamine lotion on my wrists, legs and feet. The itch subsided long enough for me to fall into a dreamless sleep.

Chapter Eighteen

Solow's howling woke me up Thursday morning. What a surprise.

"What's your problem, big guy?" For a moment I thought it was a Fluffy rendezvous he was after, until I realized I was not in my own bed in my own home. I was in Emily's bed, it was time to get ready for work, and Solow had probably howled at the burnt toast smell wafting from the kitchen. Good grief, Theda was cooking again.

By the time I was showered and ready to go, there was no time for eating. Theda handed me dark toast and a mug of thick coffee as I tried to make my escape.

"Thank you, Theda. How sweet. What's the scoop on the Lexus?"

"Warren's taking care of it. I only hope it will be back before my hair appointment at eleven."

"Call me on my cell if you need a ride. See you later." I held toast in one hand and mug in the other. I carefully opened the car door with my pinky, as all the other fingers were busy. The gator purse slid down my arm, caught on the door, jerked me and sent the mug flying onto the cream colored carpet. Burnt toast crumbs were everywhere, soaking up the coffee. I made a mental note to clean the car before returning it.

It was another sunny day at the villa. I noticed the roofers had finished applying terra cotta tiles to the various roofs. The place looked close to being finished; even the garage was finished except for clearing out the sawhorses and tools. I leaned against the side door and peeked in the window, just as Manuel pulled the door open from inside. I suddenly entered the garage without intending to.

"Hi, Manuel. How's it going?" His right arm still hung in a sling.

"Everysing ees getting better."

"By the way, did you hire Woody?" Manuel shook his head.

"I no hire dat one." He shook his head one more time and spat on the floor.

"Do you know who hired Norman?"

"Chester hire him." Manuel turned and walked away in disgust. I ran after him.

"Why don't you fire him?" He acted like he didn't hear me and kept walking. I decided to get to work. My people were already hard at it, creating art on walls and columns. The column Kyle had already finished looked like real travertine marble. I held the real marble sample up to the column to make sure. The columns would look even better after the painters added a clear coat.

"Kyle, you're a genius."

"Thanks, Josephine. Like, it's kinda' fun, ya know?"

"I'm glad you think its fun to paint because I love what you do."

"Josephine, ah, can I like, ask you something?"

"Fire away," I gave him my best motherly smile.

"Like, Kellie wants me to move in with her." Kyle's ears flamed.

"How do you feel about it?" I watched him look down at his size thirteen biker boots. "What would your folks think about it?"

"I don't want to, like, lose her, ya know?"

"So that would be your reason for moving in with her, so she won't get mad?" Kyle thought a moment.

"I guess so."

"Kyle, you need to think this thing through. It's not true that two can live as cheap as one. What you save on rent, you'll be putting into a high-maintenance female. Anyway, if she's worth your attention, she'll wait for you. Are you in love with her?"

Kyle looked at the ceiling. "I don't know."

"My best advice is to sleep on it, at least six months, then decide what to do. Why get hooked up with a girl so early in your college career anyway?" I reached up, patted Kyle's shoulder and walked to the music room feeling lucky I didn't have any decisions like that to make in my own life. The music room was cool and so was the mural, way cool!

"Allie, it's looking wonderful. I especially like the blue lupine."

"Thanks, it's one of my favorite wildflowers."

"Well, it's off to the railing wars for me. Gotta' faux the stair rail." I started to gather the paint and tools I would need, when it occurred to me someone was missing. "I haven't seen Trigger around."

"Your mom and dad were here when we arrived this morning. They took Trigger fishing. Leola said something about getting together with you for dinner. And if you're looking for Tansey, we left her at home."

I stuffed the supplies into a canvas bag and lugged it over to the massive staircase. I was having a hard time getting motivated and forgot the tarps. Back in the music room I gathered three canvas tarps into my arms and then stopped to stare out the window.

Manuel was supervising the planting of a dozen large palm trees. I watched Jose and Norman wrestle a tree into a freshly-dug hole. More palm trees waited patiently in the hot sun, their roots constricted in wooden boxes. Manuel measured and staked where each hole should be dug. Finally, he had a break from hard labor.

I tugged my mind and body back to the staircase, spread one tarp on the tile floor and two tarps on the stairs, mixed a greenish patina glaze and began rubbing the paint onto the metal with a cotton cloth. Kyle worked on the second column ten feet away. Two hours later the Boulder Creek fire siren sounded, reminding us that we should eat lunch. Actually, I needed no reminder. My stomach was emptier than a bucket with a hole in it.

Allie and Kyle relaxed on wicker chairs in the sunroom, sharing her lunch. I ducked out, hoping to find something to eat at the cabin. Theda's SUV was gone and so was she. She hadn't called me for a ride so I assumed she was riding on four new tires to her hair appointment. I spent some time with Solow, threw together a lunch and shared it with him. My stomach was happy, but my skin itched like crazy. I slathered on more calamine and waited for the lotion to dry. The phone rang.

"Hello."

"Josephine, I was prepared to leave a message."

"Hi, Theda. Sorry I had to rush off this morning. Didn't want to get fired."

Theda laughed, "no danger of that my friend. I was about to tell you that my Lexus was delivered to me this morning and I'm at my hair appointment right now. In fact, I'm under the dryer."

"So that's what that noise is. I thought a jet was flying overhead. I'm getting together with Mom and Dad for dinner tonight. Would you like to go?"

"That would be lovely. Thank you, Josephine."

"I'll see you later, bye."

Back at the villa, the solarium was full of workers relaxing after emptying their lunch pails. I sat on the kitchen steps, missing Trigger, staring at my pink-polished toenails and my chalky-pink legs below my ratty old cutoffs. Why did Woody slash Theda's tires? I felt sure he had. I wondered if Norman was involved somehow. He sat across the room from me speaking to Jose in Spanish. I had an idea. I walked out to my borrowed car and called Dominican Hospital.

"Room 243, please."

"Hello."

"Chester, this is Josephine. Remember me?"

"Yeah, I remember," he mumbled.

"Well, I called to ask about Norman Garcia, you know, one of the workers you hired?"

"Yeah, I hire a lotta' guys. What about him?"

"Does he speak English?"

"I spoke to him in English, but I don't remember him saying anything in English."

"Were you pressured by someone to hire him?"

"What do you mean by that?" Chester snapped.

"I mean, just answer yes or no. I won't tell anyone."

"There's nothing to tell." He slammed the phone down. I thought, touchy, aren't we? He could have just said, "no" but instead he went nuclear. I dropped the phone in the cup-holder and hustled back to the music room. Alicia asked me to help her paint a family of deer.

"Jo, you know I'm terrible at painting animals. That's why Kyle painted all the sheep and cows."

"No problem, Allie. Paint flowers to your heart's content. I like painting deer. Wouldn't it be awful if all three of us were good at painting the same things and bad at the same things?"

"Ok, I see your point. Thanks, Jo." Actually, deer were much more interesting to me than fauxing a railing, so why not postpone the patina for a little while? I had just finished the first deer when I heard little footsteps pounding down the hall.

"Mom. Jo. Look what I caught!" Trigger puffed out his chest as he held up two small trout on a string. "And I hooked the worms myself!" Dad stood in the doorway behind Trigger.

"This boy is a born fisherman," Dad said, as Trigger smiled and handed the fish over to Bob who put them back into his six-pack cooler.

"Honey, those are nice fish you caught," Alicia said. "I'll cook them for our dinner tonight." Trigger's jaw dropped.

"But I just want to keep them!"

"Honey, they need to be eaten right away unless we freeze them for later."

"Yeah, Mom, let's freeze 'em."

Dad winked. "That's a great idea. Just freeze 'em." I figured those little trout would stay frozen until freezer burn forced them into the garbage. I remembered the first fish I caught. I was only seven when Mom and Dad took me to Lake Tahoe and we rented a rowboat. I was so proud of my little fish and wanted to keep it forever, so I packed it in my suitcase. Driving home a couple days later, Dad stopped the car, followed the odor and extracted the fish. I was crushed.

"See you at the cabin. Six o'clock?" Mom said.

"Sure, I'll be there. Oh, I asked Theda to join us for dinner?"

"That's wonderful, dear." Dad left the cooler for Alicia and said his good-byes. We settled back to our painting projects. The small, distant deer didn't take long to paint; a buck, a doe and two fawns. When they were finished, I went back to the railing and began the tedious ragging of faux patina. Kyle was focused on applying veins to his second faux marble column using the tip of a goose feather.

I had worked on the railing for over an hour when Trigger entered the room, sat on the bottom step and sighed. I leaned down to him.

"What's the matter, big guy?"

"I wish Tansey was here. There's nothing to do." Trigger rested his chin on both knees, his arms hugging his bare legs.

"No book to read?"

"I already read the one I brought," he complained. I shoved my painty rag into a plastic bag.

"Come on, let's go talk to Mom." Alicia was taking a water break, if you call drinking water while painting a break.

"What are you two up to?" she asked.

"I thought I might take Trigger on a nature walk," I said. "OK with you?"

"Of course, it is. Take some water with you, it's hot

out there." Truer words were never spoken. It was two o'clock, the hottest time of the day. What was I thinking? Too late, I couldn't disappoint my little friend.

"Jo, I can show you where I found the gold nugget."

"OK, let's go." I figured a little fresh air would be good for both of us. Trigger ran across the front yard to a well-worn trail, maybe a deer path, heading down the western side of the mountain. I had to run to catch up to him. We passed an ancient redwood tree and some manzanitas as we careened down the steep and sometimes slippery slope. As soon as the trail leveled off, we were in complete shade under a canopy of tree limbs. The air had become cooler, not a breeze anywhere but silence everywhere. I stopped for a moment to have a sip of bottled water. Trigger wanted to keep walking.

"Jo, don't worry, we're almost to the creek."

"Show me the way. Shall I call you, Scout?"

"You can call me Trigger, but try to keep up."

"Honey, the problem is, your legs are newer than mine. We're in no hurry, are we?"

"No, I guess not," he slowed down a bit only to start running at the sound of water cascading over rocks. By the time I slid down the creek bank onto the little sandy beach, Trigger was knee deep in the crystal water. Patches of sunlight sparkled and danced on top of the stream, but the shady areas far out-numbered the sunny ones. Huge, Volkswagen-sized rocks were up to their armpits in water and moss. Old tree branches lay where they fell. Sandy areas lined the creek and the shallow waters were home for skeeters and tadpoles. Ferns covered the ground, turning chartreuse-green wherever sunlight touched them.

Trigger interrupted my reverie with a splash of creek water followed by his giggles. The water was cold and refreshing. I splashed back.

"I dare you to do that again," I shouted. More splashes and laughter followed until we were sufficiently cooled off. I flipped my sandals onto the sand next to Triggers, climbed onto a rock the size of a laundry basket and dangled my feet in the water. As I watched Trigger trying to catch minnows with his hands, I was reminded of the many camping trips I had enjoyed as a young girl. Creeks and rivers were always the main attraction. The places that provided endless entertainment.

Out of the corner of my eye I saw the glint of sun on metal not far from our sandals. I scooted off my rock and bent over the sand hoping to find a big gold nugget. Instead, I found a small circular piece of gold colored metal - the top of a shell from a bullet. I flicked sand away and picked it up, examined it and popped it into my pocket. The creek-side paradise was deceiving. I wondered if Trigger and I were alone.

"Whatcha' doin', Jo?" More splashes and giggles.

"Stretching my legs so I can chase those pollywogs." We laughed. The sun had moved to my rock so I tried another. The baby bear rock was good and shady.

"Ten more minutes, Trigger, then we have to go back."

He pulled a long thin branch out of the water with a beer bottle on the end.

"Good grief, not here," I said.

"What's the matter, Auntie Jo?" Trigger saw me scowling and flung the bottle to the other side of the creek, as if that would make me feel better.

"That's OK, sweetheart, I just get upset when people litter." Trigger immediately waded across the creek and retrieved the bottle.

"I'll put it in the recycle bin at home." He looked very proud of his decision. Suddenly rushing creek water was not the only sound around. We stared in the direction of some serious barking, not a friendly bark, but a growly bark. Without a word we slipped into our sandals and scrambled up the trail. I kept up with Trigger just fine. We never actually saw the dog, but it's bark provided plenty of incentive to keep moving fast.

After the hike, it was difficult to get back into faux painting. My mind wandered back to that beautiful little beach, the noisy water and huge boulders, all of it Munger land. I pulled the casing out of my pocket. The ranger, of course! Why didn't I think of it before? I wanted to give it to the authorities just as soon as I figured out which ones should have it. Machuca might be convinced of a few things if I gave it to him, or not. I thought about the DEA and FBI, but I hadn't seen any of them around. Oh, and I shouldn't forget good ol' Russell.

"How did you like the creek?" Kyle asked as he watched

me put something in my pocket.

"Loved it. Kyle, don't be offended, but last week when you and Trigger hiked down to the creek, did you take a bottle of beer with you?"

"Like, why would I do that? I was with Trigger, ya know?"

"I know. Just had to ask. Oh, did you hear any dogs while you were down there?"

He looked up at the ceiling for a moment, then shook his head and went back to his marbleizing. I finished a fair portion of the railing before it was time to go home. Alicia, Trigger and Kyle waved good-bye as I stood watching the Volvo disappear from view. I noticed Norman remained on the job, waiting for the Ace truck.

"Ola, Norman." He turned to look at me.

"Ola," he said.

"Do you know what time it is?" He automatically looked at his watch, caught himself and shrugged. I began talking to him in English, hoping for a reaction.

"So, Norman, why are you always the one to stay and wait for Russell?" Another shrug. "I know your mother and she says you speak perfect English." He quickly looked over his shoulder at the grounds.

"I'm sorry, Josephine. It's a long story, but I guess I can talk to you."

"I'd love to hear the long story," I said. Just then Russell drove up and parked in a billow of dust. Norman hopped in his pickup and sped down the mountain before I could say, "Hi, Russell."

The petite Ace man strolled over to the brick wall I was sitting on, his nightstick thumping his flashlight as he walked. I noticed his holster held a can of pepper spray instead of a gun. The company probably didn't trust him with a gun.

"How's the painting going? You must be almost finished," Russell said, sounding more like a 'regular person' than usual. I pulled the shell out of my pocket and opened my hand for Russell to see.

Chapter Nineteen

Thursday turned out to be a long hot day and Russell actually expected me to show him the spot where I had discovered the bullet casing. At least he was showing interest, I told myself.

"It's quite a hike from here," I said, "but I guess I could take you there." The sun wouldn't set for two more hours and the late afternoon air was invigorating, so why not go for a hike? We quickly clambered down the western side of the mountain, using our buttocks more often than our feet. We followed the steep trail all the way to the creek.

A familiar smell greeted me as I skidded on my fanny down a bank onto the beach. In the sand, directly in front of my big toe was a cigarette butt, still smoking. Russell caught up to me. His belt full of noisy hardware echoed through the woods.

"What in the world?" he said.

"Same brand I found at the barn. Obviously, the smoker just left." Russell scanned the perimeter, but saw nothing. We heard a rustling in the bushes. Suddenly an angry brown mastiff charged through the underbrush, directly toward us.

"Russell, look out!" I screamed. His body turned but his feet were stationary in the sand. He twisted and fell on his back when the muscular dog leaped through the air and landed on top of him. Russell's flailing arm wacked my chest, sending me flat on the sand. In slow motion I watched Russell put his hands over his face for protection while the dog stood on top of him, snarling and trying to get a clear shot at his victim's throat.

Visions of Trigger being attacked by the same type of dog enraged me beyond belief. My mind seemed to be sorting through all the options while the slow motion attack continued. My right hand found Russell's holster. I pulled out the can of pepper spray, pointed it at the dog and squeezed again and again. I don't know who was yiping louder, the dog or Russell.

I sat up. My eyes were smarting. I could barely keep them open long enough to see the mastiff stagger away, howling with pain. Russell cried out.

"My eyes, my eyes, I can't breathe, help!" he lay there with his hands over his eyes trying to suck in some air.

"Get up, Russell. We need to get out of here." I was blinking and hurting, but not as bad as Russell. Tears flooded his cheeks as I pulled him into a sitting position. He could not, would not, open his eyes. I helped him stand and turned him in the direction we needed to go. We fumbled our way up the sloping creek bank, holding onto each other for support. The trail was easier than the bank. We locked arms and hurried as best we could, not knowing if man or beast would come after us. I became the 'eyes' of the operation. They were open about half the time and felt like hot cinders in their sockets.

"Hang on, Russell, we're halfway there."

"Oh, God, this is awful," he sobbed. Russell's feet went out from under him. He managed to stand up and continue the climb, coughing and sucking air as he went. It seemed like hours before we finally cleared the top of the mountain. I opened a second eye when I heard voices. Dad was at my side holding me up.

"Honey, what happened?" he asked, holding me steady. I tried to answer, but nothing came out. Mom let Russell lean on her shoulder as she gave a nervous sigh.

"Oh, my, dear, what have you gotten into this time?" Why did she always remember my mishaps? I never said I was perfect. The four of us walked slowly toward the mansion, arms linked together, holding each other up. Theda stepped out the front door.

"Josephine, are you alright?" she choked.

"Actually, no." Tears were streaming down my cheeks and I had sand in my shoes and thorns in my shorts. It just doesn't get more uncomfortable than that, unless your name is Russell. Poor Russell. Mom led him to a faucet. He leaned down and splashed his face for the longest time, even longer than my turn at the other faucet beside the garage. Water didn't really help, but at least it was cold.

"So, Mom, what are you guys doing up here?" I asked as I sniffled and wiped tears away with the back of my hand.

"It's after seven and we wondered if you were working late," she said.

Dad eyed us. "So what were you two doing, if you don't mind my asking?"

"Oh, I just wanted to show Russell the creek. Everything was fine until he was attacked by this horrible mastiff, exactly like the one that attacked Trigger. I used Russell's pepper spray on the dog and it worked. Trouble is, the spray got on us too. Mostly on Russell. Should we take him to a hospital? I think he's having trouble breathing."

Theda walked over to where Russell was still dousing himself with water. I couldn't hear the conversation, but she told us Russell had insisted he was alright. I turned off the water and walked over to Russell to find out for myself.

"Hey, Russell. How's it going?" No answer, just coughs and a few gags. "I'm sorry I got you into this. Are you OK?" I waited for a response.

"Don't worry, Josephine. It's all in the line of duty." He was still bent over the faucet, splashing water on his face and gulping air between coughs.

"Sure, but if you need a doctor, we can drive you there." My eyes were longing for more cold water. He finally raised his head and opened one red eye.

"Don't worry about me. It's part of the job." He put his head down and continued drenching it with water.

"Your job is watching over the mansion, not being attacked by mad dogs. By the way, were you bitten anywhere?" Russell shook his wet head like a dog after its bath.

"I don't think so. Just a scratch on my hand." Sure enough, Russell had a deep claw mark on the back of his right hand.

"I think you better come with us to the cabin where we can clean that wound." I took him by his elbow and walked him to Theda's Lexus. My car and Russell's truck would be left behind. Theda nervously started the engine as everyone snapped their seat belts and Russell coughed. We were in for a remarkably fast ride -- equivalent to the Big Dipper at the Boardwalk in Santa Cruz.

As we jerked to a stop in front of the cabin, Mom said, "Wasn't that fun?" Which in old lady speak means, "What idiot would drive like that?" Dad just put his hands across his chest like he had just survived "The Big One."

Solow greeted us at the front door, his tail wagging the whole back half of his long hairy body. He sniffed Russell up and down, probably catching the scent of the mastiff. Russell turned and headed for the bathroom faucet without further ado.

"Leola and I will buy dinner and bring it up here. How does that sound?"

"Devine," Theda said, smiling.

"Yeah, that would be great, Dad," I said, as I walked into the kitchen, wet a small towel and held it to my eyes. "There's a Mexican restaurant called Hoffman's Tacos."

"Oh, we tried it already," Mom said. "A fun place, really. Mrs. Garcia is a dear." Leave it to Mom and Dad to find the hottest spot in town.

"Don't get into any more trouble while we're gone," Dad said over his shoulder, as if I were ten years old. Guess things hadn't changed much -- he was still my daddy. When they were gone, I moseyed down the hall to the bathroom and watched nurse Theda scrub, medicate and wrap Russell's hand. She put eye drops in our burning eyes, making us feel better.

"Theda, you would make a great nurse."

"Don't laugh, I actually went to medical school for a year after college, before I met Warren."

"Why didn't you continue?"

"Warren needed my help with a restaurant he was trying to get off the ground. In the end it failed; but eventually he invented a special tanning system and has done very well with it. By that time I forgot all about my ambition to be a doctor -- after all, I had Emily to raise."

Russell walked back to the comfy living room with a wet towel pressed against one eye, then the other. "Your dog sure likes me," he said.

"He likes the way you smell. Care for a glass of water?"

"Please." Theda jumped up and brought a glass of

water to her patient. Russell gulped it down as if he were putting out a forest fire. Poor guy probably had his mouth open when I sprayed the dog. I felt bad, but there hadn't been time to warn him.

Solow howled when Mom and Dad carried two boxes of great smelling Mexican food into the kitchen. Theda found a fifth chair and we all sat down to tacos, tamales, enchiladas and a big green salad. Mom's idea, I'm sure. She was always big in the vegetable department.

"Life just doesn't get better than this," I said. Everyone just nodded and kept chewing. Poor Russell had a hard time seeing his food through the tears, but he was determined to take advantage of the bounty. I watched him sneak a bite of enchilada to Solow, and, at that moment, my dog became Russell's friend for life. After all, Solow had discriminating taste and chicken enchilada was at the top of his list. We all looked up when someone knocked. Theda turned on the porch light and opened the door.

"Hi, I'm Norman. My mother sent me to give you this," he handed Theda a one- hundred-dollar bill. "Bob overpaid." Dad and I had already made it to the front door. Theda handed Dad the money.

"I'm sorry, Norman. I meant to give her this." Dad said, as he dug in his wallet. He handed Norman a fifty and an extra ten for his trouble.

"Gee, is something wrong?" Norman asked when he saw my red eyes and tears.

"Just a little pepper spray gone awry." I smiled as

best I could. "I'll walk you to your pickup." Everyone gave me curious looks, especially Norman. When the two of us were outside, I said, "I'm ready for the long story, Norman. Why were you pretending not to know English?" He looked trapped.

"It was a favor to Chester. He wanted me to help him stop the accidents, you know, bad stuff that keeps happening around here. He knows who's behind it but he doesn't know who is actually doing the dirty work."

"Did you discover who dropped the tile and wrote on the walls?"

"I think I know, but I don't have proof. Chester thought it might be Woody and fired the useless creep. The next day my boss lands in the hospital."

"Who do you think vandalized the mansion?"

"Personally, I think it could be Woody, just because nobody else looks suspicious."

"Did Woody's mom have anything to do with getting his job back?"

"Not really. I had already talked to Jose about Woody before Mrs. Bates pressured my mother. Jose wanted to catch Woody in the act as much as I did."

"Wouldn't it be easier to just keep him off the property?"

"This way we can keep track of him," Norman laughed, but didn't look happy.

"So, do you think the McFees are behind it all?"

"I think that goes without saying." He glanced over his

shoulder at the black, starless night. Norman said good-bye, jumped into his pickup. As soon as his tail lights disappeared, I went back in the house with more to chew on than just my supper.

"Too bad David couldn't be here with us," Theda said.

"He's crazy about Mexican food," I said, tearing into a second enchilada.

"Josephine, in the excitement I forgot to tell you. You had a call from David. He wanted to know if you could come to his house Sunday for a birthday party."

"Oh, thank you, Theda. I almost forgot Monica's birthday. What do I give a four year old anyway?"

"Give her a big cardboard box," Mom suggested. "Children love to climb in and out like a cat. Of course, you fill the box with books."

"Ask a silly question." As I rolled my eyes, I realized my eyeballs were feeling better. I managed pretty well with heavy blinking.

"Remember the three-legged cat we gave you when you were five?" Dad said.

"How could I forget old Tripod. You called him that so often I thought it was his name. Too bad it stuck. Fluffy would have been a nicer name."

"Why only three legs?" Russell asked.

"He was the son of an alley cat and the whole litter was having breakfast from an overturned garbage can. Tripod didn't get out of the way in time and a garbage truck ran over his tiny little leg." Dad's eyes misted. Mom remembered the whole thing too.

"Bob and I were downtown walking by the alley when it happened. I picked up the pour little kitten, crushed leg and all, and we drove him to the veterinarian. Doctor Foster said he couldn't save the leg and was ready to put Tripod to sleep. Well, I couldn't bear that. I said we would take him. So, Doctor Foster sewed him up and sent him home with us. Josephine was staying with her cousin, Candy, overnight. When she came home the next day and saw Tripod for the first time, she thought he was a special breed of cat, which he turned out to be."

"He was a great cat," I added.

"This orange cat with three legs lived eighteen years," Mom said.

"That's wonderful. I never had a cat ... or dog for that matter. Mother was allergic." Theda sighed. "But we gave Emily a cockatoo." Her eyes stared at a vision from the past. She smiled a sad little smile that put a lump in my throat.

Everyone looked stuffed and too sleepy to keep the conversation going, especially me. After all I had hiked to the creek twice in one day. Russell pushed his chair back.

"I better get back to my truck and do some rounds." His eyes watered.

"I'll drive you up there," Dad said "Just let me finish my last taco." Russell sat down again and relaxed for a few more minutes, wiping his eyes every two seconds. I wondered how he could do his job in the shape he was in.

A couple hours later, I woke up on the sofa. The house was quiet so I tiptoed down the hall to bed. I thought about how lucky we were that the dog hadn't attacked Trigger and me on the first trip to the creek. We would have had no defense, no hope. My last conscious thought was, "Thank you, God."

Chapter Twenty

I was dead to the world all night until five in the morning when my eyes stared at the ceiling and a zillion crazy scenarios raced through my mind. I padded into the kitchen for a drink of water and discovered Theda sitting at the table with Solow lying across her bare feet. She looked up from her crossword puzzle and wished me a good morning.

"Good morning, Theda. You can't sleep either?"

"I often get up at this time. I wish I could sleep longer."

"Well, today I'm like you. Shall I make a pot of coffee?" Theda smiled and Solow thumped his tail on the floor.

"That would be lovely. How are you feeling today?"

"Pretty good, all things considered. I hope Russell is doing as well. He looked like death warmed over last night, or was that just one of my nightmares?"

"I'm afraid it really happened," she said. "I can't imagine why a dog would be way out in the forest like that." Theda went back to her crossword puzzle after sharing the front section of the Sentinel with me. I decided there was nothing interesting there, just more problems in the world. I poured two cups of coffee and a little later we welcomed the sunrise with a homemade breakfast, courtesy of Josephine Stuart.

"You know, it's weird, I don't remember saying goodnight to Mom and Dad."

Theda laughed, "That's because you fell asleep on the sofa before they left." She took a sip of coffee. "We had a jolly game of gin rummy. Your parents have more energy than I'll ever have."

"Or me," I said. "Is Warren going to be here tonight?"

"Oh, yes, he called yesterday. Our belongings arrive Tuesday, so of course he will stay and oversee the move."

"Wow, it's exciting to see the house 99% finished. My team will finish up the painting Monday.

"Josephine, I'm going to miss you so much." Her eyes were misty.

"Once you're settled into your new home, I want you and Warren to visit me in Aromas. Maybe David would like to go with us to the Grange Hall for a terrific pancake breakfast."

"We would love to do that," she said.

"It's almost nine. Think I could have a ride up the mountain?"

"Oh, dear, I forgot your car is still up there." She grabbed her keys and we took off. I was actually getting used to Theda's spirited style of driving. She parked beside the green Volvo. I gathered up my bagged lunch and a borrowed thermos of cold tea.

"So when does the driveway get paved?" I asked as I stood by my door, choking in the dust that hadn't yet settled.

"Didn't I tell you? It will happen this weekend. Johnson Paving has agreed to do the work Saturday and Sunday. We couldn't be happier." I thought to myself, you're not the only ones. The whole world will be happy to see this thing paved.

"See you later, Theda. Thanks for the ride." I hurried toward the house before she could stir up more dust with one of her wild takeoffs. Manuel stood just inside the open front door, inspecting an imperfect piece of trim which Jose was prying off the wall with a crowbar. Jose picked up a pre-cut, nine foot piece of trim and tapped it into place. Manuel still wore his bandages and sling. It crossed my mind that maybe he liked the status quo. A few feet from the door, Kyle worked on his third faux marble column.

"Morning, you guys," I said as I passed by all of them on my way to the music room. When I got there, Alicia looked up from the field of flowers she was painting.

"Good morning, Jo. Is it true about the dog attack yesterday? I heard rumors."

"I'm afraid so. It was the craziest thing. He looked exactly like the dog that attacked Trigger, except for the plumbing." I turned to leave, but stopped when Alicia said something that sent chills up my spine and daggers to my heart.

"Maybe the dogs are related and came from the same place. Trigger told me he was frightened yesterday by the barking of an angry dog. I didn't want to take any chances so I dropped him off at his grandmother's house this morning." She turned back to her painting.

"Allie, I'm so sorry. It's my fault. I shouldn't wander around this property with Trigger. It's just not safe. It's really too bad, Trigger and I were having so much fun until the dog barked." I started to walk away, but stopped. "Did he have another nightmare?"

Alicia didn't stop painting. She just nodded. I didn't blame her for being upset. Tears welled up in my eyes as I left the room. I couldn't get poor Trigger off my mind. He must have been terrified. I made a promise to myself to be more careful in the future, especially with my dear little friend.

Halfway through the house I found Manuel on his knees inspecting a coat closet door that wouldn't close properly. He looked up as I bent down, ready to share my opinion on the door problem.

"Por favor, dee flashlight." Manuel pointed to a toolbox across the hall. I rummaged through it and handed him the flashlight.

"Manuel, did you see Russell this morning?"

"Si." He flashed the light on each of the three hinges.

"Did he look OK to you?"

"Sí."

"Nice talking to you." I walked to my faux railing project feeling like I'd been talking to a wall. I would have loved to trade places with Kyle for awhile and do some marbleizing, but everyone has their own style and all four columns needed to look alike. I organized my paint and tools, spread the tarps and began applying the fake patina. I laughed to myself at the idea of clients wanting me to make things look old and weathered. Most of my possessions actually were old and weathered. I wanted new and pretty things. I hadn't worked long when Alicia walked up to me.

"Jo, I just want you to know that I know you would never let anyone or anything hurt Trigger." My eyes overflowed as she hugged me. I felt guilty of stupidity, not only in the case of Trigger, but also in the case of Russell. I wondered if I would ever grow up and act my age, like a middle-aged adult woman. We sat on a tarp-covered-step for a few minutes, watching Kyle blend the different shades of paint into a perfect marble replica.

"This boy knows his business," I said, wiping my nose with a Kleenex.

"Sure does." She stood up and walked down the hall to the music room. I resumed my work feeling much better. By the time the noon fire siren blew, I was up to my elbows in green paint and ready for a break. We all met in the sunroom where a boombox played happy accordion music and three workmen ate their lunches. Only Jose, Manuel and another man had remained for the final touches on the mansion. My group of painters took over the whicker chairs near the north wall.

"Allie, Kyle, don't let me forget to take pictures of the murals Monday. I wonder if my camera's in the truck." That reminded me to call the Body Shop. I walked outside to the Ford, picked up my cell phone and dialed.

"Hi, this is Josephine Stuart. I'm calling about ...."

"Ms. Stuart, we tried calling you. Like, your Mazda is ready." I imagined the little tart with a hickey on her neck, snapping her gum, all worried about getting ahold of me.

"Is your shop open tomorrow?" I asked, sweetly.

"Open till two," big sigh, like she already knew I would show up at the last minute.

"Thanks a lot." I put the phone down, thought a minute and picked it up again. I dialed Chester's number at the hospital. After many rings an old codger answered.

"Hello?"

"Is Chester there?"

"Not unless he's dressed up as a nurse in one ah them white youneeforms."

"No, that wouldn't be him. Thank you." I wondered if Chester was in rehab or even better, released. I made a mental note to call the hospital information number some other time, but I was starving and needed some lunch. I returned to the solarium.

"Did you, like, call David," Kyle grinned.

"No, I didn't call David. I called about my truck, smarty pants." Kyle laughed as he washed down one of Alicia's tuna sandwiches with a cup of my tea. Fortunately, I had packed extra fruit and cookies for the poor, starving college student who never planned ahead. My lunch consisted of yogurt with a good sprinkling of sunflower seeds, almond slices and dried blueberries.

"How can you, like, eat that stuff?" he groaned, one finger resting on his tongue for effect. "It looks like something the dog ...."

"Yes, yes, I know, but you haven't tried it, have you?"

"Sorry, like, I can't get past the looks of it, ya know?" He reached for another ginger cookie from my bag. Alicia ate her lunch quietly, looking odd without Trigger nearby. Just then I spied Theda tripping across the front yard and watched her enter the solarium. She said hello to everyone, then turned back to me.

"Josephine, I have a favor to ask. Do you think you could get away this afternoon for a little trip to Felton, say about three?"

"Three would be good. Why?" Actually, I was having a hard time concentrating on faux railings and didn't mind leaving early.

"To see an antique side table for the foyer. I found this little antique shop in Felton where they have authentic antique furniture from Italy. The marble on the tabletop looks just like the marble Kyle is painting on the columns," her voice went up in excitement. "I want to get your opinion before I decide whether to purchase it. I'll pick you up at three."

I worked on the railing for a couple hours. Theda returned to the villa. I was washing paint off my hands in the kitchen sink when she found me.

"Will I have time to change my clothes before we go shopping?"

"Sure, we have lots of time. I thought we might dine in Boulder Creek on our way back home. The Brewery, Scapozzi's or Hoffman's?"

"I'll have to think it over. They're all good. Who would think one little town would have so much good food available."

"And we haven't even tried the Pizza Grotto," she said.

"I'll check on my painters and meet you at the cabin?"

"That would be wonderful. Ciao." Theda took a couple steps and turned back. "I almost forgot to tell you, Bob called to say they're going back to Santa Cruz a little earlier than planned. Something about a skin diving trip." Not a big shock there. Boulder Creek was just too tame for the likes of my folks.

"Thanks for the message, Theda."

I found my worker bees busy as ever. I wished Allie and Kyle a happy weekend and reminded them that we would finish our painting Monday. We had mixed feelings about the job ending. Mungers' Mountain was a very special place when bad things weren't happening. I walked to my temporary transportation.

Hawks soaring overhead had nothing on me. My view of the various mountain ranges, in all directions, was as good as theirs. The sun was still high when I left the mountain top. As the little Ford entered the deep shade of the forest, I thought I saw something running through the under brush. My eyes hadn't adjusted to the dim light yet and whatever it was disappeared into a thicket.

As the Ford bumped its way down the steep grade, I applied the brakes to slow the car down. They held for a minute, and then there were no brakes no matter how hard I pushed, pumped, stomped, screamed. I was practically standing on the brake peddle as the car gained speed. I cranked the wheel hard to the right, then quickly to the left, careening around a hairpin turn. A couple wheels went up the side of the bank narrowly missing a redwood tree.

Everything seemed to be happening in slow motion while my brain sorted out my options at high speed, including lots of prayer.

If I had owned the Ford for awhile, I would have known automatically how to shift down, but this was an automatic and I had never bothered to look at anything beyond PARK, DRIVE and REVERSE. I grabbed the automatic gear shift and pulled it toward my seat with all my strength. Other than a terrible grinding noise, that remedy didn't help. I yanked the parking brake to the ON position. Nothing.

Blood pounded through my veins as I barely missed going over the side of a crumbly little bank that would have dropped me into the river far below. I overcorrected and ran up a four-foot bank on the other side. The car became airborne for a second just before it hit the off-road, mulchy ground and slid over fallen leaves that were slick as snot. The Ford fishtailed from side-to-side, always downward and gaining speed. My job at that point was to try to miss the trees, never mind the gullies and bushes, and just keep steering, praying and screaming.

I began to think about departed loved ones, wondering if I would see them soon. I had a vision of Marty ushering me through the pearly gates.

Suddenly the Ford broke threw the underbrush onto a level clearing where the Munger barn used to stand. If the barn hadn't burned, I would have traveled straight through it to the other side. Since it wasn't there to stop me, the car rolled across the ashes and did a face plant in a knee-high rain ditch. Fortunately the car had slowed and couldn't jump the gully. I was stunned and practically smothered by an ornery airbag that exploded on my chest like a lead balloon shot from a cannon.

The engine clunked once and died. All was quiet except for Theda who ran from the cabin, shrieking and flailing her skinny arms. Like Wonder Woman, she yanked the battered door open.

"Josephine, what in the world ... I heard a terrible noise ... oh dear, are you OK?"

I ran a checklist over my vital parts and decided I was OK. Just shook up.

"I'm alright, but something's wrong with this car," I sputtered.

"How did you get here?" Theda gazed at the severely smashed little car, completely mystified. She reached inside to help me out, not an easy task when we were both shaking like palm leaves in a hurricane. I grabbed her hand and stood up for a second, only to crumple down on one knee. Theda pulled me up and braced my back with her arm until I could get my legs steadied enough to walk. I glanced back at the Ford with its snout buried in dirt and its backside in the air, wheels still spinning. An embarrassing position for a proud little car, I thought.

The slow motion in my head had ended when the car hit ground zero, but I was stuck with a dizzy sort of unreality. Did someone tamper with the brakes? But who, when and why? It wasn't Woody. He was in no condition to come back to work according to the Sentinel. They said he had a fractured scull. I was befuddled to say the least.

"How did you end up in the backyard?" Theda asked.

"I found a shortcut to the cabin," I giggled nervously as we stumbled along like sailors on leave, arm-in-arm to the cabin's front door. She helped me to the sofa and brought me a glass of cold water.

"Theda, I just want you to know, I didn't ask for it this time. No snooping around or anything. I just started to drive down the mountain and the brakes failed." She sat beside me, arms crossed, shaking her head.

"It must have hurt when you hit the rain ditch," Theda shuddered. "I can't even imagine what you've been through."

"The ditch was only one of a potful of ruts and gullies. Actually, I think I was lucky." Theda frowned.

"Lucky?" Her head cocked to one side.

"Yeah, I didn't fall into the river and end up like Chester, or worse," and then I remembered I wanted to follow up on him and ask a few more questions.

Theda slipped a small pillow behind my head and told me to rest my feet on her expensive sofa. My funky furniture, sure. Hers was different. She told me to do it, so I did. I sipped some water and relaxed as much as anyone could under the circumstances while Theda called 911. Solow sat with his chin resting on my knee, shivering.

Chapter Twenty-one

The clock on the mantle ticked slowly as I waited for an officer to answer Theda's call. Even her comfy couch couldn't ease my aches and pains caused by the runaway rental car. But I knew I was lucky to be alive.

"A sheriff will be here within the hour," Theda reassured me.

"Good thing the donut shop closes at five," I said. She laughed.

"You don't really think they sit at the donut shop all day, do you?"

"Don't mind me. I'm just feeling a bit cynical right now." Like, what good is law enforcement when they haven't come up with any bad guys? Even I, common citizen Josephine, had some ideas and clues. I just couldn't prove anything. Theda sipped a cup of tea and stared into space.

"I'm sorry I messed up your shopping trip," I said. "Will the store be open tomorrow? Maybe you could call and have them hold the table for you."

"Oh gracious, don't worry about that silly old table." Just then there was a knock at the door. Theda opened it and to our great surprise, Sergeant Machuca stood ready, yet again, to serve the Munger household.

"Afternoon, ladies," Machuca did a little bow. Just what we needed, a sarcastic public servant.

"We didn't expect you so soon. Would you like to see the crash site?" I offered.

"Show me the way," he said with a cheerful smirk. Theda and I looked at each other wondering when he would take us seriously, if ever. She still looked pale and I wasn't very steady on my feet, but we escorted the sheriff to the wreck anyway. Solow lead the way.

Machuca's eyes suddenly looked more awake and his mouth dropped open as he studied the major damage on the Ford which was pushing up daisies in the backyard. He inspected the crumpled front end. The side mirrors had been ripped off and the roof was a mass of dents and scratches. A small tree branch had wedged itself behind the wiper blades, like the last spear thrown.

"How did this happen?" Machuca leaned over the vehicle for a better look. My anger gave me strength. I stood with my hands on my hips, just waiting for one smart remark from the sergeant.

"Someone must have tampered with my car. I attempted to drive down the mountain and my brakes failed," I said. Couldn't he see for himself what happened?

"The driveway's a hundred and fifty feet over there.

How did you end up way over here?"

"I had no brakes, but I managed to stay on the driveway for the first few turns. The car kept gaining speed and was out of control when it bounced over a bank, then slid all the way down to where you see it know."

"Are you hurt?" he asked, checking my paint spattered outfit for blood.

"No, I don't think so. Right now I'm so angry I can't tell if I'm hurt. That's red paint you're looking at." He looked away.

"Did you notice anything unusual when you entered the car?"

"No, but I saw someone or something running through the woods. It was kind of dark going into the shade. I couldn't make out what it was. Maybe it was a deer."

"Not much to go on," he said, pulling out his notepad. "How long was the car unattended?"

"Because of a previous mishap, my car was parked at the villa overnight."

"You get a lot of these mishaps, don't you?" He scribbled in his notebook.

"More than my share, I guess." I swatted a bee buzzing around my paint shirt as if it were a field of colorful flowers. Solow went into action, caught the bee in his teeth and crunch, no more bee.

"Do you feel well enough to show me where your car was parked overnight?"

"No problem," I said. We walked to the sheriff's car

and he opened the back doors for us, Theda on the left, me on the right and Solow in the middle. For the second time in a week we were sitting in the back seat of a cop car. I directed Machuca to the exact spot where my car had been parked, just a few feet from Alicia's Volvo. We climbed out and took a look. It didn't take a genius to figure out what kind of puddle we were looking at. The sergeant bent over, stuck his finger in the stuff and wrote something in his book.

"I'll take a sample to the lab, even though I'm pretty sure it's brake fluid." He proceeded to scrape some muddy fluid into a baggie and then walked in a circle, head down, intensely looking for something, but he found nothing. Theda and I walked a wider circle.

"Got something!" I shouted, "Another cigarette butt. The guy must be a chain smoker." Machuca whipped out another baggie for the butt.

"Thanks, this might be a clue." I was steaming. Might be a clue? This guy couldn't find a clue if it was stuck up his nose. I decided it was a jungle out there. I would have to use my instincts to find answers and not hold my breath waiting for help.

The sergeant dropped us off at the cabin saying he would be in touch. Right, I thought, and you're probably hurrying back to the donut shop. I mentally slapped myself upside the head. "Get a grip, woman, he's just trying to do his job," I told myself.

"Josephine, why don't you take a nice Epsom salts

bath and then if you feel up to it, we'll go to dinner."

"Wonderful idea. Thanks." After a long bath and clean clothes I did feel better, so we headed into town, ready for some major Mexican food. As the SUV bounced its way down the curvy drive, I held onto the door with white knuckles, experiencing residual paranoia from my last car trip. Relaxing was out of the question.

The only parking available in Boulder Creek that Friday night happened to be at the library because it was closed. We piled out of the SUV and walked two blocks up Central Avenue to find standing room only at Hoffman's.

"Shall we stay or try another place?" Before Theda could answer my question, Mrs. Garcia found us and began chatting as she gathered menus.

"Good evening, Senoras. Eat ees good to see you." She motioned for us to follow her to a small table on the patio as the other groups of waiting people watched. I looked behind us wondering if we were getting special treatment and then realized the other people were in larger groups and harder to accommodate.

"Thank you, Senora," Theda said, over the loud party atmosphere. Three waiters gathered around a group of ten elderly women, all wearing red hats, sitting at a table in the center of the patio. The young waiters, wearing red bow ties and black jackets, banged spoons on metal cooking pots as they sang an odd version of Happy Birthday.

The ladies sang along, clapped and laughed, having more fun than old ladies should be allowed. One woman with a peacock feather in her red hat blew out the eight candles on her flan dessert.

"Theda, if I get to be that old, I'm not going to be afraid to make a fool of myself. The important thing is to have fun."

"Aren't these ladies remarkable?" she said.

"I believe they belong to a red hat organization," I said. "I've seen groups like this before." A young waiter walked up to our table.

"Norman, what a surprise," I said. "You're our waiter tonight?" The real surprise was how nice he looked in clean clothes.

"Hello, Josephine, Mrs. Munger. Yes, I'll be your waiter tonight." Every perfect white tooth was evident when he smiled. If I had been thirty years younger, I would have been seriously attracted to this tall, dark, Latin young man.

"Norman, dear, I'll have a crab quesadilla and a strawberry margarita please. Josephine?"

"Oh, I'll have the same with the salsa on the side."

"Thank you, ladies." He scribbled on his notepad, turned and went inside. The margaritas arrived in a flash. We sat and sipped, enjoying the jovial attitudes around us. The end of the work week party mood was contagious. My shoulders started to relax and I felt much better than I had earlier at the cabin. But as my thinking became a little clearer, I realized I didn't have a car or a ride home the next day.

"Theda, I hope you don't mind if I stay at the cabin tonight."

"Of course not. Warren and I will drive you home tomorrow."

"Actually, you can drop me at the Body Shop in Watsonville any time before two. My truck's ready to be picked up."

As Theda smiled peacefully, my brain slipped into overdrive and would not let me relax. I made mental lists of things to do and things to worry about. Number one on the list was, call Barry and tell him I wrecked another car. I made a mental note to stop thinking, chill out, enjoy the music and be thankful I was alive after a horrendous ride down the mountain, and I didn't mean Theda driving the Lexus.

"Warren will arrive late tonight," Theda said. "He has a lot of loose ends to take care of before he hands the business over to our new manager, Mr. Lowell. I can't believe we're finally going to move and live together like a real married couple again."

"I'm happy for you, Theda. It's a new beginning."

"You really think so?" she asked as a shadow of doubt swept across her face.

"Sure, look how much happier you are already."

"You're right, Josephine, and I choose to stay happy," she smiled and sipped her margarita. A few minutes later the food was served by our handsome waiter.

"Norman, did you work at the villa yesterday?" I asked.

"Yes. Actually, my last day was Thursday. Now this is my work until another job comes along. My mother wants me here, but I like construction work. I'm going to be a contractor someday."

"That's great," I said. "Back to Thursday, did you happen to see anyone hanging around my little maroon Ford parked in the field?"

"No, I don't remember seeing anyone," he glanced across the patio. "Excuse me, I need to go now." One of the red hat ladies had spilled her margarita. Norman used the towel on his arm to wipe up the pink ooze before it could run off the table onto her lap. The woman gushed her thanks and asked for a replacement drink. Norman took off for the kitchen just as his mother appeared by my side.

"Everything ees OK?" she asked as she checked to see if we needed more chips or salsa. She was decked out in a black peasant blouse and flower-patterned full skirt. Her silver loop earrings were even bigger than Theda's.

"We're fine, Mrs. Garcia," Theda said. "What a lovely skirt you're wearing."

"Gracious. Enjoy your dinner." She turned and followed Norman to the kitchen. I excused myself to go to the restroom, walked unnoticed behind them and darted into the powder room. From inside the tiny lavatory I heard Mrs. Garcia asking Norman about his conversation with me.

"Josephine just wanted to know if I saw anyone near

her car yesterday. I didn't and that's what I told her. What does it matter?" Norman sounded perplexed.

"Nora tell me not to talk to dose people. I don't want no trouble, you know?"

"What's the big deal?" Norman asked his mother. "Woody's not even working at the mansion anymore." The conversation ended.

I sneaked out of the restroom as soon as I thought the Garcia's were gone. Unfortunately, I didn't wait long enough. I walked a few paces behind Norman as he carried a tray of food toward the patio. Suddenly he stopped and turned to grab a fresh towel from a busboy. I didn't stop in time and ended up with steaming hot chili verde splashed on my pink blouse.

"Oh .... Wow! That's hot!" I wailed. Norman was ten shades of red as he briskly scrubbed my chest with a towel. His mother heard my squeals and came running.

"My dear, are you hurt? Dees ees so bad. Norman no mean to do dees." She pulled me into the tiny one-seater powder room and began scrubbing my blouse with wet paper towels. My favorite pink top had green down the front. After much effort, it became a light green stain. She grabbed more towels and proceeded to rub the bajeezus out of my shirt, leaving the material thinner, but dry.

"I tink you pretty good now?" she smiled at the thought of me not suing her.

"Don't worry," I said, "the blouse is fine and I don't think I'm burned, so I'll just go back and finish my dinner."

She opened the door and followed me out to the hallway where Theda was pacing.

"I was beginning to wonder where you were," Theda said, staring at my blouse.

"Just a little unexpected chili verde." I noticed a few beans on my left shoe. A couple shakes of the foot and, voila. "Let's finish eating and go for a walk."

"That would be lovely, Josephine." The sun hung low in the sky when we finally left Hoffman's and headed up Central Avenue. A refreshing breeze cooled the air and encouraged us to keep walking the four blocks to the other end of town, giving me enough time to convince Theda we should stop by The Brewery for dessert.

We walked into the restaurant and looked around. The bar stools were all taken, but one table was empty. Summer greeted us with her usual gush of chatter and pointed to the table against the back wall right next to Stan's favorite table. Stan was hunched over, sucking the froth off a full mug of beer.

"Evening, Stan," I said, as I dropped a Wildbrush business card on his table.

"Ladies," he said, looking like he hadn't shaved in several days.

"Would you like to join us at our table?" I smiled warmly.

"Why? Is your table better'n mine?"

"I just thought it would be conducive to friendly conversation," another smile.

Before Stan could answer, Annie arrived with menus and water.

"Annie, dear, we only need a dessert menu," Theda said. Annie turned to the back of one of the menus and pointed to the sweets and coffees.

"I'll just have a little chocolate mousse with a cup of decaf," I said.

"I'll have the same, please." Theda was probably as stuffed full of crab quesadilla as I. Annie took off for the kitchen.

"Stan, want to join us for dessert?" I asked, with total charm. He took a swig of beer and contemplated his mug for a minute.

"What is it you're after now? Can't a man drink in peace?"

"Stan, I think we're on the same side of certain issues, except I don't know where your son, Woody, stands." I watched as Theda's attention seemed to wander from the conversation. Again, I wondered why I cared so much and she so little.

"Woody's Nora's son and Annie's half brother. I'd appreciate it if you wouldn't mention his worthless name around here again." Stan sat up straight and took another swig of beer.

"Have you heard anything about Chester? Is he out of the hospital yet?"

"He might be," Stan growled. "Might be at the rehab on Mission Street." Annie served our mousse and coffee.

"Can I get you anything else?" Annie asked, glancing at her dad. I watched him send a smile back to her.

"We're fine, dear," Theda said.

"Annie, if you ever need help or anything," I whispered, "just call me, OK?" I handed her my card. She dropped it in her pocket and walked to the backroom. By the time we finished our dessert and coffee, all four of the towns streetlights were on and Mac's Bar was in full swing. A full silver moon hung brilliantly over the town like an Ansel Adams photograph. I wondered what David was doing at that moment.

Our walk back to the library took us across the entrance to the infamous dark alley between Bates Realty and the Candle Boutique. We stopped in our tracks as agonizing moans and groans traveled up the passageway. The cries seemed to be coming from a dumpster at the other end of the alley. Theda grabbed my arm and we timidly walked with baby steps down the narrow drive, wondering what kind of animal would make those pitiful sounds. Theda tugged at my arm.

"Look, someone's shoe ... foot ... leg. Oh, my!"

"Who's there?" I tried to sound bigger and braver than I was. The moaning stopped. We peeked around the dumpster and were surprised to see a young man sprawled on the blacktop, a trail of blood running down the side of his head. His shirt was torn and he held his ribs as if they were broken. The man's dark wavy hair was cut short. He was clean shaven and there was something familiar about him.

"Can we call an ambulance for you?" Theda asked, as she bent down close to his bloody face. The young man looked up.

"I'm Ok, just tripped over some ... ah, garbage." He reached for the dumpster and tried to stand up. Theda and I dropped our purses, grabbed his arms and pulled him up to his full six feet or more. As soon as he was up and steady, he grabbed his side. Sweat and blood ran down his alabaster face.

"You don't look so good," I said. "How can we help?"

"You can't. I mean, I don't need help." He pulled away from us and staggered across the alley into the evening shadows behind Bates Realty. My foot stumbled onto something lying on the asphalt. It was a wallet and when I picked it up, it flopped open in my hands. Since it was already open, I began looking for the name of the person who owned it. I found seven dollars, one business card from a local nursery with Series 700SN-Plus scribbled on the back and a door key in the change slot.

"Who carries only three things in their wallet and no identification?" I had never met anyone who didn't have at least one credit card. And where was the driver's license? I committed the Series 700SN Plus, and Tony's Nursery to memory before trying to return the wallet.

I followed the young man to the back of the building and checked out the parking lot, but he had disappeared. However, I did notice a certain rusty Dodge truck parked in the lot, all the more reason to get out of there, pronto. My heart pounded as I hurried back to the dumpster and dropped the wallet where I found it. He would be back.

Theda followed my hurried steps without question, her teeth chattering loud enough to wake the dead.

"Do you know who that poor man was?" she stammered.

"No. Do you?"

"Something about him looked familiar. But no, I don't know who he is, really," she said. I had a hunch, but kept it to myself.

We took a brisk walk to the library parking lot and wasted no time getting out of town. The SUV bucked its way up the mountain to the cabin where my sweet hound dog greeted us with a howl, much tail wagging and a bit of good-natured slobber. I took him for a short moonlight walk before we hit the sack.

A funny idea popped into my head as I lay on my bed watching the full moon from my window. I thought of David looking at the same moon and stars at the same moment in time. It was a silly thought.

Chapter Twenty-two

Even before I opened my eyes I recognized the smell of Warren's coffee. He must have arrived Friday night after I went to bed. It was great to have him working in the kitchen. Solow sniffed the air and picked up on the pancakes. I wondered if David ever made pancakes. It really didn't matter because we both enjoyed the pancake breakfasts at the Grange.

I showered, dressed and shuffled into the kitchen.

"Good morning, guys," I said, with a yawn.

"Good morning, Josephine. Care for a short stack with sausage on the side?"

"You betcha," I replied as Warren loaded my plate and poured a cup of coffee for me. "Thanks, looks great." Solow thought so too. He sat next to Warren's foot, his bloodshot eyes following the spatula. Theda put her fork down and looked at me.

"Remember the injured young man ... I thought I recognized?"

"Sure. Did you remember something?"

"He's older now and his face was bloody last night, but I know who it is. I believe it was the youngest McFee brother, Kenneth."

"He didn't look or act mean like his brothers," I said. "I wonder who beat him up." I chewed on my sausage and tried to visualize the three men as brothers. They did have similar features and dark hair, but Kenneth was different somehow. It wasn't just the short haircut or the boyish face. The youngest brother was cleaner, smelled better and I sensed he was full of sadness. Warren listened to us yammer on and finally got a word in.

"You girls get into way too much trouble. Good thing I'll be around from now on." Theda, looking lovely in her chambray pant suit, smiled and he winked back at her.

"Warren and I were talking, and we thought we would try to visit Chester on our way to Watsonville." Theda patted her lips with her napkin. "We might even have time to see the antique table in Felton. What do you think Josephine? Are you in a hurry to get home?"

"No, not at all, but I do need to pick up my truck before two."

"Don't worry, you won't be late," Warren smiled. I packed my two suitcases, my dog and his box of doggie stuff and said good-bye to Emily's room. Half an hour later we arrived at the antique shop in Felton. Only one thing wrong -- the table was gone and Theda was heartbroken. She asked the hippie-looking woman at the counter if the table had been sold.

"Sorry, ma'am, I just sold it to Abram's Antiques down the street." She pointed west. "They're open today."

"Thank you," Theda said, instantly happy again. We walked the two blocks and found Abram's door locked with a sign posted. Open Saturday twelve to five. Solow raised his leg and left his mark on the locked door, expressing my feelings exactly.

Since we only had a half hour to wait, I suggested we have an iced tea across the street at the cafe. A large redwood tree shaded the outdoor tables and lifted and cracked the sidewalk with its roots.

"That would be lovely," Theda said. And it was. We had a perfect place to sit and watch the people of Felton go about their business. I had always been an over-curious people watcher. It could have been worse. I could have been an ax murderer. Twenty minutes later we watched an elderly gentleman unlock Abram's door and go inside. We shadowed him in the door.

"It's here, look. Do you like it, Warren? Josephine?" Theda was so happy with the table that there was no way we would say anything bad about it. Actually, it was perfect for the foyer with its long, pristine marble top. Warren and I gave it a good review.

"It's beautiful," Warren assured her. Theda grinned from ear-to-ear. Of course, the table cost twice as much at Abram's, but no one seemed to care. Arrangements were made for delivery. We walked back to the Lincoln and Warren drove us to Santa Cruz.

"Next stop, Chester on Mission Street," Warren announced as he parked. We left Solow in the car and entered the large, two-story stucco building for people needing physical therapy and other services. Stan was right. Chester was on the nurse's roster and sat in a wheelchair waiting his turn with a young and pretty physical therapist.

"Jeez, what are you guys doing here?" Chester's eyes were bright, but his leg and arm were still in casts. The scabs on his face had healed, but a metal brace held his head in a straight-ahead, no-nonsense position.

"Chester, old boy, some vacation you're having with all these nurses to care for you." Warren winked and Chester chuckled weakly.

"Yeah, right. I'm thinkin' of breakin' outa' here soon as I can. Got a score to settle." Warren laid a hand on Chester's shoulder.

"Take it easy, cowboy. Let the justice system work."

"What justice?" Chester grumbled. Theda stepped forward.

"Chester, dear, I just want you to know how much we appreciate the work you did for us," she gave him a sweet smile.

"Thank you, Mrs. Munger, and thanks for the check."

"It was the least we could do," Warren said.

"Chester, you're looking better than the last time I saw you," I said.

"Yeah, I'm peachy keen."

"So let me get this straight -- you hired Norman so he

could find out who was making trouble, like dropping a tile through the ceiling close enough to scare the bajesus out of all of us." Warren creased his eyebrows together as he eyed his wife, but she seemed more interested in the various therapeutic sessions going on around the gymnasium-sized room. Chester cleared his throat.

"Norman figured it was Woody making trouble because he's a friend of the McFees, not to mention he's a slime ball who's been in trouble before. I fired Woody, but a week later, Norman convinced me we should take him back and try to catch the creep in the act. Last Wednesday I rehired Woody. That night Damon and George found me at Mac's and told me I should look for work elsewhere. I said I'd think about it. That wasn't good enough for them, so they beat the tar outta' me and later ran me off the road."

"Were they mad at you for firing Woody or for rehiring him?" I stepped closer to hear his weak voice.

"I think they thought I knew too much, but the truth is, I don't know what's going on with that bunch." Chester backed his wheelchair away from me. I followed.

"Do you know anything about the youngest McFee brother, Kenneth?" Theda heard my question and turned her head, listening to Chester's answer.

"Not much, except that he's kind of a wimp. Always does what his bully brothers tell him. Damon and George practically raised the kid since he was ten years old. I doubt if he can think for himself." Just then a tall muscled brunette in a tight sweat outfit walked up to Chester's chair and told him it was time to go to work. She turned the chair toward the weight machines. We quickly said our good-byes. I checked my watch. It was one-forty.

"Warren, we'll have to step on it if I'm going to be in time to get my truck." We dashed to the Lincoln, Warren made a quick exit out of the parking lot and we arrived in front of the Body Shop at one-fifty-seven. I saw Miss. Hickey watching for us out the window. Her day was about to be ruined. I went in alone.

"Hi, I'm Jo ...."

"Josephine, your truck's ready," she handed me the keys and asked for the keys to the Ford. I handed them to her.

"I'm afraid the Ford had a malfunction. It's not here today."

"A what?" she was not in the mood to be jerked around.

"Actually, someone drained the brake fluid out of the Ford and I drove it into the ground." She gave me a blank stare. "It crashed. All messed up. Dead car." I made the sign of the cross. "You can get a report from the sheriff's department. Ask for Sergeant Machuca," I smiled. Her mouth was still in the gaping mode when I turned and walked outside to claim my pickup.

Back at the Lincoln, Warren was pulling my luggage out of the trunk. I held up my keys and told him the Mazda was ready to roll. He hoisted the two suitcases into the bed of the truck and pulled the metal bed-top down. I hiked Solow into the passenger seat. He seemed a bit reluctant to trade comfort and luxury for primitive travel in a bumpy old truck. I didn't feel that way at all. I was very happy to see my truck in perfect condition.

"We'll see you Monday?" Theda said, as we hugged good-bye.

"I'll be there, don't worry. Bye." I rounded the truck, climbed in and turned the key. We were a family again, me, Solow and my little red Mazda. I decided to stop at the grocery store and get a fresh supply of the basics, such as ice cream and chocolate syrup. I was halfway to the market when I noticed the fuel light was on. My first thought was of Miss. Hickey and the mechanic taking a joy ride and using up all my gas. Then I did a mental slap on the head for always being so suspicious.

I coasted into the closest gas station. The prices were not competitive with the rest of Watsonville, but I couldn't be choosey. I pumped twenty dollars worth of gas and the needle barely moved. My next stop was the grocery store. Because it was Saturday afternoon, the store was packed with shoppers. I couldn't believe my eyes when I saw Robert at check stand two ringing up groceries.

"Robert, you've been promoted."

"Hi, Jo. I've been checking for three days now. It's really easy except for produce codes, food stamps and coupons."

"Looks like you can handle it. What's new?" Robert

rang up my groceries as he talked.

"Did you read about that guy in Boulder Creek? The one who wrapped his Humvee around a tree with his mother sitting in the car beside him? Sounds like he's in serious condition."

"Is that all the news from the valley?"

"Why? Did I miss something?"

"Oh, no. I was just wondering if I missed anything newsworthy."

It was late afternoon when I rolled up the driveway and stopped in front of my precious little house, where marigolds looked perky in their window boxes, thanks to David feeling sorry for them. I lugged my suitcases and groceries inside, leaving the front door open. Solow stretched out on his porch bed as if he hadn't rested in a long time. The message machine blinked its little red light until I pushed the button.

"Hi, honey." It was Mom's voice. "We're home now. We have some underwater pictures to show you next time you visit. Dad sends his love. See you soon?"

I put the groceries away and made myself a snack, a cinnamon bagel with cream cheese and pumpkin butter. I flipped through the phone book, found Tony's Nursery in Ben Lomond and dialed.

"Yeah, Tony here."

"Hello. I was wondering if you have any series 700SN-Plus?"

"Who is this? You don't sound like one of my regulars."

I could tell he was ready to hang up.

"Kenneth wanted me to call. Do you have it?"

"Kenneth bought some last spring. What's going on here? Who are you?"

"Just a friend. Bye." I decided to call my cousin Candy at her florist shop in Santa Cruz.

"Candy's Fabulous Flowers."

"Candy, this is Josephine. How are you?"

"Hi, Jo. Good to hear your voice. What's up?"

"I just have a couple gardening questions for you. My gardening skills are pretty limited, as you know. Actually, my neighbor waters the marigolds for me."

"OK, shoot."

"A friend of mine wants to know about Series 700SN-Plus?"

"Good God, Jo. Is your friend growing marijuana?"

"No, of course not. Do you know if this stuff is good for anything else?"

"Sure," she said. "It's fertilizer used for agriculture. Around Santa Cruz County it's known for its beneficial properties in the 'weed' industry."

"Thanks, Candy. You've been a big help. See ya." I hung up before she could say another word. I didn't want to tell her anymore, as it might have leaked to my folks and I hated it when that happened, especially weird stuff involving marijuana. I called David.

"Hello, David. It's Josephine. I forgot what time Monica's party starts tomorrow."

"Three. I'm glad you're planning to come. Monica will love seeing you." There was a bit of a silence on the line. "Would you like to go with me to a concert in the park tonight?" David's offer sounded good. Some nice music might help me to relax.

"I'd love to go. What time?"

"Pick you up at eight." We hung up. I threw a load of clothes in the wash and tried to think of a gift for Monica. Suddenly I remembered a special gift from my grandmother I had treasured since I was Monica's age, a tea set with miniature china cups and saucers, and a teapot to match. I loved the set when I was a child, and as an adult, I had kept it for the daughter I never had. I was excited to have solved the birthday present problem, except I couldn't remember where the china was stored.

I rummaged through two closets looking for the blue-satin box which held each piece of china safely in its own niche. I decided to check the loft where I stored items I could not throw away because of the memories attached to them.

The loft closet was a deep walk-in stuffed with eight cardboard boxes stacked floor to rafters against one wall. I pulled down the boxes and dragged them into the main room, one at a time.

The first box was full of stuffed animals. It was way to hard to throw away my 'stuffies' from childhood. I thought about Mr. Vandiveer and how happy he was to finally let go of his animal collection. I sorted through the pile of button-eyed, fury animals, trying to remember each of their names. Whitey, Bert, Blacky, Spot. The ones I couldn't name, I put in a separate pile. They would be given to the Salvation Army. Wow! That felt good.

The next box held a pink-satin prom dress and my wedding dress, both sealed in plastic bags for eternity. The rest of the box was stuffed with size-six clothing favorites that served no purpose. Somewhere, a size-six young woman might really enjoy the retro, back-in-style threads. I dropped the two special dresses into the Whitey and Bert box. The rest I would give away.

In just a couple hours I had found the set of china for Monica, filled three boxes for the Salvation Army and restacked four boxes of sentimental stuff. I felt like I had just lost ten pounds and been given the Medal of Honor.

Somehow I ended up with one empty cardboard box which worked out nicely. Monica's gift went in first and then I opened a package of balloons from my party supply and blew up seven of the red ones. The balloons filled the cardboard box and cushioned the blue, silk-covered box of china nicely. I taped the flaps closed and attached a big pink bow to the top. I checked my watch. There was barely enough time to clean up and gulp a protein shake before David would arrive.

Promptly at eight, David showed up looking smart, but casual in a baby-blue golf shirt and khaki Dockers. I wore deep-blue peddle pushers, a white tank top, matching blue cardigan and a milkshake mustache. David leaned down and wiped it away with his thumb.

"Guess you've had dinner," he said.

"Have you?"

"Sure. Let's go to town before all the seats are taken. I see your truck is back."

"Oh no!" I hadn't meant to say that but it just leaked out.

"What's wrong?"

"Nothing, I just remembered I forgot to call Barry, my insurance adjuster. I'll leave him a message tomorrow. No problem." Good, David didn't ask what that was about. I hated to worry him, but I would probably tell him the Ford story someday.

David's little convertible delivered us to the community park in Watsonville where the orchestra was already warming up. We found a place to sit on one of the many rows of wooden benches. David brought a wool blanket from the trunk of his car and draped it over our legs. Most of the audience had blankets and thermoses of hot drinks to ward off the chill of the evening fog. Warm evenings happened in September and October, not July.

David put his arm around my back to keep me warm. The music went from classical to semi-classical to jazz. I was entertained and happy. After two hours of sitting on a cold, hard bench, the concert ended and I was happy again … to be leaving.

We fought our way through traffic to the freeway and headed inland. Aromas was fog free and comfortably warm -- ice cream weather, actually. We stopped at Ducky Deli for one banana split with two spoons and two cups of decaf.

"When do you think you'll finish the Munger job?" David asked.

"Monday's our last day of work. Can you believe it? I'll miss the mountains and the Mungers, but life there can be a little hectic." More than David would ever know, I thought.

"I'll be glad when you're finished. Fluffy misses you and Solow," he winked at me. His last remark was open to interpretation.

"Well, we miss Fluffy." I winked back at him and he laughed.

"Anything exciting happen up there in the woods?"

"Not much. The mansion seems almost vacant without the hoards of workmen. Just about everything's done, and today and tomorrow the driveway is being paved. A month late if you ask me," I yawned. "Sorry, I'm just so relaxed."

"Come on. Let's get you home." He opened the car door for me and I scooted into the passenger seat. I was tired, but I wasn't anxious for the evening to end. It seemed like I was always in my comfort zone when I was with David. He didn't walk me to the door, so I waved goodnight into the headlights and coaxed my hound into the house. Solow went straight from the porch doggie bed to the bedroom doggie bed. I heard him snoring from the living room just minutes later. The message machine was flashing so I pushed the talk button. A barely familiar voice took me by surprise.

"I need to ... ah, sorry, can't talk now ..." and the message stopped. The voice conjured up a picture in my mind of a young man hurt and bleeding. How did Kenneth get my number and why was he calling? Maybe he dialed a wrong number, but he would have heard my greeting, "It's, Jo. Leave a message at the beep." He would have to know it was my number.

I sat by the phone in case Kenneth called again, but my head was so heavy and my eyes wouldn't stay open, so I finally went to bed. I no sooner put my head on the pillow, than I was asleep, dreaming sweet dreams.

Shortly after midnight the phone on my nightstand rang. At first the ringing was part of my dream, the part where milk cows were ringing their bells and asking for treats. Finally, the dream faded and I picked up the receiver.

"Hello?"

"You don't know me, but don't hang up. You helped me in the alley last night."

"I remember. Is your name Kenneth?"

"Yeah, how did you ... anyway, I need help real bad and I couldn't think of who to call until I talked to Annie. She thought you might me able to help. She says you're always getting in the middle of everything."

"Well, if you're a friend of Annie's, I guess I can try.

What do you want?"

"It's kind of complicated. Can you meet me Sunday night at eleven?"

"Jeez Louise, I live in Aromas."

"Sorry, I didn't know you lived so far away. I really need you to come to Boulder Creek," his voice cracked.

"How do I know you're not luring me up there just so you can run me off the road or blow up my truck?"

"I guess you've met my brothers."

"The hard way. I hope you're different, Kenneth. I don't even know you and I don't know why I don't just hang up." But I didn't hang up because I thought I heard sincerity in his voice, not to mention desperation.

After an uncomfortable silence, Kenneth said, "The truth is, we need help and please say you'll be here tomorrow night."

"So who's, we? I thought this was about you."

"Someone else is involved, but I can't tell you about it on the phone. My three minutes is almost up. Meet me at the entrance to the Munger's driveway, Eleve ...." An operator came on the line.

"Your three minutes are up." Guess I won't be calling him back, I thought. The phone booth could be anywhere. I checked my phonebook for Annie and Stan's number.

"Bates, in Felton, that's it!" Solow eyed me, but my excitement was not contagious. He went back into a deep doggie coma. A grumpy male voice answered the phone.

"Yeah, what?"

"Hi. I want to speak to Annie," I said, sweetly.

"I know who this is. You woke me up, ya know. She's not home yet." Slam!

"It never hurts to try," I said into a dead phone. I was wide awake and needing food for thought, ice cream to be exact. The ice cream was vanilla, so I squirted chocolate syrup and sprinkled chopped peanuts and baby marshmallows on top. It would all go to my hips, but I would be asleep in no time.

I thought about driving to Boulder Creek Sunday night. What a ridiculous thing for anyone to ask me to do, but I knew I would do it. Kenneth's voice echoed through my mind as I climbed into bed and stared at the ceiling. He had pleaded for help. I remembered his handsome young face from the night before, bloody and terrified. I couldn't let him down.

The real question was, how would I handle Kenneth at eleven in the evening and then go to work the next morning? I imagined myself driving home from Boulder Creek at one in the morning and then getting up six hours later to get ready for work. I would do it. After all, I had only one more day of work and I would be able to rest for a nice long time, until I landed another mural job.

I was dreaming again. My dream turned dark and all the cows exploded, leaving their bells chained around my neck. I waited for my turn to explode.

Chapter Twenty-three

A t first I thought I had dreamt Kenneth's call. When my head cleared and I opened my eyes, I realized it had been a real phone call. Why hadn't I just said no? Why should I help a perfect stranger? And help him do what?

After a freshly perked cup of java, I felt better and began to go about the chores of the day. I changed the bed and threw clothes, sheets and towels in the washing machine while Solow caught up on his sleep.

I attached a card to Monica's present and reorganized my purse. I dumped the contents onto my bed and sorted through scraps of paper, receipts and grocery lists. The important stuff -- penlight, lipstick, mirror, keys, firecrackers (I rolled my eyes), pepper spray, wallet and book of matches -- was all there. I added fresh Kleenex and stuffed everything back into my lovely alligator bag. The phone rang. I jumped.

"Hello." After a second of silence, a female voice came on the line.

"Josephine? This is Annie from The Brewery."

"Hi, Annie. How are you? Are you working today?"

"Actually, I have to work from four in the afternoon until midnight. That's why Kenny needs you. I would help if I could, but I have to work."

"So why is eleven o'clock so important?" I was bursting with curiosity.

"It's the only time he can get out without being noticed. It's a long story. He'll tell you tonight. You're going, aren't you?"

"I don't know the first thing about what's going on, and I don't understand why you can't tell me. If you were me, would you go?"

"All I can say is that it's important you show up. Life and death important. Kenny told me the whole story last night and asked if I would help him. There are a couple reasons why I can't."

"Is one of those reasons named Stan? Or is it Nora?"

"Something like that. Don't tell anyone. Please. And thank you for your help." She hung up. It would have been even harder to say no to Annie, than to Kenneth. I think they knew I was a sucker and couldn't stay away from trouble, especially other people's trouble. How in the world could I possibly be of help to that young man? Maybe he just needed a ride to the hospital. So, what are ambulances for?

I carried Monica's giant box down my driveway and up to David's party in his backyard, still thinking about Kenneth. Solow waddled along behind me.

"OK, big guy, practice your best party manners."

David took the box and greeted me with a kiss on the cheek. His son, Harley, red faced and dripping sweat, waved hello from the barbecue. The Randalls from across the street were there with their two boys, Dustin, five, and Casey, three, two of the most wired little towheads on the planet. Cake and ice cream would probably put them into orbit.

Dustin grabbed me around the knees, causing Monica's present to topple and land on its bow. I winced as I silently hoped nothing broke. Monica squealed when she saw me and tried to pull Dustin away so she could collect a hug. The little boy was having none of that. He let go of my leg with one hand and pushed Monica backward into the pond with his other hand.

David was quick to react. He lifted Monica up over the rocks and set her down in my open arms, dripping wet. She whimpered a couple times and then decided to get down and retaliate. Dustin ran behind his mother.

"Time for a ceasefire," I said, scooping Monica back into my arms. I carried her into the house, squirming and soaked up to her armpits.

"Monica, your pretty dress is all wet. Let's put on something dry, OK?"

"OK, Auntie Jo." I put her down and she led me through the house to her little pink princess suitcase. We agreed on a pink two-piece shorts outfit. She looked adorable with her curly red hair in pigtails, tied with pink ribbons. Her deep blue eyes and cherub smiles melted my heart.

We walked back to the picnic table where David sat with the neighbors discussing a car show coming to town. No one seemed to notice that Dustin had climbed to the top of the waterfall and his little brother was close behind.

"Look!" Monica yelled and pointed at the boys. Revenge was sweet. We high-fived each other as the parents caught up to the boys and lifted them down. I felt like Monica must have been my daughter in another life. David smiled when he saw his granddaughter in her dry clothes and me in my wet ones.

"Monica, do you think it's time to open your presents?"

"Yes, Grandpa, I can do it myself." I placed the big cardboard box at Monica's feet. She immediately ripped the bow off, and David helped her tear the box open. She pulled out the balloons and then dove head first into the box. She squirmed around and stood up with the box of china in her chubby little hands.

"What's this, Auntie Jo?"

"It's a tea set, honey. Go ahead and open it." Monica examined the contents of the satin-lined box.

"Baby dishes," she laughed and handed them to David. I noticed that none were broken ... yet.

"Thank you, Auntie Jo." A minute later the three children where in, out and all over the box as if it were the best play structure ever invented. Fluffy pranced around the box, her tail waving. Solow jumped up and started the chase, accidentally knocking Casey on his butt. The boy cried and his mother took him home for a nap. Monica and Dustin continued their play while the cat ran circles around the dog. In all the excitement, I finally noticed David staring at me.

"Something bothering you, Josie? You look like you're a million miles away."

"Who, me? I'm fine. I was just thinking about the Munger job," I said. David was so perceptive. I batted my eyes and tried to look calm, but my insides had the jitters. Why had I agreed to help Kenneth?

"How about a cold lemonade?"

"Thank you, David. That would be perfect." I watched the kids play with the red balloons while David went to the kitchen. My eyes were looking in their direction, but my brain was fifty miles away, somewhere in the dark redwood forest. It was hard for me to stay in the moment, even with these favorite people around me. David returned with a couple lemonades. We clinked our glasses.

"To my dear friend and neighbor," I said.

"May she always be near," he added. I wondered if the heat in my cheeks meant they were red.

After the barbecued chicken and sausages came the cake, a Safeway special, but thrilling to Monica with its plastic storybook characters on top. She easily blew out the four candles and then licked the frosting off each one.

After dessert, Harley carried the cardboard box into the living room where Dustin and Monica played for hours. The four adults settled into a game of scrabble.

"Harley, where does your name come from?" I asked.

"It's a nickname from my wilder years," he said. "Where do you think Dad got those gray hairs?"

"You got that right," David laughed. I saw the love and pride in the father's eyes, reflected in Harley's. I checked my watch from time to time, feeling nervous because evening was upon us and I had a weird commitment to deal with. At nine I faked a yawn and excused myself and Solow. David walked us home with his flashlight and saw me to the front door. As we stood under a full moon, he pulled me close and planted a brief, but sensual kiss on my lips.

"Thanks for coming to the party," he smiled.

"I wouldn't have missed it for anything," especially that last part! Wow. My heart was doing a fast rumba. It was the kind of kiss you never forget as long as you live.

I floated into the house, turned in the doorway and watched the light from David's flashlight waggle down the driveway. Part of me wanted to run after him and invite him back to my house. The realist in me said, "No, you don't need complications. Besides, you already promised to help someone and a promise is a promise, even if you don't know anything about this guy or his problem." I had to admit, my curiosity was peaked, but with a sense of foreboding.

Solow never made it into the house. He crashed on his porch bed, so I brought a bowl of kibble outside and set it where he would see it. Actually, he was probably so full of cake he wouldn't need to eat till morning.

It was almost ten o'clock. I quickly changed into Levis, a green knit top and tennies, turned out the lights, grabbed my gator bag and flipped on the porch light. I said good-bye to Solow and told him to secure the ranch. I don't think he heard me.

The drive south was easy, not much traffic, and I knew the way by heart. My mind was in Boulder Creek long before my truck pulled into the wide spot in the road just before the Munger's driveway. I killed the engine, turned off the lights and cranked my window down halfway so I could listen to the night.

Crickets chirped as the silvery moon rose above the trees. I looked around for another vehicle. A couple cars zoomed by, but no one stopped. Suddenly the crickets stopped their chirping mid-song. I turned my head to the left to look out the window and practically had a heart attack. A young man stood inches from my face.

"Sorry, did I startle you?" Kenneth whispered.

"I didn't see you coming. Where are you parked?"

"Nowhere. I'll explain later. Stay here a minute, I'll be right back." I watched Kenneth walk away from the truck toward the shadowy forest. He wore Levis and a black t-shirt, making it difficult for me to see him at all. It looked like he was doing something with tree branches, pulling them into a pile. He turned and ran back to my truck.

"OK, scoot over. I'll drive." Kenneth fired up the truck, flipped on the lights and made a sharp left straight into the forest. Once we were immersed in the shadows, he stopped the truck, jumped out, dragged tree limbs back across the road behind us and climbed into the driver's seat.

"Before we go any further, I need to know what's going on," I said. Kenneth didn't answer. He just drove. There was something about Kenneth that I trusted; and since he was driving, I had no choice in the matter. The narrow dirt road was basically flat except for deep left and right ruts which kept the tires centered like a train on tracks.

Tree branches slapped the sides of the pickup as we passed, like an automatic car wash without the soap and water. I cringed at the thought of all the scratches my truck was receiving. My patience was running out.

"I mean it," I stamped my foot. "How do I know you're not an ax murderer? Where are you taking me? This is Munger property, you know." Kenneth finally interrupted my rant.

"You're right, this is Munger property, but my brother's have a hard time dealing with that fact. They control what goes on down here. I'm just trying to save someone's life and I need your help." We were both quiet as the tires bounced along, caught in the grooves carved out by vehicles in rainy conditions. We made a long, slow left off the road into a clearing surrounded on three sides by giant redwoods and stopped. Kenneth motioned for me to get out. I decided to cooperate since I'd come that far, and besides, he sounded sincere and what else could I do?

"Follow me," Kenneth whispered. Each of his steps took him twice as far as mine so I had to practically run to keep up. No easy task on knee-high grass in the dark.

"Don't you have a flashlight? I have a little one in my purse." That was when I realized I had automatically grabbed my gator bag as we exited the Mazda.

"No flashlight. Keep your voice down," Kenneth warned. The meadow ended and we turned left on the rutty road that followed the contour of the base of Mungers' Mountain. I twisted my ankle in a rut I didn't see and whimpered out loud.

"I mean it. Keep it down," Kenneth hissed.

"No problem," I whispered back. I'll just hobble along and endure the pain, I thought. Just when I wondered how I could keep up with him, Kenneth stopped behind a tree at the side of the road. We both peeked around it, but I didn't know what we were looking for. He seemed to think it was OK to continue, so we left the road and walked slowly toward the side of the mountain where moonlight exposed a few giant timbers imbedded in a wall of earth and rock. Something about it reminded me of an old John Wayne western.

Kenneth reached up and pulled some cut tree limbs away from the side of the mountain, revealing more timbers and an entrance of sorts into what looked like an old cave or mine.

"Don't be afraid," he said, looking behind us and waving his arm for me to go in. I stepped through the opening, but he stayed outside. My heart skipped a beat and the slow motion panic began again as I looked around for another way out, just in case. The dim light from one candle hanging on the wall lit the interior almost as well as the moon lit the outside world. I smelled dank wood, stale air, and candle smoke. I saw a bench and a blanket, a couple buckets and a short stack of books. In one shadowy corner of the cave a person sat on a wooden box marked in big black letters, 'dynamite'.

"Hello ... you must be Josephine," the small voice said. At first I was startled, but after a couple words I realized the person was friendly and obviously female.

"Yes, but who are you?"

"You don't know me, but Kenneth tells me you work for my parents as an artist."

I moved across the room toward the young-sounding female. Finally I was able to make out her facial features and matted hair. A huge lump rose in my throat and stuck there. Tears fell freely, out of my control. I dropped my gator bag, fell down on one knee and stared into a face I had only seen in a photo.

"Oh my God! Emily?" I choked on the words. She smiled and began crying too. There was a noise at the entrance. I looked back in time to see Kenneth entering the cave, carrying an ax.

"What's going on?" he whispered. Guys have no clue why women cry. By that time, Emily and I were hugging and talking and paying no attention to the young man in the room. I was already imagining the reaction her parents would have, which made me cry all the more.

Suddenly I remembered that I had just seen an ax in Kenneth's hand. I stiffened as I stepped in front of Emily. Kenneth watched me and laughed.

"No, I'm not an ax murderer. This is for Emily." I was ready to panic until Emily put her right leg forward and rolled up her ragged jeans, exposing a strip of wide metal circling her ankle and welded to a heavy chain coiled on the floor behind her. The other end of the chain was wrapped around a timber and welded to itself. The old timbers were part of a structure that held the dirt walls in place.

The more I looked around, the more I believed we were in the entrance to a mine, maybe the gold mine mentioned in the newspaper article at the library. Candlelight reflected off three walls only. The space to my left was total blackness.

Kenneth leaned over and spread a couple feet of the steel chain into a straight line so that when he swung the ax it wouldn't clip Emily by mistake. Before I could prepare myself, he raised the ax and slammed it onto the chain. Upon close inspection, not much was accomplished. He tried again and again. It was almost impossible to hit the same spot twice, but after dozens of tries, one of the links fell away and Emily was left with eight inches of chain dragging behind her. Kenneth wiped his brow and dropped the ax on the dirt floor.

There was no time to rejoice. Emily's eyes grew big with fear as we heard men's voices, loud with drunken laughter, coming closer to the mine. Kenneth put one finger to his lips, made a dash for the door and walked out into the night.

"Hey, Kenny, get rid of the girl yet?" more laughing.

"Need some help Kenny? I got a knife and Damon's got a rifle."

"Hey, where's Thor?" Damon asked.

"Thor ran off chase'n a rabbit. I thought you guys were goin' to town to celebrate with Jose?"

"We been tah town," George laughed. "We de ... thided to come back and help you. If this thing don't git done, she could point the finner. Know what I mean?"

"Take it easy you guys. I'm taking care of it."

"Kenny, don't you need some extra muthle to tackle that little gal. Sides, we'd like to have some fun with her be ... fore it's too late," Damon laughed. George agreed they should all have some fun with her.

Emily grabbed my arm. Her hand was cold and shaky and there was a wild look in her eyes.

"Help me, please," she pleaded. My mind was already sorting things out as my heart raced and sweat ran down my spine. I dug in my purse for the penlight, found it and handed it to Emily along with the gator. I pointed to the dark end of the room.

"Go as far and as fast as you can," I whispered. She nodded and headed into the unknown. I pried open the dynamite box she had been sitting on, with pure adrenalin and several broken fingernails. I hoped and prayed that explosives didn't lose their strength with time. I pulled out two ancient sticks of dynamite.

I dragged the heavy wooden box across the floor, positioned it just short of the mine's entrance and shoved the two sticks of dynamite under the box with the fuses stretched out on the dirt floor. I grabbed the wall candle and lit the fuses. They both flamed and started to hiss. I heard Damon and George roaring with drunken laughter outside, badgering poor Kenneth and threatening to enter the mine.

"Got any more beer?" Kenneth asked, still trying to stall the brute brothers.

"Think we're gonna' share it with a good-fer-nuttin' like yer ... thelf?" Damon laughed.

"Why not, I do my share around here."

"You done a lot alright," George quipped, "made trouble for uth ... so big brothern' me gotta' take care of it." I heard Damon laughing at the top of his soggy lungs.

The McFee conversation faded out of my hearing range as I tore through the first fifty feet of the mine, tripping over rocks, wood and debris. The pounding of my heart was all I heard. The dim candle light wasn't much help, but I held onto it with a death grip, as the hot wax ran across my hand and dripped into a sea of darkness. The flame threatened to blow out at any moment, flickering like crazy whenever I moved too fast.

The dirt floor was no longer level. It had become a gentle slope, probably ending in China. Then it happened. An earsplitting blast reverberated through the cave, knocking me off my feet and sending me rolling down the rough slope. My candle was long gone and the roar of falling rocks and dirt surrounded me. I sat up, gulped some dusty air and thrashed at the dirt when it tried to cover my head. I went into a coughing fit, trying to rid myself of the dust in my lungs. And then all was quiet.

Once in a while a rock-hard piece of clay would fall from above and smash to pieces, but for the most part, the shakeup was over. I sat listening to complete silence. I called to Emily, swore at the dark and asked for help.

"Emily, can you hear me?" echoed through the tunnel. Then it was deathly quiet again. I worked at pushing dirt and small rocks off my body until I could stand. Stand on what, and where? I had no clue what to do next. There was only absolute darkness. I had successfully blown up the place, but hadn't thought of an exit strategy. I wondered if there would ever be an exit, after all, who knew where we were and did the McFees survive the explosion?

Something ran down the back of my neck. I touched it with my fingers and realized it was sticky and warm. Blood, most likely. Not much I could do about that. Various parts of my body announced they too were hurt and sore. I hoped Emily was alive. If she wasn't, at least it was a quicker death than the one planned by the two brothers. I said a fervent prayer for Emily and myself. In my mind I imagined the reaction to my death by the people I loved, David included.

Then I remembered the kiss. I sat in a pile of dirt with no hope of rescue, turning red over a kiss. I wished again that I had run after David and invited him into my house. Imagining the kiss and all that might have been was in stark contrast to the predicament I found myself in. I shuttered when I realized I might never see David again, or be able to tell him about feelings I was discovering I had.

Maybe it took an earthshaking event, like a mine blowing up, to clear the cobwebs out of my brain. But what good did it do if I was never found and just rotted into dust. Now I was really frightened, not to mention exhausted. I figured I'd better work on some constructive ideas in the realm of escape. I tried to picture digging out, but how does one dig out of a mine without help?

Finally, the exhaustion was too much and I crumpled to the ground and passed out.

Chapter Twenty-four

I awoke in darkness feeling pain in my body and grit on my teeth. Not the usual food grit, but dirt grit. Worse than a sandy picnic at the beach. My thinking was fuzzy at best as I contemplated people eating grits for breakfast. I loved waffles and sausage and Warren did a beautiful job making them. Warren and Theda came into focus.

Whoa, I suddenly remembered that Emily was alive; then I remembered blowing up the mine and I wondered if Emily survived the explosion. As I stared blindly into the dark cavern, my eyes strained to see something. Anything. I could barely see my own hand in front of my face, a hand that hurt like flesh on a hot iron. The candle wax had made its mark. My body was coated with dirt and my scalp was beyond gritty. I shook off a mountain of dirt, then stood up with great effort and shook again.

Ahead of me was a tiny ray of light coming from a two inch hole in the ceiling of the mine shaft. I figured it was an air hole and felt so grateful. God had sent me a stream of light with dust particles dancing in circles all the way down to the dirt floor.

"Emily? Emily, can you hear me?" No answer. I debated whether I should search for Emily deeper into the mine or head back to the entrance. The entrance won. Not an easy trek up hill and over tons of fallen dirt and rocks. I stumbled along for about twenty feet and came upon another ray of light coming from an air hole above me. I walked a couple more steps, stumbled, and fell over a pile of rubble.

As I tried to stand, my hand touched something soft and warm. I saw a delicate hand protruding from the pile of dirt under me and immediately rolled to one side. I stood up and saw Emily's head partly uncovered. Her lips moved, but no sound came out. My hands went to work clawing, scraping and shoving the dirt off her face and body.

"Jo ... sephine," she whispered, "I can't feel my legs."

"Hang on Emily." Only one obstacle lay in the way of her rescue. I uncovered a giant redwood beam resting against her shins, its other end still attached to the ceiling. I gave the beam a push. It didn't budge. I leaned into it with one foot. No luck. I gave it a shove with my shoulder, putting my weight behind it.

"No!" Emily groaned.

"Wait a minute, I'm going to try something." I would have given anything to have a two-hundred-pound paramedic helping us, not to mention a bulldozer. Instead, I found the largest rock I could lift, hefted it up and placed it beside Emily's right leg. The beam was pressing against her and her jeans didn't offer much protection.

I stood over Emily, my feet to the outside of hers, bent down and grabbed the splintery beam with my hands and half lifted, half pulled the thing until a portion of it rested on the rock. Her right leg still supported some of the weight. I gave it another try and finally freed the limb. One pant-leg was bloody below the knee. I ripped away some of the material as Emily tried in vain to stifle her moans.

"Why me?" I said to myself. I never wanted to be a nurse, but there I was, the only volunteer around. I rolled up her blood soaked pant-leg to reveal a palm size open wound. I fought the urge to throw up. John Wayne would have washed everything off with whiskey, but I was fresh out.

"I'm sorry, Josephine, for putting you through this."

"It's OK, Emily. I'm sorry I blew up the mine. I just didn't know what else to do." I decided to leave the injury alone since I couldn't think of a single thing to do for it. John Wayne would have ridden off into the sunset for the Doc, but we couldn't.

"Emily, are there any supplies in the mine, like water, food, medicine, anything?"

"I've never seen the rest of the mine, just the entrance area. I had a bucket of drinking water, a blanket and some apples Kenny smuggled in. He brought me food everyday, even though his brothers wanted me dead," she sniffled and wiped her eyes.

"Why did they want you dead?" I put my arm around her shivering shoulders.

"I know too much. I could send them to death row." Fear and anger gave me an adrenalin rush. I had to do something or burst.

"I'm going to see if I can recover anything from the entrance area. Just take it easy until I get back." I struggled up and over piles of dirt and rock until I came to the end of the line. Not the entrance to the mine, just the end of the line. A wall of rocks, dirt and fallen timbers stood between me and the entrance area. Ten strong men with shovels could have plowed through the pile in a couple days, but we didn't have men, shovels or days. Feeling hopeless, I turned back.

I found Emily sitting up, a good sign that nothing was broken. She looked up when she heard me shuffling through the debris.

"Josephine, did you blow up the box of dynamite?"

"You bet your sorry leg I did." I detected a small smile from Emily.

"Do you think Kenny's alive?" Her voice dropped off to a whisper.

"Sure. The blast was mostly inside the mine." I didn't want to believe my dynamite might have killed someone, especially Kenneth. I saw myself walking in chains to death row, unable to convince anyone it was self defense. I managed to put that picture out of my mind. I tried to be positive and pictured Kenny going for help.

"Emily, can you stand up?" I held one arm as she gingerly stood, wincing at the pain in her leg.

"The good news is, I can feel my legs. The bad news is, I can feel my legs," she half laughed, half cried as she took a couple steps. I was afraid to let go of her arm. "I'm good," she said. "I can do this."

"Emily, do you know if there's another way into the mine?"

"Kenny found a way in. He used it whenever he didn't want his brothers to see him visit me." We stared at the walls wondering if the alternate opening had been covered in the blast. I felt our only chance was to explore parts of the mine furthest away from the explosion.

Arm-in-arm, Emily and I slowly groped our way past the spot where I had spent the night, with the tiny stream of sunlight and dancing debris. About twenty feet further, the floor leveled off and another spot of sunlight touched the dirt. Shortly after that the tunnel divided. The cavern to the right went deeper into the mountain and was darker than Damon's temper. Dark was not an option.

Emily and I agreed we should keep to the left, staying in the original tunnel with its air holes every twenty feet or so. Those silly little beacons of hope gave us enough light to feel our way along the dank walls of clay and rock, for what seemed like hours.

"Let's sit for a minute. Here's a comfortable rock," I said. Emily giggled.

"Yes, we'll pretend it's a bench in the park." Her voice was weak as she took in deep breaths of dusty air. There was so much I wanted to ask Emily, but I was afraid it would take her last bit of energy to answer. She must have read my mind.

"Would you like to know why I'm here?" she said. I nodded excitedly. "Mom probably told you I was a junior at San Francisco State. Did she tell you that she and Dad wanted me to enroll at UCSC?" I nodded. "Well, at first I didn't want to change schools, but I had a fight with my boyfriend and decided to surprise the folks and register for the fall semester at the Santa Cruz campus." Emily wiped her eyes with the back of her hand.

"I went to my regular class in the morning, but the teacher had posted a note on the door saying it was canceled. I thought of it as a great opportunity to register for the fall semester. I picked up a burger and coke and headed up Skyline Boulevard. I accidentally spilled coke on my white Capris. I decided to stop at the Boulder Creek cabin for a change of clothes and then go on to the Santa Cruz campus from there."

"So you had made up your mind to go to UCSC?"

"I talked myself into it. No one knew I was going to sign up for the fall semester. I parked in front of the cabin and got out of my car. I noticed an old rusty truck parked near the barn. Damon and George came out of the barn and saw me. I should have gotten back in my car and left, but no, like an idiot, I walked up to them and asked what they were doing on our property. How I wish I hadn't confronted them. I was furious that they were back after the sheriff had already thrown them out. They knew who I was and just laughed at me. I got really mad and told them I was going to call the sheriff.

"So what did they do?" I almost wished she wouldn't tell me.

"George yanked my purse off my arm, and then Damon twisted my arm behind my back. I screamed and Kenny came out of the barn to see what was going on. He dropped the sack of fertilizer he was carrying and pulled on Damon's arm, trying to get him to let go of me. He said something like, "let's talk about this, you guys." Damon and George just laughed. I'll never forget that day, looking at George's yellow teeth as he cracked up over Damon decking Kenny with one punch. I liked Kenny right away."

"Don't tell me you've been in this mine since that day." I was astounded.

"I'm afraid so. Kenny was assigned guard duty over me after Damon welded the chain to my ankle. They made Kenny guard the property and do all the work while they went to town to drink. Kenny was good to me. He brought me food, water and books to read. Without something to read, I would have gone nuts."

"Did the other two brothers try to get at you like they did last night?"

"A few times, but Kenny was able to keep them away.

They were so stupid and drunk, you know, and Kenny's really very smart. Of course his brothers don't know how smart he really is."

"You're kidding. They don't know about their own brother?"

"You see, Kenny quit school in the tenth grade to live with his brothers here at their grandfather's cabin. He always kept to himself and read a lot, but he didn't talk much because he stuttered. Everyone thought he was stupid, but he's over the stuttering. All he needed was someone to believe in him. He's fine now," she cooed.

"Anyway, when Mom and Dad kicked the brothers out of the cabin a few years later, they rented a cabin from Nora Bates, behind her house, but they continued to store sacks of fertilizer in our barn. According to Kenny, there was a storage space under the floor."

"So, the sacks of fertilizer belonged to ...?"

"To the McFees."

"Why do they need ...? Oh!" Finally, it hit me like a ton of fertilizer.

"Because of the business, you know, the business of growing marijuana." She looked at me to see if I understood. I did a mental slap in the head. Everything had pointed to it, but I hadn't seen it.

"How could I have been so dense?"

"How could you know? Nobody knows, except the people involved ... and me.

Actually, you're involved now. I'm so sorry we got you

into this whole debacle."

"So do you know all about the business?" I asked. Emily nodded her head. "Are there any more people in on it?"

"Kenny told me everything. Nora Bates gets a big cut of the profit every year for arranging things and looking the other way. Woody gets a share for making trouble, spying at the new house and trying to get Mom and Dad to give up and move away. Lot's of complaints about you, by the way." Emily smiled even though her face was bruised, scraped and in terrible pain.

"I guess there were complaints about Stan and Chester too."

"You're right, there were, but those two were put out of commission. Kenny said they tried to get rid of you a couple times. You must be tough," she laughed.

"Lucky," I said. "What about the forest ranger?" Emily looked at her ankle.

"They're beasts. What can I say?" She rolled up her left sleeve to show me a four inch scar running down from her elbow. "George is handy with a knife, but Damon likes his rifle." I shivered

"So, Damon shot the ranger in the back with his rifle?"

"Yes. I wish Kenny didn't belong to the McFee family. He's not like them. He's a good person and smart, but he has no life of his own, except the time spent with me. George and Damon use Kenny, beat him and control him completely."

"Are you OK to travel?" I asked, trying not to let on how worried I was about her condition. She nodded and I helped her up. Neither of us was very steady, but we were determined to escape the damp, dark cavern.

Another twenty feet was marked by an overhead ray of sunlight. As we walked deeper into the mine, the floor was only lightly strewn with rocks and loose dirt, not at all like the havoc behind us. Narrow railroad tracks rose above the ground for the first time, probably for the transporting of the ore. I decided I could never be a miner, not in the ground with no windows.

Emily winced every time her right foot touched the ground. She stopped for a moment and I suggested we sit. She gladly sat down on a fallen timber while I stood.

"Josephine, don't you want to sit?" I shook my head. I was worried about getting up again. "Did you find any of the cigarette butts Kenny left around?" she asked.

"He was the one doing that?" My mouth dropped open.

"He was always trying to get someone down here to help me. His brothers wouldn't let him go to town or own a car or anything. They controlled his whole life and threatened him with death constantly. Guess you were the only one who noticed his little clues."

"Did he put the cell phone charger in the shop?"

"Yes, but Damon went looking for it. He was furious when it wasn't where Kenny said it was. He blamed Kenny and beat him up pretty bad." I felt awful that poor Kenny had paid for something I did. Emily looked up at me with wet eyes.

"How are my parents?"

"They're OK, but it's been a rough year for them. At first they couldn't even talk to each other. I think they're doing better now. If today is Monday, they move into the house tomorrow. I guess you know that your mom has been living in the cabin for months." Emily nodded. "Your dad made Mr. Lowell the manager of his company so he can retire and live here full-time. Theda's happy about that."

"My mom hates to be alone. Do they miss me a lot?"

"With every breath they take. You have no idea how much they miss you." My eyes stung as I spoke and a knot was forming in my throat.

"I wonder if I'll ever see them again," she sighed.

"Chin up. We're gonna' break outta' here, you'll see." I said it for my benefit as well as for hers. The negatives were piling up and the positives were nowhere in sight. I wondered if I would ever see Mom and Dad again. I figured they had another twenty years of good living and I wanted to see them all the way to the finish line.

"Did I tell you the McFees work for Nora? She handles the business, including sending money to her favorite charity in Mexico."

"You mean a real charity?" I said. Emily shook her head.

"Are you kidding? Nora's involved with a drug cartel

from Mexico." My mouth hung open as I tried to process what I had just heard.

"It's true. Kenny wouldn't lie to me. Jose and two other guys work for her, harvesting and transporting the marijuana to LA."

"You don't mean Jose, big guy from the Munger construction project? No way. The guy I'm thinking of is a very clean-cut, hard-working, young man putting himself through college." Emily looked into my eyes and nodded her head.

"I'm afraid he's not what he seems to be. Jose will be in charge of the harvest tomorrow and is also one of the drivers." Emily looked at the dirt floor.

"Right after the harvest, Damon, George and Kenny are all leaving this area." Emily could barely get the words out. "Kenny doesn't know where they're going. Damon's keeping it to himself. He told his brothers to destroy all evidence, including me, before they leave. He doesn't want Nora to be able to point the finger if she gets caught. I think Nora would have a cow if she knew I was here in the mine for over a year. I've never met her, but something tells me we wouldn't get along."

I was stunned into silence. The revelations were staggering. I became more determined than ever to find a way out so that we could blow the whistle on the detestable human debris Emily had just told me about. The dim light and stark silence was getting to me. We couldn't hear anything from the outside world, including the noon fire siren. Worse than that, no one could hear us. I swallowed my rage, ignored the hollow feeling in my stomach and tried to focus on a way out as we shuffled another twenty feet and then another.

"So who burned down the barn?" My dry lips cracked every time I spoke.

"That was Kenny getting rid of evidence like he was told. Poor boy has always done what he was told, except when it came to me."

"What about draining the brake fluid from my car?"

"Kenny thinks it was George. By the way, have you met Thor?"

"Yeah, if he's a raging brown mastiff. In fact, I've seen two mastiffs that were very unfriendly." I shivered at the thought.

"The female, Thea, wandered off and was killed. Thor is still here somewhere. Kenny said he tied the dog to a tree down by the creek so that you could help me get out of here without any barking to give us away."

"It's not the barking I'm afraid of," I put one hand to my throat for effect.

"I know what you mean. They were trained by Damon and George to attack strangers. Thor wouldn't hurt me, but you, I don't know." I thought about the day I sprayed Thor's muzzle with pepper spray and figured he would remember me.

"So, about the farm, did you say that cartel sympathizers are involved?" She nodded. "How many are there?" My curiosity was killing me. Everything Emily had said so far was shocking, so I braced myself for the next revelation.

"The way I understand it, the McFees grow the marijuana and Nora gets her share of the money when the crop is sold to Machuca. He has Jose and his two thugs harvest it and drive it to LA. They sell it to the drug cartel at a profit and, like any well-run business, everyone makes money. The cartel sells drugs to the gangs, and we all know what happens to their victims."

"Yeah, it's economics 101," I felt sick. "Do you realize this farm is helping people to ruin our youth?" I swore to myself, if I ever had the chance, I would turn these people in to the DEA, CIA, and the FBI. "Emily, do you know how much money we're talking about here? How big is the crop?"

"This year is their biggest crop, 2,700 plants, worth millions on the street." She shook her head in disgust.

"Let's just hope we can get out of here in time to stop them," I said, although I lacked a plan of any kind. The mine made a slight turn to the right and followed the contour of the mountain and the set of steel tracks. Ahead, more light reflected off the walls than we had experienced all day. Our pace quickened.

Chapter Twenty-five

Emily and I had been stumbling through the mine for hours.

"Josephine, where do you think that light's coming from?" Emily asked. Before I could say a word, someone else spoke. I jumped a foot straight up.

"Emily!" Kenneth cried out as he and Emily met in an embrace. "I was scared you didn't make it," his voice cracked.

"I was worried about you, too," she wept.

"Kenny, I'm so glad you're alright," I said, as a giant invisible weight lifted from my shoulders. "How did you get in here?" He was quite a sight with his shredded shirt full of blood stains, not to mention dirt from head to toe and a distinct limp.

"I came through the back door. Glad you're OK, Josephine." But our euphoria didn't last long. We heard a solid slam, more like a thump and then some cruel laughing. "It's Damon and George," Kenneth whispered in the dark. "They followed me."

Emily put her hands over her mouth to muffle a scream. I moved closer to the small, inconspicuous door, ensconced in the wall about three feet up from the floor. I was barely able to make out its frame because the door was closed, shutting out the sunlight.

Kenny rushed forward and threw his shoulders against the door that was constructed from thick redwood planks and framed in metal. The door didn't budge. Kenneth said it didn't have a lock, but we soon heard the pounding of many nails outside. Whatever held the door, held the door. We tried running at it as a threesome. It didn't budge.

"So, Kenny ... know any other ... way out?" I was breathing hard and finally slumped on the floor after wasting my energy on the stupid door.

"The front entrance is out. You bombed it to heck and did a number on me as well," Kenny grimaced. My face flushed. I felt bad about Kenny's injuries, but after all, we had been in a tight spot and Emily's life was in danger.

"My brothers left me under a pile of dirt and timbers. I spent the whole night there. When I finally dug myself out, they were gone. I don't think they were even touched by the blast. Next time, aim for them." His mouth twisted into a wry smile.

"I'll be sure to do that. I'm really sorry the blast caught you instead of them. By the way, what are the chances of getting out of here?"

"Well, this is the end of the mine. I don't know any other way out." Kenneth put an arm around Emily's waist to steady her. I took his answer as a less than one-in-a-million chance of our escaping.

"The mine was never a big operation. Not much gold, you know," Kenneth rattled on and on, probably out of nervousness. "During prohibition, Great Grandfather McFee made whiskey out of some of the corn he grew. His still was hidden just inside the main entrance to the mine. The story goes that one of the Munger teenagers found another way to enter the mine." Kenneth pointed to the trap door he had climbed through.

"The kid would wait until my great grandfather was napping and then fill his own bottle with hooch from the still. Amos caught him once and bit the top of his ear off. Poor boy couldn't tell anyone how he lost part of his ear because he was trespassing, stealing and drinking, all forbidden by his strict mother."

The three of us walked to the end wall with its massive timber framework over rock and clay, similar to all the other walls. We ran our hands over every inch, finding nothing but grooves hacked in the earth by a pickax many decades ago. An air hole supplied a tiny shred of light. I stared up at the two inch pipe.

"Kenny, do you think we could find a way to explore the ceiling?" He helped Emily over to an empty explosives box marked dynamite. She gratefully sat down. He finally answered.

"See any more crates like that one around here?" He pointed to the one under Emily. "I'll help you look."

Kenneth and I began our search, leaving Emily behind. Every inch of my body complained, but I was determined to find a way out. We struck out toward the opposite end of the tunnel, one step at a time until we had passed three air holes. As I checked out a shadowy wall with my hands, I tripped over something which turned out to be a wooden crate. Even though the box was empty, I needed both arms to carry it. My strength was zilch. Kenny took the box from me and limped all the way back to Emily.

I stumbled past the same three air holes and finally caught up to Kenny. He helped Emily stand up, stacking one box on top of the other under the air hole. He gave me a hand as I stepped up to the top crate. My hair touched the ceiling so I ducked my head and felt around the air hole with my fingers. Loose dirt fell as I wiggled the air hole pipe. I blinked, lost my balance and almost fell. I finally got a grip on the pipe and held onto it to steady myself. Dirt rained down on my head and shoulders. Suddenly the pipe gave way and I teetered.

Kenny quickly reached for my arm and broke my fall. He took the three-foot piece of lead pipe out of my hands. I stepped back and shook the dirt out of my hair like a wet dog after a bath. We all stared at the substantial stream of light coming from the four-inch hole in the ceiling as if it were the second coming.

"If we chip away at the dirt, maybe we can make a hole big enough for our escape," I said. No one disagreed. Kenneth helped me up onto the top box again and handed up the piece of pipe.

"Wow, that's heavy." I barely had enough strength to ram the pipe into the hard clay a couple times. A handful of dirt landed on me and the floor. Not much progress for the effort. If my hair had been clean, I was sure that a whole ton of dirt would have fallen on my head. I handed the pipe to Kenny, climbed down from the crates and leaned against the cold dank wall, breathing hard.

"I think I might be tall enough to work the pipe from the floor," Kenny offered. We pushed the wooden boxes away. He gripped the pipe, stretched his arms and took a swing. Emily walked to his side and steadied him by putting her arms around his waist. The act looked so natural. He took a few more whacks at the ceiling while I took a turn sitting on a box, breathing dust and hoping to see lots of daylight.

The most reassuring thing about the enlarged air hole was the extra light it delivered. It was like going from a five-watt bulb to a twenty-watt, but in the end, it was only a dream. Kenny couldn't stand very long on his bad knee, and Emily and I were next to useless.

Time passed and the light dimmed. I figured we should have had dinner a couple hours ago, or at least a sip of water. My mouth was stuck to itself and it was too tired to open anyway. I wandered along the tunnel dragging one hand against the cool walls of hard clay, hoping to find a miracle. I had moved away from the twenty watt light into the dim, and getting dimmer, interior of the mine.

All of a sudden I heard loud squeaking sounds, like a crowbar ripping up nailed wood. The noise came from the direction of the trap door. My heart jumped into my throat and I froze where I stood.

I watched Emily and Kenneth stand up and cling to each other as if for the last time. The small door opened and two men wearing black climbed into the mine. They hesitated a few seconds until their eyes adjusted to the dim light. I wanted to scream, "Emily, Kenny, run!" But I didn't. Besides, where could they go? Instead, I began backing up, moving quietly away, keeping to the darkest shadows. I doubted anyone besides Emily and Kenny knew about me being in the mine.

Emily wept as Kenny tried to console her. The two well-built, olive-complexioned men easily corralled the couple. One man pointed his gun at Kenneth while the other one climbed out the door. The inside man directed Emily onto a wooden crate. The outside man pulled her through the opening. Kenny stepped onto the crate and was pulled through the opening. The brute with the gun was last. The heavy door thunked and all was dark.

I didn't move for several minutes. Tears streamed down my cheeks as I thought about what would become of the young couple. I stood in the dark listening for what seemed like an eternity. Finally, I gathered enough courage to walk over to the trap door, stand on the crate and push the heavy door open a couple inches. After a long pause, I pushed it all the way open and climbed though, expecting to be captured at any moment.

The evening light seemed bright to me at first as I crouched against the hillside, studying the terrain. I saw bushes, trees and a path heading north under a deep purple sky. I heard creek water tumbling over rocks in the distance. I raised up and stood perfectly still, holding my breath, listening.

Straight ahead, down the path about thirty yards, was a narrow footbridge spanning a creek. About a hundred feet beyond the little bridge, I saw the edge of the forest and the backend of what looked like a medium-sized white U-Drive rental truck. I watched the two men in black force Emily and Kenny into the back of the truck. The U-Drive moved forward and was swallowed up by the trees.

I looked at the dense forest to my right and then the agriculture on my left. My jaw dropped as the sight gave me the equivalent of an electric shock. There was an absence of trees and an abundance of deep green marijuana plants. Eight-foot poles held a thousand yards of camouflage netting material in place, concealing the illegal vegetation from aerial viewers. The farm was just like Emily described, but I hadn't expected to see it there, sandwiched between the mine and the river.

I had a choice, go down the path and risk being seen out in the open, or go to the left and run into whoever or whatever guarded the plants. The thought of Thor paralyzed my legs. My first impulse was to go straight ahead to the stream and drink ten gallons of water. Second thought, same as the first, but follow the creek back to the highway.

Adrenalin took over. I finally had a plan, as far as it went. I broke out of my fear long enough to venture a couple feet to the right of the bushes, then darted ahead at full speed toward the creek. The sound of the water grew louder, but so did the sound of my pounding heart. Even as my whole being focused on running for my life, a heightened awareness stimulated all my senses. I was aware of the summer evening, warm and filled with the scents of lilac, bay, decaying leaves and other earthy river smells.

I aimed for the footbridge, tumbled down the sandy bank and slipped under the structure. I sat on the bank under the wooden planks, my heels tucked under my rear, quietly listening for any unfriendly sounds. All was quiet. I cupped my hands and brought water to my parched lips. At first I thought I would drink a lot of water, but just a couple handfuls quenched my thirst.

Stealthily, I crept out from under the bridge and looked around and then continued slinking alongside the creek. The sandy beach ended where thick brush began, blocking my progress. I rolled up my pants and waded into the icy water. I trudged over mucky sand, balanced on moss-covered rocks and climbed over giant boulders. Mostly I shuffled across the shallow river bottom, thankful to be wearing tennis shoes.

I slogged along in the dark, barely able to see two

feet ahead, going in the same southwest direction as the water. It pushed me along as if it knew the urgency of the situation. I knew I had to hurry and find help, or lose Emily and Kenneth forever.

Chapter Twenty-six

July's full moon rose above my head, revealing itself occasionally through a canopy of leafy tree limbs stretching over the creek. I watched beams of moonlight turn ordinary splashes of water into silvery jewels as the creek cut a path through the dark, pervasive forest full of wild animals. Fortunately I was an adult and didn't have to worry about unseen lions, tigers and bears. I told myself I was safe because nature's creatures were asleep for the night. I only had to watch out for the meanest animal of all, the armed pot farmer. That animal gave me shivers of dread.

Somewhere in the dark, an owl gave two hoots and a second later, hot breath and terrifying guttural snarls were inches from my face. I recoiled automatically, falling into the water, butt first. I scrambled toward the middle of the stream, half walking, half crawling over and around the rocks.

Glancing back, I saw Thor in the moonlight, thrashing around on his hind legs, trying to rid himself of the short rope tied around his neck. The other end of the rope was tied to a tree at the edge of the water. So that was where Kenneth left the mastiff. I was pretty sure the dog knew my scent and would like to tear me apart for old-time sake. The growling, slobbering canine tried over and over again to break free as I hurried past him and continued my trek downstream.

I thought about Solow and remembered that I had left his dinner bowl on the porch near his bed. He would need water, but I was sure he could find some on his own. Bet he's upset with me right now, I thought.

In my head I calculated the number of hours since my last meal. It had been about twenty-eight hours, give or take two, since I wasn't wearing a watch. Solow's kibble, with a little salt and pepper, would have been a welcome gourmet treat at that point.

I was wet up to my waist and the tiniest breeze sent my teeth chattering uncontrollably, but I refused to let anything get in the way of my plan to follow the river … follow the river … follow the river. The creek offered short stretches of beach from time to time, but usually I just sloshed through the water, one foot in front of the other, sometimes hopping rocks I could barely see in the dark.

Time raced forward as I dragged myself along at a snails pace, my body feeling all of its fifty years and then some. I wondered if eating more vegetables would have made me stronger. I wondered if my body would keep on walking if my mind went out of order. Were the kids still alive?

A lump in my throat nearly choked me every time I thought about the fate of Emily and Kenneth. Surely Kenny's brothers wouldn't ... on second thought, I was sure they would. I tried not to think about the McFees, Jose, Machuca and the men in black. Funny, the sergeant's name was Machuca. I wondered if they were related.

About two hours had passed when I finally found myself under the Bear Creek Bridge looking for a way up to the road. I walked along the sandy slope beside the murky black water. At the far end of the bridge a steep bank kept me from my goal. I followed the creek a few more yards and found a way up. All I had to do was push myself through a jungle of blackberry bushes, climb over rotting logs and debris and pull myself up a short cliff by holding onto tree limbs. Piece a cake. I told myself not to think about cake.

Just as I pulled myself up to the level of the road, but before I could stand up, headlights appeared from the direction of town. I thought about waving down whoever it was, but couldn't get to my feet in time. The vehicle turned out to be a white U-Drive truck. It slowed, pulled into the wide spot just before the Munger's driveway and stopped. The truck idled while the driver, dressed in black, jumped out. He ran over to the branches hiding the old road Kenny had driven on when we first went to the mine some twenty-four hours earlier.

Slow motion took over my initial panic. My brain fairly rattled, swiftly sorting out what to do. While the man in black removed branches, I darted across the road, snuck around the back of the U-Drive and entered the cab on the passenger side. I locked the door, scooted over to the driver's seat and yanked the truck into reverse. I stomped on the gas and wheels spun as sand sprayed the man in black. Finally the tires grabbed and the truck lurched backward. I looked around for "Drive", sweating like a pig on a spit.

The man pounded on my door, kicked, swore and disrupted my thought patterns. Once I had the truck in "Drive", I hit the gas and Mr. Black was left on the ground coughing out ugly words. I smiled in the dark, feeling invincible.

I headed down Bear Creek Road in a westerly direction, toward town. As I cleverly made the turns, one after another, I heard something rolling and thumping in the back of the rental truck. I remembered the black-clad thugs shoving Emily and Kenny into a U-Drive and decided to turn off the road onto a private driveway, much like the Mungers'. After a hundred yards or so, I pulled over and cut the engine. The doors in the back opened without a struggle. There was poor Kenny, duct taped and all alone. I climbed into the back of the truck and ripped the tape off his mouth.

"Sorry about all the turns. I forgot you might be back here." I petted his head, hoping nothing was broken.

"Help me get this tape off. We have to go back for Emily before it's too late." He spoke with an urgency that made the hair stand up on the back of my neck.

I pulled tape off Kenny's wrists. He sat up, leaned forward and ripped off the duct tape that held his ankles together. Hot wax couldn't have done a better job of removing body hair. His eyes were wet, but he didn't make a peep. He looked up at me as I leaned against the cold metal wall of the truck.

"You're shivering," he said. "Why are your teeth chattering like that?"

"I just finished a long walk in the creek. Where is Emily?"

"There are two more U-Drive trucks like this one and they'll be meeting at the pot field soon. She's in one of the other two trucks. I heard Jose say he wanted to take Emily with him when he delivers the pot. Said he could get a good price for her in Los Angeles." Kenny was seething.

"At least he didn't say he wanted to kill her, like your brothers."

"Yeah, Jose's two friends were going to give Emily an overdose of drugs, but he talked them out of it. You stay here in the back of the truck. I'll drive us back to Jose's truck and talk to him while you get Emily into our truck." I wasn't convinced Kenny's plan would work, but we had to do something fast.

"What about that irate guy I stole this truck from? I'd sure hate to meet up with him." My shivers started up again.

"I could go alone," Kenneth offered.

"No, I didn't mean I wouldn't go. I want to go, but to tell you the truth, I'm scared to death my chattering teeth will give me away." And then I sneezed. "Guess we'll have to work with what we've got. Let's go!"

Kenny jumped down from the back of the truck, listened to the silent, starry night for a moment and slammed the cargo doors, sending me into total darkness. If my ride in the back of the truck was bad, I could only imagine how bad it had been for poor Kenneth, all taped up, rolling around like skates on a schooner. It was hard for me to stand up, but sitting was worse. Finally I spread-eagled on my stomach, not even caring how filthy the cold metal floor was.

After a zillion sharp turns, the truck pulled into the wide spot just before the Mungers' driveway. I heard Kenny slam his door and angry voices as the truck idled. He had obviously found Jose's U-Drive, but what if the third truck showed up?

"Too bad you're not smart like your brothers," Jose said. "I'm probably going to have to kill you. Damon and George might not like that, but I don't really care."

"You'll never get away with this, Jose. Drugs are one thing, but murder will put the Feds on your tail for sure."

"I have a pistol that says you better get in the back with your girlfriend." When I heard that, I knew Emily was near, but Kenny was about to be murdered. I pushed one door open and hit the ground running, jumped into the cab and stomped on the gas peddle.

Moonlight glinted off Jose's gun as he leaned against the passenger door of the second U-Drive. I cranked the steering wheel to the left, making the gunman my bull's eye, then hit the gas peddle. Jose jumped to one side and waved his gun just in time to have it pinned between the two trucks. His gun was smashed and his words sounded hostile to say the least. The language was Spanish and the attitude was undignified.

Jose passed out with his hand still stuck between the two trucks and his body hanging in a semi-sitting position. I ran to the back of the number two U-Drive and flung the doors open. I saw nothing at first. Climbing in, I thought I saw Emily, but it turned out to be a rolled up rug. I ran back to Kenny.

"She's not here!" I yelled. His face fell and his eyes were wet.

"She must be in the third truck. I'll drive," he shouted. Thanks to me, our U-Drive had a smashed headlight so I scooted into Jose's U-Drive from the driver's side. Kenneth climbed in, turned the key, put the truck in reverse, and Mr. Jose slumped to the ground like a princess fainting from the heat.

"Do we have time to drive up the mountain and tell the Mungers? They could call the sheriff." I wished for an officer of any kind. Even Russell.

"No time. Gotta' find the truck with Emily in it." Sweat ran down Kenny's handsome forehead as he leaned into the steering wheel as if that would make us go faster.

I assumed we were headed for the Bates property on Two Bar Road.

We reached Central Avenue. Kenny stopped and engaged the right blinker in case of heavy after-midnight traffic. The only vehicle around was a white U-Drive truck speeding south. Kenny made a quick left and stayed on the truck's tail. We weren't going much over the speed limit, but once we passed through Boulder Creek, the sharp turns were more than Kenny was used to. As far as I knew, he had never had an actual driver's license or a vehicle of his own to drive.

"So Kenny, have you driven much?"

"I drive Damon's truck around the property sometimes." Just then the right front tire went up the side of a bank. I thought for sure we were going to tip over. I felt like a flight instructor who had mistakenly handed over the stick to a first time flyer.

"Would you like me to drive?"

"No time. Can't stop for anything." His tense body still leaned forward, his eyes glued to the taillights in front of us. At least there wasn't any traffic to deal with. Only drunks, derelicts and U-Drives were on the highway in the wee hours of the morning. Kenneth had started to get the hang of driving a curvy road at high speed, thank God, but I wished he hadn't practiced on my watch.

We sped through the little town of Brookdale and then Ben Lomond and Felton was only another mile away. The U-Drive ahead of us suddenly swerved over the white line and back to the side of the road, taking out a couple mail boxes before skidding to a stop. A short, heavy-set woman climbed down from the cab and checked her left rear tire. She slapped the side of the truck and kicked the tire. Finally, she looked up to see Kenny and me, hands on hips, watching her.

"Am I lucky or what?" She pulled back her mop of yellow and gray hair that covered her back clear down to the waist of her way too tight stretch pants. "I git a blow-out and help is right behind me." She had a couple teeth missing when she smiled and her skin looked like the alligator bag I lost in the mine.

"Ma'am, I'm afraid I can't help you," Kenny said. "You need to call the U-Drive office or a tow truck." He shrugged his shoulders and tried to look helpless.

"You big handsome guys are all alike. Nobody wants to help a poor woman tryin' tah x-scape from her good-fer-nuttin' old man who's outta' town and when he sees I'm gone, he'll bust his butt to git me back. I'm takin' the TV and he won't put up with that." She kept shaking her head.

"Do you have a cell phone to call for help?" I asked.

"Do I look like I got one ah them things?" Kenny stepped closer to the woman.

"Ma'am we have a situation here ...."

"You're tellin' me. I got a blowed out tire and you don't wanna help me."

"That's not the one I was thinking of. You see, we

thought you were someone else, someone who kidnapped my friend. We have to go now. I'm sorry, but we're in a hurry." He took a couple steps back. I pointed in the direction of town.

"It's only about a mile to Felton and a pay phone. When you call, would you mind calling 911 for us?"

"Right, and I'll say hey to the Pope fer ya," she said, and waved a finger. Knowing useless when I saw it, I turned and ran back to our U-Drive. I was about to suggest a trip to the phone in Felton, but Kenny wasn't in the mood. He was already whipping the truck around with a hard left, heading us back to Boulder Creek at the speed of light. Where were all the Highway Patrol cars when we needed one?

Kenneth was gaining confidence in his driving. It showed in the way he sat back in his seat and took the turns without going off the side of the road. He had been quiet most of the trip.

"So, Kenneth, how close are you to Emily? My sense is you would do anything to save her life."

"You got that right, but it's not just her life, it's also our baby's life."

"Oh, I didn't know." I turned to face Kenny. "How far along is she?"

"We think four months, maybe. It's not like she could get to a doctor or anything. I worry about her, you know?"

"I'm sure you do." I leaned over and patted Kenny's arm.

"I guess you know she's evidence and my brothers will kill her for sure if we call 911. Damon already sold her Mustang to a chop-shop in Modesto." He glanced at my face which was probably green, like his, from the dashboard lights. We were quiet again, struggling with our own thoughts and scenarios. I counted only three vehicles going in the opposite direction and not one truck.

Kenneth slowed to a reasonable speed, not wanting to attract the attention of a deputy sheriff or highway patrol officer. He flipped on the heater to help dry my clothes and keep me from chattering my teeth into nubs.

"What's your plan?" I asked, hoping he had one.

"We make it up as we go," he said. Oh, that was a big comfort.

"How do you feel about drug cartels, I mean, helping them to get money so they can perpetuate the gangs, guns, drugs and murders?"

"I know what goes on in the world. We have a TV. I hate the whole marijuana scheme, right down to my own brothers. If I ever get a chance, I'll turn 'em in." Kenneth made a sharp right onto Bear Creek road. We rolled past the turnout and the Mungers' driveway entrance. No one was there. He turned the truck around at the next wide spot and headed toward town. We passed the turnout again, drove over the Bear Creek Bridge, around one turn, made a right and then up a gravel driveway.

"Who lives here?" I asked. He shrugged his shoulders.

"Nobody I know. I just want to hide the truck so we can use it later." He parked the U-Drive halfway up the windy drive, cut the lights and listened. We left the keys in the glove box and began our hike down the dark driveway. We made a left and hurried up the highway, over the bridge and onto the hidden road leading to the mine. I noticed the sky had a red tinge. It was getting close to dawn, but not really because dawn always came late to a valley wedged between high mountains.

"Kenneth, even with your limp, I'm having trouble keeping up with you," I whispered. After all, his legs were longer than mine and he was less than half my age, not to mention I hadn't eaten anything in thirty-four hours.

"Sorry, Josephine. Are you OK?" he whispered.

"My clothes are dry and my teeth stopped chattering. Guess I'm fine." I didn't mention all the painful parts of my body that yearned for rest. I was sure Kenny was in at least as much pain as I.

It was getting easier to see where we were going. Too easy. We followed the road, staying out of sight, constantly worried someone might see us. Kenny unexpectedly made a left turn, cutting across a small meadow bordered by lots of giant redwoods. Behind the trees I found my little red pickup. I opened the passenger door and reached for the cell phone. "Drat! It's dead!" I put my hand to my mouth and looked around.

Chapter Twenty-Seven

The forest was quiet except for the many bird songs which for millions of years had served to announce the new day, Tuesday, actually. The Munger's would move into their new house while the men in black used their machetes to harvest marijuana on the same property, practically under their noses.

"Do you know where the U-Drives will go once they're loaded?" I whispered, leaning against my truck.

"Some place in East L.A." Kenneth said. "That's all we know. We grow the stuff and they take care of distribution," he shrugged his shoulders. I opened the glove compartment and took out a pair of scissors and a flashlight. I shoved the scissors into my back pocket. "Kenneth, do we need this?" Kenny shook his head.

"A flashlight will just get in the way. Now, if it was one of those big long Maglites, that would be different. We could use something like that as a weapon."

"Ok, you don't like my little pink flashlight. What about the keys to the truck? Leave them here?" Kenny nodded.

"Yeah, we might need to leave in a hurry." I figured it was his girlfriend, his problem and his escape, so I would go with his plan. Together we searched the cab for any other items that might help us. Nothing. Too bad I didn't own a gun. I remembered my pepper spray, but it was in my gator bag somewhere in the mine under tons of rock.

"I think we should walk along the creek for awhile," Kenny said. "We're getting close to the farm and the machetes will be out early."

"Just don't let Thor off the rope. He's not exactly in love with me."

Kenny nodded. We crossed the creek and headed north on Bates property. Kenny knew the woods like nobody else. He had spent the last few years stuck on Munger and Bates land, working the farm for Damon and George. And, for over a year, he had taken care of Emily. We followed a deer trail for awhile, then crawled on hands and knees under wild lilac bushes and ran like crazy across a carpet of ferns under a canopy of oaks and redwoods. It would have struck me as beautiful if I hadn't been so tired and scared.

"Kenneth, the sun's up. They'll see us," I whispered.

"Don't worry. I know my way around this place." I hoped he was right because I was lost. Nothing looked familiar, not even the cabin we were watching through the tree branches. The shortest way to the ugly little structure was straight across a dirt driveway, but that wouldn't be the smartest way.

Kenny led me in a wide circle through the meanest underbrush I had seen so far. I had stickers poking into my skin like pins on a cushion. Eventually, we came to a stop just a few feet away from the backside of the shack. Five rickety steps led to a weathered backdoor.

"Stay here and be quiet," Kenny whispered. He went inside while I stayed in my crouched position behind a couple smelly garbage cans and a fifty-gallon barrel of kibble, enough to feed Solow for a year. I saw Kenny's head through an open window near the backdoor. Just then a U-Drive came into view and raised the dust level to one hundred percent. I wanted to cough out the dust, but didn't dare.

Kenny practically threw himself out the window, landing on his bum knee. He hobbled over to the trash cans and hunched down with me. We heard the front screen door slam twice. I recognized Jose's voice.

"Grab a six pack and some ice. Let's get outta' here before the McFees get back." Jose ordered. "I'm dropping you off at the farm. I'll be back later to help load the stuff."

"My brother's gonna' be mad. You should be cutting with us."

"Just do what I say," Jose said. "My hand is killing me."

"Hey, man, there ain't no six pack in here. Look for yourself."

"Looks a little light in the food department. I think

these guys don't plan to stick around very long," Jose mused.

We heard the screen door slam twice and the U-Drive fire up. It turned around and stirred up more dust as it barreled down the driveway toward the Bates' main house. Kenny and I crept up to the little wooden shack, climbed the back stairs and entered the kitchen which consisted of a 1930's chipped white sink with grubby faded curtains hanging to the floor, a skuzzy bare-wood floor you wouldn't want to touch with any part of your body and a couple wooden cupboards seasoned with time and grease.

"I know. Don't even say it. I know we live in a sty." Obviously, Kenny didn't like his home either. He thrashed through drawers and closets looking for anything that could be used as a weapon.

"It's not your fault your brothers are slobs." I checked the fridge and was tempted to drink from the catsup bottle, but the black crud on the lip put me off. The only other thing to eat was something green and slimy in an open plastic container, unless you counted the quart of lumpy milk.

"What do you guys eat around here?"

"The plan is for us to leave this place tonight as soon as we get paid. No sense buying groceries is there?"

"No, s'pose not." I looked through the cupboards and found them foodless. The cockroaches were starting to look like steak to me, but I resisted.

"Find anything we can use, as far as weapons?" I asked.

"Nothing. My brothers must have packed last night. I bet everything's in the back of the Dodge right now." He checked out a bedroom closet and kicked the door, "How about that? They even took my stuff, but I don't think they planned to take me."

"So what do we do now?" I asked, just before we heard the mega muffler noise coming closer. My heartbeat sped up to a hundred and ninety miles per hour in three seconds. I was out the door and running before poor Kenny could make it back to the kitchen. I heard the front screen door slam as I bellied down behind the stinking garbage cans.

Behind me, just a foot or two, was shade from a grove of redwoods. That grove of trees and millions like it stretched to the northern mountains and beyond. I decided I better back up and get myself deeper into the forest before some evil yahoo discovered me hiding behind the fermenting garbage. As I crept behind some foliage I heard Damon's nasty voice.

"Well, well, little brother," he cackled. I heard him kick something wooden, like furniture, with his boot. "Change your mind? We packed your stuff and we're leavin' tonight as soon as we get the money," Damon said. George laughed.

"We got us a new plan. We're gonna stiff ol' Nora. As soon as we get paid, we get our butts outta' here before she knows we're gone," George said, laughing even louder.

I didn't stick around to hear anymore. Since I couldn't help Kenny get away from his brothers, I had to at least find Emily. I planned to circle around the shack and head south toward Mungers' Mountain. When I found the creek, I would follow it to Bear Creek Road and find help. That was my plan. Not complicated, just insanely dangerous in broad daylight.

A chicken hawk circled above the trees, probably looking me over for its next meal. Food was constantly on my mind. I figured there must be something growing in the forest, like berries, I could eat. My stomach was emptier than George's brain cavity and my energy was slipping away fast. I trudged through the underbrush in the late morning heat, my mouth glued shut from lack of spit. If someone had offered me a million dollars to spit, I would have had to decline. I pictured my brain shriveling up like a prune from lack of water. And so went my irrational thoughts.

The noon fire siren brought me back to reality and the urgency of my mission. Minutes later I found the creek, rushed into it clothes and all, and gulped some water from cupped hands. I splashed my face and reveled in the icy-cold wetness of it all. When I was thoroughly drenched, I scanned the river bank, noticing a patch of blackberry bushes with actual berries on them. I pushed through the knee-deep water and scrambled up a bank to where the berries grew. Unfortunately, most of them were red, only a few had turned black, but that didn't stop me. Sour was better than nothing. I stripped the berry bushes, netting about one handful plus scratches all over my arms.

The sun was straight up as I began following the babbling brook, tumbling over and around mighty boulders the size of hippos on its way to the San Lorenzo River. The river eventually flowed into the Pacific Ocean, but by the time it reached the beach in Santa Cruz, the water was usually too polluted to swim in. I wondered about the bacteria count where I had been gulping water. Oh, well, better to be hydrated than shriveled when the cougars came and got me. Yes, there had been cougar sightings, but no tigers or bears.

The creek was getting closer to Mungers' Mountain, only a hundred yards away. I heard the distant slashing of machetes and crouched down behind the river bank and crept forward at the speed of turtles on crutches. I rested for a moment under the footbridge, and then set off again, downstream, past the machetes and eventually past Thor who was still tied to a tree. He growled once, but knew his limitations and went back to sleep.

I had decided to pass up my truck because the machete guys might hear the engine noise. Instead, I went for the U-Drive. That decision cost me another half hour of walking. Finally, I climbed up from the river onto the Bear Creek Bridge, crossed it and turned left, down the highway and up someone's private driveway.

I passed by Jose's U-Drive which Kenny had parked in a wide spot under a giant oak, and hiked another fifty yards to the house. The house turned out to be an old cabin, boarded up and empty as far as I could see. I sat on the front porch trying to catch my breath and think at the same time. Dad always told me to, "Think it through, and then act." I tended to do just the opposite.

Fortunately, the driveway sloped downhill going back to the U-Drive. I rounded the truck, opened the back doors, and the rug almost rolled out. Hours earlier it had been near the cab. I pushed the rug back a few inches. It was harder to push than I expected and I thought I heard something like metal on metal. I pushed again, harder, stepped back and slammed the doors.

I fired up the U-Drive, biggest vehicle I'd ever driven in my life, and started down the driveway. Suddenly the noise I had heard made perfect sense and I slammed on the brakes.

Chapter Twenty-eight

I had driven the U-Drive rental truck about a hundred feet when it occurred to me there might be something important in the back. I slammed on the brakes, jumped out and yanked the backdoors open.

Already the rug had rolled toward the cab. What kind of rug rolls like that? I climbed into the back of the truck and pulled back one end of the carpet. There was definitely something inside and my heart was racing with anticipation and dread. I gave it a push and the rug rolled away from me, opening more and more as it went. My heart pounded when I discovered a delicate limp hand protruding from the rolls of the rug. I opened the carpet a bit more, exposing poor Emily, ashen and still. I held her wrist. At first there was nothing, then a faint pulse. I gently slapped her cheeks.

"Emily, Emily, wake up. Are you OK?" My fear for Emily's life was overwhelming. I tried to think. OK, I would tear up to the Mungers' house for help. Unfortunately, in my weakened condition, I couldn't lift Emily out of the truck and into the cab, so she had to suffer one more ride in the rug. I scrambled into the cab, ready to head for the Mungers', but, on second thought, I cranked the wheel in the opposite direction, toward the fire department in Boulder Creek. It would take about five minutes either way, but I thought Emily needed a professional medic, and quick.

I roared down Bear Creek Road and made a quick left onto Central Avenue. One more block and straight into an empty fire engine stall, shut the motor down and raced into the fireman's kitchen. A man about my age sat puffing on a cigar as he read the paper.

"What the ... who are you?" he sputtered, putting the cigar down and looking at me as if I were a dirty old troll coming up from under a bridge. Actually, I probably fit that description pretty well after being buried in dirt, scratched from berry bushes and soaked in the river. I saw coffee and donuts on the counter across the room and, like a robot, walked toward them as I spoke to the fireman.

"Sir, in the back of my truck ... a young woman needs medical ... attention. Please hurry." I didn't make it to the donuts. Instead I grabbed his sleeve and pleaded for him to follow me. He stood, studied my sweat-streaked face and went into action. He grabbed a white metal box with a red cross insignia on the side and we ran outside. I pointed to the back of the U-Drive. He dropped the kit on the asphalt and pulled the doors open. Emily sat on the floor, brushing dirt off her clothes and blinking at the sunlight.

"Hi, Josephine. How did I get in here?" The fireman looked at me, then Emily and

back to me. I shrugged.

"Don't you remember anything, Emily?"

"Yes, I remember now. Jose put me in the rug and I was having trouble breathing."

The fireman scratched his head. He helped her to the ground, but her legs wouldn't hold her up so he sat her half-starved little body on the truck floor, exposing a scabby knee and a piece of chain dangling over the license plate.

"Sir," I said, "she ... we haven't eaten in a couple days. Would you mind if we had a donut?"

"I'll bring them right out. You girls just rest and I'll be right back." He put his large body in gear and headed for the office door. A couple minutes later the donuts and coffee arrived on a tray and five minutes after that a sheriff's car pulled up behind the U-Drive. Obviously the fireman had made a call.

Sergeant Machuca stepped out of the official sheriff's vehicle and unfolded up to his natural six-foot-three height. He smiled at me as he shook hands with the fireman.

"We had an APB out on you. What happened, Josephine?"

"It's a very long story. I think my friend might need medical help ...."

"That's what I'm here for. You girls get in, we're going

to the hospital." He opened a back door for me, but a small suitcase was in the way. He quickly picked up the aluminum case and deposited it in the trunk. I sat down in the back seat, cleanest, softest thing I had sat on in days, and watched Machuca carry Emily to the car. He gently placed her on the back seat beside me. After a quick word with the fireman, Sergeant Machuca drove a block to Central Avenue and turned left. We were on our way to Santa Cruz, and I missed the whole trip because I fell asleep.

I felt someone shaking my shoulder. I was half awake, but didn't want to be awake at all. Finally the shaking worked and the mental fog lifted. A male nurse helped me out of the back seat of the sheriff's car and into a wheel-chair at the back entrance to Dominican Hospital.

"Is this necessary?" I asked. "Where's my friend?" The young nurse with a freshly shaved head pushed me inside the building.

"Don't worry, ma'am, everything's being taken care of. Relax, the wheelchair is standard procedure."

I felt dazed, weak and so sleepy. Baldy wheeled me through the emergency room, packed full of sick, injured and contaminated people, down a long hallway and into one of many curtained examining rooms.

Emily was lying on a narrow bed, dressed in hospital white, in front of a wall of hanging equipment and monitors. A plastic tube sent oxygen into her nose and a tube in her hand looked like it was hydrating or even medicating her, or both. I was glad Emily was asleep, but at the same time, I wished she was awake so we could talk. I had a lot on my mind and so many questions. The nurse left us.

I must have snoozed a bit in the wheelchair. Next thing I knew, somebody was shaking my shoulder again. I figured it was just a dream and refused to become conscious. A familiar voice spoke to me, and again the fog lifted. I looked up into Russell's young face.

"What ... what's going on?" I stammered.

"You're at the hospital with her," he pointed to Emily. "Just take it easy," Russell said, as he stood against the curtained wall, scratching his head. "I got the report on my scanner and came right over. It's my hobby. I listen to all the police reports, and I'm taking law enforcement classes on my day off. Did you know there was an APB out on you?"

"Yes, but I forgot who told me." Then I remembered Machuca.

"Who's your friend?"

"This is Emily Munger," I said, carefully watching Russell's reaction. He stared for a long time, trying to sort things out.

"I thought she was killed or something." He looked at me, and then turned his head to look at the patient again.

"She disappeared over a year ago, kidnapped by the McFee boys and rescued by Kenny McFee. Now Kenny's missing and we need to get him back before his brothers leave town tonight for good."

"So you think all that stuff really happened?" Russell was astonished, his eyes round and his mouth gaping.

"It's all true. Where do you think I've been for the last couple days? I found Emily rolled up in a rug in the back of a U-Drive," I said. Russell cleared his throat.

"I thought you said the guy named Kenny saved her."

"We both did," I said, pushing myself up from the wheelchair. I didn't see any reason to stay at the hospital, and I was sure Emily would want me to find Kenny. I stood up slowly and grabbed Russell's sleeve.

"Let's go. I'll fill you in later."

"Wait a minute. I still don't understand what this is all about. We can't just leave without a plan, can we?" He rubbed the back of his neck as he spoke. "Who's Kenny, anyway?"

"This whole thing is about a pot farm on Munger property. It's about kidnapping. It's about shooting a forest ranger and it's about a vicious drug cartel. Now, let's go!" I had a senior advantage over poor Russell, so he bit his lip and followed me like a good boy, past a couple of chatting nurses who were too busy to notice us leaving the building. It was early evening when we climbed into the official Ace Security pickup.

"Do you have a phone, Russell?"

"Sure do. Why?"

"Because I need to use it, OK?" Russell handed me

the phone and I dialed the Mungers' cabin while he drove north, back to redwood country. The answering machine came on.

"Hi, Theda, Warren. It's Josephine. I know this is going to be a shock, but your daughter, Emily, is resting at Dominican Hospital in Santa Cruz. She's going to be fine. See you as soon as … ah, possible." As I spoke, I spotted a discarded, half-eaten, sun-dried cookie lying on the dash. Like a frog whipping out its tongue for a fly, my hand was unstoppable. I shoved the delicacy into my mouth and looked around the cab for any other tidbits of food. Russell gave me a look.

"Are you hungry?" he asked, one eyebrow lifted.

"I'm two days and nights hungry, except for a donut and some blackberries. Got anything to drink?"

"I … ah … don't think I do. I could stop at the Quick Stop and get something."

My first inclination was to say, "no, we're in a hurry," but I didn't say it. Instead, I said, "I'll have a large iced tea and two hot dogs with mustard," I smiled like a deranged cookie monster as I watched Russell walk into the Quick Stop wearing his official baggy blue uniform. Minutes later he was back with a cup and a bag.

"Thank you, Russell."

"You're welcome. I've never seen anyone this hungry. Why didn't you eat for so long?" he asked, not having a clue, as usual, so I filled him in as best I could between bites of hot dog. By the time we reached Boulder Creek, the sun had gone down and the little town was quietly resting between floods of people. Most folks were probably home having dinner. Some would be back later for the night life. Russell asked where we were going and how to get there.

"First, I think we should drive to Nora's house on Two Bar Road. I just want to see who might be there." Russell followed my directions and a couple minutes later we passed by the old Victorian.

"Don't see any cars ... no lights in the windows. Hold it! Turn around, I think I saw something." As we made another pass by the house I saw something all right, the back end of a U-Drive parked behind the house.

"What are you looking at?"

"See that white thing behind the house? It's a truck I'm very much interested in. Park here and we'll walk."

Russell parked his pickup in a wide spot. We crossed the road and walked onto Nora's property. I scanned the yard and house, very aware of the fact that someone might be watching us. We rounded the house and examined the U-Drive, sporting a smashed headlight. The cab was empty so we turned and walked to the other end.

Russell opened the back doors and we both gasped in surprise. Even though I knew about the marijuana farm, somehow the endless stacks of bulging black garbage bags came as a shock. With my fingernail, I poked a hole in the side of one bag just to make sure. Nothing inside the bag but green leaves and I suspected they weren't spinach.

We were looking at millions of dollars worth of plants. Russell's eyes were even bigger than when Thor had attacked him down by the river.

"So, maybe we should call in reinforcements?" Russell said, his voice quivering.

"Good idea, Russ ... ouch ... let go of me!" I hissed at the Neanderthal wearing black, who grabbed my mature frame from behind and threw me up against the piles of marijuana. Skinny little Russell was thrown even harder, and I heard his head bounce off the metal wall of the truck. We lay there, stunned, as twilight disappeared with the slamming of metal doors, leaving us in total darkness.

"Sorry, Russell, guess I should have figured the driver would be around somewhere. This isn't my first encounter with these thugs," I whispered, remembering when I hijacked the U-Drive from the same guy who just slammed the doors on us. He wouldn't forget me either.

"Russell, you alright?"

"Yeah, I guess so. Who was that?"

"You mean the creep in black? That was one of the three hired machete guys I told you about." Just then the engine fired up and we were moving forward. We were definitely not going left, back to Two Bar Road. We were going right, as far as I could tell, but then again, I could have been disoriented. We bumped and swayed for a few minutes, and then the truck stopped and the engine was quiet.

"Russell," I whispered, "do you have a gun on that belt of yours?"

"Yeah, should I load it?"

"As fast as you can. Hurry!" I heard his belt clink and clunk as he tried to pull the pistol free, then it sounded like he was digging through his pockets for bullets. I hoped he had more than one, because I heard one bullet hit the floor and roll away. Just then the doors were flung open and we stared into the face of one ugly man with an evil grin pasted on his face. The grin faded when he saw Russell's gun.

I knew the gun was empty, so I decided to flee while Mr. Ugly-in-black was still in shock. Panic helped me to quickly slide off the back end of the truck and run, knees to chest, like an Olympian athlete. That lasted until I made it past the U-Drive, a rusty Dodge truck, a sheriff's car and then around the shack. I ran into the forest and collapsed on the ground, my lungs still pumping hard, struggling for air. I finally peeked through the bushes and watched Russell being dragged to the cabin by the guy in black.

Wait a minute, I thought to myself, a sheriff's car? Maybe it's OK to go back to the shack, but if it's OK, why did Mr. Machete bring us here? I longed to go to the shack and get Russell and Kenny, but I didn't know how in the world I could pull that off. Maybe the sheriff was a prisoner too.

I found my old hiding place, just a couple yards back from the garbage cans, and settled in. Poor Russell. I had a habit of getting him into bad situations. I heard the screen door slam, then angry voices and sarcastic laughter from the bullies in black. Frozen with fear, I leaned against a fallen redwood and watched the house from my shadowy position, trying to formulate a plan.

Many strange thoughts floated across my exhausted mind, like, would the machetes find me first and kill me, or would it be the McFees? I tried to conjure up some helpful ideas, but I had a hard time focusing. I decided to go through the facts and see if anything stood out. According to the vehicles parked outside the shack, a sheriff's deputy, three McFees, possibly two hired men and poor Russell were all inside. Where was Jose? Just then I heard the snapping of twigs behind me. I crouched down in the dark, only to get a warm doggie lick across my face.

"Josephine, is that you?"

"Who wants to know?" I whispered.

"It's David and I have Solow with me." My heart leaped and my eyes stung, but out of necessity, I pulled myself together, somewhat.

"Keep your voice down. That house is full of killers." Before I could say another word, David lifted me up from the ground and held me tight. I melted into his embrace as warm tears began streaming down my cheeks, utterly out of my control. After all the terror and hardship, David was there and I could finally relax and be a girl.

"You want to tell me about it?" he asked, in a husky whisper.

"I don't have time to tell you everything, but Russell, the security guard, and Kenny McFee are in that house with murderers. We have to save them right away. This is the night when the money passes hands and everyone leaves Boulder Creek for good. You'll have to take my word for it." David wiped my tears away with his thumb.

"I believe you, but now that I finally found you I don't want to put you in danger again." He kissed my forehead. "Are they armed?"

"I'm sure they are. Damon has a rifle, George has a knife and the men in black have guns and machetes. The sheriff must be a prisoner, Kenny has no weapon, Russell had a gun with no bullets and I have scissors in my back pocket."

"Well, at least we have something," David said. I felt Solow against my leg and leaned down to rub behind his ears and kiss his sweet forehead.

"How did you find me? Did Solow help you?"

"I let him smell your sheets at the Munger cabin. Solow took off like a shot. We've been at it since noon, around and around this place. I was sure he had your scent down by the creek, then he leads me back to Bear Creek Road and up to some boarded up cabin. One dead end after another. I was trying to find my way back to the Mungers' house when Solow started pulling on his leash real hard, and for good reason, as it turns out."

"Who reported me missing?"

"I did," David whispered. "I thought something was

wrong when Solow came over to my house and drank out of the pond. I walked to your house and ran the messages. One was from Mrs. Munger wondering were you where. I called her and we decided you were missing. That was Monday night. Sergeant Machuca put out an APB on you. I couldn't sleep at all last night, and this morning I packed up Solow and drove to Boulder Creek."

"I just had a thought," I said. There's only one way out of here for these vehicles, the Bates' driveway. If there was just some way to block the driveway ... or flatten their tires ...."

"You say you have scissors in your pocket? What if I slash the tires?"

"That's brilliant, David, but they might see you."

"Like you said, we have to do something fast. It's all I can come up with." He put his hand out for the scissors. I reluctantly handed them over and took control of Solow's leash. David instantly moved toward the shack, past the stinking garbage cans, and then skulked around to the parked vehicles where I couldn't see him anymore. I prayed hard for his safe return. After what seemed like two eternities, David was on his way back. He stumbled against the fifty gallon can of kibble, dumping it noisily all over the ground. Solow howled and pulled hard on his leash, dazzled by all the kibble.

"Come on, let's get out of here." David pulled on my arm and I pulled Solow along deeper into the woods.

"Did they see you?" I asked. Just then we heard the

backdoor slam and an angry Damon cussing.

"What the ... Thor ... here boy. Did you do this? You good for nothin' son of a ...."

I almost laughed. David had gotten in and out without anyone seeing him and Thor got the blame.

"How much damage did you do?" I asked, as we took a seat on a fallen tree trunk, feeling like we were far enough into the protection of the forest.

"I put holes in two tires on each truck. Cut through the rubber like it was butter. Where'd you get these scissors anyway?"

"They're my good ones, made in America. David, Jose's coming back with the third U-Drive any time now. We'll have another set of tires to slash."

"Good grief!" was all David could say. I bent down and hugged the top of Solow's head, we all took a few more deep breaths and turned around to face the shack.

Chapter Twenty-nine

Twilight had been replaced by moonlight. Crickets made their music as David plotted a brave course of action. We had been waiting in the bushes almost an hour for Jose to arrive. He finally drove into sight, parked his U-Drive truck and marched up to the front door of the shack. As soon as we heard the screen door slam, David raced to the parking area in hopes of slashing more tires.

The last U-Drive was parked further down the driveway, behind all the other vehicles, making it possible for me to watch David do his work. He bent down, arm raised, ready to stab the first tire. Someone wearing a SWAT outfit and black helmet came up behind David. I couldn't breathe. David's arm was pulled into a painful position behind his back, and as I watched, two more guys wearing black helmets grabbed his arms and yanked him into the back of Jose's truck. The doors were pulled shut.

"Oh, no, Solow, what are we going to do?" I whispered. I crouched down, stunned into silence. Half the people I knew were prisoners and a lot of it was my fault. A black sedan pulled up behind Jose's truck. A substantial woman with Dolly Parton, glow-in-the-dark blond hair, stepped out of the car and walked with her worthless son, Woody, to the shack. I stayed in my crouched position, watching with total wonder. It was like stuffing a dozen people into a phone booth.

The crickets were suddenly quiet as a shot rang out. I hung onto Solow, mesmerized by the unbelievable events. I heard furniture breaking and a woman's scream. Above all the other noise, I heard George's obnoxious laugh.

I glanced at Jose's U-Drive just in time to see the doors fly open and a small army of men in black helmets leap out and position themselves around the perimeter. David peeked out of the rental truck, but didn't leave it.

Woody opened the back door and thumped down the stairs. George was hot on his trail with a wooden chair lifted over his head. He caught up to Woody and let him have it with the chair, knocking him into the garbage cans which spilled all over the ground.

One of the black-helmeted SWAT guys came up behind George and quickly yanked his arm up the middle of his back and the other hand went over his big mouth. George was ushered to the back of Jose's U-Drive. I noticed one SWAT guy still in the truck with David and George.

Nora ventured outside looking for her loser son. She teetered down the stairs in four-inch heels, practically tipping over when she saw Woody lying in garbage. She hesitated, probably wondering if Woody was worth the trouble. Did she really want to get involved with the smelly garbage?

Again, a man in total black SWAT gear came up behind Nora, easily captured her and quietly took her to the truck. Then it was Damon's turn to look for his brother, George. He opened the back door and gazed into the night from the top of the stairs. Cautiously, Damon made his way down the stairs to Woody who was sprawled out in maggot-infested filth. Neatly, another warrior captured the irate McFee brother, and took him off to join the others in the truck.

I was busy trying to figure out how many people were left inside the cabin, how many had been hauled away and how many were unconscious. It was only a matter of time until the survivors started missing their friends. Sure enough, one of the thugs stuck his head out the door and looked blankly into the night. After a minute of listening, he returned to his friends inside.

The next one to peek out the door was Kenny. He kept going, down the stairs and past the garbage, straight to where Solow and I had a ringside seat. He jumped when he heard my voice.

"Kenneth, it's Josephine. Are you OK?"

"Yeah, I guess. What happened to my brothers?"

I think the SWAT guys have them. Nora, too." I patted him on his back. "It's going to be alright. I found Emily and she's safe." Kenny fell to the ground, his head on his knees. I was pretty sure he shed some tears. I know I did.

"Let's watch from here. I think there are only five people left in the house. Is Russell alright?"

"That would be the guy in blue? He's OK for being duct taped to a chair."

"What about the deputy sheriff? Is he alright?"

"Didn't I tell you? He calls himself, Machuca. He's supposed to pay for the pot tonight. Guess he won't have to with all the McFees and Bates' gone."

"What?" I said in my loudest imitation of a whisper. "Who is Machuco anyway?"

"He's Sergeant Machuca, local sheriff and member of a Cartel. You didn't know?"

"I was with him today. He drove Emily and me to the hospital. Now that I think about it, I'm glad I fell asleep before I could tell him who Emily was." I was beyond angry. Machuca had played us for fools. "That creep! That evil man! No wonder he never found the bad guys. Kenny, are there any more people involved in this operation?"

"Nope. They're all here tonight." He looked up from his seat on the ground, straight into a set of eyes glowing in the dark. "This your dog?"

"That's right, and he's the best. He actually led my friend, David, here just from smelling my sheets ... not that my sheets smell."

I looked toward the house again. Jose, easy to spot with his hand wrapped in big white bandages, was coming down the back stairs with the two hired hands following him. Jose yelled. "I think they went that way," and pointed toward the last U-Drive. Jose went back inside the shack as the other two men were overpowered and taken to U-Drive number three. Only Jose, Machuca and Russell remained in the shack.

I decided I needed to communicate with one of the SWAT guys, and let them know what the score was. As quietly as I could, I made my way to Woody who was still lying in the garbage, kinda' like ashes to ashes, only it was garbage to garbage. Kenny stayed in the forest and held Solow's leash while I searched for a guy in a black helmet to talk to. One of them came up from behind and put a gloved hand over my mouth. Sure enough, I ended up in the back of the U-Drive like all the others. I looked around. The whole gang was there except for Jose, Russell, Kenny and the dirty double-crossing deputy.

All of a sudden my hands were locked in cold metal cuffs behind my back. Everyone, including Nora and David were cuffed and sitting on the truck bed. My eyes met David's. He looked perturbed, but I was miserable. I was beside myself trying to get someone to listen to me. When I tried to talk to one of the SWAT guys he pointed his gun at me and told me to sit, like you order a dog to sit. My ears burned and my face was on fire I was so angry. These G. I. Joe types needed to know about poor Russell and the despicable sheriff.

I smelled wood smoke. Someone was probably roasting marshmallows over a campfire somewhere; after all, Boulder Creek was vacation country. Wait a minute! There weren't any campgrounds in that area. And then someone near the cabin yelled.

"Fire!" I heard the crackling getting louder. The guy watching over us made a call to the fire department. Minutes later the trucks appeared and men dressed in yellow pulled long hoses toward the shack.

Sergeant Machuca ran by our U-Drive carrying a small metal case which reflected silver in the moonlight. He passed by the fire trucks, heading toward Two Bar Road. I bucked and squirmed in a fit of rage, but every time I tried to talk, the gun was pointed at me and warnings were given.

I heard one fireman telling another, "It's gone. Didn't take long for that old shack to burn." I was silently screaming and then it all came out.

"No, you have to go back and find Russell!" I screamed. But my words only succeeded in angering the man behind the gun. About twenty minutes later the hoses were loaded onto the two fire trucks and one truck left the scene and then the other. A couple SWAT guys closed the U-Drive doors and we were on our way, in total darkness, but where? When the doors opened a few minutes later, we were parked on the circle drive of the Munger mansion. Three sheriff's cars were already there, along with David's convertible and Theda's SUV.

I figured it was well past midnight, but all the lights were on, inside and out. The place looked unreal, like an

Italian dream villa lighting the heavens. The lawns were immaculate, the fountain and shrubs, perfecto. SWAT guys with DEA letters on their jackets helped us down from the truck and all of us, the good, the bad and the terrible, were marched into the main entrance of the Mungers' villa.

"Josephine!" Theda cried, when she saw me. Across the room, Warren smiled as he sat with Emily on a grand, over-sized sofa. The rest of the room was filled with boxes and odds and ends of furniture to be put in place at a later date.

All the handcuffed prisoners, including David and I, were lined up against a wall of windows opposite the sofa. The front door open and Kenny and Russell march in. Kenny went straight to Emily who greeted him with open arms. Russell just stood by the staircase in a daze, taking it all in.

The front door opened again and a disgusting garbage smell permeated the foyer, followed by a very trashed and cuffed Woody Bates. Jose was right behind him.

I wondered so many things. How was it that Russell didn't burn up? How did they know we where at the mansion and why would Jose turn himself in? My mouth dropped open when the SWAT guy in charge walked to the door and greeted Jose. They talked quietly for a minute and then Mr. SWAT pointed at David and me.

"You two can go now," he said, as he freed our wrists of the uncomfortable handcuffs. David took my hand and my body warmed to the temperature of happy. I glanced at my reflection in the window. I was dirty, scratched up with a hairdo fit only for a hat, and yet, David had taken my hand in his.

Damon, George, Woody, his mother and the two hired machetes guys were read their rights, marched outside and stuffed into a black DEA van. Before Jose could leave, I ran after him. He looked down at me with fear in his eyes, as if I might inflict more damage on his person.

"Jose, is that your real name? You aren't one of them, are you?"

"I can't tell you my real name, but no, I'm not one of them. I'm with the DEA. That's all I can tell you." I gave him a hug. He was stunned, but I didn't care.

"I really liked you as Jose the construction guy. I never would have smashed your hand if I'd known who you really were. I'm so sorry. Is anything broken?"

"Several small bones, but don't worry, it wasn't your fault. You did more to catch the perpetrators than anyone. By the way, George was bragging he emptied the brake fluid out of your car."

"He'll pay for that." I grinned.

"We have everyone except the Cartel rep.," Jose said.

"Would that be Sergeant Machuca?"

"Actually, he's Sergeant Machuca, who took a trip to Mexico and came back as a representative of the Cartel. We have people following him as we speak."

"So you let him walk away?"

"That's right. We have another pot field to catch him in." Jose's smile would have lasted longer if he hadn't been in so much pain. I winced and then wished him well. I never saw him again, at least as, Jose the carpenter.

Theda pulled up a chair for me and asked if I was thirsty. I had never seen her so energetic and wearing a smile that would hurt your face if you wore it very long.

"I'd love some water, thanks, but I have to find Solow."

"Oh, yes, of course, but rest a minute first." She flew to the kitchen as Warren stood up and walked to my side.

"We were very worried about you, Josephine," Warren said. "I hope you're feeling all right after your ordeal. There's no way we can thank you enough for finding Emily."

"You can thank Kenny for saving her life many times over," I said.

"Emily has been telling us all about him. That Kenneth is quite a guy. We like him." Good, I thought, because he's going to be family soon, but I didn't say it out loud.

Russell sat down on the first step of the "Gone With The Wind" staircase, his chin resting on his knees and quiet as a mouse. I pointed to him.

"There's a man who wouldn't give up. Russell has suffered a lot at the hands of the McFees. By the way, how did you get out of the burning house, Russell?" Russell raised his head.

"As soon as Machuca lit the fire and ran out the front

door, Kenny raced in the backdoor and picked me up, chair and all. Jose came at me with a knife. I thought he was going to cut my throat, but he cut the tape instead. Jose grabbed Woody and we all took off. We circled around the area to a DEA van over by the Bates' house." Russell looked at me, and laughed.

"Gramps will never believe this one. Ever since you ran your truck into my grandparent's garage, I've been keeping them up on all your ... um ... adventures." He shook his head slowly back and forth.

Theda came back, handed me a glass of water and then handed me an envelope with my name on it.

"Sorry I didn't finish ...." I looked around. Oh ... the railing is finished." From where I sat, the faux was finished and looked great. "Who did it?"

Theda's eyes sparkled like her dangling earrings.

"Alicia and Kyle finished their work and then they got busy on the railing. They worked until seven o'clock Monday night. They were so worried about you. And poor little Trigger threw up. Apparently he does that when he's stressed." I nodded.

"He does, bless his heart." I made a mental note to call Alicia and Kyle first thing in the morning. My eyes wandered to the ceiling and the beautiful angels Alicia had painted. I couldn't stop smiling. Warren and Theda were still standing beside my chair.

"Open the envelope, Josephine," Warren coaxed.

Theda nudged me, "open it, dear." I figured it was my

pay plus a bonus, maybe. To my astonishment it was what I had earned, a bonus plus another check.

"Oh, my God!" I couldn't believe my eyes.

"A year ago, we posted a one-hundred-thousand dollar reward for finding Emily, but it's nothing compared to the gratitude we want to express," she said with a catch in her voice. I stood up and Theda and Warren took turns hugging me and then everybody was hugging everybody and rivers of tears flowed freely, happily. David had his arm around my waist, leading me to the front door.

"I hate to break this up," he said, "but we have a basset hound to find." Theda put her hands to her chest and bit her lip. Everyone nodded and agreed we should hurry and find him. Solow had obviously wormed his way into all their hearts.

The last place I wanted to be was on Nora's property again, but that was where we had last seen Solow. As David aimed his little Miata down Nora's driveway and around the Victorian to the backyard, the headlights glommed onto something four-legged moving on the back deck.

"David, look!" He stomped on the brakes and we jerked to a stop. In the moonlight we discovered Solow on the back deck eating cat food. Two cats sat a few feet away, glaring at the intruder. Solow carefully licked the bowl clean. When he was finished, he ran to us as fast as a fat, low-to-the-ground basset hound can run. David hefted him into the back seat and we headed for home sweet home.

An hour later, David parked in front of my house.

Moonlight revealed the path as he walked me to the door, kissed my forehead and turned away. After days of horror and uncertainty, I had had plenty of time for higher thoughts and realizations. I finally knew my own deepest feelings. I pulled David back to me, we kissed and went inside.

THE END